WITHIN THE HOLLOW CROWN

Margaret Campbell Barnes

"Logically constructed and finely written, and the chapter in which the young king loses Anne of Bohemia, a victim of the plague, is memorable for its depth of pathos"—*Scotsman*

"A superb delineation of the poignant, passionate, dramatic figure that is Richard of Bordeaux"—*Claude Rains*

"Full of the pageantry and pride of mediaeval days"—*Sunday Express*

WITHIN THE HOLLOW CROWN

For my younger son
John Murray Barnes

Within the Hollow Crown

MARGARET CAMPBELL BARNES

SPHERE BOOKS LIMITED
30/32 Gray's Inn Road, London, WC1X 8JL

First published in Great Britain in 1948
by Macdonald & Co. Ltd.
© Margaret Campbell Barnes 1948
First Sphere Books edition 1971

Set in Linotype Baskerville

Printed in Great Britain by
Hazell Watson & Viney Ltd,
Aylesbury, Bucks

. . . *Within the hollow crown*
That rounds the mortal temples of a king
Keeps Death his court, and there the antick sits,
Scoffing his state and grinning at his pomp,
Allowing him a breath, a little scene,
To monarchize, be fear'd, and kill with looks,
Infusing him with self and vain conceit
As if the flesh which walls about our life
Were brass impregnable ; and humoured thus
Comes at the last, and with a little pin
Bores through his castle wall, and farewell king !

SHAKESPEARE'S *King Richard the Second.*

AUTHOR'S NOTE

IN ATTEMPTING to write a novel concerning a character so hedged about with controversy it has been necessary to read and weigh up a voluminous amount of contradictory testimony. Nothing was too bad to say about the second Richard after Henry Bolingbroke had usurped his throne, and the whole tone of contemporary chroniclers changes abruptly; yet to unintimidated French historians he remained the highly civilized person who was kind to Isabel of Valois and strove consistently for peace. And the comparatively recent discovery of a manuscript written by a Cistercian monk of Dieulacres Abbey shows the capable young king in a far kinder light than is allowed by any Lancastrian historian.

In the case of the King's younger uncles and one or two other characters whose rank and titles changed during the reign, only one title has been used in order to avoid confusion.

My thanks are due to the Librarian and staff of the Epsom and Ewell Public Libraries, and to the authors of the following books :—*King Richard the Second*, Shakespeare ; *Richard of Bordeaux*, Gordon Daviot ; *Richard the Second*, Anthony Steel ; *Richard II*, H. A. Wallon, Paris ; *The Deposition of Richard II*, M. V. Clarke, M.A., and Professor V. H. Galbraith, M.A. ; *Chronique de la Traison et Mort*, English Historical Society ; *Extracts from the Bulletin of the John Rylands Library*, Manchester; *Froissart's Chronicles*, Translated by Lord Berners ; *Froissart, Chronicler and Poet*, F. S. Shears ; *Chaucer's Poems ; Chaucer and his England*, Dr. G. G. Coulton ; *Chaucer*, George H. Cowling ; *Lives of the Queens of England*, Agnes Strickland ; *England in the Age of Wycliffe*, Professor G. M. Trevelyan ; *The Black Prince*, John Cammidge ; *Lord Mayors of London*, W. and R. Woodcock ; *Men and Women of Plantagenet England*, D. M. Stuart ; *Two Thousand Years of London*, C. Whitaker-

Wilson; *History of East London*, Hubert Llewellyn Smith; *Our Cockney Ancestors*, K. Hare; *Love, Marriage and Romance in Old London*, C. T. S. Thompson; *Old London Illustrated*, H. W. Brewer and Herbert A. Cox; *The Tower of London*, Canon Benham, D.D., F.S.A.; *Everyday Things in England*, C. H. B. and M. Quennell; *History of Pontefract Castle*, Richard H. H. Holmes; *History of Bodiam Castle*.

My thanks are also due to Edna St. Vincent Millay for the charming lines which I have used on pages 262 and 363.

Epsom, 1948.

PART

I

" Tout ce qui est de beau ne se garde longtemps,
Les roses et les lys ne regnent qu'un printemps."

—Ronsard

CHAPTER I

YOUNG Richard Plantagenet knelt by a richly blazoned tomb in Canterbury Cathedral while priests and monks chanted prayers for the repose of his father's soul. Every now and then he made a valiant effort to recall his wandering thoughts and leash them to the solemn meaning of the Latin words ; but it was difficult not to drowse in an atmosphere so heavy with incense and packed humanity. He was only fifteen and this was the fifth anniversary of the Black Prince's death—and even when he had been alive Richard hadn't cared for him with all that passion of loyalty of which he was capable.

Not that he would have dreamed of telling anyone so, of course—unless perhaps it were his closest friend, Robert de Vere.

Such an unnatural confession would hurt his mother and shock his uncles, besides seeming to admit some rather shameful lack of appreciation in himself. For hadn't all these people crowded into the Cathedral year after year on the Black Prince's birthday to pay homage to a national hero ? And wasn't all England still mourning for the martial, grown-up king they might have had instead of a useless minor like himself ? But unfortunately his illustrious father had always been too busy fighting to play with him when he was small and Richard remembered him mostly as an irritable invalid, blighted in his prime by some unpleasant disease picked up in the Spanish campaign.

Actually, he had preferred his old war-horse of a grandfather, Edward the Third, who had lived a year longer and anxiously bequeathed him the crown.

At last the long Requiem chants died away in a series of lovely, diminishing echoes that pursued each other upwards from choir to clerestory and out through the open arches, one hoped, to the feet of God. Richard eased his knees from a faldstool and seated himself beside his mother to listen to the usual eulogy of their dead. Sudbury, the Archbishop, spoke proudly of how the late Prince of Wales had carried the renown of English arms like a flaunting banner across the Continent—of his courage at Crécy and his generalship at Poitiers. His effective voice was like a clarion call to the new, untried generation, and Richard, in common with other youngsters of his age, gazed with apologetic awe at the recumbent effigy of the proven warrior, flanked by a hardy company of living comrades-in-arms bearing the famous black armour and the captured ostrich feathers of Bohemia. He had been brought up on the names of Crécy and Poitiers. The overworked words had been dinned into him until something inside him sickened secretly at the sound of them. He felt that people used them unfairly, like pikes to prod him with, so that in self-defence he tried to avoid the warlike things they stood for. Unconsciously, against such high-sounding standards, he was always striving to keep inviolate that precious indescribable thing which was *himself*—the spiritual quality which so many well-meaning people tried to encroach upon. And being both imaginative and intelligent, he could usually find plenty of alleys of mental escape when he didn't want to listen to them. Even now, while formally trying to fill a chair of state which was considerably too big for him, he was able to give the primate's eloquence the slip and enter into the intimate, satisfying world of his own conceits.

He couldn't be bored for long in so exquisite and interesting a place. If his father's war cult left him cold, the boy had imbibed his mother's cult of beauty. He loved the rich colours of vestments and stained glass, the cool mysterious perspective of dim aisles and the grandeur of tall arches soaring into the vaulting of the roof. By sliding forward a little in his chair he could catch a glimpse of the worn steps leading to Becket's golden shrine and relive the well-known tragedy of a previous Plantagenet's anger and remorse. What must it feel like, he wondered, to be murdered. How must poor Saint Thomas have reacted when he saw the King's knights invading his sanctuary? Had he suffered much? Richard shivered involuntarily, miserably uncertain whether he himself could ever face the violence of four assassins with the bravery of Becket. "Priest or no priest, he set about some of them first!" he recalled, reconstructing the thrilling scene which he and Robert de Vere had pestered their tutor to recount so often. From the time when he had first come from Bordeaux it had formed a favourite theme for their "play-acting"; and what with his own vivid imagination and Robert's dramatic skill, they had managed to scare themselves deliciously. And as soon as they were a bit older they had ghoulishly searched the Cathedral floor for bloodstains.

But all that had been in the untrammelled days when he was only the King of England's grandson. Richard suppressed a yawn and tried to ease the heavy ermine cloak about his shoulders. For want of something better to do he fell to contemplating the queer little faces of men and beasts and angels ornamenting each stone corbel. He liked to picture the monks of William of Sens' time scaling ladders or standing on precarious stagings to carve each small perfection so that it reflected their own laughing, Christ-loving souls. Setting those quaint little oddities so humbly high up—so removed from the earthbound glances of the righteous—that they seemed almost intended for an intimate, tender jest between craftsman and Creator. There was one harsh, self-important face that reminded him of his Uncle Thomas, a handsome one like Uncle John and a grotesquely puff-cheeked figure of Gluttony that might have been meant for Uncle Edmund of York when he was hungry. The fortuitous resemblance delighted their unregenerate nephew so much that he almost forgot the solemnity of the occasion and laughed aloud. Mercifully he was hidden from Thomas of Gloucester by a massive pillar, York was dozing gently, and John of Lancaster—the eldest of the uncles—was up north trying to finish off some peace negotiations with Scotland.

While the familiar recitation of his father's virtues drew towards its concluding homily, Richard turned his attention to the newly restored nave with its half-finished aisles. In spite of workmen's scaffoldings it was packed with people who had come surging after the royal party through the great west doors. He often wondered why they came so far and stood in such discomfort to see him. The men always shouted for him good-naturedly, the women sometimes cried a little because of his youth; and he on his side was always careful not to show his repugnance for their frowsty clothes and sweating bodies. For even if his mother spoiled him, at least she insisted upon good manners. And whenever he had complained about the way some of them stank, his tutor, Sir Simon Burley, had pointed out that no one who had seen inside their houses could expect them to wash much. Naturally, this was one of the things Richard had immediately wanted to do, but no one would let him for fear of the plague. But when he *really* began to rule he meant to do something for them, poor wretches, if only because of their unbelievable patience. Patience was the virtue Sir Simon was always exhorting *him* to have—particularly with the uncles—and he found it the most difficult of all to acquire.

Although he often speculated about the common people and the queer, brutish lives they led, he hadn't, of course, an idea of what they thought about *him*. Being a decently modest lad, he supposed that they had followed him into the Cathedral mostly for his father's sake, and he was unaware of the reassuring picture he made for their anxious eyes. During the four years since his grandfather died he had learned to face their gaze with composure, so that even grudging, hard-bitten Thomas of Gloucester had to admit that he held himself well. The grandeur of the building made a fitting background for his fair and flawless youth and the glow of innumerable tapers

16

warmed his smoothly burnished hair to the ruddy hue they associated with their kings, so that they were able to see in him the incarnation of those vaguely stirring, inarticulate ideals which lift even the coarsest clod above the beasts he tends, to some dim consciousness of his mislaid divinity.

At last the Archbishop's hand was raised in final blessing. Richard glanced sidelong at his mother. Tears were slipping like chaplet beads between her white, perfumed fingers and falling desolately on to the grey flagstones as she knelt. This annual Requiem Mass was no formal anniversary to her. For all her frail frivolity she had loved her last husband passionately and nursed him devotedly. Because their first-born son had died, the only remaining one was doubly precious. She wanted to keep and cosset him. Richard understood this and adored her. But he often resented the cosseting and thought how much pleasanter it would be to be loved wholly for one's own sake.

Monks and choristers were beginning to file out into the ambulatory with a gentle slither of sandalled feet and he stood up beside his mother, protectingly. He took her missal and carried it for her before any of her women could offer to do so—partly because he loved the smell and feel of the soft tooled leather and partly as an excuse to touch her hand encouragingly. And although her lashes were still wet, she smiled a little, thinking what an understanding lover he would make. Unlike most of the Plantagenets, the Black Prince had not been a tall man, and she could almost imagine for a moment that it was he himself walking down the aisle beside her. This child of their passion, so inconveniently born at Bordeaux in the midst of men's preparations for battle, was shooting up and would soon be leaving boyhood behind. " You must grow up like *him*—and I shall be so proud ! " she whispered inevitably.

" Yes, madam," murmured Richard dutifully. But as they came out into the summer sunshine together, the half-hearted promise was borne away on the frantic cheering of the crowd.

17

And he didn't really *want* to grow up like his father, always careering about Europe killing people. Nor like anybody else. All he asked was to be allowed to grow up in peace as himself, unheroic and ordinary, with all his keen young interests vibrant and unthwarted. He didn't want to be moulded by his dictatorial Uncle John, nor his ineffectual Uncle Edmund, nor his bellicose Uncle Thomas—nor even influenced too much by her. . . .

Edmund of York was at his elbow now, fussing about the lateness of the hour. " A splendid sermon ! " he observed, although he had dozed through most of it. " We are fortunate—you and I, my boy—in having been sired by such fathers ! "

" Yes, sir," agreed Richard again. It always saved argument to agree with the uncles. But he wasn't so sure. Without being able to put the matter into words, he was beginning to find out that being the son of some public hero like his father or his grandfather precluded the possibility of being liked without comparison. He lingered a little in the pleasant Cathedral precincts, tossing the hot ermine cloak to a page and telling his groom to tighten a girth. Truth to tell, he still felt a bit diffident about riding before his mother and his uncles. But of course all these paunchy grown-ups would be wanting to get along to the Archbishop's palace for their dinner. Their show of grief hadn't, on previous occasions, he recalled, affected their appetites. And a small surge of superiority and precocious insight possessed him, remembering how when his puppy had died he had been too desolate to eat for days.

Footsteps that he feared—yet knew only in the depths of his soul that he feared—roused him from dalliance and drove him instinctively towards his horse. Thomas of Gloucester, the youngest and hardest of Edward the Third's batch of sons, came striding out from the violet shadow of the west porch, a lean figure resplendent in ceremonial armour and emblazoned jupon. " So you will not be journeying back to

18

London with us, Joan?" he inquired briskly of his sister-in-law.

The widowed Princess of Wales gathered up her scalloped crimson reins. As a good Kentishwoman she liked to spend a week or two shopping and seeing friends in Canterbury. "You know that every June I come on a pilgrimage to the shrine of blessed Saint Thomas on my poor husband's birthday," she reminded him, in the virtuous tones of a woman who knows herself to be disapproved of.

"Killing two birds with one stone, eh?" observed Edmund of York, settling his flabby weight in the saddle with a grunt. He wasn't particularly tactful at any time but probably, thought Richard, his mind was running on the chances of episcopal capon.

"Well, don't hurry to return, dear sister, until your native air has restored some of those wild roses to your cheeks," urged Gloucester, ignoring his brother's unfortunate contribution to the conversation. "The odours from the Fleet ditch aren't too healthy in hot weather, and you can rest assured that I will escort the boy safely back to Westminster."

"I make no doubt you will, milord," agreed Joan, turning to stare pointedly at an armed troup in his livery which far outnumbered the young King's modest retinue. For the briefest moment the glances of mother and son met in guarded amusement. She made no secret that "the fair maid of Kent's" complexion came out of a paint box these days, and they both knew that the longer she tarried in Kent or any other county the better the uncles would be pleased. They always had resented the confidence her husband had placed in her, going over their heads to make her co-governor with the Duke of Lancaster; and her absence gave more scope for avuncular interference.

It had been decided that they and Richard must leave directly after dinner to attend a Council meeting especially convened because of the widespread discontent about the new poll tax. Michael de la Pole, one of the most astute members of the

Council, and Walworth, the Lord Mayor of London, had both sent messengers urging them to come. But after all, wondered Joan, was this wretched meeting so important? It wasn't as if it were about some imperative matter to do with the wars in France or Spain or Scotland. What did it really matter what a lot of ignorant shopkeepers and swineherds thought here at home? They were always grumbling about something. If it wasn't taxes it was wages. . . . She leaned from her white palfrey to lay a hand on Richard's shoulder. " Couldn't you stay, Dickon, and return with me next week? " she suggested.

She could feel both uncles glaring. She knew well enough that if the late Prince had decided his son was to go somewhere at a certain time, he would have had to go; and that Burley, who had been tutor to both of them, was hovering disapprovingly somewhere in the background because he hated the idea of Richard's being brought up softly. She knew that they would all tell her for the hundredth time how bad her inconsequent vacillation was for the boy's character. But they ought to remember that he was all she had left. And he was such a charming companion. The monotony of widowhood was leavened by his gaiety and affection. He wasn't always bragging about his prowess at sports like Lancaster's tedious boy, Henry—nor dumb about everything but military manœuvres like the two hefty sons of her first marriage. Not but what she adored her two grown-up sons, of course. . . . But Richard had more of the woman in him. He could take an intelligent interest in music and clothes and things that interested her. Though even he, of late, had been less amenable to her extravagant devices for their mutual amusement. " We could go and choose the cloth for your new hunting coat," she coaxed. " I've got the Flemish weavers down by the river to design some delicious green stuff specially for you with little white harts embroidered all over it."

A month or two ago the suggestion would have tempted him. But now, pausing with one foot in the stirrup, he only looked up to laugh at her naïve cajolery. He was exceedingly proud of this beautiful mother of his, with her pink and white skin and red-gold hair. Although she was growing plump and in her early forties, she still retained the charm that had enslaved so many men. He liked going about with her and knew that if he stayed they would have a good time together, taking a ridiculous little boat down the narrow Stour and dressing up with her ladies in the weavers' fascinating stock of fabrics. But there were other things to be done. He wanted to get back to London to put in some practice for the tournament the Lord Mayor was giving at Smithfield—back to his friend, Robert de Vere—to the book of poems Geoffrey Chaucer had given him and to his new puppy, Mathe. For once he even wanted to attend the Council meeting. For this time it wouldn't be about war. Michael de la Pole was sure to open the debate on the conditions of the working people—and de la Pole always talked sense.

So Richard lifted the persuasive hand from his shoulder and kissed it gallantly, but shook his head. He could see Archbishop Sudbury, newly changed from his vestments, bearing down upon them—full of further homilies on living up to the Black Prince's reputation, no doubt. So he swung himself into the saddle and signalled hurriedly to his Master of the Horse to move off.

Out beyond the fine new city wall which his uncle of Lancaster had built against the marauding French he caught a glimpse of sunlit fields, framed like a piece of green tapestry in the grey archway of the Pilgrim's Gate. And winding through them like a dusty white ribbon the road to London. *His* London. The city where so many interesting people lived and so many exciting things happened. The port where ships brought strange cargoes from all over the world.

He was impatient to get dinner over and be on the way. Life beckoned enticingly. Perhaps after all it wasn't so bad being a very young king. One would grow up. And then people wouldn't be able to prevent him from doing all the lovely things he planned.

Richard's dreams stretched before him like a golden pathway leading to a city where craftsmen made buildings beautiful and poets poured out a fantasy of words. Where merchants from all countries met in peace on prosperous quays. Where hovels and stenches and disease were swept away, and all the wisest scientists gathered to cure the plague. Nebulous, shining, adolescent dreams—remote enough from the standards of his world to catch the smile of the Christ. Or a crazy jumble of impracticable whimsies which would have shocked the uncles to their unimaginative souls!

CHAPTER II

THE TILT yard at Eltham was a pleasant place in June. The scent of box hedges and sun-drenched thyme drifted across from the palace garden, and red and white roses nodded their heads over the wall. Slim squires and pages, brighter than any flower border in their short tunics and parti-coloured hose, stood about holding spare equipment and laying bets ; for the King and his friends were practising for a junior event in the Lord Mayor's midsummer tournament. And the attention of all of them was centred on a well-worn quintain set up in the middle.

Tom Mowbray, the Duke of Norfolk's heir, had just cantered back from a thrust barely good enough to save him from the backwards swing of the beam. "Your turn next, Robert !" he panted, as he passed de Vere.

"Robert won't escape the sandbag ! He never takes the trouble to practise," prophesied Lancaster's son, Harry Boling-broke, who rose at dawn every day of his life to do military exercises, as behoved a nephew of the Black Prince.

"I'll wager you a florin he does !" countered Richard Plantagenet from his perch on top of a mounting block. But he spoke out of loyalty rather than conviction.

"Make it two !" urged Bolingbroke, who was always comfortably sure of his own convictions—and usually so annoyingly right.

But for once his judgment was out. Or was it that Robert de Vere had a genius for doing the unexpected, wondered Richard, noting the negligent way his friend couched his lance and how a kindly little gust of wind sprang up from the river and stirred the swinging target just at the right moment.

Tom Mowbray hooted with good-natured laughter.

"The wind blew the thing straight onto his lance !" said

Henry disgustedly. But he called the page who was holding his purse and handed over the coin without resentment.

" Milord of Oxford is always lucky ! " grinned Bartholomew, the Master-at-Arms, chalking up a score equal to Mowbray's.

" Does that go for love as well, Barty ? " chaffed Richard. Being completely bilingual, he had been alternately singing snatches of a Provençal ballad and shouting ribald English comments at his fellow competitors ; and everyone laughed because the handsome Earl of Oxford had ousted stocky young Tom from the fickle favours of one of the Princess of Wales' wards. But Robert, who was taller and older than the rest of them, rode back with a disarming grin, seemingly equally indifferent to his conquests in either field.

Richard rolled over lazily onto his stomach. It was pleasant lounging there in the sunshine, watching his two cousins' exertions and his friend's indolent grace. If one half closed one's eyes the bright morning light made all the people in the tilt yard look like little figures cut out of paper with their own violet shadows neatly folded over backwards for stands. There was old Bartholomew in his leather jerkin, Bolingbroke all done up in his first suit of armour, small groups of multi-coloured squires and—a little apart in gown of sombre velvet —the dear, familiar figure of Sir Simon Burley, who usually came to watch their sports. It was one of those golden moments when time stands still enough to paint itself upon a page of memory. Somehow Richard knew that in after years he would only have to turn back to this scene to recapture the quintessence of a youthful summer day, and was vaguely saddened because the bright sands of boyhood were slipping all too swiftly through the hourglass of his life.

But all fanciful illusion was suddenly disturbed by a scattering of pages and servants, a spectacular splutter of sparks and the thud of Henry's heavy stallion charging purposefully across the yard. Success was a foregone conclusion ; but the sun blazed so on his breast-plate that it was difficult to see.

"A perfect thrust!" cried their delighted instructor, above a howl of applause.

"Perhaps if we too had worn our new armour——" murmured de Vere a little maliciously, drawing rein beside the mounting block.

"Old Barty didn't say we need. And it's only a quintain practice anyway," yawned Richard.

Sir Simon Burley turned to frown at their deplorable flippancy. "That thrust was the effortless result of regular discipline," he was heard to observe. "None of your chancy successes achieved on the strength of spasmodic efforts just before tournament time!" He was addressing Sir Thomas Holland, Richard's grown-up half-brother who had strolled over from the palace. But the criticism was evidently for their benefit.

Richard jumped down and greeted his half-brother affectionately. He enquired politely after Thomas's wife and gave him news of her ten-year-old son, whom he had recently taken into the royal household as a page. It made him feel pleasantly mature, being an uncle. But he wished Thomas hadn't chosen that moment to arrive. A couple of men-at-arms were steadying the quintain in readiness for a fresh essay and the redoubtable Master-in-Arms was coming in his direction. "Your turn now, sir," he invited, with that exasperating mixture of deference and command which he had perforce to endure from all his instructors except Sir Simon.

Richard mounted his white mare without more ado, gentling her to the starting point. He even made some gay quip to the young squire who handed him his lance. But his grip on the thing was a thought too tense, his brows knitted. He wished now that he hadn't waived his right to ride first. How could anyone be expected to tilt immediately after Bolingbroke? To compete with his expensive armour and his solemn practising and his one-track mind? The morning had been so enjoyable until now, he thought, screwing up his eyes almost angrily to sight the target. In a moment he would be charging across the enclosure, filled with exhilaration. But first there was always that split second of shivering fear. Fear of what, he wondered for the hundredth time. Fear of being afraid—of making a fool of himself? Did other lads experience it? Or was it because there was always that extra little hush before *he* sped a hawk or pulled a bow? Just because he happened to be a king. . . . And because he was always aware of Thomas or someone watching to see if he were shaping like his father.

Thomas Holland thought the world of his illustrious step-father and had been knighted by him on the field in Spain. How paltry all this childish pother about a contest with light-weight lances must seem to him! The bare thought of it made Richard spur Blanchette into a nervous start.

But he was off and the breeze was in his hair. That cold, silvery feeling like plunging into the river for a swim had braced him. His slim, lithe body felt supple in the saddle. Life suddenly was a joy, an adventure. He and Blanchette were as one and his blood warmed to a lovely confidence. Onlookers, repressions, criticism—all were forgotten in the thrill of thundering across the Eltham yard. Only the quintain swam before his vision—a worn wooden post and crossbar transformed by imagination into the splendid figure of some doughty opponent. At the right moment he raised himself in the stirrups. With perfect timing arm and lance swept back ready for his own graceful, unorthodox thrust; so that Thomas and Burley and the grizzled Master-at-Arms almost fancied they saw the Black Prince ride again. Then all in the last few yards Richard had to remember Bolingbroke's correct and carefully perfected thrust—and Burley's approbation. He, too, wanted the old man's approbation. The quintain was flying towards him. Richard's quick brain flew faster. " If I draw my elbow in now—just a fraction, the way Uncle Thomas is always nagging about—I've still time. . . ."

According to all military ethics the effort should have been successful. He put all he had into it so that the thrust shook his slender frame from toe to shoulder. But the lance caught only the edge of the target and glanced off, almost unseating him. And as he ducked instinctively the heavy bag of sand at the opposite end of the bar swung round and hit him soundly on the back. The ignominious fate ingeniously designed for all who muffed their stroke.

Even when he had pulled his mare, sweating and slithering, to a standstill the blow still jarred. To tough, stocky Mowbray or steelplated Bolingbroke it would have meant little. Robert was clever at concealing all he felt. Richard hated himself for being sensitive and unaccustomed to rough handling. He stopped to pat Blanchette because he was blinded by tears. Tears of rage and shame. His companions' laughter reached him from a long way off. " How *dare* they laugh at me ! I am their King," he caught himself muttering childishly; but strove to chase the ignoble thought away. Of course, it was the same good-natured fun he had been poking at them—all part of the precious good comradeship which had made him purposely forgo his prerogative to ride first. Only—only—there was something in him—some part of him—that no man must laugh at. And it was so difficult to know which part of him minded so much that humiliating, body-shaking thwack—the cosseted mother's darling who would probably bring up his breakfast because of it—or that part of him which he inherited from his father's father, right back into the austere past, and which he had to guard from indignity.

He wheeled his mare and looked with envy at the others, untrammelled by such dual personalities, and rode slowly back to them. His back was a little more rigid, his chin held a little higher. Only Robert and Sir Simon would know by the wet brightness of his eyes how awful he felt.

" Better luck next time, Dickon ! " called Thomas, trying to swallow the slur on the family prowess.

" I'd better have stayed at Canterbury—making an exhibition of myself like this . . ." muttered his shamed relative.

Thomas was fond of him and told him not to be a young

fool. "You're not up to their weight," he pointed out with rough kindliness. And Burley came and stroked Blanchette's sleek neck and smiled up at him. "Plenty of other people make exhibitions of themselves, Richard, and haven't the wit to know it," he said. He was thinking particularly of Gloucester and his friend the Earl of Arundel when they lost their tempers in Council but, attracted by a sudden burst of merriment, his keen grey eyes passed from his pupil's flushed face to the spectacle of an unseated horseman in modish pink picking himself up from the dust, and he was glad to accept the opportunity of pointing his words more lightly. "Look at young de Vere there! A worse miss than yours—and he's laughing all over his impudent face!"

But no laughter lightened Richard's. "Any one can afford to," he answered bleakly, "who does it purposely to keep a friend in countenance."

The sun climbed higher and the practice went on. But the roses had begun to languish and the early morning enchantment to fade. It was often so when one grew tired. Bolingbroke's swagger became more insufferable and Bartholomew's voice more raucous. Richard felt hot and sticky and wanted to be sick. Although he never stopped the sandbag again he achieved no spectacular success. "I could have killed you for doing that just now!" he broke out irritably, when at last he and Robert found themselves alone again.

"Doing what?" asked de Vere guilelessly, reining in in the shade of the wall. It wasn't always easy being friends with a fellow who was as clever as he was sensitive.

Richard had had enough. He dismounted wearily and sat down on a bench, pulling off his lance hand gauntlet. "Oh, I admit you're a good actor. But you can't fool me—or Burley. Muffing your thrust just because I'm so in-c-competent!"

"You're not incompetent." Robert handed over his horse to be rubbed down with Blanchette and came and stood argumentatively before him. "Look here, Richard, if you'd only use that devastating perception of yours where it's needed you could figure it out for yourself. Don't you see you're up against some of the best trained athletes of your age? I wager you in a few years' time, Harry and Tom will be two of the most famous champions in Europe. I'm just erratic, of course. Brilliant at times—hopeless at others. But you—in any other company at all—would be steadily well above average."

"Oh, I've had the best instructors, if that's what you mean!" agreed Richard bitterly.

"Steadily and deservedly above average," repeated de Vere, ignoring the interruption. "And that in spite of not having a powerful physique."

Richard swung the gauntlet moodily between his knees. "It's not only physique. I let outside things affect me."

De Vere sniffed derisively. "Would you like to be smug and stolid like your cousins?"

Emerging from his glumness, Richard glanced across at them and smiled.

"Very well, then," said de Vere. "Let's thank God we are not as other men and go on being temperamental!"

"It's all very well for you—you can hide it."

"Everything's easier for me—or for any of us, come to that."

It was just such flashes of intuition that made Robert so precious; and Richard had wanted that particular sympathy so much that it almost unmanned him. "People don't realize —how awful it is sometimes—being me," he stammered incoherently.

"They *must* be fools!" said de Vere quietly.

Richard picked up his discarded lance and began stabbing savagely at a little tuft of toadflax that reared its yellow glory bravely from the beaten earth. "And then there's my name— the same as that first Richard Plantagenet's. The very sound of it makes men expect miracles."

De Vere flicked distastefully at the dust still clinging to his pink tunic. "I don't see that his military prowess did England much good," he observed.

"No," agreed Richard, wondering if military prowess ever did—except that the lack of it left one open to attack and only a clod wouldn't want to fight efficiently in defence of his own land. "I often wish my brother Edward had lived. I scarcely remember him. But being three years older than I he always seemed so much stronger and more—more like they want me to be."

De Vere stopped a passing page and told him to bring some wine. He always knew by the fading colour in his friend's cheeks when it was needed. "But Richard, you know most of the time you enjoy being King——" he objected.

"Yes, in a way I do—in spite of *ces maudits oncles*." Richard laughed ruefully and made room for his companion to sit and drink beside him. "Perhaps it's the only way I can get even with self-satisfied fellows like Harry Bolingbroke."

The young Earl of Oxford tossed off his wine and stretched his elegant long legs before him. "But that isn't the only reason," he said, regarding his well cut hose with satisfaction.

"No, it isn't." Richard sat sipping thoughtfully while the pages collected his gear. "I suppose one always enjoys doing anything one can do well. And sometimes—oh, I know it sounds conceited—but if only they'd let me alone I believe I could do and say the right thing. Preside over my Parliament —get hold of the people. . . ."

"Your sense of the dramatic should help."

"Yes, I suppose it does. And I've enough imagination to know how they're feeling—like holding someone's pulse . . . If only Uncle Thomas and that beast Arundel wouldn't keep butting in, riding bald-headed at everything——" The colour had come back into Richard's face and he leaned forward with a sort of shy eagerness. "You know, Robert, when the Arch-bishop anointed me something really d-did happen," he explained with the slight stammer which caught him only in moments of diffidence or anger. "I *am* different. There's something inside me that no one can touch—only God per-haps. Something I've got to guard from ridicule or—or any sort of indignity. That's why, although I'm not in the least ambitious personally, I feel I must struggle to do even the things I'm not good at well enough not to make a fool of myself in front of people. You see, it isn't just *me*. . . ."

If Robert de Vere was too sceptical to share his friend's idealism, at least he had the wit to envisage his unique loneliness. He loved Richard for his very naïveté; but, having lost his own, there was little he could say in comfort. " I should talk to old Burley about it," he suggested, with unaccustomed awkwardness.

But Burley had walked back to the palace with Sir Thomas Holland, who was worrying at a problem of his own. Both he and his younger brother John had inherited the Holland features; but nothing, he was thankful to reflect, of their mother's fragility and rose petal skin. " Young Richard looks almost like a girl at times," he was complaining.

Simon Burley reassured him. " You needn't worry, Thomas. He's perfectly healthy. Only a bit highly strung. And after all, one wouldn't want——" He left the sentence unfinished; but, like de Vere, he glanced back significantly at the rubicund cheerfulness of Mowbray and the insensitive toughness of Lancaster's cub.

But apparently Holland's anxiety wasn't wholly for Richard. " My own small son is with him so much these days—he's growing very like him," he said.

" I've certainly noticed a great improvement in his manners," agreed Burley dryly.

Holland threw cloak and gloves to a hovering page. " His mother was set on his being at court. And I must admit Richard's very kind to him." The great banqueting hall where the late King had been wont to feast his royal captives was crowded with people waiting to dine at the lower tables and, blood-relation as he was, Holland had the sense to lower his voice. " But I don't want young Tom to blow his nose on a square of silk and grow up effeminate and slack about sport like—" noting an icy sternness in Sir Simon's eye he floundered a little—" like that scented young fop de Vere."

Just as well, thought their tutor, that de Vere was negligible and debonair—seeing that men so often substituted his name when they dared not use the King's. " Slack about sport ? " he repeated, with simulated density. " I should have thought that after this morning . . ."

" Child's play tournaments ! " sniffed Holland, fresh home from Acquitaine. " If the Prince were still alive you know as well as I do that Richard would have been sent campaigning abroad like young Bolingbroke of Derby. Why, I don't suppose the boy's so much as seen a man killed ! "

" Would it do him any particular good, do you suppose ? " inquired Burley, stopping a passing clerk who was carrying some books Richard had recently chosen for his growing library.

" It might make a man of him," declared Holland, in his high-handed way. " What does he know or care about laying waste a city or raising a siege ? "

Old soldier as he was, Burley lingered lovingly over the pile of richly bound volumes. Froissart's *Chronicles* and Chaucer's *Romaunt of the Rose*. Really, the boy's taste was growing remarkably good. " There *are* other things, you know," he submitted, a trifle absently.

Holland stared at him doubtfully. " Poems and stuff, you mean ? " he inquired, viewing both clerk and burden with uneasy contempt.

" Why, yes," agreed the King's tutor blandly. " And the building of cities and encouragement of trade——"

Unfortunately the last part of his remark was drowned in a rather inopportune outburst of catcalls and cheering from the direction of the village. " Our tradesmen don't sound as if they needed much encouragement at the moment ! " snorted Holland, turning an indignant head to listen. " What with mere prentices and journeymen agitating for Guilds of their own, and these unlicensed preachers inciting them at every street corner, we shall soon need half our foreign levies brought back to keep order at home ! "

" Too true," admitted Burley, ever the least contentious of men. And certainly the labour situation was growing grave when peasants dared to demonstrate under the very walls of one of the King's palaces.

Holland was hungry. He wished his pernickety young step-brother would hurry out of his bath and come to dinner. " And anyway, we're at war," he added, clanking towards the dais with much ringing of spurs.

It was the cliché that had terminated most conversations during the past twenty years. Burley was an old man now and even he could scarcely remember the beginning of all the bickering in France and Spain. " Yes," he sighed, reluctantly closing the delectably illuminated *Romaunt*, " we're still at war."

CHAPTER III

RICHARD and his friends rose early next morning so that they might reach London before the noonday heat. Leopards and lilies on a silk banner drooped motionless from the tower in the oppressive air and thundery grey clouds were beginning to roll up along the river flats. Their horses had been brought round into the cool shadow of the gatehouse and while they were mounting a man in the Lord Mayor's livery galloped into the forecourt covered with sweat and dust. He muttered a *Deo Gratia* at seeing they had not yet started and, scarcely stopping to make obeisance, asked urgently for Sir Simon Burley, who was just coming down from the great hall to see them off.

"Some last-minute arrangements about the lists perhaps," suggested Tom Mowbray, who could talk of nothing but his first big tournament.

"They won't get such big crowds anywhere as at Smithfield," asserted Harry Bolingbroke, confident that his own performance would be well worth watching.

But Thomas Holland, who was escorting them to London, dismounted in silence and went to join Sir Simon and the gesticulating messenger at the foot of the steps. It seemed to Richard that they stood talking there for an unconscionable time, and that they kept glancing anxiously in the direction of his gay little cavalcade of impatient youths and restive horses.

"I wish Sir Simon were coming with us instead of crossing to Calais," he said. For although Burley wouldn't pass over a fault he always *wanted* one to do well. Burley *believed* in one. That was why he was such a comfort at public functions, always giving one confidence and unobtrusively heading off the people who destroyed it.

"Why does he have to go abroad?" asked Mowbray.

Because he lived most of the year on the Bigods' vast estates in Norfolk, he was always asking questions when he came to Court. And de Vere, out of sheer boredom, made a pass at him, trying to tousle his countrified thatch of straight brown hair. "Didn't you know he has to scour Europe to find Richard a bride?" he answered teasingly.

But before Mowbray could pursue the exciting bit of gossip, Burley himself came across to them. Evidently he and Thomas had arrived at some decision at last. "I'm sorry to keep you waiting, Richard," he apologized. "But we think it will be wiser to augment your escort."

Richard looked up quickly. "You mean in case of more trouble about this wretched tax?" he asked.

Besides being the King's tutor, Burley was Vice-Chancellor and had attended all the Council meetings. His fine, lean features were unwontedly grave. He, too, was sorry that he had to go abroad just then. He came and gentled Blanchette's high-bred nervousness with a gesture which seemed to include her rider. "Only as a routine precaution, of course," he explained quietly.

So things were as bad as that. "Was that all the messenger came about?" Richard asked levelly.

Burley turned so as to include the whole gaping group. "It's bad luck on all of you after the hours you've spent practising, but Sir William Walworth has regretfully decided to postpone the tournament," he announced.

A howl of wrathful disappointment went up from competitors and attendants alike. "Why? At the last moment like this?" they wanted to know.

Burley spread a deprecating hand. "It appears there has been rioting at Dartford, and now the peasants at Canterbury and Maidstone are refusing to work."

Bolingbroke stared uncomprehendingly with eyes expressionless as hard brown pebbles. "You're not suggesting that they could be *dangerous*?" he said.

Burley strove to be patient with the blind egotism of their

youth. " You must all realize that this new poll tax the Commons have pushed through Parliament is grossly unfair to the poor," he reminded them.

" Of course it is, sir," agreed Bolingbroke readily. " But surely they wouldn't dare to *do* anything about it ? "

It was the comfortable assumption that had held so long. The assumption on which the families of all of them existed. But would it hold forever, wondered Burley ? Tolerant, far-seeing men like Michael de la Pole and himself sometimes found themselves comparing the handful of people who fixed the taxes with the hordes who paid them. And the numerical comparison could be quite frightening—if one assumed that sufficient provocation might one day produce a leader for the people who paid . . . It was an ugly train of thought. " Well, quite annoyingly, they have," he observed dryly. " According to this man of Walworth's, they've even stoned to death one of the tax collectors ! "

After he had turned back to the palace there was a deflated silence. Even a postponement of their personal triumphs and petty wagers paled before such glaring impertinence aimed against their kind. " Surely you don't believe that's more than an isolated case ? " asked Bolingbroke of no one in particular.

De Vere, who had had one of the grooms walk his horse up and down, stood drawing on his gloves. " Well, if it isn't, I see no reason why people should be so amazed about it," he drawled. " After all, they're the same men who fought at Crécy and Poiters. Our fathers called out all our villeins and pushed pikes into their hands and expected them to do something *then*."

" But under proper leadership." Bolingbroke's fierce black stallion had been chafing so long at the bit that only firm horsemanship could hold him. " Good Heavens, man——" he argued, between stampings and uprearings—" you don't suppose they've either the brains—or the initiative——"

" Perhaps empty stomachs can be equally inspiring," suggested de Vere, stepping back a pace to avoid the beast's plunging hoofs.

The earnest young Earl of Derby always found such flippancy baffling. It stifled all serious argument. " What a queer fellow you are, Robert ! " he complained, showing off his skill in a few more equestrian contortions. " One would almost suppose you sympathized with the treacherous scum."

" On the contrary, it's a grievous blow about the tournament—particularly as I appear to be on top of my illusive form and might have unhorsed you ! " explained de Vere pleasantly. " But I've enough imagination to wonder what it must feel like to see one's wife starving and not be able to buy her any bread."

" And imagination's so uncomfortable, you know," murmured Richard.

Bolingbroke was never quite sure when they were getting at him. " But of course they've enough to eat ! " he blustered. " You know very well, they're always grumbling about *something.*"

" Well, thanks to Gloucester's expensive military fiasco in Brittany it looks as if they've got something to grumble *about* this time," said de Vere, with asperity. " And for God's sake keep that brute still, can't you ? He's simply covering me with dust."

Tom Mowbray turned to the cousin who had so far contributed least to the conversation. After all, he was king. And a king should know. He had to attend enough boring debates. " What's it all about *really*, Richard ? " he asked, with a disarming trustfulness which always made him seem younger than the rest of them.

Richard, who had been calculating whether his mother would have left Canterbury before the trouble started, came out of a rather worried abstraction to smile at him. He had suffered so much loneliness and uncertainty himself that he was always considerate to youngsters less experienced than himself. " The only really fair method of taxation, Tom, is assessment on property ; not so much per head, regardless of people's income."

37

The boy ranged his mount alongside Blanchette, whom he adored. " But we had a poll tax before," he recalled. " When everybody had to pay a groat a head for your *father's* wars."

Richard had a shrewd idea that more of the groat tollage had gone to pay for his grandfather's mistress in England than for his father's battles in Spain. But he had disliked them both and probably the money had been wasted either way. " That was a kind of experiment, I imagine—to see if the people would endure it," he said.

" Somebody's got to pay for the wars we fight," observed Bolingbroke, who never let them forget that he had once gone campaigning with his father.

" Quite," agreed Richard. " Though—as Robert remarked just now—the bowmen and people have to fight them too. *Without plate armour.*" He regarded the stallion's spiked panoply with aversion and turned back to his other cousin. " The trouble that first time, Tom, was that people didn't pay enough. I remember a lot of tedious old men discussing it for hours at my first Parliament. The tax didn't hit the common people too hard but unfortunately it brought in only about a third of the deficit. So now Uncle Thomas's Brittany campaign has to be liquidated by everybody paying a shilling instead of fourpence. Which means—if only they'd the sense to see it— that the tax is bound to be at least three times as unpopular. Hence all this unrest."

" What did they say when you pointed that out to them ? " asked Mowbray, with more enthusiasm than tact.

Richard couldn't very well admit that they had said nothing at all. That they had, in fact, all been shouting too excitedly themselves to notice that he was trying to speak. " The only concession Burley and I could wring out of them was a raising of the assessment age limit from fourteen to fifteen," he reported, with a rather pitiful attempt at pomposity.

De Vere hastened to relieve his friend's discomfiture. " The equality of payment need only be nominal," he pointed

38

out. "I've told my stewards to help out all our workers and I'm sure any decent landowner will do the same."

It didn't sound so bad put like that. In most cases amounts would be adjusted and probably the whole storm would blow over. "De la Pole is urging the same method of collection in the towns," Richard told them. "But I knew it would make a muddle if each mayor were left to divide the amount between his population as he thinks fit."

He was glad when his half-brother arrived with an armed escort and they were able to set off for London at last. They rode for the most part in silence. The others were still inclined to be aggrieved about the tournament, but Richard himself felt relieved. And secretly ashamed of being relieved. But he had been tilting badly of late through over anxiety to do well. Only the accident of his high birth would have driven Bartholomew or anyone else into pretending that the opposition wasn't too strong. Had Richard been older or wiser, the measure of his relief might have warned him of the unfair strain.

He would have been glad of a few weeks at Westminster to arrange his new books and train the young deerhound his Uncle John had sent him from Scotland. He had been looking forward, too, to visiting Mundina Danos, his nurse, in the new home he had bought for her wedding present and for the housing of his wardrobe when she had married his tailor. It would have been fun visiting an ordinary gabled house in Carter Lane. But if this silly unrest went on among the working classes he would probably have to attend a lot of dull debates instead.

The prospect was as depressing as the clouds that were beginning to blot out all the summer blue. Council debates always seemed to be about money or war, or both; and in any case they meant wasting hours of sunshine sitting at the head of a table listening to the same men arguing about the same sort of things until he knew just what they were going to say, and could even see through the self-seeking speciousness of most of their arguments. There were brighter moments, of course, when some amusing old pirate like Sir Edward Dalyngrigge was called in to describe how he had driven out the French when they burned Rye and then raided their coasts in reprisal; or when the bishops got all worked up about some heretical rector called Wycliffe and the danger of his followers being allowed to preach without authority from Holy Church. Or when shrewd business men like Nicholas Brembre and Richard Whittington complained about the growing wealth of the Flemish wool merchants. Richard had inevitably absorbed a good deal of knowledge about government and often of late he had felt he would like to join in some of these domestic discussions—not bickeringly, like Gloucester and the testy Earl of Arundel, but pleasantly and constructively, considering both sides of each question, so that they might really arrive at fresh ideas. And *do* something. Couldn't the bishops, for instance, be persuaded to curb the scandalous self-indulgence of some of their own friars before picking holes in the Lollard preachers? And instead of trying to tax away all those foreign ships which were pouring lovely, useful things into England, couldn't the jealous City Guilds build more ships of their own and compete in all the trading ports of the world? And not be too proud to improve their wares by sending their goldsmiths and weavers and dyers abroad to learn still more about their crafts? But whenever he offered suggestions his obdurate, old-fashioned Councillors would listen politely for a few minutes and then go on arguing with each other as if he hadn't opened his mouth. Treating him as if he were half-witted as well as young. So now he seldom bothered to speak, but just put his Great Seal to the papers they brought him, reserving to himself the rather spiteful satisfaction of knowing· that they couldn't really pass any affairs of state without him.

But there was a part of him that wasn't wholly content to leave it at that, and he knew that it wasn't just pique at being ignored. His mind was far too active and intelligent to register nothing but boredom or amusement. Richard often saw some of the Councillors' faces, close up and mouthing, in his sleep, and often he dwelt upon them with a kind of frustrated hatred during the daytime. He was thinking about them now, and disappointment about the tournament damped the morning's enthusiasm. So that it was not until they had come miles from Canterbury and Ralph Standish, his body squire, brought him his cloak that he noticed heavy, sluggish raindrops presaging the promised storm. He looked around and noticed for the first time that his party was approaching a village and that there was an extraordinary number of people abroad.

"Is it a fair or a saint's day or something?" he asked, wondering what all the excitement was about. But before Standish could swing the crimson velvet across his shoulders Thomas Holland, who had been riding ahead with the captain of the escort, came cantering back with a military cloak on his arm. "Better put this on instead—at any rate until we're through this rabble," he said hurriedly.

Richard opened his mouth to protest haughtily. He was very particular about clothes.

"For Christ's sake, don't make a fuss!" besought Thomas.

Richard noticed that the raindrops running down his half-brother's face looked like beads of sweat, and that the lowering light cast a greenish hue over the tanned leather of his skin. And, roused to understanding of his urgency by an excited band of farm louts brandishing pitchforks who pushed rudely past them, he suffered the rough frieze to be draped about him.

Evidently they had run into the very kind of demonstration Walworth and Burley had feared. Even in his wildest dreams of promotion, the young captain could scarcely have desired the responsibility so suddenly thrust upon him. He warned his charges to keep close together and cover up their jewels. But the high-spirited sprigs of nobility were tense with excitement. "Who are all those ragged wretches over there by the pond, Sir Thomas?" asked Mowbray, agog to see all that was to be seen.

Holland didn't answer. He was reconnoitring the layout of the village in case of trouble and biting angrily at his clipped moustache. But young Mowbray's voice had a piercing quality, and a verminous beggar, sheltering under the hedgerow, was only too glad to volunteer the information. "Thieves and felons they be, young sir—freed by the breakin' open o' the gaols," he chuckled through toothless gums. "And the Lord o' the Manor, he can't do nothin' about it." The wretched man couldn't go and help in the lawless work because he'd lost both his legs at Crécy, but probably nothing half so exciting had happened to him since.

The gilded youth of England averted their gaze hurriedly from the pitiful spectacle of his helpless torso. In their fathers' heyday he would have been a hero. But since Poitiers and Limoges and Najera there were so many maimed men begging about the country that they had become merely a nuisance. They tossed him a groat or two and looked with all the more interest towards the village green where scores of idle labourers augmented by the toughs with pitchforks were clustered round the bewildered prisoners they had released. One of these gaolbirds had clambered onto the steps of the pillory and began haranguing the rest. His shrill, penetrating voice carried across the green above the rumbling thunder and the exciting jostling of his audience. "Good people, things cannot go well in England until everything shall be in common, till there be neither vassal nor lord, and until all shall be equal." Although without grace of any kind, the man had book learning of sorts; and his experience in swaying a crowd suggested that he might be some sort of unfrocked priest.

"One of those mad Lollards probably," shrugged de Vere, pulling up the high collar of his riding cloak to protect the cherished pink velvet.

Yet it seemed to Richard that there was a certain sanity about his plaint. Perhaps it was only because it was so disconcertingly new that it sounded mad. "Why are they, whom we call lords, more masters than we? What have they done to deserve it?" the man demanded, obliged to shout still louder against the annoying hoof-beats of the company jogging

nearer along the road to London. " If we came from the same
parents, Adam and Eve, what reason can they give why they
should be more masters than you and I ? "

" He looks like the wall paintings of John the Baptist,"
tittered a perky page, more aptly than he knew. And his
companions laughed gustily.

Better to dismiss such ranters with concerted raillery than to
let their words sink into each personal consciousness and have
time to remind one of the words of Christ. And he *was* like
John the Baptist. They had drawn almost level with him now
and could see him clearly. His emaciated body glistening wetly
through the rents in his rough brown soutane, his wild hair
and prophetic gestures, and the burning intensity of his eyes.
Perhaps one had to be all burnt up with zeal like that before
one really cared about some cause—enough, anyway, to start
doing something about it that nobody had done before ! If
so, thought young Richard Plantagenet, how few men ever
really cared about anything ! . . .

" They make us toil that they may spend," the Lollard ranted
on, inciting the illiterate crowd so that they began to cheer and
press closer. " They are clothed in velvets and fur, while we
are in rags. They have wines, spices and good bread and we "
—he swept a gaunt arm in a telling gesture towards his fellows
from the gaol—" we have only rye and refuse and straw, and
water to drink. They have manors and palaces and we have
nothing but the toil and the work, the wind and the rain in
the fields."

They certainly had the rain in the fields. A rising fury in his
voice and an even fiercer deluge of rain coloured the eloquence
he had culled from the pages of Holy Writ as yet withheld
from ordinary laymen. In the common tongue encouraged by
Chaucer he was putting into words comprehensible both to
them and to their masters the inarticulate, smouldering resent-
ments that had lived so long in their hearts. Showing them
what it was that made their lives drudgery instead of joy, and
whom it was they really hated. Setting light to the straw.

43

Trained in the art of cheap oratory, he used every passing symbol to press home his point. "It is from us and our labour that they get their wealth," he cried, pointing with lean accusing finger at the cavalcade of valuable horses and rich men's sons so that his audience turned and stared dangerously as their oppressors trotted past, and saw in the trappings of each horse enough wealth to keep their hungry families for a year.

They saw an armed guard, too, before whom—in twos and threes—they would normally have cringed. Soldiers who might at any other time have dispered them with a single threatening motion of their pikes, or answered any show of resistance by sweeping them into their own duckpond. Actually, the captain had halted them with some such intention. But the peasants' mood was ugly. They seemed to close together, crouching a little ; and the eyes of all of them were fixed warily on the men-at-arms. And presently they began to sing, taking up the theme of the agitator's words. Singly at first as if to keep up their nascent courage, then united in a kind of mass hysteria.

> *When Adam delved and Eve span—*
> *Who was then the gentleman?*

An exultant note crept into the doggerel words until they become a chanted challenge. Without having the least idea who the wealthy travellers were, they began to sing *at* them.

> *When Adam delved and Eve span,*

The captain had enough sense to change his tactics, contenting himself with putting his men like a shield between Richard and the staring crowd. "It's only a popular song," he apologized, red to the neck that the King's ears should be so shocked while in his care.

"Oh, I've heard it before, Beverly," Richard assured him

cheerfully. " He's culled it from one of those interminable sermons I have to endure at Paul's Cross. The Bishop of Rochester, on humility, I think. He always saves up some crushing couplet like that for Lent, doesn't he, Henry ? Specially when your father comes riding up from the Savoy with so many retainers they get stuck under Ludgate."

Somehow his easy allusion to ordinary happenings made his elder's anxiety look faintly ridiculous. They were not sure whether he realized the danger or not. But at any rate, it seemed easiest to adopt his insouciant attitude and hope for the best. " Let's push on quickly. I'll be glad to get into some dry clothes," muttered Holland rather shamefacedly.

Beverly was glad to give the order and the mob seemed equally glad to see his men move on. The party had served their purpose as an illustration to the preacher's exhortation, and official interruption had been momentarily staved off. But before reaching the end of the green the horses were all in a huddle again.

" What on earth's the matter now ? " asked Richard, who could see little for the soldiers in close formation about him.

A page hurried forward to investigate. " It's milord of Derby, sir," he reported. " His horse has cast a shoe."

" Scarcely surprising, considering the way he was pawing up the forecourt at Eltham!" De Vere laughed, with the forced hilarity of a man released from a nerve-racking situation.

" There's a forge over there by the church. We may as well all go and take shelter," Holland shouted, above a prolonged clap of thunder.

Richard was nothing loath. The borrowed cloak was rough and sodden against his neck. But at the bend of the road he looked back at the rabble on the green. Some of them had pulled sacks over their heads, but they made no attempt to shelter from the downpour. Even as he looked a vicious streak of lightning played over the scythes and billhooks in their hands. Yet they stood as if drinking in words of salvation. The priest on the pillory steps was still waving his arms about and his voice carried faintly across the stagnant water of the village pond. "Let's go to the King, who is young," he was urging. "If we go together"—some of the words were caught and torn away on a gust of wind which stirred the osier beds and ruffled among paddlings of ducks— "all manner of people . . . will follow us to get their freedom."

As Richard came in sight of the long, low smithy, the solid Norman tower of the church hid from view both pond and green. He lagged behind a little, head down against the storm. What had seemed a communal jest a few minutes ago was now something which concerned him poignantly. He didn't want it to. He didn't want that man's damned eyes coming between him and the colourful luxury of mimes and tournaments, his words spoiling the taste of good food. And yet something in himself—something generous and eager and untarnished— leapt up to meet the challenge.

"Let's go to the King, who is young——" their preacher had suggested. Not to the Uncles or the Councillors, who were old and experienced. Nor yet to the Commons, who should represent them. For what, after all, was the good of going to any of them? *They* never *had* done anything to help. This idea of equality was a new idea—an idea for the future. And perhaps one had to be young—to have the kind of imagination which hurts—to know, as Robert could, how it must feel to see one's wife starve and be forced to spend on someone else's unsuccessful war the money that might have bought her bread. Even those very small scraps of stale bread he had seen offered like gold and frankincense to the released prisoners. Perhaps one had to be young to *care*?

Parliament had all the figures and statistics, but the people were coming to *him*. For the second time that day Richard felt that there might even be advantages about being young—and a king. . . .

CHAPTER IV

IT WAS dark in the forge except for the red glow from the furnace, and the place appeared to be already full of men. The tenseness of their attitudes could be felt rather than seen, and as the royal party entered they stopped talking and drew defensively about the anvil. But even between their clustered bodies the hissing, white-hot iron threw into relief the strange looking object upon it; and the great, leather-aproned smith paused with uplifted hammer to glower at the newcomers from beneath his bushy brows.

"Look! He's beating a ploughshare into a thing like a sword. What's the idea?" whispered Tom Mowbray, rather overawed by an interior so reminiscent of all the macabre paintings he had seen of Hell.

No one answered until de Vere laughed, a trifle nervously, "Let's hope *we're* not! " he said, in French.

The blacksmith took a pair of tongs and lifted the crude weapon from his anvil. He cooled it in a vat of water and thrust it beneath a pile of sacking which might have concealed the beginnings of an armoury. But there was nothing furtive about his movements. It was rather as if he warned strangers to mind their own business.

"A good thing *someone* in this village is working today!" remarked Thomas Holland with asperity, as Bolingbroke's limping horse was led in.

The smith shrugged tolerantly. Whatever his personal sympathies, his was the decent independence of an essential tradesman. Ploughshares or horseshoes, his furnace must still roar.

Richard's eyes were becoming accustomed to the gloom. He noticed that the posse of labourers were drifting away by some back entrance through the house. Thomas pushed him towards a rough bench against the smoke-grimed wall where the

47

shadows were deepest. " Go and sit over there," he ordered, without ceremony.

Richard was glad to discard the dripping cloak, and sat down obediently. It was the first time he had been in a public smithy and it was interesting to watch the blacksmith's assistant work the bellows that blew the dulling embers to leaping flames.

The smith had backed the black horse into a kind of wooden frame and lifted a forehock onto his knee. He was probing for a stone. His strong, work-worn hands were amazingly gentle. Whether it happened to be blacksmith, goldsmith, fletcher or bowman—Richard loved watching an expert at his work. He felt exasperated when his half-brother began fussing about wine and food, and wondered why old campaigners should consider it such a calamity to miss a meal. He saw the smith look up at Holland's peremptory demand and fancied it was not altogether the glow of the furnace which kindled such sparks in the man's fine brown eyes. " There is water in the well," he answered curtly.

But Thomas Holland had been hardened by the necessity of victualing armies in a ravaged land. " The young squire sitting over there is not over-strong," he insisted.

Richard could have hit him. But he had the grace to realize that probably both he and Beverly must be feeling extraordinarily worried about having brought him into such strange contacts.

" My daughter may have some bread," admitted the smith sullenly, and sent his assistant to find out.

The man went to a ramshackle door at the back and called " Rose ! " and presently a girl appeared. A tall girl with white skin and straight, honey-coloured hair. She had brought a pitcher of water and a wooden platter with some pieces of bread. Not the dainty manchets of white bread they were all accustomed to, but hunks of dark stuff, made of rye and bran and beans such as they had seen the hungry prisoners devouring. She stood hesitating for a moment or two, embarrassed at finding herself in such well dressed company. Then, dazzled by the outstanding elegance of de Vere, she carried the platter straight to him.

He refused it hurriedly. " Take it to the squire over there," he told her, with an apologetic grin at Richard. But she was oddly attractive in her grave, peasant way and he could not resist teasing her, and presently some of the other young men were ogling her too. Richard couldn't hear what they were saying for the roar of the bellows, but he saw the ingenuous blushes dyeing her neck and forehead and wished they would leave her alone. The girl was too simple for their sophisticated badinage. She was obviously in an agony of shyness—village bred and timid as a doe.

When at last she broke away and brought him the bread he spoke to her with grave courtesy to make amends. She kept her eyes cast down, and he could see her breasts were still rising and falling quickly with agitation beneath the thin blue garment she wore. But she stayed close beside him, away from the others, as if she felt safe there. He ate a piece of the sour tasting stuff out of curiosity, and looked past her through the open doorway. The place appeared to be reasonably clean. A pot was simmering over a few sticks and the remainder of the loaf was on the table. " Do you live in there ? " he asked.

" We all do," she said.

" All ? " he questioned. It didn't look big enough to house a couple of dogs. Yet in spite of such overcrowded conditions, she smelled sweet enough.

She overcame her shyness sufficiently to look up, quizzing him with candid grey eyes that even held a hint of mockery. " My younger brothers and sisters, of course—and my father and I," she explained. He seemed quite a nice squire—less high and mighty than some—but, living in some noble's palace or knight's manor, he was probably quite stupid about the world outside.

Richard stood up so that he could see more of the puzzlingly bare interior. " But there's no bed," he said, looking for some sort of curtained four-poster.

Rose gave vent to a giggle and pointed to a pile of miller's sacks folded tidily in a corner. "I shake them every morning," she volunteered, wondering why he was so curious.

Richard coloured at his own clumsiness. Even at Eltham and Westminster some of the servants slept on the floor, he supposed. "But your mother?" he persisted, under cover of the clanging of the hammer. Surely a woman would want a bed.

"She died," Rose told him. And because of the way her eyes suddenly suffused with tears he sensed that it must have been very recently. Instantly all that he had been taught about the danger of going into the common people's homes came back to him. Instinctively, he drew away from her.

Living so close to the crude fears of life and death, Rose recognized them immediately. "Oh, no, not the plague!" she assured him, laying a hand on his fashionable sleeve with the same sort of mothering gesture she might have used towards one of her brothers. But the withdrawn uncertainty was still in his eyes, and she wanted to bring him back to friendliness. There had been some quality in it that she had never so much as glimpsed in village lout or patronizing gallant. And because she knew that people often lied about the plague lest their neighbours should refuse to come near or bring them food, she spoke in an urgent whisper which seemed to wrap them apart from his companions. "Truly, it wasn't, sir! It was just that she was going to have another baby—and there wasn't enough food for us all——"

Richard put the remainder of the bread back on the platter. It was true, then, in spite of the easy assurances—some of these people *were* half starved. . . . And yet she and her father and the forge looked relatively prosperous. He would have liked to ask her how it came about that a blacksmith's wife should die of malnutrition, but just then there came an angry commotion outside, the shuffling approach of many ill-shod feet, catcalls and jeering. He sprung up and was conscious that all his friends did likewise. The blows on the anvil hammered no harder than their hearts. They were only a handful—the hated handful who had manors and velvets and wine—and for the first time in their lives they realized how dangerous it was to be in a social minority. The rabble they had left on the green were coming along the lane. They were making straight for the forge with the crazy Lollard egging them on and half a dozen men riding in front. Holland, de Vere and Standish whipped out their swords and came and made a little circle of steel about Richard. Beverly rapped out an order and the men-at-arms lounging outside scrambled into their saddles. Only the blacksmith appeared to be unperturbed. "It's not your lordships they're after—it's those damned snooping tax-collectors," he told them, as well as he could with a mouth full of nails.

It was only then that they realized that the half-dozen horsemen in front were the pursued and the target for so much ribald venom. Sheepishly they put up their swords and relaxed. And the rabble, at sight of the soldiery whom they had previously defied, slunk back a little, suspecting a trap. As yet they dared not stop the tax-collectors doing their hated work. The lean, vulpine individual in charge had Parliament at his back. With his ink horn and stilo he appeared to be some sort of lawyer's clerk. He pulled up in front of the forge and consulted his assessment roll. "John Hilliard?" he read out inquiringly.

The smith answered civilly enough. "John Hilliard lies in the churchyard yonder, but I am his son."

The collector rested the roll on his saddlebow to cross out the name of the deceased. "And now the forge is yours, eh? What name shall I put?" Knowing the temper of the people, he was trying to be conciliatory.

"Walter Hilliard."

"Married? I'll be wagered you are, a fine figure of a man like you!"

But Walter Hilliard, bending over the black's hoof, held no

truck with lawyers, facetious or otherwise. " I am a widower,"
he said, driving in the last nail. " And all my children are
under fifteen."

" Then I must trouble you for your shilling, Walter Hilliard.
And your man there. What's his name ? "

The scraggy little assistant, who had been trying to make
himself as scarce as possible, came out from behind the bellows
babbling excuses. He'd been shaking of an ague ever since
serving with the Prince of Wales in Spain. . . . He hadn't his
health as other men. . . . He hadn't the money. . . . . He
would pay if their Worships would give him time. . . . But
his master shoved him good-naturedly on one side. " He's
served me well ever since he was disbanded, and I'll pay his
shilling as well as my own. And God curse all wars ! " he
said. He fumbled beneath his leathern apron for the purse
hanging at his belt ; but his fingers were all foul from his
work. He looked round for his daughter and saw her standing
close to a pretty, auburn-haired gallant, whose flattery would
probably do her no good. " Come here, my girl," he called,
" and take two pieces o' siller out o' my wallet."

Rose moved obediently from the shadowed obscurity by
Richard's side, and he thought she looked like a sliver of silver
birch bark against the massive outline of her black-browed
father. " 'Tis all we have," she whispered, full of domestic
concern, and stood holding the coins doubtfully on her open
palm. But the smith smiled down at her as if, in a world where
loss and injustice turned a man sour, she were all that kept life
sweet. " Go give them to the scrivening vultures and be done
with it," he bade her, careful to keep his great hands from
soiling her gown. " There be things more precious than
siller."

She went outside the shop and held them up to a coarse
looking ruffian who had the moneybags tied to his saddle. The
rain had almost stopped and a shaft of watery sunlight breaking
from the bondage of two clouds caught at the lights in her pale
gold hair. Her uplifted face was sweet with innocence.

Richard saw the man's brutish face as he looked down at her, and it spoiled the sunlight. Saw him hold on to her hand as well as the money and presently heave his bulk from the saddle and stand over her, pawing her bare white shoulder. Here was no young man's harmless ogling, of which he himself had been half envious; but the calculating lasciviousness of middle-age. Involuntarily, he glanced back at her father to see if he had noticed.

But Hilliard had other preoccupations at the moment. The officious clerk was not satisfied. "I see it is written here that John Hilliard had but one son who survived the wars and the Black Death," he observed, running a stubby finger down his records. "And that son was at one time apprenticed to a tyler in Essex."

Bolingbroke's horse stamped his newly shod hoof on the ground and was released with a friendly pat. "I am Wat the Tyler, if that's what you mean, Master Lawyer," answered the smith, turning at his leisure to face the assertion. "But my family was large and my wages small. So when news came that my father was like to die and no son to carry on, I came home to Kent."

The Earl of Arundel's minion pursed his thin lips disapprovingly. "You could have been branded for that, you know, my good man," he alleged, in pompous imitation of his master, "taking advantage of the shortage of able-bodied men to sell your labour from place to place."

"There've been Hilliards working this forge since Doomsday," the smith barked back at him. "And like enough they'll go on working it in spite of sharp-nosed busybodies like you!"

A new voice joined in the wrangle. "Since when are the highways of England free only for upstart lawyers and idle popinjays with decked up horses to move from place to place?" the aggravating Lollard wanted to know.

Arundel's man ignored him. The crowd behind him had drawn unpleasantly close; but the courage of the obstinate was his. He had been trained to pry, and he went on prying.

"I take it you paid your heriot dues to the Lord of the Manor here when you came back and took over your inheritance?" he inquired, determined to catch out this insolent giant.

But Wat Hilliard wasn't even looking at him. Having finished his shoeing job, he was free to observe what was going on. Particularly the press of labourers behind his tormentor and their menacing attitude. Some of them were neighbours he had known all his life, and some he had never seen before. But they were all on his side. His hardships and injustices belonged to each of them. And the tall, prisonbird of a priest, without an ounce of muscle to his arm, had dared to bait these well fed Parliamentary scavengers in his defence. Wat was usually a peaceable man. But for the first time it dawned on him that he wasn't just one man protecting his own private affairs—that the comic ploughshare swords hidden away under his corn sacks might come to mean more to him than just an ill-paid job done out of neighbourliness. When he turned again to confront the lawyer's clerk his actions were more self-conscious and he raised his voice so that his defiance would be heard by all down the road. "What is it to do with you whether I paid heriot or not?" he demanded. "You were sent here to collect the King's taxes, weren't you? And you've got your filthy money, haven't you? Poll tax for two— which is about as much as I earn in a month!"

A titter ran through the crowd, brittle and ominous as flames crackling before the wind through dried bracken on a common. And still the official seemed unaware of the fire he was starting, and the underling in charge of the moneybags chose that moment to come swaggering into the forge dragging the girl. There were no blushes on Rose's cheeks now. Innocent as she might be, she knew evil when she met it, and she struggled at every step. "He's still cheating you, master," the ruffian laughed boisterously. "Don't tell me this tall, bed-ripe lass isn't sixteen!"

The smith swung round and saw his daughter with mute terror in her eyes. "Lay your foul hands off her, or by the

Mass I'll kill you ! " he shouted, in a voice so terrible that the very tools seemed to jangle on their hooks and the royal party, preparing to mount, stopped in their tracks.

But the man was either a born fool or drunk. Lust so licked him that he paid no heed even when one of his fellows warned him that up in Essex a bawdy tax collector had been stoned. Standing in the middle of the workshop, full in the brightening sunlight, he jerked the girl to him so that her clean, childish body merged obscenely with his own. " If you dodge the poll tax, friend smith, you can pay leyr-wite on her instead," he crowed, dragging the fresh linen from her shoulder to cup her tender breast in the grossness of his hand. And in spite of their sour-faced chief's disapproval, his mates laughed coarsely. For even the youngest page present knew that whereas merchet was money a villein had to pay to his overlord when his daughter married, leyr-wite was what he paid for her shame if she merely became pregnant.

Richard sprung to his feet, caution burned up in a sudden gust of impersonal anger. But men's eyes were on stark drama and there was no need for speech. Wat Hilliard, tyler turned smith, had already—with the patience of his kind—suffered much. Provocation had at last produced a leader for the people who paid. His muscles were like whipcord and the hammer still in his hand. He swung it high above his head and it came down like God's vengeance out of the unsuspected shadows and split the tax collector's skull. Brains and blood spattered against the blackened post where de Vere had so lately lolled, and the ugly body slumped with no sound but a dull thud among the discarded horseshoes on the ground. Rose Hilliard would have gone down too in the ghastly embrace had not de Vere caught her as he was moving away towards his horse. He set her gently on a stool where she sat staring dazedly at a great splash of blood crimsoning the front of her bodice.

Silence held the forge, so recently alive with the clang of iron and warm, human voices. The immobility of actors in some *tableau vivant* held all present, arrested in whatever they were doing. The hirsute smith glaring without remorse at his victim; Henry Bolingbroke staring down with mildly surprised eyes at the lumpish thing which had so recently been a man; and Tom Mowbray, loosened from the last leading strings of childhood, trying not to avert his eyes from the first really toughening lesson of his manhood.

Holland, inured to such scenes of violence, glanced across at his half-brother with concern. He hoped to God the pampered youngster wouldn't faint or become hysterical like some of those idiot pages whimpering in the background. Even in the red glow from the embers Richard's face showed white, and he moved aside fastidiously so that the sickening stream of blood should not touch his shoe. But he stood erect and gave no sign of what he felt. "He's gamer than I supposed," thought Holland, forcing himself out of the tenseness of the moment to take some sort of command.

"Your cursed horse is ready at last," he snapped at Bolingbroke, "so let's get out of here before there's a riot."

Before leaving, Henry Bolingbroke slipped a gold florin into the smith's slack hand. Wat's gaze shifted slowly to stare at it. It was payment enough to keep his family for months, but obviously he took in nothing of its value. His mind was still a consuming fire fed with the freshly perceived wrongs of his kind.

Drawn by a sense of catastrophe, the crowd had come closer and were craning over each other's shoulders to see what people were looking at on the ground. Something gruesome enough to divert their interest from a party of gentry resuming a journey. Particularly as their men-at-arms seemed far more anxious to get on their way than to mix themselves up with a local brawl. Let them depart to their fine houses in London or wherever they were going. And to ultimate perdition, no doubt. . . . For had not John Ball just told them, with an inconsistency they were incapable of appreciating, that riches were a burden? "For verily I say unto you, it is as easy for a rich man to enter into the Kingdom of Heaven as for a camel to pass through the eye of a needle." They'd never seen a camel but no animal they *had* seen could do that—and it was written, he said, in the Holy Book. And if John Wycliffe got his way and had a printed Bible put in every church, anyone who knew how to read could see it for himself. As it was, of course, the priests read out only what suited them. And many of the priests were rich men themselves. Why, even the Archbishop of Canterbury had allowed himself to be made Chancellor, and the Prior of the Knights of St. John of Jerusalem was Treasurer of England and had their hard earned savings in his hands. . . .

Their simple heads were full of these things and of this new sensation created in their own village by Wat Tyler—as they had always called him to differentiate between him and his brothers—that they even made way obligingly for the noble party to depart. And the lawyer's clerk was quick to see that it would be safest to ride in company, particularly as they would be without the brawny keeper of the moneybags. " This will mean the gallows for you ! " he called back to Hilliard, putting the final touch to his morning's work by making a desperate man of him. But he dared not lay hands on him then. " Put your mate's body across his horse," he ordered his men hurriedly, " so that we may take it back to Dartford as proof and give him decent burial.".

A page who looked as if he might be sick at any moment was holding Blanchette at the door and, at a nudge from de Vere, Richard pulled himself together and went out. As he passed Rose Hilliard he thought that she kissed his trailing over-sleeve. She was sobbing quietly and Wat's huge hand lay in awkward compassion on her shoulder. The hand of a man with natural affections who had been provoked to murder.

As he took the reins of his horse, Richard came face to face with the Dartford men bearing their gruesome burden. He found himself shaking with ungovernable Plantagenet rage. " Throw that dog's body into the nearest ditch ! " he called

savagely. " And when you collect this cursed tax call it the
Commons—or Arundel's if you like—but not the King's ! "

He was aware that Wat the Tyler was staring after him, that
some of the more intelligent labourers were whispering together and that his half-brother was hurrying him away. As he
cantered up the London road ahead of the rest he realized that·
he had spoken ill-advisedly. That the Council, if they came to
hear of it, would be furious. But something warm and exciting
glowed within him, displacing his disgust and sudden anger,
because he had found that when he spoke like that people
obeyed him. Neither Thomas nor the tax gatherers had dared
to gainsay him, young Mowbray regarded him with ludicrous
awe and even that bombastic Lancastrian cousin of his followed
at his heels like a chastened cur.

CHAPTER V

IT TOOK only that journey from Canterbury to London to convince even the most sceptical of the King's friends that the revolt of the peasants was a reality. Not one of them but was thankful to lie safely in the Tower that night.

Naturally, Richard had been disappointed at not returning to Westminster, but he knew that Thomas's decision was right. If the royal apartments lacked the spaciousness of a modern palace, at least the Conqueror's great white Keep looked impregnable and Richard Coeur de Lion had known what he was about when he encircled the whole area with strong walls. Whatever happened outside in the streets, no danger could possibly penetrate such defences.

After supper the young king climbed out on to the leads of the Lantern Tower. The wind took away his breath for a moment as he emerged from the dark, winding stair and stirred his hair beneath its slender gold circlet. By craning over the parapet he could see a corner of the privy garden, peaceful and pleasant in the evening light. But all around him were towers and battlements and the whirring of ravens' wings, and below him the dark waters of the moat. Here and there about the sprawling mass of buildings the setting sun reflected on steel, picking out a sentry standing motionless in the shadow of some arch. Beyond the Byward Tower the drawbridge had been raised before curfew as a precaution, and beneath the wide arch of the water gate the ugly teeth of a portcullis shut out all unauthorized craft from the wharf. When Richard had lodged in the Tower before his coronation he had taken these things for granted as part of the grim atmosphere of the place; but now he reviewed them with a more calculating eye.

Across on the Surrey shore the Marshalsea prison stood up gaunt and grim beside the road to Eltham. Only that forenoon he had passed beside it on his way across Blackheath. Seen from the Tower of London the heath was merely a strip of blue distance, of course; but he could remember only too well how it had looked a few hours ago, with little groups of men camping on either side of the road among the flaming gorse. They had not seemed out of hand like the peasants he had encountered during the thunderstorm, nor even particularly antagonistic; but there had been something far more ominous about them for the very reason that they were organized. There had been men of better type among them—tenant farmers and tradesmen and here and there a parish priest—lending a more serious aspect to the uprising. And as Henry Bolingbroke had pointed out, many of them were obviously old soldiers—trained for the French wars in the levies of the masters they had risen against or in the "hue and cry" bands of town sheriffs. One could see it in the way they handled a bow and made camp. And judging by their confident and unhurried movements, they awaited reinforcements. It was as if all the wild protests which had been disturbing the various countries for weeks had crystallized into action here on the outskirts of the capital, and the whole green and gold heath had put off her holiday mood to await the issue.

As the royal party had trotted down to the river at Southwark, some rougher elements of townsmen had come streaming up from the beer gardens and brothels of Bankside and recognized them. They had shaken their fists at Bolingbroke—for no other reason apparently than that he was the haughty Duke of Lancaster's heir—and shouted for "King Richard and the trusty Commons!" But all the same, Richard had been glad to see the strong escort which Sir Robert Knollys, one of his father's trustiest comrades-in-arms, had brought out to meet them; and he was ready to wager that all his companions were as thankful as he to hear their horses' hoofbeats echoing once more beneath the battlemented towers of London Bridge.

Once across on the north bank, life had seemed normal enough. Flemish ships were unloading as usual at the Steelyard wharf, prentices' voices shrilled their wares from the direction of Cheapside, and all along Thames Street merchants and customs men and porters jostled each other as they went about their business.

But inside the Tower there was tension. The Lieutenant's lodgings seemed full of people. Thomas of Gloucester was there, and the Earls of Warwick and Salisbury and Sir Thomas Percy. Noticing John Legge, the hated author of the poll tax commission, talking anxiously to Hales, the Treasurer, Richard supposed that they must have come there for safety. But he had scarcely waited to speak to them. He had hurried straight to his private apartments, hoping to find his mother returned from Canterbury. All the way back from Eltham his anxiety for her had been mounting, for she, too, would have to pass across Blackheath. But no one had news of her and vivid pictures of violence immediately began to assail his imaginative mind. While Thomas Holland's boy held the basin for him to wash his hands, Richard had been annoyed to find them far from steady. But, noticing how scared the boy looked, he had managed to speak casually as he tossed back the fringed napkin. "Have them send someone to Westminster to make sure your grandmother, the Princess of Wales, hasn't gone there," he had ordered, suspecting that in concern for their own safety his older relatives had forgotten all about her.

Throughout dinner people had cursed the peasantry. Characteristic remarks of each of them came back to Richard as he stood out on the Lantern Tower in the freshening breeze.

"It's the fault of the small landowners—pandering to hired labourers and giving them any wages they ask," declared Warwick's resonant bass, seeing things only from the angle of his equals who still kept their own retainers.

"I suppose they've got to get their corn cut somehow, poor devils!" observed de Vere's lighter tones with lazy tolerance.

"A pretty pass the country has come to when our own villeins exploit us!" grumbled Gloucester, glaring at Richard as if the very fact of his being a minor made it his fault.

And then Richard recalled his own voice wearily taking up the implied challenge. "Isn't it the inevitable result of dragging on the war and draining our manpower? Perhaps if we can keep at peace for a few years, now that Uncle John has concluded this treaty with Scotland——"

And that, of course, had set Uncle Thomas off like one of his own incalculable cannon. "What's anybody got to gain from a patched-up peace?" he had snapped, in the grating voice which sounded as if he might explode at any moment. "Why, the peasants in this country are simply stuffed with loot from your father's conquests. That's just what's the matter with them. They've never been so well off and it's gone to their heads. Besides, if it comes to manpower," he had added, reaching rudely for the salt, "the Black Death killed far more of them than the wars."

After that Richard had let the conversation flow over him unheeded. Useless to suggest to a pig-headed militarist that returning armies might have carried the contagion. Useless, come to that, to argue at all about the plague—a calamity so devastating that it swept through a country mowing down nearly half the population and creating an unheard of situation where there were not enough labourers and servants to go round. No doubt, as Warwick and Percy kept contending *ad nauseam*, it was iniquitous of the survivors to seize upon the aftermath of a common misfortune as an opportunity to rise up against their masters. But just conceivably, mightn't some of the iniquity be on the masters' side? Impossible to doubt, for instance, the sincerity of that wild-eyed priest who claimed that in the eyes of God all men were equal, or the provocation of the blacksmith. And there had been the girl, Rose, as clean and sweet as any fine heiress about the court, subjected to hunger and insult—and yet all the fine laws of chivalry in

62

which he and his kind were so carefully brought up did absolutely nothing about distressed damsels of *that* sort.

For the first time in his life Richard found himself looking tentatively over the top of the code that shielded him. And he found there was something there—something alive and logical. Food for thought at any rate. This absurd rising would have to be put down, of course. It was becoming a menace to all the decent comforts of life. But he couldn't feel that the poor ignorant wretches were his enemies. He was touched that they should have appealed to him for help; rather set up, too, to find that they believed he had that much power. And he wished he could think out something to do about it.

That was why he had given the others the slip after supper and come up here, telling Standish to say that he was tired after his journey. Often of late when he wanted to sort out his mind he had used this subterfuge, without realizing what a handle it gave the Lancastrian clique to stress his supposed delicacy. Indeed, he scarcely believed that such a clique existed. There might be people who thought it would be better for the country—or for their own private ends—that his powerful, experienced Uncle John should reign. Yet the man who always *seemed* to be clutching at the power was his youngest uncle, Thomas of Gloucester.

But up on the battlements in the limpid evening light, with the sky turning to a pageant of crimson and gold behind the towers of Westminster, all these problems seemed rather a nuisance. And very remote. Why, only yesterday he and Robert and the rest of them had been tilting at the quintain, and tournaments and river parties and all the pleasant things of summer had still seemed quite important. Richard wished it could always be summer. Instinct in him was the desire for warmth and colour. These long June days were the nearest semblance now to the fading memory of his beloved Bordeaux and could wrap him in the old contented indolence against which Burley was always urging him to struggle.

A clatter of horses hurrying along Thames Street roused him from his southern habit of day-dreaming, and the sight of a gaily painted charette in the midst of them suddenly drove all other thoughts from his mind. His mother was coming home. The drawbridge was going down over the moat, the sentries at the Byward Tower were springing to attention. Peasants and problems forgotten, Richard Plantagenet dived down the dark spiral of the stairs, taking the worn steps at dangerous speed. By racing along a gallery he arrived in the courtyard just in time, no dignified king but an eager boy with shining eyes and wind-swept hair.

He had outstripped his half-brother, who was coming more soberly from the hall. Grooms and pages he waved aside and, swinging himself onto the high steps of the charette long before the lumbering vehicle had come to a standstill, he thrust his head through the unglazed window. Chattering women filled the barrel-roofed interior with the flutterings of an agitated dovecot. But his mother was there, illuminating the dim interior with the russet flame of her hair and the unfailing radiance of her smile.

"I've been so worried about you, precious!" he cried, kissing the soft hands which were the only part of her he could reach.

Joan of Kent made quite a to-do fussing herself and her bunched-up skirts and flowing sleeves through the narrow wooden doors, so that he had to stand aside and let her tall firstborn, Thomas, lift her down. Between tears and laughter, she embraced them both. But there was mud on the satin of her gown and her high, veiled headdress lay crushed and torn in the hands of her youngest lady, who skipped out after her.

"It was those ruffians on Blackheath," she tried to explain, as Gloucester and Bolingbroke and her small grandson crowded round to welcome her.

"What did they do to you?" asked Richard, tenderly wiping a smear from her cheek with his newfangled handkerchief.

Although obviously still rather breathless from some recent ordeal she was quick in their defence. "Oh, my men couldn't help it, Thomas," she expostulated. "There were simply swarms of people and somehow or other they had collected a lot of pikes and things——"

"They could easily have murdered us all!" dramatized the dark vivacious girl carrying the crushed headgear.

Apparently Gloucester felt there were worse calamities. "Or held you as hostages," he scolded. "And then our hands would have been tied!"

Holland met his glance with full appreciation of what seemed to both of them a crazily lost opportunity. "Thank God they hadn't that much sense!" he concurred piously.

But Richard wasn't concerned with military tactics at the moment. "They didn't really *hurt* you, did they, madam?" he persisted, urging his mother to come in and rest.

Her musical, full-throated laughter was reassuring. "No, no, of course not, *ma mie*. Why should they? They've nothing against *me*." As she walked buoyantly into the hall she was human enough to glance round with malicious enjoyment at Gloucester and the rest. All men whom the insurgents had reason to hate, presumably, since their consciences told them they would be safer in the Tower. "The people don't forget that I am the widow of their idol. Besides which, they've always liked me for my own sake." She preened herself provocatively before the empty hearth in her plumage of blue and green and gold, and laughed beneath her painted lashes in the way that always made Richard feel uncomfortable. "Why, I believe if I'd been a statesman I could have twiddled them round my little finger. Made them do anything. . . ." She stood twiddling the rings on her fingers instead and most of the men watching her shuffled themselves into a sheepish, admiring semi-circle that mutely admitted her Circean powers.

"Everything except go away, madam," her youngest lady presumed to remind her, with a sidelong smile at the attractive king. Lizbeth de Wardeaux was both amorous and pert, and

Richard often wished that his mother would box her ears. But Joan was the soul of good nature and allowed her household far too much licence. And noticing the strained lines round her eyes, he was more concerned for her than with the wiles of a pretty Sussex heiress. So he called for food and wine and coaxed her a little apart from the barrage of questions her women were answering so excitedly.

" You were really badly frightened, weren't you, my sweet ? And only trying to put up a brave show so that those fools shouldn't panic ? " he asserted intuitively, unfastening her cloak.

Joan drooped a little in the comfortable chair Ralph Standish set for her, letting a shower of small possessions slide from her lap and enjoying a brief luxury of self-pity from which all assumption of bravado had vanished. Her other two sons were obtuse and violent, but somehow one could always tell Richard even the silliest things. " They crowded round so. Such a lot of strange, rough faces," she murmured, leaning back gratefully. " I didn't mind so much until they insisted upon climbing on the carriage steps and kissing me. . . . Because I am a Kentish women, they said. . . ."

Richard's face flamed as if someone had struck him. " Kissing you ! *That* filthy rabble. . . . How dared they ? Oh, how dared they ? " he shouted furiously, unwittingly drawing attention to the indignity she had suffered.

Joan drank a glass of spiced wine and felt better. " I think they only meant to be friendly," she said, and seeing how profoundly she had shocked the assembled company found herself struggling with an urge to hysterical laughter. She was able to view them objectively. They were all so solemnly blue-blooded, whereas she, although a Plantagenet's grand-daughter, had seen other aspects of life and begotten her first batch of children in a commoner's bed.

" Friendly—with *you*, madam ! One might as well speak of swine singing to the stars ! " reproached Robert de Vere.

Richard looked round appealingly at his uncle and the lords

66

enjoying his hospitality. "Let's go out now," he urged. "Take every available man-at-arms and clear the heath."

His arresting young voice rose so confidently above the jumble of horrified questions and exclamations that Joan, anxious for his safety, immediately began to make light of the affair—although actually she need not have bothered, for there was no eager response from the indignant nobles. "They didn't mean any harm, Richard," she hastened to assure him. "In fact, most of them were quite respectful. It was only that they smelled so vile."

Seeing that he was not yet dissuaded, she sought to create a diversion. "I can still smell their grimy fingers," she complained, shaking out the folds of her dress with fastidious fingers. "Tell them to prepare me a bath, please, Ralph. And Lizbeth, run and get that French perfume the King bought me. Give me an arm, Robert de Vere, you born flatterer!"

She rose from her chair with all the ruffle of an acknowledged beauty, accepting gloves and purse and herbal nosegay with a smile that made men feel privileged to pick them up. The very austerity of the old stone-walled room warmed to her presence as she paused to stroke the soft texture of milord of Oxford's ringed velvet sleeve. "You must tell me your tailor's name, Robert," she coaxed with laughing envy, "and I'll have him make me a dress in that same becoming shade to replace the one that smells of peasants." She played up to his compliments with affectionate badinage, then yawned and thought she would go to bed; so that Richard was forced to abandon his sensible project and—drawn by her smile—accompany her to her room.

Once there he lingered of his own free will—as no doubt she had intended. The riot of richly coloured tapestries without which she never moved and the lovely garments her women were unpacking served to divert his interest, and ever since he was small he had loved to watch them brush her hair.

"Oh, Richard, I forgot to tell you. There was one man who didn't smell at all, although his hands were work grimed," she said. "A fine black-browed giant of a man who seemed to have made himself their leader. He had the most marvellous brown eyes——"

Richard smiled at her contentedly. When she sat like that by candlelight with her burnished hair about her shoulders it didn't seem at all ridiculous that she could still thrill to the sight of a handsome man. "And did he kiss you too?" he asked, with only a trace of his former resentment.

Lizbeth de Wardeaux had been clever enough to find the French perfume among the mountain of his mother's baggage, and he stopped her to take a leisurely sniff at it as she crossed the room with the painted Venetian phial held carefully between her tapering hands.

"I think it must have been he who crushed my poor head-dress," admitted Joan, her voice not wholly disapproving. "But you needn't be so sanctimonious about it, Dickon, because I remember now he said you had called in at his forge on the Eltham road and taken notice of his daughter."

The disdainful toss of Lizbeth's high-born head was wasted on Richard. Subtle French fragrance of mignonette was wiped out by a vivid recollection of the reek of smoking horseflesh. He was back in that beamed smithy, and he suddenly felt sick.

"He told me you took her part against some brute of a tax collector who had insulted her," went on his mother's voice, half muffled by brushed-out strands of gold. "It wasn't very wise of you, but they all seemed tremendously set up about it."

Richard replaced the stopper of the phial and handed it back abruptly. "And did he tell you that I had seen him split the man's skull?" he asked savagely.

The little lady-in-waiting stifled a scream and Joan was all concern at once, her shallow habits of vanity drowned as usual in the flood of her warm affections. "Oh, Richard—you poor thing!" she exclaimed, waving brush and tiring women aside. "And here have I been vexing you with the petty experiences of my own journey!"

Encouraged by the familiar sound of her sympathy, he put

both hands to his eyes as if to shut out the distressing picture—the kind of dramatic gesture which had always proved effective with both mother and nurse, insuring sweet consolation. But almost immediately, clutching at that manlier part of him, he walked nonchalantly towards the door. " It wasn't a particularly pleasant sight," he admitted, aping de Vere's habit of understatement.

Either way he was play-acting, and miserably conscious of the fact.

His mother, who had given birth to him almost on a battle-field, guessed that he must suffer abnormally from such sights and longed to comfort him as she had been wont to do when he was younger. These new efforts at self-reliance and reserve seemed to drive a wedge between them and she resented them as the handiwork of her brothers-in-law—and even Burley—who wanted to harden him. But she had the sense to realize that the boy must grow up, and pressed him no further.

" There is just one thing, Richard, before you go," she said hurriedly, seeing that his hand was on the latch.

" Yes, madam ? "

He waited politely and she rose and came to him, more troubled still about her second son. " Could we not have John fetched from the Savoy ? "

Richard always found the younger of his two half-brothers rather exhausting. " Why ? " he asked, without enthusiasm.

" Because I'm worried about him, being in your uncle of Lancaster's household. As I came across Blackheath I heard men shouting ' Burn the Savoy ! ' "

Richard had heard it too, together with a lot of other wild suggestions. " Don't worry, my dear," he said soothingly. " Walworth won't let them get into London. He'll raise the movable bit of the Bridge first."

But Joan was still uneasy. " Richard, why do they keep singing that ridiculous song ? Something about never wanting another King John. As if Lancaster were trying to make himself . . ."

"Oh, just because he has built himself a fine palace on the waterfront and likes to order people about and keeps ten thousand men, I suppose. You don't believe there's any truth in it, do you?"

"No. But *my* John's so hot-headed. He couldn't tamely accept their insolence. If he heard them, he wouldn't let people even *say* it. He'd rush out and start a fight or something. . . ."

"If he wants a fight why didn't he go with Uncle to Scotland?" asked Richard.

But their mother scarcely heard him. "He sees no fear," she was murmuring complacently.

Richard laughed without much enjoyment, quick to appreciate her unconscious comparison between John Holland and himself. It was so unfair, when she had just headed him off from rushing into danger on her behalf.

"He's your favourite son, isn't he?" he said, more as if he were stating a well-known fact than asking a question.

But one couldn't expect her to answer an impertinent remark like that, and when she looked at him in hurt reproof he felt a brute. "Of course I'll send for him," he promised, kissing her reassuringly. "Tonight, before the tide turns. But Thomas or the Lieutenant will have to sit up for him. I'm going to bed."

CHAPTER VI

At the foot of the stairs leading to his bedchamber Richard found de Vere and Mowbray waiting for him. "I've come to say good night and ask you to excuse me, Richard," said Mowbray, stepping forward into the circle of light thrown by a torch stuck in an iron bracket on the wall.

So many things had happened since they left Eltham that Richard had almost forgotten a messenger from Norfolk who had waited upon him. "Ah, yes, of course. Your people want you to go up to Framlingham until all this bother has blown over," he recalled. "I think you'd be wise to get away early, Tom."

But Mowbray hung about scowling at such womanish caution, evidently hoping that Richard would disregard his relatives' wishes. "I'd much rather stay," he muttered. "It's horrid missing all the fun."

"It may not be so funny as you think!" consoled de Vere, without moving from the shadows where he was standing. Through an arrow slit in the thickness of the stair turret he could see an angry red glow of which the others were unaware. Somewhere on the opposite bank up Lambeth way.

Mowbray ignored him. He wasn't the only one who was sometimes annoyed by the confident way in which de Vere answered for the King. After all, the fellow wasn't even related to him except by some distant marriage. "Good-bye, Richard," he said with grave sincerity. "I would far rather stay with you—particularly if things *do* get worse."

It was nice of him, Richard thought. He grasped his hand and resisted the usual temptation to rumple his hair. "I know," he answered, with mutual regret. "A pity we couldn't have had a few days together at Westminster so that I could have shown you the new pup. Mathe, I've called him. And I've a colt out of that dappled grey." He and this country cousin of his had a passion for dogs and horses and hawks in which the more sophisticated Robert did not share, and some of their happiest hours were spent pottering round the royal kennels and mews. " *We're* safe enough here, Tom, but see that your men are well armed," he warned with a sudden access of concern for him. " The Lieutenant of the Tower was telling me at supper that a fellow with the ridiculous name of Jack Straw is making trouble *north* of London now, up on the Hampstead hills. Oh, and Tom——"

" Yes ? "

" You'll be riding out of the City through Aldgate, won't you ? I wish you'd tell Geoffrey Chaucer he's welcome to move into the Tower if things get ugly on that side. He lives over the gate, you know."

" Yes, of course I will," agreed Mowbray, glad to have at least some small behest to do. " You mean that waggish-looking little man who controls the Customs down at the wool wharf ? "

" And writes such amazingly good verse—although you'd be no judge of that ! " teased de Vere. " He's been a sort of household necessity with one member or another of the Plantagenet family for years."

He and the King stood together watching Tom go—a pleasant, dependable-looking lad without any social graces. Richard had always felt an easy affection for him; but some-how tonight—when everyone seemed keyed up and different —he was conscious of parting with a doglike devotion which might be precious. Naturally de Vere's feelings were different. " The heir to the mighty Bigods goes home ! " he remarked, as if his departure left the two of them free to take up their undivided companionship in peace.

Richard noticed the faint sneer in his voice. " You don't really like him, do you, Robert ? " he asked regretfully.

Not to have noticed it before was one of those naïvetés

which de Vere loved in Richard, but which at times he found exasperating. " Isn't the shoe rather on the other foot ? " he laughed. And seeing that Richard, already part way up the stairs, looked round at him inquiringly, he shrugged with suitable diffidence. " I wish I had your modesty, Richard ! " he said. " Can't you see the fellow's jealous of me ? "

He had stepped into the patch of wavering light and Richard wondered almost resentfully why a few people should be so unfairly favoured and self-possessed. " Oh," he said unresponsively, and lingered a little, vaguely comprehending the kind of hurt he must often have dealt his more defenceless cousin. But a page came along at that moment to light him to bed, and instead of pursuing the subject he called carelessly over his shoulder, " Come and talk while they undress me, Robert".

De Vere followed him into his room, lounging over to the deep-set window while Richard sat on the edge of the bed for Standish to unpeel his long silken hose. Although normally the exquisite Earl of Oxford would have left so menial a task to the servants, he was careful to draw one of the heavy tapestry window curtains so as to shut out a warmth from the west which might have passed for the afterglow of a June sunset. " Did you hear that some of the colleges up at Oxford are seething with Wycliffe's tenets and all in sympathy with this rebellion ? " he asked tentatively.

" And what Oxford thinks today London will think to-morrow ? " mused Richard absently, staring into a small fire of scented cones.

De Vere rose and began to prowl about the room, picking up a book here and a jewelled trifle there. " Richard, you do want me to stay with you, don't you ? " He chose the moment when his friend's bright head was momentarily eclipsed by a freshly warmed nightshirt. " You don't feel that perhaps I ought to go back to Oxford ? Naturally, my presence would stop any nonsense on my own estate."

Richard, whitely arrayed, handed day shirt and belt to a

kneeling page and began thoughtfully smoothing the soft doeskin of his discarded tunic. "I don't know. I'm not sure. Perhaps you *had* better go, Robert. You could start out with Mowbray in the morning. Some of the eastern counties are affected and we don't want this thing to spread."

An almost inaudible sigh of relief passed between de Vere's even teeth. "But you won't have anyone to talk to—anyone reasonably young, I mean," he began to protest, taking the furred bedrobe from Standish and putting it almost tenderly about the King's shoulders.

"I shall have my cousin Henry. And if the worst comes to the worst he'll be able to advise me about withstanding a siege," said Richard lightly.

"And what he doesn't know your bellicose brother Thomas probably does," laughed de Vere.

But Richard hadn't yet quite outgrown the younger-brother attitude fostered by his mother. "Have you noticed, Robert, that he hasn't been looking too well lately?" he asked anxiously, standing up to belt the soft folds of fur about him. "Sort of thin and yellowish, like my father was. . . ."

"He's probably caught the same bug in Spain," suggested de Vere flippantly. He had nothing in common with Thomas Holland and rather resented the respect Richard showed him.

Richard didn't answer. He was hurt that Robert should have taken his dismissal so much more readily than Tom.

"You don't really mind my going?" asked Robert, quick to sense this.

But Richard had moved to his *prie-dieu* and looked somehow sacred and aloof with the lighted tapers on either side him. They seemed to kindle a flame within him. "You know I mind horribly," he said, turning the vellum pages of his missal. "But there is England to be considered."

He had looked like that at his coronation and Robert de Vere, who understood him even better than he loved him, knew that in such exalted moments he had gone away somewhere far beyond his influence.

CHAPTER VII

WHEN RICHARD rose next morning his two best friends had gone, but the Tower seemed more full of people than ever. John Holland was there, of course, protesting loudly that he had only been persuaded to leave the Savoy in order to allay the nervous apprehensions of his mother. And the Archbishop of Canterbury had just ridden in.

In these changed circumstances Richard was genuinely pleased to see Sudbury, but surprised that he should have brought so many of his clerks and servants. " What brings your lordship here so early ? " he asked, wondering how on earth his poor harassed steward was going to feed them all.

" Haven't you heard, sir ? " quavered Sir Robert Hales, hovering anxiously round his spiritual superior.

" Heard what ? " Richard looked sharply round at the whispering huddle of relatives and nobles and back to the ageing primate's agitated face.

" The rebels marched to Lambeth last night and burned down my palace," said the Archbishop tonelessly, as if he had learned to repeat the words but still couldn't believe their import.

Richard stared aghast and led him to his own chair and made him sit down. " My poor Sudbury ! All your priceless books and pictures and everything ? "

" And your Grace's Chancery records." Even losing his home had not deprived the conscientious servant of Church and Crown of his fine sense of stewardship.

" They would have killed milord Archbishop, his clerks say, if a travelling friar hadn't warned them in time," said Bolingbroke, coming to join them.

The Princess came too and seated herself beside the old man, full of consolation. " If they will do this to their own primate they will do anything ! " she cried indignantly.

In spite of his shaking limbs Sudbury managed a wan smile. " I think it was less because I am an archbishop, madam, than because I am—or was—Chancellor of the realm. Their poor minds have room for one idea at a time, and at the moment, they are full of taxation."

" Why do you say 'was Chancellor'? " asked Richard, wondering if the shock had unhinged his mind.

But Sudbury was wiser than most of them—and probably less self-seeking. Fumbling in the folds of his gown, he brought forth the seal of the Chancery and laid it in the King's hand. " I think, sir, it would be better for you—and for all of us—if you appoint someone else in my place. It is the idea of churchmen holding state appointments which the people hate," he brought himself to admit, with an apologetic glance in the direction of his colleague Hales, who was both Treasurer and Prior of St. John's of Jerusalem.

" His Lordship is quite right," agreed Gloucester, before Richard had time to answer.

Of course, in the absence of his elder uncles it was for Thomas of Gloucester to advise him. But Richard's gaze clung to the broken old man who had at least always been kind to him. It was a big decision to make—to change the Chancellor of England all in a hurry like that. Parliament wasn't sitting and it would probably mean putting in someone of Gloucester's choosing. The boy's safe, normal world was slipping away from him on the tide of this incredible uprising of a class that had hitherto been negligible, and he wished with all his heart that Burley were there to tell him what to do.

" I suppose we had better hold a debate," he found himself saying, and thought how amused Robert would be at the mere idea of his suggesting such a thing.

And so, quite informally, this handful of important people taking refuge in the Tower held the strangest debate at which Richard had ever presided. If, in fact, he could be said to preside at all. For—having given up his chair to the Archbishop—he perched for a while on the arm of his mother's, and then wandered restlessly to the window from whence he could see houses burning all along the opposite bank of the river. About the table, in no particular order of degree, crowded his uncle and half-brothers and his cousin Bolingbroke, Warwick and Salisbury, Hales and his satellite Legge, the dignified Lieutenant and a sprinkling of privileged squires like Standish and Bolingbroke's man, John Ferrour. And into this worried assembly walked Walworth, the Lord Mayor, and Nicholas Brembre, one of his sheriffs, bringing a breath of the outside world. Apart from their civic rank, one was Master of the Fishmongers' Guild and the other a wealthy grocer; but in the eagerness for news even Gloucester and the pompous Warwick moved willingly to make room for them. Richard himself greeted them quite simply as welcome friends. Brembre's clever, simian face had always fascinated him, and Walworth's experience and poise made him an asset at any meeting.

In answer to a bombardment of questions they confirmed the bad news about Lambeth and reported that the Marshalsea prison was now ablaze and the prisoners at large.

" And joining the rebels," surmised Gloucester.

" Which introduces a definitely criminal element far more difficult to cope with," added Brembre.

" Then nobody's property is safe ! " cried those of them who had town houses.

But Walworth was able to give them a certain amount of reassurance. Those two totally diverse characters, John Ball the Essex priest and Wat the Tyler, who had made himself the Kentish men's leader, still appeared to have the mob well in hand.

" You mean to tell us that starving dogs like that saw all Sudbury's priceless stuff and could be leashed back from looting ? " scoffed Thomas Holland, in the light of whose experience such a miracle seemed impossible.

" Something of the crusading fervour seems to have entered into it," explained Brembre, with his wry smile. " This gaolbird priest preaches that riches are accursed, and that those who enjoy them in this world will inevitably find themselves garnered with the goats on Doomsday."

"I am afraid he has also inflamed them with the damnable notion that all churchmen—with the possible exception of a few friars who have thrown in their lot with the people—should be exterminated," warned Walworth, on a more serious note.

Hales shuddered visibly.

"The man must be mad!" murmured Joan.

Sudbury, who had regained his composure, laid a soothing hand on hers. "My dear lady, he has been going about the country railing against our greed and lasciviousness for years. That is why I have more than once had to imprison him."

Whatever the ethics of the case, Walworth couldn't help thinking that it would have been better for the Archbishop had he burned Wycliffe for a heretic and let this political extremist go. He could almost see the crowd tearing him limb from limb. "If you imprisoned Ball, I would advise your lordship to keep out of their way," he said curtly. He and his sheriffs had enough responsibility with the King in the midst, and he felt that the primate's presence on this side of the river was the last straw.

Richard watched them all from the window seat, taking in the mounting gravity of the situation. For the first time in his life he felt glad that Uncle Thomas was there. He would know what to do. Undoubtedly, he himself had often behaved like a presumptuous puppy and there was good reason for the value these seasoned warriors set upon themselves. He looked hopefully from his uncle's glum face to a reflection of the same type mirrored in the hard, younger faces of the Hollands. Surely any minute now they would take the situation in hand— rise up and issue orders in the decisive way they were always advocating. Orders which would alter the complexion of things in a few hours. But unfortunately all their experience had been on foreign battlefields against armies who moved and countered-moved according to orthodox rules of strategy. And there had been nothing laid down in the rules about thousands of fellow countrymen armed with pitchforks, growling like bloodthirsty curs against their gates. Moreover, none of them was gifted with much imagination. So they just sat there, dazed by a series of events for which they knew of no precedent or formula.

" We must do *something*," the Princess was saying, looking from one to another beseechingly.

And because nobody else answered her, Richard got to his feet and said the only thing he could think of.. " Why not send Sir Robert Knollys to disperse them——" he suggested, remembering how that trusty, brutal old campaigner had come to meet him and how the audacious pirate Dalyngrigge had been conspicuous in his train.

Those round the table shook their heads. It was true that Sir Robert had scorned to come into the Tower. He was still in his City house. But his forces were inadequate. " Besides, he may be of more use where he is if there should be trouble later on *inside* the City," Walworth reminded them grimly..

" You mean they may try to rush the Bridge ? " asked Richard, wishing his voice sounded a little steadier.

" They are right up to it now," said Walworth. " All night they've been burning the brothels along Bankside, and they're threatening to burn down Southwark church if we don't let them across."

" Burning the brothels—whatever for ? " exclaimed Gloucester. In any warfare he'd ever had anything to do with they were the one part of a city one might reasonably expect to be spared.

" Haven't you noticed that almost every stew is kept by a Fleming ? " laughed the younger Holland.

Simon Sudbury surveyed the handsome young know-all with a nice blend of toleration and dislike. " Not frequenting them myself, I'm in no position to judge," he said, in his quiet, humorous way. "But I have long deplored the Londoners' prejudice against the Flemish woolstaple."

"If Sir John's observation be correct your lordship must admit that our citizens have some provocation," grinned Brembre. "After all, two of our most flourishing industries in the hands of foreigners——"

"I'm not sure that's the only reason for the burnings," said Walworth, with a meaning glance at Prior Hales, who fidgeted uncomfortably and hoped that only local sheriffs and such would know that the Bankside property was his. After all, when he had let it to the Flemings at a soaring rental he had been careful not to inquire too closely into their affairs. "And the poor—er—inmates?" he asked hastily, with a virtuous clearing of his throat.

"This fanatic Ball had them dragged out into the road and put to death," Walworth told him. And Sudbury, who was neither cruel nor a hypocrite, was heard to murmur something about finding someone to cast the first stone.

Richard had scarcely been listening. The fate of a few tumbledown stews concerned him not at all. But the fate of London did. "Has the drawbridge at the other end of the Bridge been raised?" he asked sharply.

"Yes, sir. And the tower on the bastion this side of it fortified." The Lord Mayor turned and answered him at once, as if jolted into surprised recognition that his orders mattered. "Walter Sybyle, of the Mercers' Company, is alderman for that ward, and I have offered him reinforcements. Though the fool will probably refuse them out of jealousy for his Guild!"

"As long as it *is* only jealousy, and not treachery!" muttered Brembre shrewdly. "I don't altogether trust that man."

"Then let us send a company of pikemen and be done with it," advised Thomas Holland sensibly. But it appeared that they would give such offence to London pride as to jeopardize the citizens' much taxed loyalty.

Finding it useless to wait upon other people's advice, Richard's mind was beginning to work clearly on its own account. In fact, this thing was becoming rather fascinating, like a game of chess in which one enjoys outwitting a wily opponent. " Don't forget that raising the movable part of the bridge will let shipping through into the Pool," he pointed out. " These insurgents won't dare try to get across in the comparatively few rowboats moored on the other side. But you'll have to see that all big ships tie up below bridge on this side, or Tyler may try to board them as they pass through and use them for transport."

" Too true ! " admitted Brembre. " We must send word to Chaucer to stop them before high tide."

" And Aldgate ought to be fortified against these fresh forces from Essex," blustered Gloucester. And he and the Hollands began telling the civic dignitaries how to do it.

The word Aldgate started a train of thought in Richard's mind. If Gloucester had been in the Tower for several hours before his own arrival, it was a pity he hadn't begun telling people how to do things a bit earlier ! " If Robert de Vere and Thomas Mowbray were able to leave by that gate this morning," he asked, cutting across their confusing spate of directions without apology, " why were no messengers sent through before I got here to rouse the unaffected shires ? Surely there are plenty of my knights sitting comfortably in Midland manors who would have come to our assistance ? " He looked straight at Gloucester as he spoke and was aware of his mother ranging herself joyfully on his side—probably more because it was the first time she had ever heard him openly call one of his uncles to account than from any sense of gravity of the omission.

Thomas Plantagenet stopped giving orders but said nothing. It would so obviously have been the sensible thing to do that most of the older men looked sheepish. But Henry Bolingbroke took up the idea. " There may still be time," he said, in his unflustered methodical way. " If Walworth can send these knights the exact disposition of the rebels, a relieving party could approach under cover of darkness and attack them in the rear. And that would be *our* moment to ride out in two separate parties and outflank them."

"After all, London is as good as besieged, isn't it?" said Richard, backing him up.

It was the idea of Youth—chancy and exciting—and it appealed to several present. But others objected on the ground that it would take up too much time.

Joan, who had been thinking how this new touch of brisk masterfulness became Richard, withdrew her adoring gaze from him and turned her mind to the business in hand. If the men couldn't settle something, she must. She dealt with it much as she might have dealt with a plague of mice or some troublesome servants clamouring for higher wages. "If you're sending out messengers at all, why not send them to Blackheath and Highgate and ask these people exactly what they want?" she suggested. "Then perhaps we can appease them and they will go home."

Men cunning in council turned to look at her in shocked surprise. Put like that the whole business sounded absurdly simple. Her suggestion went straight to the heart of the thing, of course; but then, women's minds worked so differently, always putting common sense before pride. And if one heeded them, why, there'd be no wars or anything. . . . Nothing to sit in Council *for*, or feel important about. But at least one man besides Richard beamed upon her. The Lord Mayor was grateful to her for making it easier to say what he had really come to say. "I have already taken it upon myself to do so, madam," he confessed.

In spite of themselves the others looked relieved. "Quite right, Walworth—quite right!" approved Warwick. A tradesman could do that sort of thing, of course, and it would save men of noble blood from demeaning themselves. "And what did they say?"

Walworth got up and looked with respectful diffidence towards the raised window embrasure where Richard was standing. "They refused to treat with us at all—but only with the King. They want to tell *him* their grievances. They seem to think that he——"

Whatever more he said was momentarily drowned in indignant shouts of "Monstrous!" and "Impossible!" Only when his listeners had spent their indignation were his concluding words audible. "They want him to go to Blackheath."

The words came to Richard as a shock. They wanted *him* to go—not all these warlike adults arguing around his table. The thought of going back to Blackheath—to a Blackheath no longer ominously orderly but swarming with wild beasts who burned down palaces and killed prostitutes like helpless sheep in the streets—was a far more terrifying challenge than any he was ever likely to encounter in the lists. Across the heads of the rest he met William Walworth's steady gaze, and it was as if the man had thrown down a gage. A gage for which the prize was London. Only instead of cantering across some flag-decked lists he would have to ride out from these strong encircling walls into a hostile world where violence and class hatred ruled. Into a strange, inverted world where, like Gloucester and the rest, he didn't know the first thing about the rules. He felt miserably inadequate, but something in him —some heritage stronger than himself—made him nod assent to the inquiry in Walworth's honest eyes.

"Is it necessary for *anyone* to go?" asked his elder half-brother, anxious for his safety. "After all, bread doesn't grow on Highgate or Blackheath. Tyler and Straw can order their men about but they can't feed them. Not all those thousands."

"Keep them out of London for another twenty-four hours and their empty bellies will tell them to go home," agreed the Lord Lieutenant.

Walworth and his sheriff exchanged uneasy glances. "If we can," they muttered in unison.

But Gloucester had evidently been turning over some new project in his mind. "I don't see why the King shouldn't go out to them," he said unexpectedly. It was his first contribution to the discussion for some time.

"My dear Duke, consider the boy's age!" protested the Archbishop. And Salisbury backed him up with the very objection which Gloucester had been swift enough to mention when the rebels had waylaid the King's mother. "Doesn't it occur to any of you that they may keep his Grace as a hostage?"

"And then they might demand *anything!*" spluttered the Prior, well aware that his own head would be one of the first things they would want.

In response to his mother's imploring gaze Richard had returned to the table and was standing by her chair, but evidently he was not giving in to her arguments. "If he goes, I shall go with him!" she declared. "When my father was Duke of Kent he made most of his serfs free. For the love they bear him and the Black Prince and myself they will do us no harm."

"Then we will all ride with you, madam!" cried Standish and several others, stirred by her courage and trusting rather bleakly in her optimism.

They were almost all on their feet now, arguing more fiercely than ever. Richard was grateful to Bolingbroke for ending it. "Listen, milords!" he called out, rapping the table with the quillons of his sword to make himself heard. "There's no need to ride anywhere. Why can't Richard go by barge? Down the river to Rotherhithe or somewhere. He can summon the leaders to the bank and hear what they have to say from midstream. Then there will be no danger of hostages or trickery."

Old soldiers like Warwick and Salisbury were half ashamed of themselves for not thinking of so simple a solution. This son of Gaunt's was a likely looking lad, mature for his age and quick to seize an advantage. And—much as they hated to admit it—new situations called for adaptable young minds.

"An excellent idea, Harry!" approved Richard, and sent

for his bargemaster before the others could think up some argument against it. "We'll go this afternoon."

John Holland, not to be outdone, sprang up with such clumsy haste that he upset his stool with a bang. "Why not now—this morning?" he demanded pugnaciously.

Richard and Henry were bending over a map of the Thames valley which Standish had had the forethought to bring along and which he had just unrolled across the table before them. For once these two grandsons of Edward the Third were in absorbed accord, fair head and dark almost touching. "Because this morning, my dear John," explained Richard without even looking up, "my watermen would have to pull back up-river against the tide. Whereas this afternoon the tide will be on the turn and we can come back quickly—if we should need to."

CHAPTER VIII

RICHARD had told Ralph Standish to wake him early on Corpus Christi day so that he might attend Mass. But he had slept badly and lay still in his bed for a while, thinking over all the disturbing events of the previous day. After dinner they had gone down the river in the state barge as Henry had suggested. The meadows at Rotherhithe, usually so lush and green, had been black with insurgents, and the royal party had stayed off shore for a little while talking with their leaders. A very little while it seemed, looking back upon those confused and nervous moments. And then they had taken advantage of the turning tide—just as he himself had shocked John Holland by suggesting—to row back a great deal quicker than they had come. Because they were afraid. They—the supposed cream of English nobility—afraid of that ill-fed, ill-armed rabble on the bank.

Richard Plantagenet groaned with shame at the thought of it, turning closer into the blessed privacy of his tapestry bed hangings.

Even now he could scarcely believe that they had behaved so cravenly, and was prey to a tantalizing conviction that if only they might go again they would do better. What had happened to all the inherent dominance of the ruling classes—to all their warlike training and lessons in high chivalry? What must these serfs and labourers—whom they had ordered about all their lives—have thought of them? And—above all—how could they themselves go on respecting each other? Once back in the Tower they had avoided each other's eyes. But the fact remained that not even the bravest of them, tried on many a battlefield, had had any idea that a mob, once free from their crushing heel and aware of its own power, could look—and sound—so alarming.

Richard's waking senses became aware of sounds unusual to the hour. Surely the same sounds as at Rotherhithe—that murmuring of innumerable voices and shuffling of innumerable ill-shod feet? But that was impossible, with the width of the Thames between. It must be some horrid trick of memory born of a sleepless night. He knew that he would be late for Mass, yet burrowed a rumpled bronze head deeper into the softness of the pillows. But it was all of no avail. The mob really *was* howling beneath his windows. He sat up starkly and called for Standish to pull the tapestries.

" What is it, Ralph ? " he asked, and knew the answer before his squire spoke.

Standish was white beneath his healthy summer tan, but he began laying out his master's shirt and hose with steady, accustomed hands. " The rebels have been pouring into the City all night," he said.

Richard's blue eyes were points of demanding intelligence in the disordered wideness of the bed. " You mean they rushed the Bridge ? "

" It is thought to have been treachery, sir." Standish guessed that the King had slept but little and tried to curb his own rising panic. " One of those accursed aldermen went across to talk with them and told them the bridge was held by friends. And all the unruly prentices and some malcontents already planted in the City made sure that it was so. They either persuaded or overcame Sybyle's guards."

" But I sent a messenger to say that the charters I promised at Rotherhithe would be ready for them this morning—so that they can go away. As you know, I took a clerk with me in the barge specially to write down their main grievances, and after supper we all composed a sort of free pardon embodying most of the things they asked. Some fool started writing it out in Latin, but I turned it into plain English for them myself and told those idle clerks of Sudbury's to sit up all night making copies of it."

The King slid his legs over the side of the bed and hastily

pulled on his hose. "It appears, sir," said Standish, stooping to smooth out the slightest suggestion of a wrinkle from ankle to thigh, "that this treacherous Alderman Horn borrowed a City banner from the Town Clerk to give him the semblance of authority and forestalled your messenger."

"God damn his insolence! I'll see that Walworth has him hanged for it!" Richard sprang up and ran shoeless to the window. All he could see was his privy garden spread out like a neatly patterned coloured kerchief. The dew on the grass was not yet dry and cobwebs glistened like glass lace across the rose bushes. But with such tumult going on outside the walls it seemed incongruous that roses should bloom at all.

"Some of us have been to the top of the Keep. You can see everything from there," Standish was saying excitedly. "As soon as the drawbridge was down on the Southwark side the devils began coming across in little companies and you could see their friends on this side giving them food. But now hundreds of them are ransacking the Vintry and private houses in Thames Street. And whole gangs of them were rushing shouting along the Strand."

"But that howling noise is coming from the opposite direction."

"St. Catherine's hill. If you come to this side of the window, sir, you can see a bit of it behind the wharf. Tyler's got his main forces assembled there. And they're yelling for blood!"

Richard leaned out and listened, trying to recognize the words they were shouting. It was the most terrifying sound he had ever heard. The pleasant open space, so often thronged with Londoners taking their evening stroll, was now packed with an angry, surging mass of labourers shaking fists and home-made weapons at the fortress wall which baulked them of their prey; for now it was not charters they were asking for, but lives. When Richard drew his head back into the room he, too, was white. "They sound like wild beasts!" he said.

Standish returned his horrified gaze. For the moment they were no longer King and squire, but a very young man and a boy facing up to a common danger. "It's the poor Archbishop they want. And Prior Hales, of course. And Legge."

"I know. They sent a deputation about them almost as soon as I got here, and my uncle would have turned them out to their fate." Richard began pacing restlessly back and forth. "I don't mind what happens to that rat Legge. By all accounts he started most of the trouble. It wasn't only the accursed tax. It was the way it was collected. You saw what happened in that forge." Fetching up before the empty hearth, he sighed and stretched, graceful as a girl in his silken underwear. "Lord, how long ago that seems!"

"It's a mercy the Duke's in Scotland," said Standish, clapping for the pages and making an effort to resume his normal duties.

Richard knew, of course, that when anyone said just "the Duke" like that, that they were referring to his eldest uncle. Back at the window, again, with all his attention centred on a fresh cloud of smoke, he caught at his squire's arm as he brought him his fashionably pointed shoes. "Look, Ralph! You said they rushed shouting down the Strand. Surely that's the Savoy burning now?"

Ralph looked, and an awed silence fell upon them. "The Londoners almost burned it before—when the Duke tried to take the City government from the Lord Mayor and Corporation. At the time of Wycliffe's trial. Do you remember?" Ralph whispered, above the scurrying of the frightened pages.

Richard nodded. "The beloved Bishop of London intervened. But what's to prevent them now?" he asked bitterly.

Yesterday he had watched several houses burn, but somehow it was different when it was a home belonging to a member of one's own family. A place where one had gone in and out familiarly—eaten meals, had favourite rooms and petted dogs. Perhaps he should have been glad—all cock-a-hoop because the people hated his haughty uncle. One of the uncles who had kept him in leading strings. But the times were too critical for that; and Richard was not naturally revengeful. Besides, oddly enough, of all three uncles he disliked least the one whom rumour persistently represented as his rival.

Apparently other occupants of the Tower had been astir early at their windows, for Richard was still in shirt and hose when his half-brothers and a posse of excited hangers-on invaded his bedroom. They seemed on the verge of panic. "The fiends really *have* fired the Savoy!" shouted the younger Holland.

"And Hales' Priory at Clerkenwell," added the elder. "So it's no longer a question of the rebels being starved out. It's we who are being besieged." He stopped gloomily before the open psalter on his nephew's *prie-dieu*. "And it's Friday the thirteenth," he added, with all the pessimism of a man sickening for something.

Pages coming from the kitchen with hot water were too scared to hold their ewers steadily. They slopped it over people's feet and were cuffed by their overwrought betters; but Richard thought they were scarcely to be blamed, considering the poor example they had been set. He coaxed and rated them into dressing him somehow and was thankful to hurry down to the courtyard and betake himself to the bare old chapel in the Keep. Glad, too, to find Archbishop Sudbury waiting to celebrate. Here, at least, where his ancestors had worshipped, there was peace. The thickness of the Conqueror's walls shut out the murderous howling of a crazy new world, and between massive pillars of Caen stone it was easy to slip back into a familiar age when feudalism was unquestioned and secure. Watching the Archbishop move serenely before the altar, it seemed absurd to think that the old man's life was in danger. All the crescendo of ugly scenes which had filled the last few days were muted to a dream so that Richard, on rising from his knees, could almost imagine it was any ordinary day and that he was free to go hunting at Sheen or Windsor.

But realization came sharply. He separated himself from the rest of the congregation and followed Sudbury into the sacristy. It was true he had been shriven, but he was missing de Vere and felt need of more informal confession. So he stood around watching a clerk divest the primate of his chasuble until Sudbury, sensing his desire for privacy, sent the young monk away. Even then Richard lingered over the vestments spilling their gorgeousness from a great carved chest, so that his bright hair and the richly embroidered materials made a pool of colour in the dim, pillared gloom. Suddenly aware that he was being observed, he lifted his head and spoke impulsively, cutting out all preamble. " I was afraid yesterday in the barge—horribly afraid," he said.

The clear-cut words seemed to echo almost startlingly against the stonework of his hardier ancestors. Sudbury laid down the jewelled mitre in his hands and smiled at him. " Who am I to judge you, my son ? " he asked gently. " I, who was asked to stay in hiding."

Richard waved his diffidence aside. " But you can tell me— not as priest but as friend—was it ignoble of me to let them row back before my conference with these insurgents was completed ? "

The Archbishop found such grave, youthful conscientiousness very touching. It seemed so unfair, too, that this boy whose burgeoning ideas about statecraft had been so consistently ignored should now, for the first time, be left by his managing relatives to conduct his own conferences. " You had a woman with you," he reminded him, seeking to restore his self-respect.

Richard let the cope he had been examining fall back across the coffer lid. " My mother *would* come," he said. " For love of me, probably. Or out of fear for John, because he is of the Lancastrian household. As you know, milord, she is much more courageous than most women. But when she saw the numbers of insurgents she nearly fainted. It *is* the numbers that are so terrifying, of course." He paused for a moment or two as if reliving his own sensations at sight of them. "Naturally, I was anxious about her. But I wanted to get back to save my own skin as well," he added, with meticulous candour.

Sudbury had gone down to the Tower steps to meet them on their return. "Judging by their complexions there were older men in the barge who were not exactly loath to do so either," he pointed out dryly. "Although I noticed afterwards that most of them, at one time or another, made your lady mother their excuse."

Richard knew this to be true, and when the Princess had retired to her own room and they had been discussing the expedition at supper he had hated them for it. "If they hadn't kept urging me I might have stayed to hear more," he admitted. "I wanted to. Actually, it was extraordinarily interesting hearing about life from a viewpoint so absolutely opposed to our own."

"A rare experience for a king," smiled Sudbury.

Richard drew near. He had been wanting to tell someone about it. Somebody who would understand like Burley. "Their spokesmen were quite intelligent and I feel we might have come to some real agreement. But it was difficult, shouting from a swaying boat and trying to understand their rough country speech. And unfortunately I missed a lot because people in the barge kept talking across me. Saying they could see dangerous-looking trained bands on the bank— crack shots as likely as not who had been at Poitiers—and what was the good of coming by water, anyway, if the men ashore had bows and arrows? Even my bargemaster whispered to me that he thought we ought to be going. Then one of my mother's ladies, who is very young but would come with us, screamed out that there was a man hidden behind one of those drooping willows taking aim at me." Richard stammered a little at remembrance of her embarrassing concern for him. "Though I think it was really Henry he was aiming at," he explained confusedly, "because some peasants were shouting 'Down with Lancaster!' and when I moved in front of him the man lowered his bow."

Sudbury studied the fair, sensitive face which showed no trace of the Black Prince's hardihood. "You did *that*, Richard?" he said. "And you come and ask me if it was ignoble to be afraid!"

Richard reddened uncomfortably. It sounded as if he had been bragging. "Oh, well, that was different. Things one does on the spur of the moment like that——"

"Are usually the outcome of habit and therefore a true indication of character. But I always thought that you and he——"

"There's no love lost between us, if that's what you mean. But we're all in this together and he's been more helpful than some of those wordy old Councillors. After all, he stands in as much danger as yourself; but he didn't get sent for by anxious relatives or—or find more pressing business elsewhere."

If the Archbishop recognized a tinge of bitterness in the King's words and guessed at the cause, he was too wise a man to remark on it. And, as their import reminded him, he had enough urgent trouble of his own. "I am an old man now and prepared to die," he said, as they came out on to steps of the Keep and heard again that unappeased howl for blood. "But I too have been horribly afraid. Afraid of being torn limb from limb by those ravening wolves."

Richard offered him his arm with charming courtesy. "I could have bought our immunity that way two days ago," he said. "But you are my guest, milord, and surely these walls are thick enough to reassure you."

The people's hatred had come as a great shock to a man who had been wont to pray for them. "Then they asked for—my body?" he quavered, as they descended the steps.

Richard nodded gravely. "Yours and Hales' and Lancaster's—which last is not in my hands, thank God!"

Half-way across the courtyard Sudbury paused a little breathlessly, and in his preoccupation rested a hand on the King's shoulder almost as if the lad were his own son. " Richard, I have been thinking——"

" Well ? "

" If Hales and I could get away, too, it would make it easier for you all, wouldn't it ? When I was down on the watersteps yesterday one of the fathers from Crutched Friars was getting into a little boat. Taking Extreme Unction to some poor passing soul aboard one of those galleys bound for Venice, no doubt. And I wondered if I, too, could——"

Richard was quick to take in his thought. " It is worth trying," he agreed.

" Except that today the insurgents are all along *this* bank, watching," sighed Sudbury as they came through the privy garden to the royal apartments. " So that unless something should divert their attention——"

" Don't worry, Sudbury. I will see that there is a diversion quite soon," promised Richard, unconsciously adumbrating his father's brisk decisiveness. " Before dinner, if I can get my own way, for once ! "

He looked back from the doorway so that the last the Archbishop saw of him was his bright, boyish smile, unclouded as yet by cynicism or distrust. " God keep him like that always," prayed the old man, " with his goodness shining out of him ! "

CHAPTER IX

RICHARD found most of his friends and relatives gathered in the Lantern Tower. From thence they could look down on a part of London. They seemed stunned by this invasion of the City and were herded together in anxious groups in one half of the bare, circular room. As if by common consent they had left the westward window to Henry Bolingbroke, who stood with his back to them staring at the dying flames which were all that was left of the Savoy.

In spite of this fresh tragedy, Joan of Kent was seated at a little table breaking her fast. " You see how right I was about John," she said as soon as Richard appeared at the top of the winding stair. He noticed that although Lizbeth de Wardaux was spreading her a fresh slice of bread and honey the dear, inimitable woman spoke in a hushed whisper as if she were still in church—out of deference to her detested nephew, he supposed. He smiled and bent to kiss her, then went straight to Henry. Seeing that desolate gap in the fine river frontage for the first time was like having a bit of one's everyday life suddenly shore away. " I'm terribly sorry, Henry," he said. " It was one of the loveliest buildings in London ! "

Henry himself cared considerably less about its architectural beauty, but it had been his home ; and a reflection of the conflagration shining in his dark eyes revealed his burning rage.

" You're sure the Duchess got away safely ? " asked Joan, rather ashamed of her preoccupation with her own loved ones. She never had liked the Lancasters, but at a time like this one couldn't help being sorry for them.

" I hear she reached our castle at Kenilworth, madam," answered Henry. " But even up there feeling runs so high against us that I doubt if the Constable would dare to let her in." His words sounded wooden and callous; but the present duchess was only his step-mother—and part of a political bargain at that. For, as everyone knew, John of Gaunt had married her solely to substantiate his pretensions to the Castilian throne. She couldn't even speak English, and the upbringing of his first wife's daughters had been left to Katherine Swinford, the family governess.

The name of Swinford must have reminded Joan of someone in the household for whom she *did* care. "How awful of us to forget about Chaucer's wife!" she exclaimed; and when the Port Controller came hurrying into the room she half rose in consternation as if this beloved servant were one of themselves.

Chaucer had married Katherine Swinford's sister—a woman of gentle birth—and adored her. Perhaps the very fact that they had served in separate households had perpetuated the sweet flowering of their love. His finely chiselled features and normally fresh-coloured cheeks were ashen, and tearing anxiety had dulled the kindly humour of his glance. Having lived with various members of the Plantagenet family for twenty years or more, he went straight to the King without embarrassment. "I have just seen the roof fall in," he said, without wealth of words and still panting from the turret stairs. "Philippa, my wife—as you know, sir, she is one of the Duchess's ladies—I believe they got away, but . . ."

Richard stepped forward and took the blindly groping hand which had written so much lovely poetry. "For God's sake, Henry, give him what comfort you can!"

Bolingbroke was sorry enough for the fellow, although of course he couldn't show it as Richard did. He rather despised poets, but this Chaucer was a man of parts. He had fought and even been taken prisoner in France, and the late King himself had ransomed him. So he hastened to assure him that his Philippa had gone north with her sister in the Duchess Constanza's train.

Even while voicing relief and thanks, Geoffrey Chaucer was

swift to realize that the room was crowded with distinguished personages with whom he was far less at home. He began to realize, too, that they were all avid for news. " It was hearing the screams as the roof fell in that was so awful," he apologized. " Some poor drunken wights must have been still in the gutted cellars, besotted with wine. Not being sure about my wife, I tried to land from my revenue boat. But the flames were too fierce. That fanatic Ball was there, shouting to his followers to throw the Duke's treasures into the water. One could hear his voice above the cracking of the rafters, telling them that all who possessed riches were damned. I saw priceless paintings floating like rags . . ."

" And what about the wharves on either side ? " asked Gloucester.

Chaucer was becoming his normally coolly observant self again. " Our own they have spared, sir. But the Flemish wharves are a shambles. Even from midstream I could see the wrecked weighing sheds and every Fleming who had not escaped lying headless in his own blood."

" How can a man who forbids looting allow murder ? " demanded Richard indignantly, wondering how on earth he was to placate the Flemish government.

" It seems they have got beyond his control," answered Nicholas Brembre, who had gone as far as he dared by road and come back to report. " Some faint-hearted citizens with more money than sense have been trying to buy favour by opening their cellars to the rabble. They forget that most of these peasants have never in their lives tasted anything stronger than cheap tavern ale."

" And most of the great vats down in the Vintry have been broken open," confirmed Chaucer. " I was there only this morning, hoping to conclude the sale of my late father's warehouse."

" Having moved up and up until you live over a City gatehouse and no longer need it ! " laughed John Holland boisterously. He never could understand what his august relatives saw in the insignificant wine merchant's son to trust him with important offices at home and private missions abroad which he would have liked for himself.

But Chaucer could afford to ignore him, and went on talking to the King with that happy blend of candour and respect which makes a family servant a friend. " They'd cleared out everything. The good Gascoigny and Rhinish that my father used to supply to yours, sir—and even your own favourite vintage."

" My poor Geoffrey ! " commiserated Richard, wiping out John's jibe with an arm briefly laid about a sensitive man's shoulders. He turned back into the centre of the room with a rueful laugh. " And to think that I've got to go out and talk to them while they're inflamed with my own Bordeaux ! "

He spoke with intentional lightness, but everybody stared at him as if he were mad, and Joan rose abruptly with a hand both pressed to either cheek. "Oh, *no*, Richard!" she protested.

He knew that both she and Lizbeth had lost their nerve since the Rotherhithe episode. " You saw how reasonable the peasants were yesterday," he reminded her. " This morning I propose to meet some of the Essex men, and Walworth says they're not nearly so savage as your Kentish toughs." He turned to his uncle and the rest, unaware of how slight a figure he looked in their midst. " I thought it might appease them if I offered to meet them all in that meadow at Mile End where the prentices hold their sports. How far would that be, Brembre ? "

" About two miles, I should say, sir."

Richard went and perched on the table, which was still littered with his mother's impromptu meal. " That should be far enough to draw this howling mob off from here, shouldn't it, Uncle Thomas ? And to give all decent citizens time to arm under Sir Robert Knollys ? "

For some reason or other Gloucester looked quite pleased with the suggestion. " It should give time for quite a lot of things to happen," he agreed civilly, after a moment or two's cogitation.

But as usual the Hollands were clamorous and argumentative.

"Why humble ourselves to them like that? They'll probably all be dead drunk in a few hours, and we could plan a night attack and butcher the lot," suggested the elder.

"Words! Words! What's the good of words, Richard?" the younger wanted to know.

But the Earl of Salisbury, whose courage no man could question, upheld his King. "If you think you can really appease them by fair words, sir, it will be so much the better," he said quietly. "For if we take too high a stand and fail to go through with it, it will be all over with us and our heirs, and England will be a desert in their hands."

Richard drew resolution from the man's personal liking and his patriotism. For once two people of experience and standing had backed his own ideas. "Then are you ready to ride with me, gentlemen?" he asked, turning to the rest of them.

They had expected him to beg for their advice—to shilly-shally and spin out the morning in safety. But the words were less of a question than a command.

Blank surprise was in their faces, and cold fear in their hearts. But rather than be shamed before his fellows each man muttered assent. All of them must have known that sooner or later Gloucester or Walworth or one of the Hollands would have to sponsor some desperate sort of action; but so far, in spite of all their united military experience, no leader had been forthcoming. And it had been left to this boy of fourteen to rouse them. A leader as unexpected as he was inexperienced. It was preposterous, of course—and damaging to their pride. Small wonder that their grudging admiration was mingled with scepticism. It was only youngsters like Bolingbroke and Standish and adventurous opportunists like Brembre who caught something from the flame that kindled him and began to rally round.

But already Richard was beginning to organize the affair and as he called for messengers and ordered the horses some of them caught echoes of his father's crisp, decisive tones.

"Well, if we've got to do this crazy thing, for God's sake let's put on some armour," grumbled Thomas Holland.

Richard was concentrating on the wording of a message which he and Salisbury were trying to concoct. "Not obviously—it would spoil everything," he objected. "Under our tunics, if you like."

"And by the same reasoning it would be provoking trouble to take any archers," pointed out Salisbury.

But the sight of her two elder sons quilting themselves against dagger thrusts and the youngest allowing a mesh of mail to be belted about his immature body was too much for Joan. "All three of you!" she cried, covering her face with both hands. "After yesterday, I can't live through it— waiting for you to come back!"

Thomas stopped half in and half out of the quilted jacket his squire was slipping over his head and looked across at this incalculable, fair-skinned young brother of his. For years he'd been trying to make a decent sportsman of him, and here he was calmly arranging for people to ride out into the teeth of a drink-crazed mob. And on a morning when one's bowels were already as water. "Don't you think one of us ought to stay, Dickon?" he suggested hopefully.

His head rose like a sallow cheese above the jacket; two of his front teeth had been knocked out in a recent tournament and this ridiculous changing business had so disarranged his hair as to make it obvious to all beholders that he was beginning to go bald. For the first time Richard viewed him dispassionately and wondered why he had always looked up to him as such a magnificent person. It was Thomas, he recalled, who had been loudest in making their mother his excuse for returning so hurriedly yesterday. "Henry will be staying," he answered briefly, bending to put his signet to the message.

Bolingbroke, who had been swifter than any of them in

getting into his armour, began to protest, and Richard understood well enough how one of his temperament must resent the indignity of being left behind with a lot of women and priests. "Obviously, Henry, it will make things easier for us all," he pointed out patiently.

Reluctantly, Bolingbroke motioned to his squire, Ferrour, to help him disarm again. "Of course, if you put it like that——"

But Richard laid a detaining hand on the immaculately polished hauberk. From where he stood he could still see smoke drifting from the Savoy palace, and it seemed scarcely likely that a city's hatred would be spent with the flames. "I shouldn't take the thing off until all this business is over, if I were you," he warned, lowering his voice. "Maybe you didn't see that archer yesterday——"

Bolingbroke's strong, spatulate fingers dropped from the buckle he had been sullenly wrenching at. "Yes, I did see—and I'm grateful," he muttered, avoiding Richard's eyes. It didn't come easily to him to say thank you—or to owe his life to someone whom he had always considered rather a milksop. And because generosity was not inherent in his nature it didn't tend to make him like this important cousin of his any the better.

There were hasty farewells and a mounting of corveting, ill-exercised steeds in the courtyard. Already the howling of the mob was stilled and watchmen on the walls reported that on receipt of the King's message there had been a consultation of rebel leaders and a general drawing away of forces in the direction of Mile End. Great crowds from St. Catherine's were already gone.

It had been decided to go out by the postern in the eastern wall, striking up northwards just outside the City boundary and joining the Mile End road outside Aldgate. But when the small gate was opened the King's party saw that hundreds of rebels remained, grim, watchful and silent—close under the Tower walls.

"They've tricked us!" exclaimed a dozen voices, as men and horses jostled in the entrance.

"Tyler's been too clever for us again, dividing his forces," observed Nicholas Brembre, almost admiringly.

After the first moment of dismay, Richard turned instinctively to rate the Lieutenant of the Tower for allowing his men to report so ill. But the man was nowhere to be seen, and there was nothing for it but to go forward.

Neither he nor any of his companions had keyed themselves up to be confronted immediately by that battery of hostile eyes, those rows of grimed arms holding bills and hooks and stones. Until that moment Richard himself had had little time to think of the danger of the enterprise—to consider what his own reactions would be. The moment Blanchette's dainty hoofs tapped the planks of the narrow drawbridge in full view of that still, formidable crowd the old familiar chill of fear gripped him. It took away his breath, like plunging naked into icy water. He would have given anything—anything—to turn back into the security of the courtyard. But a great swearing and pushing of flanks behind him forced him forward, and inevitably the feeling passed, to be followed by a lovely excitement and sense of exhilaration. Adventure lay before him, and the joy of personal endeavour. He rode out bareheaded into the summer morning.

All eyes were upon him. He was conscious of that hush which always prefaced his movements, and acutely aware that his demeanour held the crowd. As his senses accustomed themselves to such exposed publicity he became capable of secondary thought. Out of the tail of his eye he saw a small boat put out stealthily from below the arches where the kitchen sluice fell into the moat. But to his dismay it withdrew almost instantly before a spurt of cruel jeers and the splashing of many stones. "Poor old Sudbury!" he exclaimed, in bitter disappointment.

Gloucester, pushing forward to ride beside him, looked at him sharply. In the anxiety of the moment his hard, light eyes were less carefully veiled than usual. " So you're doing this hare-brained thing to save him ! " he snarled. And by the ill-concealed violence that emanated from him, Richard knew that he didn't want Sudbury to be saved.

But the sudden illuminating thought was drowned in present reality. The postern drawbridge was already up and all retreat cut off. Each man must have turned towards Aldgate feeling as if his heart were in his throat. Soon they had skirted the City wall and turned sharply right on to the Bow road. It stretched like a straight, dusty ribbon between Hackney marshes and the river. No more insurgents were in sight. But some of the King's small, outnumbered company had been badly shaken. He could hear them keeping up their spirits with shaky jests behind him, and addressing each other with an unwonted cordiality born of nervousness. And presently he was aware of Thomas's harsh voice, croaky with distress, complaining of the pains in his belly and the ague which made it almost impossible for him to hold the reins.

Richard turned and looked at him. The man really did look ill. And they were just nearing the White Chapel where the good Carmelite brethren would care for him. " Better go in there and rest until our return," he shouted back, remembering with compunction how his war-tried father had often looked like that. And for once Thomas took his advice.

" It's all this worry," thought Richard, ingenuously. But for himself, in spite of worried days and sleepless nights, he felt fit and clear-headed. He had no idea what he would say to those hordes of Essex men waiting at Mile End, but he would let them air their grievances. This time, whatever happened, he wouldn't run away. And—given goodwill on both sides—no doubt they would be able to come to some lasting agreement. After all, their comrades outside the Tower could have hewn him in pieces just now, but they hadn't. And for the moment it was enough that he was no longer afraid and that the sun shone. Sunshine to him was always worth more than ten score archers, and he even broke into a gay French song, grinning widely at the curious antics of John Holland's rawboned horse. It was the kind of mount that neither he nor Mowbray would have been seen dead on. " How *can* a man of your experience be such an appalling judge of horseflesh ? " he broke off to shout banteringly.

John didn't answer him. And then, quite suddenly, the most extraordinary thing happened. Without excuse or apology or any word of warning his precious half-brother set spurs to the fidgeting brute, cleared a ditch and bolted across a field of rye towards the lonely safety of the Hackney marshes.

Clearly, his nerve had broken.

The whole party reined in to stare after him. All of them had been called upon to witness some amazing incidents during this last week, but this was unbelievable. John Holland, who would prick a man in the gizzard as soon as argue with him, disappearing like a common craven in a cloud of dust !

" Perhaps it was your Grace's untimely singing unnerved him," suggested the irrepressible Brembre. And Walworth laughed contemptuously, for there was no London tradesman but had felt the scorn of the younger Holland's haughty tongue.

But Richard burst out laughing. " If only Robert could have seen him ! " he spluttered. It struck him as excruciatingly funny that his mother's fire-eating favourite who was always sneering at him should have bolted like that. And it gave him too, a warm surprised feeling of superiority, so that he patted Blanchette forward almost eagerly and even grimaced cheerfully at his uncle.

After all, there was something in being a Plantagenet.

CHAPTER X

IT WAS long past noon before Richard rode back into London, but he felt neither tired nor hungry. In a few short hours he seemed to have become a different person. He had laid hands on his heritage and it had not eluded him. Some of the very men who for personal ambition had tried to stamp out the flame of his spirit had stood silently by and taken second place in this strange emergency. Their assumption and his own consequent fears that he might not rise to the splendid record of his own family had proved false. He had seen Thomas of Gloucester tongue-tied and the Hollands skulking among monks or flying like poltroons; while he— the youngster whom they chose to think effeminate—had kept his head.

For three solid hours he had talked with the insurgents. Not from any barge or battlements, but pushing his horse in amongst them as his interest grew. Moreover, he had liked them. They were honest, upstanding men upon whose drudgery the country depended; and they turned to him naturally with their grievances, ignoring all the complications of Councils and the pretensions of his uncles. This time, being neither hurried nor flurried, he had found that he could follow the roughness of their speech and even appreciate the racy virility of phrase which Geoffrey Chaucer always chose as the medium for his verse.

They had laid before him facts and demands undulled as yet by the tedious circumlocution of Council chambers. And his own mind had worked like quicksilver, following their arguments. Heriot and merchet, for example, were dues which he and his kind had always extracted from them as a matter of course; but seen from their point of view these old feudal usages looked less reasonable. Why should a man who worked hard all his days be fined for dying or pay to get his daughters married? And then there were the old vexed questions about a villein's right to buy and sell in open markets, to snare rabbits on manorial lands and to take his little bit of corn to be ground at any mill he chose.

That serfs should clamour to be freemen, paying money for their strips of land, seemed understandable. They were willing enough to work for their landlords, it seemed—even to fight for them if need be—but they were determined to work for a wage and hold their fields by rental and not body service. Richard had learned enough of economics to realize the power this would give them—particularly in a land suffering from a war-depleted population where wages were already soaring. But by some intuition of his own he perceived that somehow it might put new vigour into the exhausted country and raise the whole standard of living; so that he soon found himself discussing the average value of land and what the average peasant could afford to pay for it. With the impulsive quickness of youth he referred the matter there and then to some of the rich land owners who were with him so that it could be practically settled before submitting it to a lot of long-drawn-out legislature. And before he left, a standard price of four pence an acre had been agreed upon, which seemed fair enough to all.

In the same friendly spirit he promised the insurgents written pardons. And, realizing that his uncle and the Lord Mayor were far more concerned about getting the mob away from London than with any agricultural matters, he promptly had a number of his personal banners distributed among the leaders so that they might begin to march home immediately, feeling themselves to be under his protection.

Bitter grudges which had been growing for years had been wiped out with a little common sense and co-operation in a few hours. The crowd had cheered him again and again with a spontaneous gratitude which made all the hostile demonstrations around the Tower seem like a forgotten dream; and he had been able to look back at Mile End village and see the surrounding meadows almost cleared.

" A good morning's work, sir ! " Nicholas Brembre had declared. And Salisbury, Walworth and the rest had given him credit, congratulating him with a sincerity which made him blush with pleasure. Only his uncle and some of the older lords had hung back a little, shamed and disapproving.

But Richard cared little for their disapproval now. He even hugged himself to think now much Uncle Thomas must be hating it all. The cheers of the people were still ringing in his ears as he passed through Aldgate, tasting for the first time what it felt like to be a real king.

He and his supporters would return in triumph. No more sneaking out at back entrances for him. They would go past Barking church and round by the main gatehouse of the Tower. Already all the malcontents seemed to have melted away from St. Catherine's. Looking towards the wharf one saw only blue sky and the masts of shipping bobbing on a full, slapping tide.

The sight of ships reminded Richard of Sudbury. No need now for the poor old man to go slinking off to some Flemish port. Hadn't he—Richard the Second—settled it all ? Brought back safety and peace of mind to London and to all his friends ? Now that the actual work was done a happy sense of drama enthralled him. Too bad that Robert and Burley couldn't be there to see him returning to the city he had saved—bareheaded and valiant in his gold damask tunic with the new-fashioned up-standing collar and his fine green worsted hose. And what a pity the bells weren't ringing as they had been for his coronation ! Richard loved it when St. Paul's and all the other churches clashed their bells, filling the narrow streets with a delirium of sound. But his mother would be sure to come out to meet him. There would be the warm welcome of her laughing embraces and the adoring glances of that doting minx Lizbeth. And the guards would cheer from the battlements as they heaved on the winches to let the drawbridge down. . . .

But nobody seemed to be about. The tall houses mirrored in Barking Creek had a blank, deserted air. Doors were bolted and windows shuttered, and the only sign of life was a mangy cur routing among the gutter garbage. Rounding the Tower wall, Richard noticed that the drawbridge was already down. But no one was watching from the battlements, nor were there any sentries by the gatehouse. The great oak doors stood wide. The gatehouse itself yawned open—with a broken pike lying across the flagstones and the twisted iron of a torch sconce banging in the draught.

His retinue reined in against the moat and stared aghast.

"It looks like a house that has been burgled," said Brembre, who must have seen plenty of them during the past few days.

"No one could possibly break into the Tower!" scoffed Salisbury.

"Unless they were helped in," said Walworth, remembering how the insurgents had been helped over London Bridge.

The word "Treachery!" sprang to men's lips. Only the Duke of Gloucester, who for once had been keeping himself in the background, made no comment.

Like Salisbury, Richard couldn't believe it to be true. He tried to shake himself out of such a ridiculous nightmare. He wasn't going to have his beautiful bubble of a day rudely pricked like this. "Send for the Lieutenant and I'll have him answer for those defaulting sentries—*and* this morning's watchmen," he ordered, in a fair imitation of his grandfather's angriest voice.

Before anyone could obey, Standish had scrambled from his saddle onto the wall of the moat. "Look, they're coming out to meet us now!" he called down from his vantage-point.

But it was ragged peasants, not soldiers in the King's livery, who came swarming out across the bridge. Most of them were drunk, and all of them yelled, hoarse with excitement, as they came. Some clutched golden bowls and some brass candlesticks. They trailed and tripped over precious tapestries they had looted. And leading the way were brawny, bare-armed men carrying something aloft on a pole. The rest danced round it and clawed up at it with obscene gestures, and as the whole bacchanalian rout wedged itself to a momentary standstill on the drawbridge it was possible to see what the thing was. For a moment or two it mopped and mowed in the direction of the silent spectators—a battered, sightless head with the merciless sunlight glistening on a silver tonsure matted with blood.

"Simon Sudbury! Oh, my poor Sudbury!" shuddered Richard, covering his face with both hands and letting all the bitter mockery of his triumphal summer day wash over him.

There were other heads on other poles. "Hales—Legge—some unfortunate clerk in Lancaster's livery——" counted Brembre, between set lips. But the whole venom of Tyler's men was concentrated on the prelate who had imprisoned John Ball, the creator of their dream. They never even noticed the royal party. "To the Bridge! Stick them up on London Bridge!" they yelled, and bore their horrid burdens westwards to the river behind the smouldering wharves.

"If they have done that to Sudbury, what must they have done to my mother?" cried Richard, spurring forward almost before they had passed. A dozen hands caught at his bridle. He fought wildly to get past, striking at them indiscriminately with his riding whip. "I've got to get in . . . I must see for myself. I must find that damned Lieutenant—he'll know . . ." he raged hysterically. But for some reason best known to himself, Gloucester was equally determined that he should *not* see the Lieutenant. "Don't be a young fool!" he shouted, wedging his great Flemish roan across the boy's path. "Half those maniacs are probably still in there. They're drunk with power and blood as well as wine. You don't want to come out with *your* head on a pole like Sudbury, do you?"

It was sound sense, of course, but in his frantic anxiety Richard slid to the ground and tried to slip beneath the mare's body. He even drew his dagger and would have struck at the friends who detained him had they not made way just then for Geoffrey Chaucer, whose everyday aspect appeared to pull things back into the realm of sanity. He had come walking up from one of the wharves, staff in hand, just as Richard had seen him dozens of times coming from his daily work at the Customs office. Chaucer of the shrewd, kind eyes—Chaucer who always understood. "The Princess is quite safe," he said at once, in that soothing voice of his.

"Where, Geoffrey? Where?" In his relief Richard leaned against him, clutching at the familiar texture of his brown livery gown.

"We took her to the Wardrobe in Carter Lane. To the house you gave Mundina Danos when she married your Grace's tailor. It was the only place I could think of."

"Then Mundina is with her?"

"Yes, sir. Plying her with her famous remedies. The poor lady fainted when she saw that vile rabble surging into the private apartments. They were tearing down the hangings and disporting themselves on the beds. But that pert, dark de Wardeaux girl has the courage of a tigress. She bethought her of the boat the poor Archbishop had hoped to use and we got the Princess away in that."

Richard sheathed his dagger shamefacedly. "Oh, Geoffrey, Geoffrey, what should we all do without you?" he said, feeling rather like fainting himself. He was thankful beyond words for his mother's safety; but it had all been such a shock—such an ugly ending to so promising an adventure. Couldn't Life ever let him play his fine ventures to a conclusion? He heard Salisbury asking sternly what the guards had been about and his uncle inquiring with genuine anxiety for his nephew, Henry Bolingbroke, and felt how much more dignified it would have been to concern himself with these matters than to let himself get all worked up and behave like a hysterical idiot.

"About the guards, I can't say, milords," he heard Chaucer answering in his unruffled way. "None of us saw the beginning of it. I was checking up accounts with the King's steward and when I opened the door the rabble were upon us and my one thought was to hurry to the Princess. But, looking back, it seems to sit in my memory that on some of the stairs the guards stood back and let them pass." He paused a moment and looked strangely at Gloucester. "And when I got to the Princess's room milord Derby was there, about to leave by some backstair. That squire of his, John Ferrour, was bundling him up into one of her women's dresses and said he could hide him in his own home somewhere in Southwark. I think they must have got away while those brutes were murdering the Archbishop and the Prior at their prayers in the chapel."

Richard had forgotten all about his cousin, but he had the decency to try to strangle an involuntary wish that Sudbury might have been spared instead.

The morning's work at Mile End must have been more of a strain than he had realized. He was suddenly terribly tired. Almost with indifference he heard Chaucer telling them that it would be impossible to lie in the Tower that night—that Tyler's men were tumbling the kitchen wenches in the King's own bed. And loyal old Salisbury swearing that he would string them all up before they could live long to boast of it.

Was everybody going to stop in an ignominious huddle all afternoon, discussing what they were going to do, he wondered irritably. For himself, he was going to Carter Lane. To his mother and his beloved nurse, whose lovely tenderness beckoned like the only lighted candle in a drab and cruel world. He mounted without a word. Dejectedly he rode off down Thames Street, and dejectedly most of the others followed.

Probably they had nowhere else where they dared go. But Richard didn't want them. He would have given anything to go to his own womenfolk alone. And after talking with men who sweated for their daily bread he felt ashamed of the way his uncle and other rich lords took Jacot's and Mundina's hospitality for granted, crowding their house and straining the unwarned resources of their larder. He himself could eat but little. The sight of those mangled heads had turned him sick.

But he sat watching his mother who, with her usual resilience, was recounting her experiences. And he let Mundina's ministrations flow over him and heal him.

The strange evening passed in a babble of discussion; but the topic was always the same. How had the insurgents got into the Tower?

Was it the Lieutenant's fault? Had he—as Gloucester suggested—either through slackness or dishonesty left the place too ill-victualled to withstand a siege? Were the men-at-arms themselves really in sympathy with the revolt? Had they been bribed? Had someone promised Wat Tyler access to the hated Treasurer and Chancellor once the royal party were out of the way? And if so, who?

Probably they would never know. And since the thing was done, thought Richard with an access of his old southern indolence, what matter? But when there came a tramping of mailed feet on the wooden household stairs and his uncle brought in the Earl of Arundel bearing the late Archbishop's Chancery seals, he thought he could make a pretty good guess. Nothing that he would ever be able to prove, of course— since Gloucester had been clever enough to ride with him. . . . But if Sudbury were still alive and the Court not in a state of emergency even Gloucester wouldn't have dared to make his shifty crony Chancellor of England without consulting either Parliament or his elder brothers.

After Richard had been coerced into signing the necessary documents, he lay awake for a long time in the strange, gabled room upstairs. It was the first time he had ever gone to bed in an ordinary private house. The windows overhung the street and it seemed strange to hear footsteps padding up and down the lane and to see a rushlight burning in the window of the opposite house only a few feet away. But although it was a typically English house he fancied a faint scent of almond blossom hung about the bed linen. Probably the sheets were some that Mundina had brought in her presses from Bordeaux in Aquitaine.

The nostalgic fragrance carried him back to the carefree days he had spent there in her kind and indulgent company, when his father was away at war and his lovely mother and sometimes his elder brother had come to play with him. He had been a lonely child and loved their visits. Except that his brother Edward had been rather self-opinionated and full of himself. But then he had been heir presumptive to the throne of England and all the French possessions, whereas he himself had been a comparative nobody.

Lying there in the darkness with the horror of Sudbury's bleeding head before him every time he dared to close his eyes, Richard wished with all his heart that he were a nobody still. And he prayed that Simon Burley or even John of Lancaster might come home soon. For if there was one person he loathed and mistrusted more than his Uncle Thomas it was Richard, Earl of Arundel.

CHAPTER XI

SATURDAY morning dawned warm and cloudless—just like any other June day. Except that London was in the hands of ruthless rebels and the King and all law-abiding citizens virtually prisoners. As Brembre had feared when the gaols were broken open, it was largely criminals who remained behind, and all lawyers against whom they had a grudge were being vindictively murdered in the streets. Trade was at a standstill. Churches were closed and priests afraid to venture abroad to shrive the dying. And instead of busy booths along Eastcheap the extremists, fanned by the growing fanaticism of Ball, had set up an execution block.

For years all the best brains in the country had been concentrated on Continental wars while sores festered too long at home. Through sheer reaction Richard could see, by that gift of vision which most of his mentors had done so little to develop, that to reconcile the claims of rich and poor would be a finer job than either Crécy or Poitiers. But in the end it was irritation that drove him again to action.

Such was his antipathy towards Arundel that he could scarcely breath in the same house with him. By every word and gesture the arrogant, tactless earl did his best to make the young king feel of no account; and, like most sensitive people, Richard was apt to become very much what his audience thought him. Yesterday he had risen above himself, cast off the fetters of tutelage, basked in the approval of all. Today Arundel and Gloucester, their nerve restored, behaved as if they had been in charge of everything and talked across him as if he were some witless page.

" Of course, it's absurd trying to placate these canailles," snorted Arundel, who had never been called upon to come face to face with them. " You think you've made them generous concessions and they crop up somewhere else shouting for disendowment of the Church, a general holocaust of all laws and lawyers and the right to roam about our woods and kill any game they fancy."

"But they went away reasonably enough yesterday when I talked to them and gave them my charters and banners," objected Richard, realizing as soon as he had said it how childish the words sounded.

Arundel turned and stared down from his great height as if he had only just noticed that he was there. "What's the use of a few fancy bits of vellum and silk?" he asked rudely. "Hundreds of them 'em are still here—killing Flemings and dragging out poor devils who've taken sanctuary in the churches."

Gloucester reached for the last spiced cake from the little tailor's depleted table. "If you ask me, most of them are staying less because they want more concessions than because they want to make sure of looting London before the scum of half a dozen other counties get in. You always get that when you think you've cleared up this sort of thing," he said, as if he had had life-long experience of dealing with insurgent mobs.

Richard almost choked over his cup of Rhinish. "Then I sup-p-pose you two think everything I did yesterday was w-wasted?" he said, stammering with rage.

"Well, they say now that this Wat Tyler proposes to make himself King of London and split up the rest of England among his down-at-heel lieutenants!" laughed Gloucester, goading him. The man had got up in too much of a hurry to shave, and his nephew watched the masticating movements of his bristly blue jaw with loathing. "Does he?" Richard said, with dangerous quietness. "Then let's go out at once and find him."

"If we knew where to look," shrugged Arundel indifferently, without troubling to move.

Richard glared at him and sent a page for his horse. "Well, anyhow, I'm going down to Westminster," he said, with calculated insolence. "At least a man can sometimes hope to be alone in his own house."

But apparently even that was to be denied him. His mother laid a restraining hand on his arm. "Wait a while, Dickon," she advised. "You remember how the governor of the Marshalsea prison escaped? Well, Brembre says the poor wretch took sanctuary in the Abbey and a pack of rebels are down there now trying to drag him out."

"If you take my advice, madam, you won't listen to everything that pert grocer says," snapped Gloucester.

But even to the most irreligious of them violation of sanctuary was a serious matter. It must be dealt with. For who knew when they, too, might stand in need of such protection! And having braved the mob once at Mile End they were not so much afraid, particularly as they were still wearing the same mail beneath their ordinary clothes. All except Richard, who had intended to stay in with his mother and Mundina. But only his body squire would know about that. And when Standish would have gone to get it, Richard pulled him by the elbow. "For God's sake don't make a commotion now," he muttered. "It will only upset my mother again and we shall never get out!" And a moment or two later he was hurrying out into the forecourt and leading the way down Ludgate Hill so that he wouldn't have to look at the self-righteous backs of men who thwarted him at every turn.

As he and his followers crossed Fleet Bridge a breeze caught them from the river, ruffling the bedraggled velvet of their horses' trappings. Along the Strand the sun poured impartially on rose bushes in walled gardens and stiffening bodies half submerged in gutters that ran blood. It shone on the smouldering site of the once proud Savoy and on the fine new hall at Westminster. And as the party passed through the little riverside village of Charing it glistened unexpectedly on a golden cross borne by a long, winding procession of monks coming out to meet them. A scandalized fraternity chanting dirges over the woeful desecration of their abbey.

The rebels had been to Westminster and gone. According to the Abbot they had dragged the unfortunate prison governor from the very shrine of the blessed St. Edward and taken him away to butcher him in Eastcheap. And God had not struck them down. There was nothing Holy Church could do about it. There was nothing stable or sacred any more.

Shocked and sobered, the King and his followers went in and prayed. And because they knew that sometime today, sooner or later, they must come to grips with these vandals and end it all or be themselves destroyed, they made humble confession of their sins. Laying a hand on the pillar to which the wretched victim had clung for life, Richard wondered with good reason how it would feel to die; and then—more irrelevantly—what sort of things his uncle and Arundel were confessing. It seemed so unfair that the only sins he himself could think of at the moment were the very spite and anger they had provoked in him; whereas only yesterday he had made so fine an effort, created harmony and understanding and been at peace with the world.

All thought of retiring to his rooms in the Palace to enjoy his books and his dog had been purged from his mind. There were sterner things to be done. Gathered in the chapter house, where the Commons normally sat, he and his party tasted the Abbot's famous wine and tried to draw up some plan of campaign. Because of the deserted streets scarcely anyone would know that they had left the Wardrobe. All the country westward lay open to them. The rebels were occupied with their horrid business in Eastcheap. It would be possible to reach Windsor before nightfall, disperse in various directions and raise a loyal army to march on London and encompass it. " That would be the safest thing to do," urged Gloucester.

" Safe for us, milord—but not for London," pointed out Walworth, to whose valiant heart the city represented a sacred trust. " If someone had had the sense to do that a week ago it would have been the soundest policy, I grant you," he added pointedly. " But if we leave London now, however large an army we raise, there may not be much left that is worth fighting for when we come back."

"Then we may as well ride back unmolested the way we came," said Thomas Holland, who had at least had the grace to return from the White Chapel and join them.

But Richard, looking from a window at a panorama of walls and streets and spires sprawling to the feet of St. Paul's, shared the Lord Mayor's feelings. These things had been handed down to him from his ancestors and were worth fighting for *now*. "At least let's go back a different way and *chance* an encounter," he urged.

Nothing loath, Standish took up his master's sword from the Abbot's long table. It was a big, bejewelled weapon which had belonged to Edward the Third and was far too heavy for Richard, who seldom carried anything more formidable than a dagger. Before handing it to Sir Robert Newton, whose privilege it was to carry it, the King's squire ran a tentative finger along the naked edge of it. "It seems shameful somehow," he observed thoughtfully, "that although these dogs have killed a mort of honest men, so far we've never so much as struck at one of them."

Apparently there were many of the same mind.

"Then let's make a detour. . . ."

"Better not go by Eastcheap—just now. . . ."

Richard was always impatient of argument. He drained his cup and bade the unhappy Abbot farewell. "Ludgate, Newgate, Bishopsgate, Aldgate, Aldersgate, Cripplegate, Moorgate—seven gates to London," he chanted, spinning a frivolous coin close beneath the new Lord Chancellor's aquiline nose. "With milord Mayor's permission, does it matter very much by which we enter?"

The wine had warmed him. *He* would show this inflated blacksmith who was King of London!

CHAPTER XI

IT SEEMED fantastic to be riding in broad daylight through silent, deserted streets with danger lurking round every corner. It was very depressing when one thought of all the pleasant things one had hoped to do in London.

It wouldn't have been so bad if Robert had stayed with him, or if Nicholas Brembre could have been diverting him with amusing gossip of all the latest disputes between the City Guilds. But Gloucester and Arundel insisted upon riding on either side, while pompous John Newton followed behind with the ceremonial sword. So absurd of them, thought Richard, to make a formal progress of it when they all knew they were going in fear of their lives !

In order to escape the tedium of their conversation he closed his mind as much as possible to present reality. He wondered what his friends were doing—whether Robert were having similar adventures in Oxfordshire and if poor Tom were chafing with boredom at Framlingham. What a lot he would have to tell them when all this fracas was ended ! Always provided, of course, that it *did* come to an end and that he himself were alive to tell about it. . . . A sudden horror impinged upon his vivid imaginings. What if the sunshine and the wind in the trees and his friends' cheerful voices were to go on, while he was speechless clay—like Sudbury and that poor devil who had been dragged from the Confessor's shrine. . . . But that didn't bear thinking about. Not while one was young and attractive, with all life clamouring to be tasted. One must grow up and buy beautiful things, make love and marry.

Deliberately, to still the rising panic in his mind, he turned his thoughts to the bride Sir Simon even now might be negotiating for. Who would she be ? There had been talk of one or two princesses but probably it would be that Bohemian girl, Anne, whom he had heard them wishing onto him in Council because she was related to the Emperor and her Flemish ancestry would improve the wool trade. He hadn't been much interested at the time. Boylike, he had been thinking more about the breaking in of Blanchette. But now he wondered what she would be like. Would she have warm dark eyes like Lizbeth, or mousy hair and thin lips like Henry's sister Blanche? Honey-coloured hair and white skin like the girl in the forge, or red-gold loveliness like his mothers? On the whole he hoped she would be a blonde. He rather wished he had been more explicit with Sir Simon. But Burley was a man of taste. He wouldn't bring him a perfect fright of a woman for all the wool in Christendom. And it wouldn't matter much, decided Richard in his youthful insouciance, so long as she had pleasant manners and smelled sweet. . . .

He was brought back to earth by a smell that was anything but sweet. He looked about him, sniffing, and became aware of the dismal lowing of penned beasts and a stench of rotting entrails. He remembered encountering it before and knew they must be nearing Smithfield.

From a modish sleeve he drew the gay handkerchief which his uncles regarded as the last word in decadence, pressing it to offended nostrils. "I thought we passed a bill forbidding butchers to do their disgusting slaughtering so near the City walls?" he complained, turning to catch the Lord Mayor's eye. "You should really speak to the alderman of this ward about it."

But neither Walworth nor Brembre paid any attention. A sudden silence had fallen upon the company so that only his own petulant words and the clatter of hooves on the cobbles seemed to be audible. They all appeared to be listening to something else. Warned by the strained gravity of their faces, Richard forgot the offending stench and listened too. And presently he distinctly heard the familiar muttering of a mob.

Coming to the end of a narrow street, and emerging from the protection of over-hanging eaves into the great open space which served Londoners as meat market, lists and fair ground, they reined in involuntarily.

Smithfield. The very place where the Lord Mayor's tournament was to have been held. Richard saw it all. The huge arena of trodden brown grass. The mass of sturdy Norman buildings which he knew to be St. Bartholomew's Abbey. And the mob. But for them he might have been tilting in this very place. He and Robert, Henry and Tom. Pitting their promising youth, with keen rivalry and careless laughter, against half the chivalry of England—just as they had practised at Eltham. Trying to win the bets they had laid that happy summer morning when they had jeered at each other, tilting at the quintain. And a fine, cloudless day the spectators would have had for it ! Only here were no multi-coloured pavilions and banners and fine ladies. No trumpeting heralds and knights in shining armour. Only a countless mass of drably dressed peasants lined up in the deep shade of the Abbey. The threatening rise and fall of their uncouth voices, and the still more ominous silence that fell upon them as they perceived the gaily dressed band of nobles. Taken equally by surprise, they stared back like defensive curs or stooped with primitive cunning to pick up stones. And riding up and down in front of them, barking out harsh orders, was a huge hirsute man on a gaunt black horse. A man Richard had last seen swinging a hammer in a humble workshop—beating ploughshares into swords—roused to murderous fury by the sight of insult to his daughter. An honest tradesman, turned brute. A desperate man, with a price on his head. The man who would make himself King of London.

Richard's gorge rose at the sight of him. So this place was, after all, to be the lists. This day his trial. And here, ready to hand, his opponent. No stripling of his own age. But a giant, spoiled by power and popularity, who could snap him in two with a twist of his mighty hands. Backed by ten thousand toughs, drunk with undreamed-of power.

Richard glanced round at his own supporters—a mere

handful of men whose names were part of England. They had spread themselves out funnel-wise on either side of him as if it were some state occasion, making an alley through which he could pass. Their eyes were watchful and measuring. They stood there firm enough. But they waited for him to go first.

He understood perfectly.

When it was a matter of choosing his own bride or deciding about the advisability of taxes, he was only a foolish, temperamental boy ; but when it was a moment for dangerous action on which the fate of the whole country might depend, then he was the King.

He accepted his destiny, but would have liked some older man's advice. " Well, milords ? " he prompted, searching their eyes for help. Thomas of Gloucester, Richard of Arundel, his own half-brother, Thomas, mighty Warwick, kind Salisbury and hot-headed Percy of Northumberland. . . . But no man answered. They even seemed to huddle a little closer together as if withdrawing from a decision which must inevitably entail such momentous praise or blame. If only for their own sakes, they would have helped him if they could. But, warmongers as they were, they just did not know what to do. Whether to go on or to turn back.

So Richard bent to give Blanchette's soft white neck an encouraging pat, and rode forward. And as he passed close between Gloucester and Arundel he looked deliberately into the abashed face of each of them and laughed contemptuously.

This was his day ! He would show them that a man who loved beauty was not necessarily decadent. He would teach them he was born to be their master. And—being young— he cared nothing that they would never forget or forgive a look which stripped them before their fellows for the paltry things they were.

As he emerged into the sunshine a sense of buoyancy sustained him. This time there was no cold shock of fear to overcome. He might have been the first Richard riding forth to meet the Saracens. The same spirit was in him, so that he felt it was a fine thing to confront his enemies. For enemies they definitely were. All his sympathy with the decent Essex folk had been betrayed. He had been fooled. His lodgings—his very bed—had been fouled. And old Sudbury's head, mouldering on London Bridge, cried for vengeance.

Faced with such fantastic odds, he stood implacably for authority and for his own friends. By his own wits he must save them.

He could see Wat Tyler still prancing up and down in front of his rabble. With keen young eyes he noted every braggart gesture. But he had met the man before in his own home and knew him to have decent instincts. " Go, my good sword-bearer, and bring that man to me," he called back over his shoulder. " Tell him I will talk to him only on condition that he tells his men to stay where they are." He spoke in such ordinary tones—so much as if he were summoning a defaulting servant or a competitor who had cheated in the lists—that the luckless Sir Robert had no choice but to obey ; and the rest of the company were almost charmed into believing that they were in a position to make terms. Seeing their king, so slight and valiant a figure in that great space, most of them were moved to follow him a few yards. But all the same Richard passed a hand grimly over his thin, summer doublet, regretting the mail he had spurned ; and felt grateful when Walworth and Standish closed in on either side of him as if to protect him with their own bodies.

Evidently Tyler was as surprised as they. He laughed boisterously at the coolness of a boy who couldn't see when he was cornered, but years of accepting orders had left him a prey to any confident command. He came as he was bid, half sheepish and half truculent. He had no idea how to address royalty and he was a very poor horseman. " You see all those men over there, King ? " he asked.

" Naturally, I see them," said Richard. " Why do you ask ? "

" Because they are sworn to obey me. There are ten

thousand of them, and at a sign from me they will do whatever I want."

Seeing them straining forward, taut as a strung bow, Richard had no doubt of it. He knew that if he made the least sign of fear the stones and arrows clenched in their hands would be unleashed and centuries of resentment assuaged in blood. The lives of his followers were in his unarmed hands. He looked Tyler straight in the eyes, feeling like a lion tamer holding ravaging cruelty in check. "And what *do* you want?" he asked evenly.

The man had had his unreasonable demands glibly enough to tongue all morning, but never before had he voiced them in the presence of the gorgeously dressed master-men against whom they were aimed. Their contemptuous stares began to fray the bluster with which he bolstered up a peasant's natural discomfiture. Their very stillness unnerved him. He glanced over his shoulder at Sir Robert, who still kept close behind him. "I'd be better able to tell you if the gold-trimmed minion of yours would put down that sword," he said rudely.

"It is the King's sword," explained Newton, purple with indignation.

"Then give it to me. I'll hold it for him," offered Tyler, still showing off before his gaping ten thousand. "He and I have met before."

"A dog like you isn't fit to touch it!" cried Sir Robert, holding the jewelled weapon out of his tormentor's reach so that it flashed in the sunlight. Inevitably there was an unseemly struggle, with Tyler turning his lumbering horse so inexpertly that the beast's ill-docked tail flicked Blanchette's delicate nostrils, causing her to shy.

Richard kept his seat and his temper. It was just the sort of thing he had been afraid would happen. The spark for a petty quarrel which might well blaze into disaster for them all. "Better put the sword down, Sir Robert," he advised, swallowing his pride. He knew how unpopular such an order would be with his haughty relatives, but if bloodshed were to be avoided he must handle this thing in his own way. Still soothing his mount, he looked up at the half-placated blacksmith. " It is true that I saw you in your forge," he said, trying to appeal to what had seemed fine in the man. " You were an honest tradesman, sorely tried by an insufferable insult to your daughter. You were no traitor then."

" I'm no traitor now ! " protested Tyler. His hot brown eyes considered the King more sanely, seeing him less as the figurehead of a hated class and more as an individual. More as he had seen him then—a frank-faced youth who hadn't looked at him as if he were a dog—who, for all his fine clothing, had spoken to his Rose with gentle courtesy. Perhaps if one could talk to him alone one could gets things altered. Those burning injustices which had been all that he cared for then—those things which *really* mattered. . . . For a moment Wat Tyler forgot the ugly mounting ambitions which had gone to his head—forgot all about making himself King of London. He could talk reasonably as those Essex fellows had done. After all, it would be more comfortable to be done with this marching about and get back to his forge and Rose, who must be worrying her pretty head sick about him. . . . " I'll tell you——" he began, lowering his voice so that those other proud pieces shouldn't hear, and clutching at the King's bridle.

But in his ignorance and encouraged by such kindly reference to his home, he clutched over-familiarly—thrusting his face close to Richard's as he might have done with a friend with whom he wished to speak intimately. Unfortunately, too, his right hand was still upon the sword he had half drawn while arguing with Sir Robert. Richard knew he meant no harm. He felt no fear, only repugnance for the man's garlic-scented breath. But it was more than Walworth could endure. His dagger leapt from his belt. Close before his face Richard saw it plunge into the bare, muscular column of Wat Tyler's throat and felt the man's hot, nauseating blood spurt over him.

The bold brown eyes looking into his seemed to start from their sockets in agony. Clutching and slipping, the great body toppled from clumsy saddle to trampled earth. Such was his strength that even then, with his lifeblood flowing from him, Tyler half rose again to grapple with his assailant. But Ralph Standish sprang lithely from his horse to finish the business with his sword, straddling the mighty body where it had rolled in the dust.

The unpremeditated incident was all over in a few moments. In their hot loyalty and indignation, those closest to the King scarcely comprehended the dangerous crisis they had created.

" Good God, you fools, must you get us all torn to pieces ? " cried Arundel, eyeing the advancing mob. They had already broken ranks and came straggling across the trampled field, and he had just dodged a sharp flint as he spoke. Mercifully some of those at the back, having seen the uplifted sword and then the empty saddle, still believed the King had been knighting their leader. " For Christ's sake, what had we better do ? " asked a dozen different voices in panic. " They will be upon us in a moment and massacre us ! "

" We'll have to make a dash for it," decided Gloucester, measuring with a soldier's eyes the distance to the road by which they had come. " Once in the narrow streets a handful of us might hold them."

But they all knew that once they moved away from Wat Tyler's dead body it was unlikely that even the most swiftly mounted of them would make it alive.

Richard ignored him and spoke to the abashed slayers. " Don't you see that our only chance is for me to ride forward —*alone* ? To seem to leave you and side with them ? " he urged.

They looked at each other, desperate but loath to let him go.

" His Grace is right. It's a chance——" said Brembre, who understood the temper of the people.

" If he has the nerve to do it," muttered Arundel.

Richard overheard him and the words were like a spur.

Walworth rode a few paces with him. " Try to lead them away from London," he entreated.

"There are open fields at Clerkenwell," Brembre whispered in his other ear. "We'll ride back and rouse Knollys and the citizens—and meet you there——"

The moment they had wheeled their horses Richard heard them galloping hell for leather back into the City. He knew that his uncle and the rest were gathered into an irresolute huddle behind him, and that Tyler's bleeding body must now lie exposed to view. He knew it by the savage roar that went up from the rebels' ranks. But his mind worked like quicksilver. Before the wild beast in them had time to spring he was cantering across Smithfield right into the midst of them. And they were so astonished that they stayed each in arrested motion, like so many statues, gaping at him.

He pulled Blanchette to her haunches, hailing them with upraised arm. "Tyler is dead," he called, his clear young voice cutting across their confusion. "But I—your King— will be your leader in his place."

He was good to look upon with his red-gold hair and his peacock green tunic and his white horse. To their untutored minds he was all-powerful. Because he was put forward on all state occasions, they had no idea that the men whom he had forsaken really ruled. And he was offering to befriend them and champion their cause. Bewildered by the whirlwind twist he had given events, they were suddenly abashed and dumb. One by one they let fall their stones and gathered about him. And with shining eyes he rode through the midst of them. Some of them swore they saw a flame about him. Some even crossed themselves, thinking the ghost of a tall crusader rode with him. But probably it was only the noonday sun on the brightness of his hair.

Cunningly, while they were still bemused and at a disadvantage, he turned northward past the gatehouse of poor Hales' smouldering priory. And they followed like sheep. Looking back over his shoulder, he saw the strangest procession he had ever led and wondered just how ridiculous he must look. None of them, he supposed, had the least idea where they were going or why. And he himself wasn't too sure of the way. But somehow or other he must keep them in good humour—keep them together and unsuspicious until someone came to round them up. So, to cover his inclination to laughter, he began to sing as he rode, choosing popular ditties like " When Adam delved and Eve span " so that they could join in the choruses.

He ambled purposely, taking several wrong turnings. And by the time he had found Clerkenwell fields he saw, to his unspeakable relief, that Walworth and Brembre were already there with a considerable force of armed men. They must have worked with amazing speed. Sir Robert Knollys had been ready *cap-à-pie*, of course, and it was apparent now that all those shuttered houses must have held a veritable army of loyal citizens only waiting a chance to muster. Well, he himself had given them the chance. And now all that remained was to lead his poor fools of peasants into the trap. It was like throwing the deer's carcass to hounds at the *curée*—so easy that he rather hated himself for doing it. But he would be glad not to have to see or smell them any more for a while. It would be wonderful to live normally again. And to enjoy the thrill of being a hero, of course.

Once the rebels had been rounded up, people crowded round him. In their excitement they wrung him unceremoniously by the hand and called him the saviour of London. Even old soldiers like Warwick and Northumberland, who had hitherto disapproved of him, called down blessings on his head.

Some of the people from London had even had the fore-thought to bring him food, and suddenly he found that he was famished. And while he sat on a thyme-scented hillock con-suming cold pigeon pie, Walworth had Tyler's body brought and shown to the discomfited followers, and someone rode up in a cloud of dust to announce the good news that the mad priest, Ball, had been caught as well.

So the rebellion was really over. All around him men of the ruling classes were rejoicing because this hitherto unknown taste of subjection was lifted from them. But even that was a small thing to young Richard Plantagenet compared with finding the assurance of his own manhood. Bareheaded among the golden gorse, he faced the warm splendour of the dying sun and knew that the flame of courage that had illumined most of his ancestors was in him too. That from now onwards he could afford to disregard men's taunts—to laugh in his uncles' faces when they called him " peacemonger ", and enjoy without self-searchings the beautiful, constructive things which appealed to him. And never more would he be afraid of fear.

Reluctantly he withdrew himself from the moments of ecstasy during which he had let his soul browse upon her new-found treasure. Although his face was radiant, there were tears in his eyes. " Why are all the bells ringing ? " he asked, looking beyond his companions at a silhouette of City churches.

Walworth, proud unemotional man that he was, bent a knee in the dust and kissed Richard's hand. " Because you have saved London," he said. And Richard guessed that the wealthy fish merchant was all the more grateful because his own hasty act had endangered it.

" It was rumoured in the City that you had been killed, sir," added Brembre, his humorously puckered face more serious than usual. " And they have just heard that it is untrue."

Richard smiled at him ingenuously. " Do they care so much ? " he said softly. Then, realizing that his mother must have heard the rumour too, he ran down from his gorse-clad hillock, calling for his horse. " We must get back to Carter Lane," he said, seeming to mount and make for London all in one movement.

The rest cantered willingly after him. But above the cheerful bustle of departure he heard the peasants calling after him. Knollys' men were rounding them up, while Dalyngrigge's desperadoes, trained in despatching raiding Frenchmen, stood ready, knife in hand. With only a few seconds between them and Eternity, the peasants' voices rose to a beseeching scream.

Richard reined in before his father's implacable old captain. "What are you going to do?" he asked, breathlessly.

"Kill 'em," grunted Sir Robert. "It's all the swine deserve. If your Grace hadn't outwitted them they might have killed *you*."

It was true enough. But on such a joyful day Richard couldn't bear to be the cause of so much suffering. He lifted an arm to stay Dalyngrigge's men. "Any fool can kill," he said. "I led these poor ignorant wretches here and I'll not betray them. I pray you, good Sir Robert, stop this butchery and send them home."

It was sweet to have the power to reprieve men's lives and to hear a thousand blessings mingle with the music of the bells. And because this day he was the idol of all classes, Gloucester and Arundel bowed unquestioningly to his will.

CHAPTER XIII

IT WAS in the dusk of a drear February afternoon that Richard
came again to the Wardrobe house in Carter Lane. His
mother was wintering at Berkhampstead and the Court had
just returned to Westminster. He disembarked from a hired
shallop with only Standish in attendance, and climbed Black-
friars steps through the mizzling rain, wrapped in his squire's
cloak. And because they had given his uncles the slip they
hugged the shuttered house fronts like a couple of cut-purses,
and knocked almost furtively on Jacot's door.

It had been one of those leaden grey days which depressed
Richard to the soul. But inside the house all was warmth and
welcome. The dapper little tailor bowed and beamed and sent
his servants scurrying in all directions. No one was more glad
than he. Now that the King was back from the County assizes
and most of the rebel leaders hanged, London would come to
life again. There would be new houppelardes to fashion and
new winter furs to buy. Jacot could scarcely wait until his
master had been warmed with wine before showing him the
mulberry velvet he was itching to make up for the Twelfth
Night revels. It wasn't often a Court tailor had a patron with
a figure like Richard's, and an easy grace that set off satorial
genius to such advantage. "Straight from Utrecht," he
murmured, unrolling the precious stuff. "And tones perfectly with the new scented gloves your Grace had from
Paris."

The wine in Richard's glass was no richer than the colour
of the velvet. He sauntered across the room to finger it. At
any other time he would have been enchanted. "It's exquisite,
Jacot. You did well to buy it," he approved absently. "But
I'm not wanting anything just now—except Mundina. Will
you send for her?"

Yet in the midst of his depression he spared a smile that charmed away the man's disappointment and left him contentedly calculating the extra inches he would have to add when cutting the new tunic. And when Mundina came *she* noticed how much taller and older the King had grown. But she noticed, too, with a woman's eye, that some spontaneous enthusiasm had gone out of him.

He kissed her on both cheeks, French fashion, and restrained her from ordering a meal for him. "No, I have dined," he said, impatiently. "It is just that I wanted—to come home."

Mundina understood. She left Standish and her husband to finish the wine and led the way upstairs to her own room. Richard thought it had a more comfortable, lived-in look than rooms in palaces ever seemed to achieve. A bright fire burned on the hearth, and candles had been lighted and curtains drawn against the river darkness—and against his other world. A sheet which Mundina must have been mending still trailed from the seat of a high-backed chair. And he recognized with pleased surprise many things which he had used or played with in childhood. Even the small four-poster was the one he had slept in at Bordeaux. Glancing from its faded tapestry to the bolted door, he wondered if Mundina's husband ever came here. He had often wondered why she had married Jacot. Probably she lay with him dutifully enough in the best bedroom they had given up to him that awful night when the Tower was taken. But Richard felt sure, somehow, that her soul lived here, apart in this sanctum over the forecourt gate.

Understanding his mood, she took up her sewing in silence, seating herself unbidden in his presence as she used to do. She let him wander round picking up a remembered toy here and a trifle there, until the memories conjured up by each had wiped the listlessness from his face.

He came to her soon with a small worn shoe in his hand. "Dost thou love me as much as all this, that thou must needs keep my old clothes ? " he chided teasingly, slipping into the intimate *tu-toi* of her native tongue as they always did the moment they were alone.

She looked up sharply from her work, and it was not only the firelight that kindled a deeper colour in the southern olive of her cheek. She was a woman of strange reserves, and had not meant him to find the thing. But since he had . . . " I would give my body to be burned for you," she said, in matter-of-fact tones which precluded sentiment.

Richard knew right down in his soul that she would. He put the shoe back very carefully between a little mother-of-pearl box his uncle John had brought him from Spain and his first lopsided drawing of a horse. He took rather a long time about it because hot tears were pricking at his eyes. " Then go on loving me like that, Mundina Danos," he ordered with his back to her. " For God knows I have need of it to combat so much hate ! "

Her dark eyes surveyed him anxiously, adoringly. He had gone away a laughing boy. But tonight he looked more like eighteen than sixteen, she thought. " Something or someone has hurt you, ma mie," she said, biting off a thread with a jerk of strong, white teeth.

Richard sat down on the edge of the bed. It was still hung with the set of crimson baudekin curtains which had been specially bequeathed to him in his father's will. The face of each gold embroidered angel was familiar as only one's earliest recollections are. " You can't have everything you believed in broken and stay the same," he said slowly. " Do you know where I have been all these months, Mundy ? "

" Everybody knows you went on a sort of Circuit with Tressilian, the new Chief Justice, and milords of Gloucester and Arundel. Cleaning up the counties and trying those vile rebels. Your mother said it would be good experience for you," she said, picking her words carefully.

She knew that he was holding himself in check. That he probably had been ever since she last saw him—that day when he had been so radiant and confident, and the people had cheered him so. She knew, too, that when his mind had accustomed itself to the ease of being alone with her—the rare ease of being alone at all—the full flood of his feelings would overflow the dams built by his unique position. And, being a wise woman, she knew that only that way could relief come. But she was to be badly shaken by the accumulated bitterness laid bare.

" Yes, it was experience all right," he agreed, turning the folds of baudekin about until he found his special angel and then staring at it with a sort of blank estrangement. " Up till then I had believed that the men who ruled England wished her well. And that this chivalry which was crammed down our throats meant keeping our word."

"So it does, my dear," argued Mundina. " When your father captured King John of France didn't he keep him over here as an honoured guest, and then trust him to go back to collect his own ransom ? "

" Yes. Because he happened to be a king. But he butchered the women and children when he took Limoges." Richard let go of the curtains so roughly that they slid back along their rods with an angry swish. " I see it now. Chivalry is only for the rich. Even my mother thinks that."

Mundina went on stitching and let him talk.

" When I promised better conditions to those poor wretches at Mile End, I meant it. And—Christ help me for an unfledged fool—I thought the others *knew* I meant it. But they just laughed—Uncle Thomas and Warwick and that cur Arundel —and said I'd acted beautifully." Richard ceased sprawling on the bed and sat up. His blue eyes blazed. " But I wasn't acting, Mundina. For once, I wasn't acting ! It was the best and most sincere thing I'd ever had a chance to do. Don't you see ? My life's been like a golden cage—and I was in contact with real life at last. And overjoyed to find myself able to cope with it." His voice went suddenly gruff the way it did now adolescence was upon him, and he leaned forward and covered his face with both hands. "But they've killed my joy and covered me with shame."

Mundina laid aside her work. "Who, Dickon—and how? You rode through the counties in state, didn't you?"

"Yes. And they made me sit in evil-smelling courts while they condemned to death the very men I'd pardoned. Condemned them in my name. The Bloody Assize, men called it, in Essex. Tressilian wasn't really trying them. He was avenging his fellow lawyers on any peasant he could catch. And when he couldn't convict in court his soldiers used to stab them after dark in the woods. I've lain in bed many a time, at Havering, listening to their screams. And when Uncle Thomas broke up their camp at Billericay it was just plain murder."

"Ugly things have been done here too, Dickon," she said, trying to distract him. "The few Flemings left alive were encouraged to avenge their countrymen on that block in Eastcheap. They say that even the Flemish widows——" But she saw that he wasn't even listening.

"At Waltham they humiliated me by making me eat my own words," he raged. "Convicted peasants used to turn to me. They thought I'd save them at the last minute as I was able to that day at Clerkenwell—that happy day when all the church bells were ringing. 'Serfs you were, and serfs you still are!' I told them." He thrust out his hands before him, staring first at one upturned palm and then the other as if they were stained with blood. "I saw the look in their eyes—the slow realization that they were being betrayed. . . . And I had to sit there like Judas seeing my people's love slip away from me."

It was pitiful, knowing how hard he had striven to obtain it. "But couldn't you have refused?" asked Mundina, with small conviction.

"Have you ever been alone with those two men?" laughed Richard shortly. "It didn't matter how I raved and argued— they always bullied me into doing what they wanted. Even my brother Thomas, who was dealing with his own Kentishmen, insisted that unless we crushed them once and for all our lives and property would never again be safe. I know it's true— *now*—the way they've bungled things. But it could have been the beginning of some new brotherhood—some better basis between craftsman and master. . . . I *had* started something."

"You couldn't expect men like your uncle and Arundel to see that."

"No. They're so beastly. D'you know, Mundina, when I sent some money to Wat Tyler's daughter, they thought in their stinking minds I wanted her for my amusement. They even had the poor frightened innocent brought to my bedroom. Hoped she would take my mind off arguing, perhaps. . . ." He broke off in youthful embarrassment. "As if a man can't have a decent impulse, like pity ! I had the devil's job to reassure her—and then to send her home before that leacher Arundel got at her."

Mundina had heard plenty of stories about Arundel desecrating convents during the French wars. "The world would be better without either him or Gloucester," she said grimly.

Richard laughed suddenly, as at some cherished recollection. "You should have seen their faces when I rode past them to meet the peasants at Smithfield ! " he said, quite boyishly.

"But don't you think that's just what they're trying to take out of you now, my love ? That, and your ability to take command ? "

"Yes, I suppose so," he agreed, more soberly.

Mundina raged inwardly because she could not bear these burdens for him. "Sir Simon will be coming home soon," she reminded him.

"And Uncle John's on his way down from Scotland. Gloucester's never quite so horrid when he's here." He seemed to brighten considerably, and got up, settling his rumpled collar. "Poor Uncle John ! It will be a sad homecoming for him. I wish it had been Gloucester's place at Plashy that had been burned."

"How terribly you hate him, Richard!"

"Why shouldn't I, Mundina?" he demanded sharply.

Although she had had the upbringing of him, Mundina offered him no moral platitudes. "Because it is so bad for you, Dickon," she said simply.

He came instantly and hugged her for her candour. "Mundy, *ma chérie*! Your heart always did outrun your hopes of Heaven, didn't it?" He laughed and pressed his cheek to hers, then moved away sadly. "But how few people realize what cause I have! If Lancaster wants my crown, I sometimes think Gloucester would like to destroy my soul."

He went and stood before the fire, with the warm glow leaping up over his straight, slender thighs, and his handsome face in shadow. When he spoke again his voice sounded strained with anger, and his clenched fists beat against the hooded chimney. "When I tried to stand up to them about keeping my word—tried to go on being *me*, the King—that presumptuous swine, Thomas Plantagenet, dared to remind me of what happened to the second Edward!"

Mundina listened with absorbed attention. She had read a good many books about sciences in which women were supposed not to dabble, but few about English history. "He was deposed, wasn't he?" she hazarded.

Richard's fists ceased their angry tattoo, and dropped almost resignedly to his sides. "And with some reason," he admitted. "Although he was an anointed King."

"What did he do, Richard?"

"Oh, he filled all the best places with his favourites. He'd a pig of a French wife. He put a fop called Piers Gaveston in her place—fondled him in public—and worse in private, so she plotted against him with her lover."

"I remember now." In spite of the warmth from the fire a shiver shook the Aquitanian woman's gaunt frame. "He was murdered, wasn't he?"

"Horribly."

The same *frisson* seemed to touch him too. She leaned

forward from her chair and took one of his quiescent hands. "Don't think about it, child," she urged, as if he were still her nurseling.

He flung round on her, half angrily. "Not think of it! How can I help thinking of it—*now*? Although he was my great-grandfather, I never knew till now. Only what everyone knows. That they hounded the poor, scared wight from prison to prison, until finally he died mysteriously in Berkeley Castle."

One of the candles, burning low, hissed itself out in its own grease, and Mundina let go the King's hand to snuff the other. She might have been an image carved in brown wood, with her dark gown and intelligent face, and the half-light from the fire centred on her wimple and the sheet lying in white folds about her feet. "And your uncle took care to tell you?" she prompted.

· Richard swallowed hard. His eyes were fixed unseeingly on the tester of the little bed behind her, and he began to speak monotonously like an indifferent actor repeating his lines. "Yes, he told me first, of course—in front of Henry. Sneered, and supposed a lily-livered exquisite like me, who couldn't bear to see a few miserable peasants hanged, would faint if he told me what happened at Berkeley. Of course, I laughed. Carelessly, like Robert does—and said that as *I* hadn't hung back at Smithfield for someone else to go first, no doubt I could sustain it—if he and Henry found that sort of thing amusing."

A log fell with a thud to the hearth, shaking out a shower of golden sparks only to leave a deeper darkness. And young Richard Plantagenet's tortured voice dragged on. "And so he described it—in that horrible ill-lit room at Waltham. And I just stood there, leaning against the window—trying to look like Robert. And wishing to God I were. . .

"Oh, my poor poppet!" Out of the shadows Mundina's deep voice was a caress.

"It wasn't so much what he said as the way he seemed to tower over me. His tall, menacing shadow on the wall—and the hatred glowing like twin coals in his eyes. As if—as if he were doing it all over again—to me. . . . And taking joy in it——" Richard flung up his hands to cover his eyes, so that the words seemed to force their reluctant way through his tense fingers. "And Henry standing there, so unmoved by pity—although I swear he had never heard it before either——"

Mundina got up swiftly and went to him. "What did he tell you, Richard?"

"It's not fit for a woman's ear," he mumbled. He would have turned aside, trying to spare her, gripping at his manhood. But her strong hands were on his shoulders, her dark fierce eyes compelled him. And suddenly he was clinging to her, his copper-gold head hidden in the gauntness of her sterile bosom. "Oh, Mundina, Mundina, take it from me! For Christ's sake, take it from me! Like you used to exorcise those dreadful dreams when first I knew I would have to be King."

She coaxed him to the edge of the bed and sat facing him, knee to knee, his cold hands beneath her own. She knew that only speaking of this thing could help him.

"He told me they kept him for days at the bottom of the garderobe tower, up to his waist in human filth," he said, tearing away a hand to toss back the damp hair from his forehead. "Slowly the rats gnawed him, and his gaolers starved him slowly. And then, when he could suffer no more, they pretended he was to be freed. Took him back to his own apartment, lit torches and mocked him with a feast. But before he could slake his hunger on the first dish two killers were upon him. They stripped him and threw him upon the table among the overturned food and spilled wine. They'd red-hot irons ready in the next room and they thrust them up his body, burning out his bowels. 'This—and this,' the sadist devils shouted, 'for Piers Gaveston!' They say that through the vast thickness of the walls his screams were heard down in Berkeley village." The second Richard flung himself across her knees, the full flood of his suffering gushing forth in tears. "And he was a young k-king," he stammered between rending sobs, "whom the people had been taught to hate!"

What thoughts corroded Mundina's mind, what vows of vengeance seared her soul, this child of her heart would never know. When he was quite exhausted she laid him back, trembling, on the bed. He turned his head from her so that it was hidden in the pillows. She rose stiffly and lit fresh candles, and left him. When she came back she had a little wooden bowl and pestle in her hands with which she ground some white powder while she stood watching him. Presently, when his limbs became still, she put a pinch of powder into a cup and filled it with water from a ewer, and bent over him. "Drink this, Dickon," she said, in the cool matter-of-fact way which had never failed to control with sickness or tantrums when he was small.

He raised himself obediently, looking at her with drenched, dark-circled eyes. His face was drained of all colour. He was too shamed for speech. He drank docilely as a child. Whatever happened to his world, he trusted her utterly.

"You will sleep peacefully here in your own bed as you used to sleep in the happy sunshine of Bordeaux," she said, her voice so sure and soothing that she might have been chanting some incantation. "And whenever you feel that you can no longer live in the same world with this fiend Gloucester I have enough powder to put *him* to sleep—for ever."

Richard smiled faintly, his hot hand fumbling for hers. "Even to rid the world of *him*, I couldn't let you endanger your soul. Suppose I got to Heaven first—and you weren't there . . ."

His voice fluttered out, his wet lashes came to rest upon his cheek. Mundina stood holding the empty bowl until his breathing became light and even as a child's. Then she looked around the room for something in which to put the rest of the powder. She put half of it in a phial and half in Richard's little mother-of-pearl box. Then she went in search of Ralph

Standish. Strong woman as she was, she walked wearily, for much virtue had gone out of her.

"You may as well go to bed, Ralph," she said. "The King won't want you again tonight. He is fast asleep."

Standish rose from the table where he had been dicing drowsily with her husband "He hasn't slept properly for weeks. Not ever since we left Waltham. You're an angel, Mundina!" he exclaimed, with relief.

Her tight, thin lips relaxed into a grim smile. "Better be careful whom you say that to, young man," she warned, with asperity. "Because I have more book learning than most men and my father was an alchemist, plenty of people are more disposed to call me a witch." But she caught at his arm in passing, so as to draw him apart while Jacot grovelled for a dice which her sleeve had swept as if by accident onto the floor. "Take this, Ralph," she urged in an undertone, thrusting the phial of white powder into his hand. "Keep it in some secret place. And whenever the King is overtired or excited, or those uncles of his have been at him, mix a little in his cup. As much as you can put on a florin, *but no more*. There is no taste that he will notice."

On more than one occasion Standish had proved his devotion to his master, but he was not without caution. He held the phial suspiciously on his palm. "It is a risky game," he demurred, "putting powder in a king's cup."

Mundinâ Danos gave his arm a friendly, reassuring push so that he should slip the stuff into his pouch before her husband joined them with the missing dice. "Yet most of us would play riskier games than that," she scoffed, "for one so lovable and so ill-beset as Richard of Bordeaux."

PART

2

" So passeth al my lady sovereyne,
That is so good, so faire, so debonayre,
I pray to God that ever fall she fayre . . ."
—Chaucer.

CHAPTER XIV

THE NEW Bohemian Queen sat at her embroidery frame in a room at Westminster Palace. Every now and then she paused in her stitched creation of a tree to look round at her new friends and relatives. She knew that, like all royal brides, she was a pawn in the politics of Europe. But the first pangs of homesickness had passed and—being an adaptable creature—she thanked God daily that her lines had fallen in such pleasant places.

It was one of those lovely leisure hours when the King summoned Chaucer to read aloud to them. And although Anne could not always understand the people's English which he wove into such wonderful verses, she loved the lilt of them. She loved, too, the fine books and hangings and goldsmiths' work with which the King's apartments were garnished. Shame always covered her now when she remembered the disdain with which she had viewed her parents' proposal to marry her to Richard Plantagenet. She had believed England to be a rude and uncivilized place. And then Sir Simon Burley had come to Prague, and she had found him to be one of the kindest and most courteous men she had ever known.

She looked up now to find him watching her speculatively, and returned his smile without embarrassment. It was he who had described her future husband to her, making her see Richard from the first as someone infinitely lovable. She did not realize, even now, how skilfully the ageing statesman had predisposed her unformed mind, nor how much of Richard's none too ardent courtship he had conducted for him. All she knew was that Sir Simon had done her a score of unobtrusive kindnesses, that a tender understanding had grown up between them, and that, in some undefined way, he looked to her to do a great deal for Richard.

While the rest of Geoffrey Chaucer's small, intimate audience followed without effort the lively sense of his words, Anne allowed her mind to wander a little, resting affectionately on each of them. There was her mother-in-law—indolent, extravagant and kind—attended as usual by that pretty minx, Lizbeth de Wardeaux. Richard's eldest uncle, suave and handsome, home from the wars. And Robert de Vere. Few women, Anne supposed, could look upon Robert with disapproval. He had been her husband's friend for years, and she might have been jealous of him. But Robert was so amusing, so disarmingly *léger*, and at the moment all his attention appeared to be devoted to her favourite lady, the Landgravine Agnes Launcekron. It was reprehensible of him, of course, seeing that he had a wife in Oxfordshire. But, if he must philander, one could not but commend his taste. For Agnes was very lovely, besides being a beloved bit of home.

But however much Anne's eyes and thoughts might wander, they always came back to the attractive figure of her own husband. He was standing by the open window looking out over the river, with the afternoon sunshine streaming over him so that it seemed as if he were dressed in gold. But whether he stood in sunshine or in shadow, there always seemed some quality of brightness about him which made all the other people in her life a mere background for his beloved presence.

"I love that bit about the river and the seemly knight," he was saying, as Chaucer finished the last verse. "It just *is* London, isn't it, Robert? Read it to us again."

Chaucer's gaze, too, turned towards the busy Thames which was so much a part of their daily lives. But for all his versifying, he was obliged to see it sometimes with the practical eyes of a Customs official. "There's a wool ship due out for Ghent with the turn of the tide," he made so bold as to remind them. "And unless I keep my eye on the tally of export tax——"

"Forget it!" urged Richard, with lovable enthusiasm.

"But your Grace's income——"

" Is never enough to pay for all the people he invites to dinner ! " laughed de Vere.

" With this niggling Parliament I certainly need all the wool taxes you can rake in for me," Richard agreed ruefully. " But money can't buy golden words like that. How did it go, Geoffrey ? ' London, thou art the flower of cities all——' "

Chaucer's smooth cheeks grew pink with pleasure. Most of the martial nobles of the late King Edward's vintage regarded his literary efforts as so much time wasted from Government affairs, so that it seemed rare good fortune to serve a sovereign who, though scarcely twenty, really saw and loved the images one made. And to find at court an audience of young people, modern and good to look upon, yet not too full of their own exploits to hang upon a poet's words. Chaucer's mind moved nimbly enough with the times to see this as a crucial compliment. He unrolled his script again with delight and picked out the piece which had caught at the King's fancy.

> " *Above all ryvers thy ryver hath renowne*
> *Upon thy streets go'th many a seemly knight*
> *In velvet gownes and in chains of gold . . .*
> *Strong be thy wallis that about thee standis*
> *Wise be thy people that within thee dwellis*
> *Fresh is thy ryver with his lusty strandis ;*
> *Blith be thy churches, wele sownying by thy bellis ;*
> *Fair be thy wives right lovesome, white and small . . .* "

No one spoke until the poet had taken his leave. And even then his words seemed to linger in the pleasant room, long after him, building a town somewhere between fantasy and fact.

" I'm afraid that last line wasn't meant for me ! Though time was when my waist was like a wand," laughed Joan of Kent, who was reclining like a comfortable and comely Ceres on a damask-covered pallet, nibbling at a dish of comfits.

"Nor for me," smiled Anne, to keep her company. "I'm only a foreigner."

"And Agnes and I are not even wives!" sighed Lizbeth, pivoting on her little carved stool so as to turn the full play of her lustrous eyes upon the King.

"Not *yet*," agreed Anne, with the faintest little pucker of annoyance spoiling the neat serenity of her plucked brows. And because she *was* a foreigner she was careful to appeal to the mother-in-law whose importance she had in some measure usurped. "Richard and I must see what we can do about it, mustn't we, madam?"

But growing infirmities made Joan loath to part with her devoted little lady, and so far Lizbeth had managed to elude her pack of suitors and remain where she could see the King almost daily. Richard himself avoided the issue. "I expect Chaucer was thinking of his own wife," he remarked negligently.

Anne tossed a badly ravelled skein of silk into the Landgravine's lap, hoping that some occupation might keep *her* out of mischief. But Agnes Launcekron only encouraged de Vere to help her with the task until their hands were even more disastrously entangled than the silk. "Is *your* wife lovesome, white and small?" she teased wickedly.

"She is white and tall," muttered the newly-married earl, well aware that everybody in the room was watching him with covert amusement.

It was the first time Richard had heard his friend's temper fray like that. He began to think his wise little wife was right. The sooner they made some matrimonial plans for Agnes, the better. He was glad when Anne pierced the little nut tree she was embroidering with a purposeful needle and remarked very distinctly that in her opinion Philippa, Countess of Oxford, was an extraordinarily nice woman. There was a quiet precision about Anne's remarks which matched the poised grace of her smallest movements.

Richard glanced across at her approvingly. Since their

marriage, life certainly had been easier. Even if Gloucester and Arundel irritated him on every possible occasion, there was respite for his frayed nerves at home. He found it pleasant and restful sitting in this sunny room with those he loved best about him. Mathe, grown into a stately hound, pressed against his knee and grew somnolent beneath the fondling of his hand. A set of designs for his new School of Heraldry lay beside him on the cushions. But John of Lancaster rose from his chair, a man consumed by restless enterprises. "Well, whatever the shape and colour of our wives, we shall soon have to part from them!" he said decisively, going to consult some maps which the King's invaluable secretary, Medford, had left ready on a table.

"And set forth for Scotland," agreed Richard.

"You seem only just to have come *back* from there, John, and I thought you had signed a peace treaty," yawned Joan, too inured to military preparations to protest against the partings they presaged.

But Anne looked up sharply. It was all very well for Lancaster, with his greying hair and a second wife whom he had married only in the hope of ruling Spain. But she, Anne of Bohemia, was still almost a bride. "Richard and Robert, and Tom Mowbray have been full of it for days. But why must you invade Scotland?" she asked.

The Duke turned to her courteously, unrolling a map with fine white fingers. He had so much of Richard's manner that she always found it difficult to be angry with him. "It is less a matter of invading Scotland than of defending ourselves," he explained plausibly. "The French have made a landing in the Firth of Forth."

Anne wrinkled her adorable nose in perplexity. "But surely that is the King of Scotland's business?"

"My dear Anne," laughed Richard, "have you lived in this contentious country all these months without finding out that the prospect of a battlefield *anywhere* is inevitably the business of my uncles?"

"Not your uncle Edmund's," murmured Joan, with a sugared almond in her mouth. "He'd sooner any day be fattening capon at Langley."

John Plantagenet surveyed his nephew quizzically—almost one might suspect, hopefully. "Of course, if you'd sooner stay and bear him company——"

"God forbid!" expostulated Richard, turning sharply from the window. "I've never been to Scotland. Besides, don't Uncle Thomas and Arundel keep dinning into me that it might win back my popularity which they lost for me if I go to war somewhere?"

"Surely you can afford to ignore their venom—after Smithfield?" suggested Simon Burley quietly, going to join them by the table. And Anne noticed how Richard slipped an arm through his one-time tutor's as they talked, and how the little flame of bitterness was instantly snuffed out. "Come over here, Robert," he called with his usual cheerfulness, "and get our route settled while my uncle John is here to advise us. I'm having you and Stafford ride with me—and perhaps Tom Mowbray. I hope the heather will be out on the hills!"

"I thought we were supposed to be going to war," laughed de Vere, disengaging himself from the wiles of Agnes and lounging across the room.

"Of course we must push the French back into the sea and teach the Scots not to endanger us so treacherously," said Richard, momentarily relapsing into his best Council Chamber manner.

Perceiving that the men were aching to get down to crossbows and cannon, Anne stuck her needle into her work and rose. "I must go and be fitted for my new dress, Richard," she excused herself charmingly. "It is nice of you to lend me Jacot and I am afraid I have already kept him waiting an unconscionable time."

Richard crossed the room immediately and began gathering up her scattered silks. "What colour is it to be?" he asked.

"Purple," answered Anne bleakly. "I'm afraid it doesn't suit me at all. But it seems that for this Garter ceremony I must wear purple."

"Yes, of course. And I must certainly see you received into the Order before I go."

Anne stood with down-bent head and took the deftly arranged skeins he held out to her. Not for worlds would she have him guess how her whole body hungered at the casual touch of his hands. "How soon will you be starting?" she said softly.

"Oh, quite soon. In a few days, I hope." In his eagerness for this fresh experience he scarcely noticed the forlorn drop in her voice, and because he looked so fit and radiant she hadn't the heart to remind him that it would mean months of anxiety and loneliness for her.

But Joan knew all about women's part in war. She called Lizbeth to help her rise and to gather up her diverse possessions. "I will come with you, if I may, Anne," she said. "I adore new clothes."

Anne waited for her gratefully. Richard had already rejoined his fellow campaigners and, looking back resentfully from the door, she saw them clustered about their precious maps. Their four bent heads were illuminated by the late afternoon sun. Burley's white hair in sharp contrast to Robert's dark curls, John of Lancaster's distinguished iron-grey head rising from the high collar of his houppelarde and Richard's like a splash of eager copper. Their crisp, technical conversation seemed to exclude her. "In a few days this room—this happy room—will be empty," she thought, her soft brown eyes filling with tears.

Joan laid a hand on her arm as they went along the gallery to the Queen's apartments. "One gets used to it," she said. "My other son, John, will be going too. As Lancaster's constable."

Anne was all compunction at once. "Of course, madam, it is twice as bad for you."

"Thomas, the elder, hasn't been well of late. But John couldn't be kept out of any fight," boasted Joan, a shade too complacently.

Anne was scarcely listening. She didn't care much for either of them. "When the Black Prince went campaigning he always took you with him, didn't he, madam?"

"Yes. And that was sometimes worse. Richard was almost born on a battlefield," answered Joan, with her warm reminiscent laugh. "That is probably why he hates them so."

Anne's eyes opened wide so that an arrested tear toppled over the thick fringe of her lashes. "But he doesn't hate them. Not for himself, I mean—and if they are necessary," she expostulated. "It's just that he hates unnecessary killing and brutality. . . . Don't you see how glad he is to go?"

They had reached Anne's apartments and Joan sat down on the first chair she came to. Exertion or the least emotion brought on unwonted pallor and breathlessness these days. Anne, in common with the rest of her family, was much concerned about it, but Joan refused to be fussed over. The thought of being treated as an invalid was wholly repugnant to her. "I don't think we need worry unduly about our men this time," she said, still panting a little. "They probably want to impress the Scots with the size of our forces and I don't suppose there will be any very bloody fighting as there was in France."

Anne waved aside the woman whom she had called to open a window. "Then do you think that I could ask Richard if I may go too?" she asked eagerly.

"You could. And, being Richard, he would probably say yes. But seeing that he himself hasn't suggested it, I think it would be scarcely wise—or kind."

The Queen's little oval face went white as if she had been struck. "Kind?" she repeated. "Do you mean—he doesn't want me?"

"I mean that this is a man's jaunt. And that he will have much more fun without you. Which isn't at all the same thing." Joan leaned forward with kindly amusement and took her daughter-in-law's slim, restless hands in her own beringed smooth ones. "Don't you see, he's probably picturing it all in his own mind as some shining adventure. Living in tents, washing in streams and all that sort of thing. The austerity that a king so seldom gets a chance to taste. And when a young man's set on a thing, it's best to let him get it out of his system." Seeing that Anne still looked forlorn, she let go her hands impatiently. "Listen, my dear. I've had two husbands. And I can tell you this. The more lightly one lets them go, the more ardently they come back. And perhaps this time next year we shall all be rejoicing and the bells will be ringing for an heir."

Anne's pallor turned to burning embarrassment. She knew that this was what all England waited for. And that somehow she had failed them. She turned away and sent her women to fetch Jacot and the material for her dress. But as soon as they were gone she came back to her mother-in-law and touched the undimmed gold of her hair wistfully. "When Chaucer was reading just now I was looking around at you all—you and Agnes and that de Wardeaux girl. You were all ' right lovesome ' like the wives he described in those verses Richard liked so much——"

"My poor child! You're terribly in love with him, aren't you?"

Anne nodded dumbly. All her dainty pride was in the dust before this discerning woman. But she had to tell someone— turn to someone for advice. And instinctively she knew that Joan was built on too generous lines to betray her. With one of her swift, graceful movements the young Queen was on her knees beside the elder woman's chair. "I wouldn't mind his going so much, if only I were sure that I held his heart." With her two hands she made a lovely cupping gesture against her own. "As it is—he likes me, he is kindness itself; but then, he is kind to little Tom Holland, or to Mathe . . ."

" It is only that a woman is born years older than a man, and that he hasn't quite waked to maturity yet."

" And when he does ? He will live like other men, campaigning. Because he is handsome and a king, girls throw themselves at him—like your Lizbeth."

Joan laughed at her, kindly and comfortably. " Richard isn't a philanderer like Robert."

" No. But he is so devastatingly charming, and I have so little to hold him with. I wish—oh, I wish I were beautiful ! "

The sigh that accompanied the words seemed to flutter right out of Anne's heart, so that the woman whose beauty had been a household word was filled with understanding compassion. She tilted up the girl's dejected face, looking searchingly, critically, at the intelligent brow, the candid eyes and delicious mouth. She told no lies in the cause of kindness, but her gaze dwelt longest on the kindness of Anne's mouth. " If I were a man——" she began, rather as if words she had not intended to utter were being forced from her.

" Yes ? " breathed Anne.

Soon they would be talking lightly of fripperies and fashions, but in that still moment they were both aware that to a mother who has put much of herself into her son it is sometimes given to see other women through his eyes.

Through an open door at the far end of the room they could see Jacot coming, carrying the precious purple velvet on uplifted arms as though it were the Host, born along by an ecstatic wave of admiring women.

Joan rose to her feet abruptly, seeming almost to spurn Anne from her side. " You have something which the rest of us haven't, however beautiful we may be," she said harshly, almost grudgingly. " Something that could hold a man like Richard to the gates of Death—and beyond. . . . Not only his body, but his whole soul." It was not easy to know that she herself, with all her allure, had never been loved like that. To feel that she was giving place. Yet, bigger than her own sense of blank finality, a new prescience informed her, making her fear for this most problematic of her sons. " If only," she murmured, " he isn't too light a fool to find it | "

CHAPTER XV

ANNE FOUGHT down her own disappointments and handed Richard his unspoiled adventure with a smile. Agnes might weep and cling and make things difficult for de Vere. But *her* man must go to war with undivided mind.

She rode out of the City with him because he wanted her to see the final muster of his forces at Highbury. And a fine muster it was. Almost every nobleman in the country appeared to have taken the field, and the common land for miles looked like a gigantic mosaic of richly coloured banners and surcoats and shining steel.

"Most of them are Lancaster's, of course," admitted Richard. But seeing the pride in his eyes and being borne forward on the surge of excitement that animated his friends, she almost forgot that she herself was not English. And she could have kissed the crowds for cheering his military enterprise, knowing that their voices must be balm to heal his bitterness.

"A good thing the Queen rides side-saddle, or she would be wanting to lead a charge in person!" laughed young Lord Stafford, who had been chosen as the King's aide-de-camp but whose gaiety and good nature made him popular with all parties.

In the last few minutes before departure he and de Vere and Tom Mowbray crowded about her. And Anne knew that it wasn't just because she was Queen. There was a bond of gaiety and youth between them. Mowbray was particularly intrigued by the foreign saddle she used, and the others were teasing her and Agnes about the tall, horned head-dresses they were making so fashionable among their own womenfolk. "Though of course no Englishwoman can wear the ridiculous gauzy things with such an air as you Bohemians," allowed de Vere.

"How can you expect them to when their husbands won't let them shave the backs of their necks?" retorted Agnes.

"The Bishops say it's sinful," said Mowbray doubtfully. "But apparently Richard doesn't mind."

"Richard is civilized," boasted Anne.

"Besides, the Bishops aren't supposed to watch women dress. And I'd rather see my wife sinful than slovenly any day!" laughed Richard negligently. He had dismounted to gather a few sprigs of broom for luck and now, seeing Anne so piquant and gay in the midst of so much masculine attention, he came to her side and laid a hand on the queer wooden stirrup bar where her feet rested. "Planta Genista—my own flower. Does it grow wild in Bohemia?" he asked, handing her up the little nosegay. "It's funny, but everything always happens to me in June—when the broom is out."

Anne shook her head and tucked the golden sweetness into the tight-fitting bodice of her *cote-hardie*. "Nice things or nasty?" she asked, spreading the spikes so that they showed bravely as a badge.

"Both," he answered a little absently, his eyes still bright with excitement. "My father died in June. It was June when I first came to England. And then there was that awful week when the rebels held London. And now this. All the important things . . ."

"It was winter when we were married," murmured Anne.

But either he did not hear, or he missed the sad little implication. His gaze was still on the satisfying pageantry of his army, and it was not until a trumpet shrilled somewhere and their companions tactfully withdrew, that he realized the moment of parting had come. He turned to her then with his endearing smile. "Well, it is good-bye now, Anne," he said. "I have told Medford to see that you don't stay in London during the heat. There was a case of plague at Charing last week."

She managed to smile down at him without showing any of the wretchedness in her heart. "I shall go to Sheen tomorrow," she assured him.

" You like that better than Eltham ? "

" I love it best of all your palaces."

For a moment she felt his hand, hard and friendly, gripping her ankle. " Then I shall give it to you," he promised. " And you won't be too lonely, with my mother away at Wallington?"

Already Anne was living a moment ahead of time and knew just how lonely she would be without his impatience and his laughter. " Oh, Richard ! " she whispered urgently, seeing the uncles and a posse of important people coming to take leave of her.

Something of her urgency seemed to impart itself to him. " My dear ! " he whispered back, with a new tension in his voice which showed that he recognized her as something essential and permanent in his life as opposed to even the most exciting episodes.

Instinctively their hands met. He pressed closer to her dappled jennet and she bent over him. " You will write to me, Richard ? "

" Because you will miss me ? "

" Because I shall be so anxious. I must know, Richard. Suppose—suppose you were wounded——"

She saw him no longer as he was, erect and smiling, but lying on the cold earth, earth-cold himself and dabbled in blood. And now that his mind was wholly centred on her he read the thoughts that pictured him so.

The adventure took on a more sombre aspect.

" Of course I will write," he promised gravely.

Thomas of Gloucester was bearing down upon them, tearing without delicacy through their precious moments. Anne glanced at his hard face with loathing. " Soon ? " she urged.

" As soon as we reach Scotland, sweet." Richard kissed her hands, then released them quickly as though his uncle's detested presence profaned the action, and snapped his finger for his waiting groom.

In his thrustfulness Thomas Plantagenet had overheard their words. His clanking armour and blood royal jupon blotted out the summer sun. "Once we get to Scotland we shall need every man," he observed dourly. "It will be no time for dallying."

Instantly Anne became a stiff-necked little piece of imperial pride. Rudeness always made her like that; and spiritually or physically, she would sooner starve than be beholden to this bully for a crust. "I will send Sir Meles with you as my messenger," she said haughtily, beckoning to one of her own Bohemian followers.

Richard was in the saddle, gathering helmet and gloves from a page. Only his wife's example kept him from an outburst of rage. Anne never lost her temper or flared out at people, yet underneath her politeness there was a sharp edge of anger on his behalf. And somehow, deep down in that hidden part of him which had always feared Gloucester, he no longer felt alone. "If Sir Meles will ride in my own company we will make ourselves responsible for his comfort," he said formally, trying to emulate her self-control. "Stafford, we commend this honoured Bohemian knight to your charge, so that once we are safely across the border he may return with news for the Queen."

Anne's quaint, elusive beauty flamed like a rose. Although they both ignored Gloucester, the romance of a private pact had had the bloom knocked off it by publicity. "It will be the first love letter I have had from you," she said half reproachfully, as Richard, wheeling his horse, passed close beside her for a final word.

He looked back at her with warmth and laughter in his smile. She could almost have sworn that a spark of the passion she waited for was in his eyes. "I will see that it is a good one," he promised.

Another shrilling of trumpets—a stirring of seried ranks—a trembling of productive soil beneath the beat of martial hoofs. Quite unself-consciously, Richard turned to wave to her from the head of a column where the proud banners were thickest. And then he was gone. A normal, peace-loving young man swallowed up in a welter of war.

June slid into July, and all through the long summer days the sun shone mockingly at Sheen. Anne walked restlessly about the beloved gardens, waiting for her letter. She even begged for the big painting of Richard, gorgeous in his coronation robes, to be brought from Westminster. But the portrait was stiff and wooden. The lips wouldn't break into a smile for her, nor the eyes light up. And anyhow, she couldn't remember him like that.

So she sent for young Tom Holland to keep her company. He looked more like Richard than did the portrait, and it had nearly broken his heart when it was decided that he was too young to go to war. To cheer him and herself, Anne had Richard Medford fix a large map across an embroidery frame. And every day the three of them would hang over it, measuring the distance the army must have travelled. "Your Uncle Richard must have reached Oxford today"—or Coventry or Derby—Anne would say, sticking one of her new-fangled silver pins into county after county, always farther and farther northwards. And long after the lovable lad was asleep and dreaming of future laurels she would lie awake listening to the breeze stirring the riverside willows and telling herself like any sentimental dairymaid that the same stars shone over her love.

But when at last Sir Meles came riding in it was no love letter he brought. Only a hasty, outraged scrawl telling her that Stafford had been murdered.

"Not *Stafford*!" she cried, letting the slim, red-sealed roll of parchment flutter to her lap half-read. "Everybody loved him. He was what Chaucer calls 'a gentle parfait knight.'"

"Surely no one could pick a quarrel with *him*," cried Agnes, who was in attendance.

"I'm afraid the quarrel was picked on our behalf," their compatriot told them sadly.

" By whom, Meles ? By whom ? "

Meles didn't answer immediately but asked leave to send Tom Holland on some errand. And Anne, with heavy heart, read the full sum of her husband's rage and humiliation. " I see now why you sent the boy away," she said slowly. " It was his uncle. The King's own half-brother, John Holland, Agnes. Oh, how awful ! "

Both women looked to Sir Meles to fill in the details. " It all started with a servants' brawl," he explained. " Some of these English can't abide a foreigner and Holland's men lost no opportunity of jibing at mine. When we were come to a town called Beverley they jostled us out of all the best lodgings, and Stafford's men, knowing the King's hospitable wishes, rushed out on our behalf. A squire got killed. Accidentally, I believe. But it had to be John Holland's favourite squire. And as soon as it was dark he rode like an avenging devil through the streets and stabbed milord Stafford as he was riding home from supping with the King." Horrified silence greeted his words, and hung in the room. " Apart from the killing of his squire, that younger Holland always was jealous of any favour shown to another, they tell me," he added.

" And Stafford ? " asked Agnes.

" Poor Stafford was taken unawares—bemused by a pleasant evening and singing as he rode. He hadn't even had time to sort the matter or to offer his regrets. And Holland stabbed again and again and left him lying between blood and garbage in the gutter."

Anne covered her face with both hands. The letter she had so longed for lay, a besmirched thing, among the rushes at her feet. " Oh, Meles ! " she shuddered. " And only the other day I was talking to him, and he was so kind and cultured. Richard thought the world of him." She looked up anxiously. " Whatever will the King do ? "

Meles went thoughtfully to the window where Agnes was standing. Without subterfuge he handed her a letter from Robert de Vere, but she hadn't the heart to open it. " What *can* he do, madam," he asked, turning back to the Queen, " but have him put to death ? "

Anne stretched an entreating hand. " But, Meles, his own brother——"

" There is no love lost between them."

" I know. But don't you see—his mother . . . *Their* mother. Oh, no, the King can't have him put to death ! It would break her heart—and his, too, because it would always come between them."

But, moved by her distraction as he was, Meles took the man's view. Only a few days ago he had had to look upon a much more passionate grief. " What about Stafford's father ? " he argued. " With a son so full of promise. Stiff-jointed as he is, the old Earl has already ridden all those miles to beg justice from the King."

All those miles. Richard so far away with all this worry on his mind, and she not there to ease it. Anne rose and joined the others. " Don't you see, my friends, that I am in some way responsible ? If only I hadn't fussed about that letter ! "

" It was only natural, madam, with a husband going into battle," soothed Meles.

But instead of soothing her, his words only brought to mind that vivid picture of her young husband lying grey-faced on the ground. Perhaps even now the only battle that mattered was over. . . . And his last thoughts of her had been tinged with annoyance. . . . " How Richard must hate me ! " she cried, twisting her handkerchief into a fevered ball.

Agnes Launcekron only laughed and put kind arms about her. She who was too happy-go-lucky ever to spoil a present moment by dodging a future which had not yet caught her. Romance for her lay warm to hand, in Robert's letter ; and she was a woman who exuded happiness. " Nonsense, dear Anne ! All these weeks of anxiety are making you morbid," she declared. " Don't you remember how the very day we last saw Stafford, you were boasting to that solemn cousin Mowbray that Richard was civilized ? So why should he be unreasonable and blame you? It was *he* who should have thought about exchanging letters. As Robert did."

Anne had to smile at her friend's shamelessness. "That is just what Robert *shouldn't* have done, seeing he is married," she pointed out. "But go along now and read that letter, do, before it burns your pocket! And tell them to get Sir Meles a meal."

"And you will try to persuade the Pope to get Robert a divorce?"

"I will think about it."

Left alone, Anne allowed herself to savour the unintended hurt in Agnes's consolation. "Richard isn't in love with me as Robert is with her," was the persistent burden of her thoughts, outweighing even the worry of this family scandal.

CHAPTER XVI

EVEN THE joy of Richard's return was spoiled by Stafford's murder. Bells pealed and balconies were draped with costly tapestries and London cheered the triumphant army. But many of the banners and balconies were draped with black, and men were whispering everywhere, " Where is John Holland ? Will the King pardon him ? " Richard knew that the common people were watching him, waiting to see if he who had hanged their relatives when they rose in a just cause would condone a brutal murderer because he was of his own blood.

And inside Westminster palace Agnes Launcekron was asking the same question of the Queen.

" I don't know, Agnes. I wish I did, for my mother-in-law's sake," sighed Anne.

" But haven't you asked Richard ? "

The Queen and her favourite lady were already dressed for hawking and breaking their fast, but after the previous day's celebrations most of the warriors they had come to welcome were still abed. Anne shook her head as she set her small white teeth into a medlar. " They looked so fit and had so much to tell—he and Robert—that I hadn't the heart——"

Agnes arched freshly plucked brows. " Surely last night——" she began, but observing Anne's uncommunicative air she pursued the matter no further. " Their sunburn suits them, doesn't it ? And although they had such an exciting time they were both ridiculously glad to be home, weren't they ? " she babbled on, glowing over her own happy recollections of the last twenty-four hours.

" Robert at least had good cause to be," said Anne.

It was not like her to speak caustically. But she had noticed enviously how early they had both excused themselves from the festivities. Whereas Richard had sat up late, laughing and talking with Brembre and Walworth and the Masters of the Guilds who had given him civic welcome. She knew what pleasure he took in their forthright company, their practical outlook and their constructive plans for the everyday problems of London—particularly when he had been for long in the company of his uncles. And last night he had been in brilliant vein, describing the more human incidents of the campaign with a vivacity which everybody found infinitely more amusing than Bolingbroke's tedious statistics. But it was ages since she had seen him alone, and he might have shown some of Robert's eagerness. She had lain in bed shaken with lonely frustrated sobs until her head ached and her eyes were all puffed and ugly; so that when at last she had heard his hand on the latchet of the door she had turned her head away and feigned sleep. He had stood awhile by the bed. She had felt him gently replace the tumbled coverlets. And then she had been unreasonably angry because he had tiptoed out again for fear of waking her. It had been one of those lost, ill-synchronized hours that beset the path of matrimony.

Anne looked up and saw him now, coming into the room with Mathe beside him. His eyes seemed to be searching for her, but whether with sheepishness or reproach she could not tell. "Why so soberly dressed this morning after all yesterday's gorgeousness?" she asked, knowing that the clothes he wore always indicated his mood.

"Business," he answered crisply, helping himself to salted almonds from a plate which Agnes held up to him.

"You sat so long with City merchants last night that you are beginning to talk like one," laughed Anne lightly, so that he might know he was forgiven.

"Well, Parliament, then. I find I am expected to go down and tell the Commons how the money they voted for this expedition was spent. Already some of them are beginning to suggest that it was hardly a success."

"Not a success!" exclaimed Agnes indignantly. "But you took Edinburgh."

Richard's immaculate, sun-tanned fingers dived again among the Provençal almonds. " True, my dear Agnes. But it seems there weren't enough people killed."

He was in one of those flippant, aloof moods which Anne recognized as a kind of armour against unimaginative criticism. She laid aside her platter. " Surely it was much cleverer to have frightened away the French and impressed the Scots without much bloodshed," she said.

" That is exactly how I felt about it," agreed Richard. " I took such a large army that the Scots avoided a pitched battle. It cost a good deal of money, of course. And I suppose the paunchy gentlemen who sit here at Westminster prefer spending soldiers' lives to spending money." Accepting a cup of wine from a page, he strolled over to where his wife was sitting. So often the sight of her quenched his bitterness, much in the same way as Simon Burley's quiet words. " And each man's life means a broken home," he went on thoughtfully. " I saw inside the home of a blacksmith once. And I've talked with the people, Anne. At the time of the revolt. They've minds and hearts and hopes the same as we have. And so pitifully little besides."

Anne looked up at him with shining eyes. She had seen something of the aftermath of war on her journey through Flanders, and she loved it when he spoke his thoughts to her with that complete naturalness.

"Robert feels like that too," murmured Agnes, with the pride of recent surrender softening her face. " But I supposed it was because he is partly a poet."

Richard was conscious of vague resentment, and not a little envy. What was it about this new-born passion which gave people possessive knowledge of their lovers' minds ? " We used to hold forth about it when we were youngsters," he said with studied negligence. " I suppose there were so many amusing things we wanted to do that all the hours spent on preparing ourselves for war seemed a waste of precious time."

" ' The life so short, the craft so hard to learn,' " quoted Anne, in her lovely voice.

Richard laughed at her affectionately. " Quoting English poetry at me already, you clever little Bohemian ! " he teased, bestriding a stool before her. " I suppose you read Chaucer because he's besotted with you. Your charming head-dress, your exquisite gowns, and your demurely coiffed face, piquante as a nun's. Shall I tell you a secret, Anne Plantagenet ? " He lowered his voice to a momentous whisper and winked at Agnes. " I believe the man's writing a poem about *you* ! "

Anne clapped her hands in delight. Her brown eyes danced. " Oh, do you mean it, Richard ? "

" Of course I mean it. And of course you'll get unbearably conceited. With all my knights wanting to wear your favour at tournaments, too. Why, Tom Mowbray nearly drove us crazy singing some tuneless song about you up in Scotland. And only the day we parted from you Stafford said——" Richard stopped abruptly, appalled afresh at the loss of a life that held all the promise of an opening epoch—all the gifts that would have helped the cultural renaissance craved after by the youth of a war-weary age. To cover their mutual emotion he snapped his fingers to Mathe, trying to make the great gentle brute nuzzle Anne's hand. " This is the only purblind creature who hasn't the sense to love you best," he said.

" Nothing less than a king will do for Mathe," she laughed ruefully, ruffling the hound's reluctant head.

But whatever they spoke of, it was really the Stafford tragedy that filled their minds. Richard touched a fold of Anne's riding skirt, smoothing the rich green velvet absently. " It was nice of you to go to see my mother so often while I was in Scotland. Has she really been as ill as the doctors say, Anne ? "

" It's her poor tired heart, Richard."

" I'm not surprised. Dragged from campaign to campaign. And then nursing my father through all those years of illness."

Anne waited until Agnes had gone to join de Vere in the herb garden. " Why don't you ride over to Wallingford and see for yourself ? " she suggested.

" You know I would. It would be the first thing I should do. But now—it's so difficult . . ."

" Then it's true what Burley tells me ? You've decided your brother must die ? "

" He's not my brother," snapped Richard.

" Your half-brother then," Anne corrected herself patiently. " Won't you pardon him for her sake ? "

" And have my people think that I have one set of laws for them and one for the nobility ? That I twist justice how I like ? Besides, John Holland is detestable. Everywhere he goes he makes trouble with his bombast and his brutality."

Anne knew that he was right. But her heart ached for Joan. " In that case I suppose it would take a lot of courage to go and see her," she observed.

" And listen to her heart breaking," he agreed with a sigh.

Because Anne had finessed him into it he got up there and then to go, but mother-love forestalled him. Before the horses could be saddled Joan herself was at the door. And it didn't make it easier for Richard that she—a sick woman—had come to him. Women, for him, were creatures to be comforted and cherished. He hated to see her suppliant. Because he was furious about the ugly thing which had come between them he greeted her formally, so that all joy in seeing each other was spoiled. Yet in his miserable constraint he was grateful to see Anne show his mother the tenderness he could not.

The Princess had been brought in a closed litter and her servants had carried her upstairs. She still held the letter John Holland had written her and it was clear that she had risen from her sick-bed and come at once. " You will spare him, Richard ? " she beseeched. It had been some time before she could speak, but her eyes had been asking it from the moment she came into the room.

By an almost imperceptible gesture Richard begged Anne to

stay. He wanted her to see for herself how circumstances always hounded him to do the things he hated—to understand, and to be on his side. He himself leaned defensively against a table in the centre of the room. The change in his mother's face alarmed him, and he averted his glance with loathing from the desperately scrawled appeal in her hand. "He sent you here to beg for his life when all the physicians say you must rest," he broke out. "Wasn't it enough that he had to come crawling to me at Beverley?"

"I should have come anyway," countered Joan faintly. "Don't you see, Richard—whatever he has done, he is my *son*?"

"Your favourite son."

"You said that before. You've always been jealous of him," accused Joan, with a spurt of anger.

Moved by some uncanny dog-sense, Mathe growled as though his master were being attacked, and Richard pulled absently at his ear to quiet him. Somehow the warm, silky contact helped to soothe him. "Curiously enough, I'm not," he said slowly. "I just—dislike him. I dislike in him the same things that I dislike in Henry Bolingbroke. Except that when Henry brags he usually has something to brag about. One can't be jealous of someone who doesn't count."

He looked up as if glad to make the discovery, and his mother's anger melted before the grace of his reasonableness.

"I know it must have been difficult, to stand his sneering— his lack of understanding. And I know he has never loved you as Thomas does. I'm not upholding him, Richard . . ."

Richard said nothing. He was thinking of that crazy ride to Mile End. Seeing Holland and his horrible raw-boned horse disappearing across Hackney marshes in ignominious haste. At least he had been able to spare her knowledge of that.

But apparently others had been less kind. Her next words shook him out of all thought of his own reactions. "It was generous of you—not to tell me—about the time he ran away."

That she—the Black Prince's widow—should have to speak such words . . . He was across the room in a few strides. "So you knew?" he whispered, dropping on one knee beside her as he used to do.

"I've known all the time," she said, the great slow tears of spent grief welling in her lovely, faded eyes.

"Then surely that makes it—easier?"

Such knowledge seemed to Richard a bigger thing than knowing that one's son must die. If he had seen any son of his turn tail like that, he would go on loving him, he supposed, but all joy in him would be gone.

Joan only shook her head. All his life Richard had adored her as the fount of gaiety and loveliness, and it hurt him horribly to see the helpless tears course unheeded down her raddled cheeks. "Even Uncle John—though Holland is his own son-in-law—agrees that there is nothing else I can do," he argued, in self defence.

She made one last bid. She clutched at his encircling arm. "Dickon! Dickon! By all the loving joy we had together in your childhood——"

He released himself gently and walked away so that he should not see her agony. "I can't. It's only common justice," he flung back at her. "You are here pleading with me now to spare his miserable life. But in my mind's eye I can still see Stafford's father—at Beverley, only a few days ago—weeping for *his* son. And Stafford was the sort of knight we all of us, in our better moments, hope to be."

Joan's hands fell with defeated limpness to her lap. Simultaneously with the knowledge that John must die came the realization that Richard was no longer a malleable boy, but a man with a streak of obstinacy in him whom she could no longer melt. Her reign was over. If anyone moved or moulded him now it must be Anne.

"I don't know how John comes to be your son, my sweet," he was saying pitifully. "We all of us have vile tempers, I know. But his violence is a destructive, uncivilized thing—

part of this professional warmongering—and I mean to pluck it out of England."

Despairingly, Joan looked across at her daughter-in-law. Anne's sweet face was pale with pity and distress. But she said nothing. She sided with her husband. Involuntarily, she moved closer to him. Through her tears Joan of Kent saw them standing side by side. And it was as if for the first time and with prescient clarity she saw them facing life together. Only they were facing it with a completely different code from the one she and her husband had known. In whatever they did they would be moved less by traditional impulses, more by their own young minds and consciences.

"You can see him to say good-bye," offered Richard. "After I refused to pardon him he ran away—again. But I will have him brought to you."

When her women came for her he went with her to her litter. He took her hands tenderly and had his own physician accompany her. But he could not kiss her. Through no fault of his own he had been made to feel like Cain.

And he never saw her again.

Only a few days later her tired, generous heart was stilled for ever. They would have fetched him home from hunting but Anne insisted upon breaking the news to him herself. "Let him have a few more joyous hours," she entreated, knowing how remorse would always gnaw him. How all the happy memories of his mother's radiance must be blurred by regret.

"If only I had let John go!" he kept saying over and over again, when the first storm of his grief was past.

"It couldn't have made much difference—only a few days or weeks perhaps," comforted Anne.

"But she would have gone out happy—with a smile on her face." He covered his own face with both hands. "Every day, as long as I live, I will pray for the repose of her soul," he vowed with intensity.

It was already dusk but the servants had not dared to come in and light the torches. Richard began to pace up and down the room, while Anne, etched in half-tones against the uncurtained window, watched him from a high-backed chair. "It wasn't only what Holland did to Stafford," he burst forth presently, sensing her compassion. "But how could I tell her more?"

Anne stretched out a hand as if to halt his tortured progress. "What else, Richard?"

He stared at her consideringly for a moment or two. He was wont to see her as some witty, exquisite being, surrounded by gilded youth—the pampered daughter of an emperor. Ever since she had come to him as a bride he had thought of her as a charming companion for his leisure hours—someone to say pretty things to, or go hawking with to the accompaniment of jingling bells and carefree laughter. Someone who must be sheltered from the sordid things of life, just as her delicious gowns must be protected from the splash of mud. It had never occurred to him to make a serious confidante of her. But his mother was dead, and Mundina was at Wallingford laying her out. Rare, unshockable Mundina whom he had been wanting so desperately . . . "Weeks before Stafford was murdered an old friar came to me with some story about Lancaster wanting to betray me to the Scots," he said, half ashamed to begin talking to his young, foreign wife about these miserable, ever-recurring state intrigues. "People are always telling me Lancaster is treacherous."

"Perhaps only because he is so powerful, and they are jealous," she suggested reasonably. "What did you do?"

Richard resumed his maddening tramp across the sweet-scented floor rushes. "Do? Why, what anybody with a grain of common sense would have done. Changed our route at the last moment so as to avoid the alleged ambush, and had the monk detained in the nearest castle until I had time to go into the matter. I wasn't concerned with the tale-bearer himself. I wanted to get at the people who sent him. To settle once and for all if there's any truth in these rumours, and who spreads them. It's so important to know if I can trust Lancaster."

"And did you find out?"

"No. That cursed half-brother of mine went back secretly to the castle and tortured the poor wight. Tortured him so horribly that even the men-at-arms refused to have anything to do with it, and he and his friends had to do the beastliness themselves."

Anne shuddered, but would not break his mood by moving nearer to the fire. "How can men do such things?" she murmured.

"God knows! And men we have both sat at meat with. The poor devil died in spite of everything the constable of the castle could do for him. And now, thanks to those inhuman fools, I shall never know whether there really was an ambush or not."

"Weren't you furious?"

"So furious that I hit one of Holland's friends in the face. A bishop, I believe. I behaved like a maniac. And then I come back and preach at my poor mother about John Holland's temper!" He laughed harshly, then fetched up penitently before her. "But I'm not really like that, Anne. You know I don't get wild unless other people do something vile first. And at least I'm not smug. Tell me I'm not smug, Anne!"

"I can't imagine you ever being smug, Richard," she assured him gravely. In the gathering darkness he could not see her lips twitching into an almost maternal smile.

"I know only too well afterwards when I've behaved badly."

"And suffer for it."

"Yes. I suppose that if one chooses to indulge in ideals one must often suffer shame. And now I can't even show the people my fine gesture about justice."

"You mean you won't have him——"

"How can I have him put to death after this? It's as if *she* had already paid his debts, and I've no longer the heart. He'd better go on a pilgrimage or a crusade or something. Anything, so long as I don't have to look at him for a very long time!"

Richard stood there staring out at the drizzling rain, too wretched even to call for torches. There was a flurry of silken skirts behind him and suddenly it was Anne, his impeccable little wife, who was playing penitent.

"Oh, Richard, please don't hate me!" she entreated, clutching his hand and pressing her smooth cheek against his sleeve.

He swung round, surprised by her vehemence. "I—hate you?" he repeated vaguely.

"For causing all this. For sending Sir Meles——"

"That was Uncle Thomas's fault." His jaw set savagely, as if almost glad to discover one more score against the man. "It was all Uncle Thomas's fault, damn him! If he hadn't butted in——"

Anne disliked Thomas of Gloucester intensely, but she had not witnessed the years of bullying frustration that had built up Richard's loathing. And sometimes the deep-seated intensity of it frightened her. "But it was I who fussed about getting a letter from you," she reminded him hastily. "I wanted one so badly."

Richard drew her down on to the window seat and into the comforting circle of his arm. "Dear Anne," he comforted, the kindness of his smile seeming to illuminate her life again. "And I never wrote you a proper love letter after all!"

CHAPTER XVII

RICHARD lay full-length on the daisy strewn lawn in the privy garden at Westminster. His green hose and tunic made him as one with the grass but his head looked like a splash of copper against the grey coping of the lily pond. He rolled over on to his stomach and began indolently tickling the golden carp with a bullrush reed. The scent of red and white roses, for which the palace gardens were famous, drifted over him and the warm afternoon sunshine warmed him through and through.

All morning he had sat in a stuffy Council chamber where tempers ran high—and his own, in the finish, higher than any —and after dinner he had come out here to be alone. But somehow it seemed a king never *could* be alone. People had to be near him to feel they were at the centre of things, or because they were afraid of missing some favour—or sometimes, of course, simply because they liked his company. Robert de Vere, stretched on a stone bench near-by, wrapped in the throes of composition with his lute, was quietly companionable. But now Lizbeth de Wardeaux must needs come running out from the Queen's apartments and seat herself unbidden on the grass beside him.

Richard glanced from one to the other of them without enthusiasm and returned to his preoccupation with the fish. At least in line and pose they detracted nothing from the peaceful beauty of the garden. Robert with his lute and Lizbeth with her ridiculous daisy chains. Richard had had his fill of looking at ugly, quarrelsome faces round the Council table. He could bear it for so long, at first with bored indifference and then with a sort of exasperated patience, and then when they started picking Michael de la Pole's foreign policy to pieces or being rude to Burley, he would cut in with some sarcastic reminder of the business they were really there to settle. And then it would always end up with Gloucester or Arundel criticizing *him*, and he would fly out at them. Each time he would go to a meeting determined to emulate Burley's polished calm, and each time he would lose his temper. And losing his temper took so much out of him. It was so much more exhausting if one cared tremendously for the principle of the thing involved. He couldn't go home and eat a good dinner like Uncle Edmund, for instance, who could argue like an obstinate mule just for the sake of hearing his own voice. Half closing his eyes until pink and yellow water lilies merged themselves into a waxy carpet of exquisite colour, Richard admitted to himself that he felt tired in mind and full of lassitude in body. "But perhaps it's only that I'm missing the strenuous exercise of the campaign," he thought.

Lizbeth edged closer to him. For all her demure looks and sober mourning damascene, he felt sure that she, too, had come to argue about something. "It is just three months now since my dear lady the Princess died," she sighed, looking up appropriately to watch a flight of white pigeons flap upwards towards the blue sky. But as Richard took no notice she dropped her daisy chain and the guilelessness of her childlike pose. "It is true, isn't it, sir, that I am *your* ward now?"

"I suppose so," said Richard, chivvying an obese carp to sanctuary beneath a lily pad for no better reason than because its protruding eyes and rapacious gills reminded him of Richard Arundel.

Without looking around he sensed that Lizbeth was settling her skirts in the deliberate way of pretty women who intend to stay until they have got what they came for. "Well, what are you going to do about me?" she asked, her impertinence excused only by the informality of the hour.

"After a morning with Lancaster coveting the crown of Castile and Edward Dalyngrigge wanting a permit to build a new castle, I should imagine the King came out here precisely because he didn't want to have to do anything more about anybody," observed de Vere, pausing in the middle of a stanza to tighten a string.

But Lizbeth only made a grimace at him and defied convention still further by taking off her tall head-dress and setting it on the stone coping, where it stood like a miniature church steeple.

" I've had you brought here as one of the Queen's maids-of-honour, haven't I ? " pointed out Richard. " What else do you want me to do ? "

Lizbeth regarded the back of his comfortably relaxed body with exasperation. " You might take an interest in me, for one thing."

With a ponderous sigh he abandoned his piscatorial pursuits and sat up. She was so pretty that he could only review her pouting persistence with amusement. " I'm sorry," he apologized charmingly. " But judging by the way half the eligible bachelors and widowers in the country plague me, I should say that quite enough men are interested in you already."

She tossed her head so that her loosened curls made delectable little shadows against the whiteness of her neck. She probably knows, thought de Vere, how enticing she is without that tight wimple affair. " I don't want dozens of men," she was declaring. " And you know very well they are interested only in my money ! "

Richard forgot the aftertaste of political wrangling and began to smile. " I'm not exactly disinterested in it myself," he reminded her, tossing a pink water lily into her lap.

She tucked the blossom absently between the coral buttons of her tight-fighting corsage. " Oh, I know that's why you all want wardships. So that you can sell us poor girls to the highest bidder——"

" Oh, come, Lizbeth ! I'm not as mercenary as all that."

De Vere laid aside his lute. He was always interested in a girl whose amatory technique surpassed his own. " But it would help to pay for some of those banquets and tournaments the Commons were complaining about," he pointed out, hoping to prod her into a fury. Lizbeth, he knew, always looked her best with her passions unleashed and he wished that Richard would stop being such a monkish fool about her.

"And to pacify the Commons you'll send me away to marry a Percy in the wilds of Northumberland or a Courtenay right down in Devon?" she protested.

"My dear child, I can't afford to forgo my wardship fees," began Richard reasonably. "And surely every respectable girl wants a husband——"

"I'm not a dear child!" she raged.

"Nor fundamentally respectable," murmured de Vere.

"I'm nearly the same age as yourself, Richard Plantagenet, and we've known each other practically all our lives. As long as you've known that versifying nincompoop over there. And I won't lie in any fat baron's bed! Nor bear his vacant-looking brats. I'd murder him first!"

Both men burst out laughing. But Lizbeth was very seductive with the tears in her eyes and her little pointed breasts heaving indignantly. Richard reached over and tumbled her into his arms. "My precious poppet," he expostulated. "You don't suppose I'd marry you to any man you really loathed, do you? Or that I forget how brave you were that day you helped Chaucer to get my mother away from the Tower? But you're so beautiful and so alone in the world that you need protection, don't you?"

"Yes," murmured Lizbeth, with her lips against his tunic.

"And you can't stay virgin for ever."

"No," murmured Lizbeth, with still more conviction.

Her little marauding hands clung tighter and she nearly swooned with ecstasy when she felt Richard's cheek lightly caressing her hair.

"And only last night the Queen was saying that it was high time we——"

Clever as a cat, Lizbeth detected the teasing note in his voice and guessed that all the time he was fondling her he had been grinning at de Vere across the top of her head. She sprang up, rigid against his encircling arm. "You're mocking me—as if I were some light-o'-love offering you the infatuation of an hour!" she accused, her angry eyes searching his down-bent, laughing ones. To be made a fool of before de Vere was more than the undisciplined little spitfire could bear. Too quick for thought she freed an arm to slap Richard's face. She forgot that he was King of England. He was just a terribly attractive young man who always inflamed her desire by his indifference, until her senses were consumed by him. Mercifully, he was even quicker than she and caught her hand in time. His eyes went light, warning her momentarily with their cold fury. For a split second she caught a glimpse of that other Richard—white, austere and anointed—usually hidden so successfully behind the radiant, colourful personality he showed to every-day friends. And then it seemed that they were just sitting there normally as before—two young men and a girl in the sunshine—with the arm of one of them casually about her. But each of them had been sobered by a revealing flash of fundamental emotions. Even Lizbeth realized that but for Richard's quickness she must have been sent away in disgrace. She drew a deep breath. "I know why the Queen wants to get rid of me," she said with desolate defiance, staring straight before her at the shadows of the darting fish.

Richard knew too, with the invitation of her body still against his own. He knew that when he held Anne in his arms he did not feel like this. Anne was so exquisite and always charming about his inexperienced love-making. She never asked for more than he could give, nor made him feel inadequate. One couldn't imagine her pushing her wares, so to speak. But he had married so young, and with so little sex experience. And the complete, all-consuming union of Robert and Agnes dangled before him, like a mirage that he never reached. He, too, wanted to taste life to the full. With all his heart he wanted it, sensing that nervous irritability and frustration could be drowned in that well of sweet oblivion. That, caring less for all else by comparison, he could draw new strength of character from its depths.

He often wondered about it. Was there some virility lacking in him? To achieve such felicity did one have to take some delicious, Eve-old child like Lizbeth? Or be promiscuous, like Arundel and the uncles? Even Lancaster, with his greying hair and suave manners, took his daughters' governess, Katherine Swinford, to bed. "Into the same bed, naked, with his bargained Castilian wife," people said. De Vere and some of the other officers, slightly drunk in Scotland, had been bandying coarse jests about it. . . . But, of course, it couldn't really be true of a cultured man like Lancaster. Just back-stairs gossip, no doubt, because the people hated him. . . .

Richard shook himself out of the erotic train of thought. "You'd better get up, you little baggage," he said, purposely giving Lizbeth's thigh a callow push and trying to speak lightly. "And if you'll give me some indication of the sort of husband you'd like I'll see what I can do about it."

He sprang lithely to his feet and pulled her up beside him so that they stood hand in hand, facing each other. Her demure grey dress was crumpled and the daisy chain lay broken at her feet. But she still looked at him with demanding eyes. "I don't mind what he is like as long as he lives at Court," she told him shamelessly. "Please don't let them send me away, Richard!"

She walked away obediently enough between the rose bushes, swinging her expensive headgear by its veil. Both men stood to watch her go, shaken by the unexpected power of her passion. Somehow, their sophisticated baiting hadn't been so amusing after all. And presently Richard joined de Vere on the bench. "Well, that's that," he said inadequately.

"Not all of it perhaps," suggested de Vere, looking after Lizbeth with grudging admiration until a door in the palace wall swallowed her up.

The summer afternoon was spent. The sun was beginning to dip down towards the river, so that already the water in the lily pond looked brown, and the long shadow of the Council chamber reached across the garden. It crept like a menacing finger to where they were sitting, symbolic of the shadow its dictates could cast across a sovereign's life. Even if one went out into a garden or dallied with a girl, thought Richard resentfully, one couldn't forget it for long.

"What a herd of obstructionists in there this morning!" he exclaimed, nodding towards the splendid Norman building, so that de Vere wasn't certain whether he were deliberately trying to change the conversation or whether the thought had been there all the time, hagriding his mind.

"Gloucester faced with a new idea is like a ringed bull with a freshly unleashed dog. His only reaction is to tear it blindly to pieces, head down," laughed de Vere. "I thought he would literally have gored poor Michael de la Pole across the table when he brought up this new plan of establishing our wool staple at Bruges instead of Calais. Quite sensibly, I thought, considering that most of our trade comes from Flanders."

"A pity you didn't say so," remarked Richard.

De Vere shrugged fashionably padded shoulders. "What was the good? With everybody so worked up already."

"It might have added weight to the proposed bill."

"Or damned it straight away. My dear fellow, can you imagine *my* approval making any bill more popular? 'The King's echo!' some wit has only to whisper behind his hand. And then what happens? Arundel and Gloucester sneer, Burley or Lancester tries to pour oil on troubled waters, you rush in with some stinging sarcasm and then can't eat any dinner."

Richard had to laugh at so accurate an epitome of the familiar scene. "Oh, Robert, I suppose you are right," he conceded, flinging himself full-length along the bench while his friend strolled over to the pond. He lay supine for a moment or two, poignantly aware of the muted twittering of birds and the peace preceding eventide. From the Abbey near-by a bell began to drone for Vespers. Idly, he picked up Robert's lute and began trying to fit a ribald little chansonnette to the sonorous under-tones of the bells. " I wonder if I was wise in letting Lancaster go to contest Aunt Constanza's claim in Spain ? You know, I could like Lancaster—if only I were *sure*," he murmured. And then, giving up his weird harmonic experiment, " Wouldn't it be wonderful if we were irresponsible again ? Or else knew whom we could really trust ? " Suddenly, restlessly, he swung both scarlet shod feet to earth again. " Come to think of it, Robert, there are precious few. One could almost count them on the fingers of one hand." He laid aside the instrument and began to do so. " Burley—de la Pole—Tom Mowbray. Henry, I suppose, in a way——"

" And Anne," supplemented de Vere, watching him from across the little pond.

" *Cela va sans dire*," agreed Richard. " One's wife is part of oneself."

" Not always."

Richard knew that it wasn't so with Robert. And here was another matter that he supposed he should have done some-thing about. But, hotly resenting interference in his own pri-vate concerns, he had purposely refrained. " You made no objection when we arranged your marriage with Philippa de Courcy," he reminded him reluctantly.

" I'm making no objection now," countered de Vere. " She's your own distaff cousin. She's very rich. And her people seem to own half Devon."

" Oh, for God's sake, stop being cynical ! " snapped Richard.

De Vere stopped immediately. His whole manner changed. " Don't you see, Richard, that for once I'm not ? " he said. " A man can't live on money and high places alone. One wants something beautiful, glowing, intimate—to warm the loneliness we all try to cover from the world—the love of someone utterly responsive to oneself——"

" Like Agnes ? "

" Yes, like Agnes."

Their glances met and held and gradually the spark of

authoritative anger died out of Richard's. "It's real this time, Robert?" he said.

"Yes, it's real."

Richard tried not to envy him. But one couldn't have the Queen's most intimate friend living in open sin; and nothing, he knew, would ever placate the de Courcys. "It's damned unfortunate," he muttered.

De Vere flashed out at the word. "Not unfortunate for us. A thousand times no!" he protested. "However little our official marriages mean, Agnes and I will have *lived*." He looked across at the lovable figure of his friend, a person at once so vulnerable and so capable of ecstasy; and all that the worldly Earl of Oxford would have deemed best in himself rose to the surface. He wanted Richard to share this bigger experience, just as they had shared all the fun that came to them as boys. "You're so—young, somehow!" he exclaimed, with a kind of fond exasperation. He came and rested one foot on the garden seat, leaning eagerly towards Richard with gesticulating palm. "You think *you're* fortunate, Richard, because you're married to a very charming girl. She isn't haughty and reserved like Philippa. Your fears about her being a stranger to you were all dispelled by the fact that she speaks perfect French. She's witty, and you're proud of her in public and enjoy paying her pretty compliments. But there's something more than that—something you haven't tasted."

Richard was aware of it, and his very awareness seemed a disloyalty. But when he would have sat silent de Vere added impulsively. "Why don't you take that bewitching trollop Lizbeth?"

Richard knew that Lizbeth wasn't a trollop. That, with all her seductiveness, she had never seriously tried to tempt any man but himself. "I don't know," he said truthfully. All he knew was that something always held him back. Not morality. Fastidiousness, perhaps. . . . Or just because he was waiting for something better. . . . And anyhow, his parents had always been faithful to each other, and he had been brought up in that sort of household.

"Good God, man, is your blood made of water?" urged de Vere. "All these months, when she throws herself at you, I've been wondering how you can resist her!"

Richard knew that whenever he tried to make peace with France there were people who said contemptuously that he wasn't the Black Prince's son at all, but the son of some Bordeaux priest. Gloucester himself had slandered his sister-in-law's memory by taunting him with the tale. Gloucester might even have started it. And because he was an uncle, and a Plantagenet, Gloucester must go free.

He sprang up from the seat. "Then I wager you I'll take her before the week is out!" he cried.

"Done!" De Vere clapped a hand to his. "And I hope you win," he added, turning away, his own casual self. "Then perhaps you'll be more kind to Agnes and me."

Richard began to brush the bits of grass from his hose preparatory to going in. "I don't see what I *can* do," he admitted ruefully. "Half the powerful families in England are related to the de Courcys. And already they are champing about the insult to Philippa."

"One of the reasons you were seeking for my unpopularity, no doubt."

"And you're supposed to have a bad influence over me," grinned Richard. "A charge which you can't very well deny!"

Even de Vere, who deliberately posed for publicity, sometimes tired of the venom of men's tongues. "If only the things I *really* do were half as bad as the things they invent," he sighed wearily. "You've forgotten the worst charge of all."

"Which charge?" asked Richard negligently, breaking off a red rosebud and pulling it through the top buttonhole of his tunic.

De Vere shifted his stance uncomfortably. "Oh, you know, Arundel's masterpiece, that fits so well with his filthy mind.

The thing quite a number of people are beginning to say about us."

Richard was still contorting his neck in an effort to enjoy the rose's perfume. "And what are they saying this time?" he inquired, between appreciative sniffs.

De Vere didn't answer at once. He was beginning to wish he hadn't mentioned the subject. But since Richard chose to be so dense—"What *do* people say about two young men who are always about together like us?" he asked, with a deprecating shrug. "Particularly if one of them happens to be fair-skinned like you."

Richard's head shot up. His face blanched visibly. He stared at de Vere in horror. "So that's why Gloucester's forever referring to our being 'inseparable!'" he muttered at last, in a strangled sort of voice.

"I thought you knew," muttered de Vere, flushing beneath that unwavering stare. "Why, even young Mowbray's got hold of it now. He called me 'Piers' the other day as if by mistake, and then apologized elaborately in front of a whole anteroom of people, including Gloucester and Arundel, of course——"

"Mowbray said *that*?" Richard's eye blazed with fury.

"Oh, more in sorrow than in anger, I imagine. Mowbray is very religious. So I suppose it was the only way they could think of to knock you off your pedestal." In order to cover his embarrassment, de Vere was talking much too quickly and saying more than he had intended. "Arundel's trying to strengthen their party by persuading Tom to marry one of his daughters. Didn't you know? And even a thick-skinned fool must see that he'd have to kill Tom's devotion to you before dragging him into the detestable family circle."

Part of Richard's brain asimilated the unwelcome information; but he scarcely appeared to be listening. "Mowbray said that," he repeated, "and you didn't k-kill him?"

"But Richard, what does it really matter—since it isn't true?"

" You mean you don't—mind ? "

De Vere was hanging on desperately to the shreds of a fast fraying temper. " Of course I mind. But what can I *do* ? Nothing would have pleased them better than for me to have challenged Tom and blared abroad their horrid whispering campaign. And anyhow, I can't tear the thought out of men's minds, can I ? "

It was true enough—once those arch-fiends had planted it in fertile soil.

" No," agreed Richard, relaxing slowly into normal movement. " But I can see that it withers, stillborn. I can make you Duke of Ireland."

" Duke of Ireland ! " Such an idea had never occurred to de Vere, who enjoyed most of the privileges that fall to the proverbial " king's favourite". He wasn't even related to the royal family and was sane enough to visualize the outcry that would ensue. " But I thought that you were keeping the title for your late uncle's son—Edward of March—because he's heir presumptive ? "

" By the time he's grown up Anne and I may have children. And I don't mean just take the title, but *go* there."

It was de Vere's turn to be appalled. " By the Holy Rood, Richard, you don't mean me to go and live there among a lot of illiterate, half-savage chieftains ? What do you suppose I should do in that God-forsaken, bog-ridden place ? "

" Rule it, I suppose," said Richard coldly. In that moment he almost hated any man whose name had been so coupled with his own. " At least it will show Arundel's dupes that we are *not* inseparable."

De Vere saw that he was in deadly earnest. " I am honoured, sir," he said formally. " But I wish to God I hadn't told you !"

" And I am unspeakably grateful that you did."

" Grateful ? " He glanced at Richard's ashen face. " But you are suffering hideously."

" It is better to suffer and be warned," said Richard quietly.

" Warned of what ? The thing is done."

"But done for a purpose." Richard seemed to have got a hold on himself and, seeing his friend's perplexity, he tried to speak with some sort of patience and dignity. "You don't understand, Robert. This isn't just one of their malevolent little thrusts at my happiness. Nor merely another insult to humiliate me. It's part of a deliberate plan. A plan to keep me in subjection. To keep the power in their own hands after my majority. To prostitute my abilities. They're hideously afraid sometimes because they know—and Burley and Michael know —that, once given the chance, I am capable of ruling this country a great deal better than they do. You don't believe me, perhaps? Well, all I can say is, you haven't had to bear with Arundel's veiled hints about the second Edward being dethroned. Or listen to Gloucester describing exactly how brutally he was murdered——"

"Richard! They wouldn't dare——"

But Richard was staring past his friend's protestations at the stately outline of Westminster Hall, seeing only an intangible world of intrigue where there was no pity at all. "This calumny is but the first step to what they want to do. I see it now. I'm not unprepossessing enough—I haven't done anything unconstitutional enough—— With a popular bride beside me I'm not *hated* enough. . . . So they thought of *this*— and cast you for the part of Piers Gaveston. . . ."

De Vere was staggered. Realizing that he could touch only the fringe of that troubled, inner world his most intimate friend must live in, all worldly wisdom was momentarily knocked out of him. "And I've treated you as if—as if I knew so much more than you," he said awkwardly, coming to lay a hand on Richard's shoulder. Anything, he thought, to pull him out of that wrapped, bleak mood.

Richard laughed harshly, but he withdrew his inwardly focused gaze and smiled at him. "I told you long ago that it was a fool's game, giving me your friendship," he reminded him. "Have you forgotten Mundy's queer expression? How she always spoke of me as being ' ill beset ? ' "

Robert walked soberly to the seat to retrieve his lute. Something in the cheerful look of it, with its streamers of coloured ribbons and its companionable gaiety, drove home to his mind the incredible role Richard had thrust upon him. Banishment, that is what it would be. Glorified banishment, to kill a rumour. Because of some rather far-fetched suspicion that his crown and life might be in danger. Plots and suspicions lurked everywhere with so young a king. But why should his own pleasant way of living be sacrificed, while Richard stayed here with all the delights of love and culture about him? Chivalry demanded that one serve the King. Give one's life for him, if need be. . . . And this would be only *living* it for a time in intolerable circumstances. But Robert de Vere wasn't quite big enough. He swung round to clutch at his departing companion's trailing over-sleeve. " I couldn't carry Agnes off to Ireland. It would start a Bohemian war or something. For God's sake, Richard, need this spoil our lives ? "

But he had come up against that streak of firmness, or obstinacy. Richard looked at him for a moment in genuine surprise. " Your private life is your own, for men to say of it what you let them," he answered, turning on his heel towards the palace. " But mine is not. It belongs to England. And what men say of me will be remembered."

CHAPTER XVIII

Dusk was wrapping itself round the Queen's favourite palace at Sheen. It blurred solid towers to a grey, ethereal outline and began to extinguish the bright hues of stocks and larkspur in the gardens. The withdrawn river, shrunk to a flat sluggish ribbon between the wide mud flats of low tide, flowed silently in its narrow bed. Stiff reeds, fringing the ooze, had ceased their brittle lisping, and along the banks below the terraced garden the dripping fingers of sad willows shrouded the embrace of summer lovers.

All Nature's perpetual whispering seemed to have transferred itself into the palace, where officials held anxious consultations and bewildered servants huddled here and there awaiting orders. Something had happened which was completely beyond the range of their accustomed duty. For a whole day the King had been in residence. Yet no meats had been borne into the great hall and no minstrels made music in the gallery. No one had called for hawks to be unhooded or hounds unleashed. No torches flamed through the state apartments. Only a couple of candles burned in the window of the King's bedroom, palely visible from the barge-walk below.

Yet men-at-arms in the guardroom swore to having seen him ride in with the dawn, a startled groom had taken his horse and the Constable had been summoned frantically from his bed.

The strangest thing of all was that the King had come alone. They were so accustomed to seeing him surrounded by sportive nobles and laughing ladies. But there was not so much as a squire in attendance, nor even the great grey wolfhound that was his devoted shadow.

The King had not even eaten.

He was standing now between the candles, staring out at the depressing mud. He himself was stained with mud. Stale, hard mud that had splashed up from muddy lanes to stick upon cheek and hose and tunic. Just as that uglier, more tenacious mud which had been thrown at him might stick upon his reputation.

He turned a page or two of a psalter on the book desk beside him, trying to take in the soothing sense of words penned in some peaceful monastery. But his mind was too busy piecing together the events of the last twenty-four hours. He glanced round the room in search of some starting point. The great state bed behind him was still tumbled where he had thrown himself across it in the early hours. He must have bolted the servants out, he supposed, and slept. Slept until late afternoon. But then, he had been riding all night. He couldn't remember where except that he must have pounded past the gibbet on Hounslow Heath, lost himself in the darkness of woods and followed the familiar track through the deer park. Anywhere, to get away from Westminster and to find himself eventually in the healing quiet of Sheen. He had had to exhaust himself physically before he could burn out the fires of hatred that possessed him.

He remembered leaving Westminster. He had given de Vere and the rest of them the slip. Someone had brought his horse. His new roan, Barbary, who had carried him so tirelessly in Scotland. People had looked at him queerly as he mounted. And then Ralph Standish had brought his cloak and been importunate about coming with him. And in his irritation he had struck at Ralph. At Ralph, who was one of the best swordsmen in the country, and who couldn't hit back !

Richard hated himself very thoroughly. His sweaty, unwashed body and his rage-dishevelled soul. A wave of affection for his squire swept over him, engulfing him until it grew big enough to include all his household. At least his clerks and servants loved him. Only last week, passing through the kitchen courtyard, he had seen a scullion stoop furtively to kiss his shadow as it fell across the flagstones. Probably it was the aftermath of some forgotten kindness. But the boy had looked such a clod in contrast to the unconscious beauty of the gesture that all the facile sympathy in Richard had stung momentary tears to his eyes. And now the devotion of even the meanest scullion looked precious against the treasonable cruelty of greater men. All that was quick and generous in Richard wanted to champion them, to reward them with something better than blows. And, as if in judgment on him, before the night was out he had needed that proffered cloak. It had come on to rain, he remembered, passing exploring hands over the creases in his sodden summer tunic.

Sudden anxiety seized him for Barbary. He had pushed the poor brute hard. He recalled the feel of her steaming flanks as he had slid stiffly from the saddle. He crossed the room to pull back the bolt, and a couple of wide-eyed servants almost tumbled into the room. They expected the King to call for comforts for himself. But all his concern was for the roan. Had she been properly rubbed down? Where was she bedded? Had the head groom remembered to give her a hot mash?

Quick on their heels came the perplexed Constable. He was horrified at the mudstains. It was unthinkable that there should be no gentlemen-of-the-bedchamber. He would have a bath prepared with scented herbs. The cooks were preparing a meal and the tables laid in the hall. The King's grace must be famished. He had had nothing—nothing at all when he arrived—except some wine to quench his thirst.

That had been just the trouble, thought Richard, suddenly remembering a good deal more about his thirst and his arrival. Too much Bordeaux on an empty stomach. Robert's wager and Gloucester's taunts all mixed up in his mind, and an overpowering desire to forget everything. "I gave you a message last night—or was it this morning—for my ward the Lady Lizbeth de Wardeaux," he recalled tentatively.

The man bowed in confirmation.

" Telling her "—Richard passed a hand through his matted hair, trying to remember exactly what he *had* told her— " telling her that I lie at Sheen and wish to arrange about her marriage."

" Yes, sir."

Well, that should certainly be good enough for anyone as amorous and as enterprising at Lizbeth. Richard made no doubt she would come before nightfall. He even smiled a little, picturing her eagerness. " I hope you entrusted the message to someone—circumspect ? " he said.

" I sent my own son, sir, thinking perhaps——"

Not being a practised philanderer Richard looked up sharply to see what the Constable *was* thinking. But the old man had been in the Plantagenets' service for a long time and took it for granted that Kings could send for any ladies they fancied. All that appeared to worry him was lack of sleep.

Richard's preoccupation broke into an indulgent smile, remembering that the man had been badly wounded at Crécy. "Go to bed, Gervase," he ordered, with his own happy blend of authority and badinage. " I shan't want you any more to-night. How should I, when I'm expecting a lady ? And tell the cooks they can go to bed too and I'll taste their patisserie to-morrow. I'll have a chicken or something sent up here—and a flagon of that twelve sixty-eight vintage you've got hidden away in the cellars. I don't want any fuss. Only for God's sake have them bring me a bath and a clean suit of your son's."

But Richard got neither suit nor bath. Before the servants could bring either there was a stir outside the door. It appeared that the lady had already come. The departing Constable spent a long time bowing and scraping to her in the doorway, but, rather surprisingly, made no attempt to detain her. Richard had certainly intimated that she might be admitted without any fuss, but to walk into his bedroom unannounced. . . . Even for Lizbeth this was a piece of unwarrantable impudence. Antagonism rose in him. Doorway and arras were in shadow so that all he could make out was a girl's slim hooded figure. She had him at a disadvantage with his unbuttoned tunic and dishevelled appearance illuminated by the two tall candles. And showing unusual diffidence, she must needs linger just inside the room.

" Come in, if you're coming ! " he called, standing very still and erect as he always did when he felt his dignity was being infringed.

The girl obeyed him immediately and he let out a startled, hastily stifled oath.

It was not Lizbeth, but Anne.

And even in his amazement and through swift dissembling thoughts he was conscious of a great sense of relief. He knew that he had only wanted Lizbeth as a kind of antidote.

For a crazy moment he supposed that Anne might somehow have heard about his message and come to upbraid him. But her look of strained anxiety changed to relief at sight of him. " We have all been so worried about you," she explained. " When you didn't come to supper—and then when night fell. I had the gardens searched because that de Wardeaux girl said she had last seen you there. I even began to think perhaps there really *was* some plot of Lancaster's—or that John Holland had come back for revenge——"

Richard hadn't thought of that—nor realized what a constant burden of anxiety a royal husband could be to a girl. He hurried to take her cloak and make her welcome. " I'm so sorry. I ought to have let you know," he said. But in the light of all that had happened his words sounded formal and inadequate. Almost as if he were apologizing to his Aunt Constanza or the Duchess of Oxford for being late for some trivial party.

But he couldn't say more. And anyhow, the servants were back in the room, bringing more lights and laying a meal. " Haven't you eaten yet ? " Anne asked. She stood sipping some wine from the glass he had handed her, her eyes ranging over the informal assortment of food. Even before she noticed, Richard saw himself betrayed by the stolid laying of two covers.

Such a contretemps would never happen to Robert, he supposed, suppressing a grin. But one could scarcely expect a couple of bewildered chamber grooms, acting on hurried instructions, to have the wit to cope with so unexpected a situation. Anne set down his priceless Venetian goblet hurriedly, realizing that it had not originally been intended for her. " Oh, I see," she said bleakly.

Clearly, Anne was seeing several things. Her gaze turned from the table to her husband. Divorced from all elegance and ceremony, there was a sort of amused virility about him. She saw that for all his gentle courtesy, he was quite as capable of having love affairs as Robert, or any other personable young man—that for all she knew he might have had several. And that because he was a King he could do what he liked, and neither she nor anybody else would dare to reproach him. She saw, in fact, that if she wanted to keep him she must fight for him. All these months they two had lived together on the shining surface of things—so charmingly, so conventionally —that it was a nasty jolt. " You must be badly disappointed," she stammered. " But I will go soon."

Richard didn't answer. If Edward the Confessor were his patron saint, as people said, he must have leaned from Heaven to lay a finger on his lips, knowing in his wisdom what a taste of honest jealousy can do. This was a new Anne—less controlled, more comfortably human. He liked that spark of anger in her, brittle and dangerous as burning sticks. It flattered him, when most he stood in need of something to restore his self-respect. And beckoned to all those primitive urges which had been crying out for satisfaction.

To ease the constrained moment Anne looked round the ill-prepared room, taking charge like any housewife. It was her right and unconsciously she used it as a challenge. Before the servants withdrew she asked them sharply why they hadn't lit a fire.

" It is June and I hadn't told them to," Richard said in their defence, as one of them came and set a torch to the brushwood stacked against October on the hearth. Watching the man's unresentful back, he wondered irrelevantly how it must feel to be a servant and not be able to retort that the King had been in a vile temper and had barred them out.

Anne sat down and began peeling a peach, scraping at it with little vicious dabs, waiting for the man to go. " Yes, it is June," she said.

Richard caught the allusion. Standing with a chicken bone poised between his fingers, he set his teeth to it hungrily. Yes, all the important things had happened to him in June. Good things and bad. And now—but perhaps after all, this thing that Robert had let slip wasn't really important enough to count. The fire was blazing up, the good old vintage warmed him. Turning his head to look towards the darkening river he found that the dreary vista was already blotted out. Tomorrow the Thames would be full and sparkling again. What, he wondered, would happen to him *this* June ?

" How did you know that a fire would make everything so much better ? " he asked boyishly, as soon as they were alone.

Anne wiped her fingers on a fringed napkin. Throwing a cushion to the hearth, she knelt on it, warming her hands at that extravagant blaze. One oughtn't to be cold in June— unless one were dying, or driven away from the warm intimacy of a man's love. . . . " Because you're the sort of person who needs a fire for spiritual comfort as much as for bodily warmth," she told him, trying to forget her own stab of misery. " Were you so frightfully wretched, Richard, that you had to ride about all night until you were wet through? "

" Of course not. It was just that sitting around a Council table a man needs exercise. I suppose that is one of the few arguments in favour of war——"

" Must you lie to me ? "

He stopped exploring for favourite morsels among the dishes, a silver cover still upraised in his hand. " Oh, my dear ! After you were sweet enough to come to me——" He covered the steaming frumenty carefully, trying with compunction to answer her first question. He wasn't particularly hungry any more. "It was just that yesterday afternoon I found out something that makes me want to be sick," he said.

Anne jerked up her proud little chin. The riding hood had ruffled her hair, making her look less *soignée* and remote. "That happens to most of us—sometime or other," she reminded him, spreading her fingers to the blaze.

"And every time I look at Gloucester and Arundel I could commit murder," he went on, unheeding the implication of her remark.

Anne slewed her exquisite little body round on the great, tasselled cushion. "And don't you suppose I feel sick every time Lizbeth throws herself at you? Don't you suppose I could murder her now—when she's managed to take you from me?" she demanded.

Richard, who had been ranging back and forth dramatically, stopped in his tracks. "Anne!" he exclaimed, gazing down at her. A great excitement began to rise in him, crushing out all smaller emotions. "I didn't know—how could I—that you felt like that."

She sprang up then and faced him. All her poise and elegance were gone. She might have been a gypsy's daughter, not an emperor's. "Well, it's natural, isn't it? I'm your wife. And I've always known you're not in love with me. And I imagine it's Lizbeth you were expecting here tonight?"

"She didn't throw herself at me this time," said Richard.

Anne began to laugh, rather piteously. "Oh, I've landed myself in a queer situation, haven't I?" she said. "And you're being very patient with me." For the first time she understood that—although he had never said so—he wanted everything. Everything that a woman could give. And that a woman couldn't give everything until she had thrown away her dainty pride—even her pride in not letting a man see that she gave more than he did. But now, probably, it was too late. . . . "Please believe me," she added, still gathering the remnants of that pride about her, "that I wouldn't have followed you here if I hadn't supposed you needed comfort——"

" Followed me ? "

" Oh, not immediately. But I didn't need sending for. I guessed that if you were in trouble or hurt you would come to Sheen—just as I should myself. . . ."

Richard came closer, taking her by the shoulders impatiently. " But who told you that I was hurt ? "

" Agnes, of course." She lifted candid, troubled eyes to his. " Oh, Richard, how could you make Robert Duke of Ireland ? She's in floods of tears because she can't go there officially. And just imagine what the uncles will say ! He'll be their equal. And our children's. If we ever have any now ! "

But Richard wasn't attending. Uncles and titles and other people's troubles left him cold just then. He was looking down at his wife's white, sensitive face. " Wait ! Let's get this straight," he insisted. " If Agnes told you all that, then you know about—what people are saying. . . ."

" Of course. You know Robert tells her everything——"

Meticulously, he lifted his hands from the tight sleevetops of her gown. " And you still don't mind my touching you ? "

" That's why I came," she said simply. " I thought you might need me—tonight."

He still stared down at her without moving. " You care about what happens to me—more than about what happens to yourself ? " He hadn't supposed that any woman did, except Mundina. Marriages were made—very often, in his own walk of life, without the man and girl meeting—and they usually turned out successfully. Even cold-blooded Philippa of Oxford, for instance, would consider it her duty to " make Robert a good wife ", bearing his children and never letting him down in public. But here was Anne caring desperately what happened to his own private soul. Coming all alone on that ridiculous sidesaddle of hers, no doubt. Putting aside her pride. He could imagine what it must have cost her to come.

"Oh, Anne, my poor darling! That you should have to know that—loathsomeness!"

"But I also know that it isn't true," she said, with regained serenity.

"How do you know?"

That generous mouth of hers, which his mother had foreseen would be his undoing, curved tenderly. "Don't you know there's a sort of shining quality about you? In the way you walk and when you smile. A kind of—of flame. And if this slander were true it would be—put out."

He stood there with puckered brow trying to understand what she meant. And because at the moment he looked such a very ordinary young man to say such things about, with his shirt open at the neck and mud on his clothes, Anne began to laugh. It was so seldom they found themselves unsurrounded by ceremony, and she adored him like this, unshaven, waiting on himself and smelling a little of saddle leather. Perhaps it added to her passion for him that he had been caught out in an affair. But actually they had both forgotten about it. "Oh, Richard, don't be ridiculous!" she exclaimed, catching at his arm. "If it were true how could I possibly love you as I do!"

He pulled her roughly into his arms. His breath caught in his throat. His eyes shone with elation. What if here—here all the time—were the perfection he had been waiting for? Here on his own hearthstone. "You mean—you love me—like that?"

"Shamelessly, Richard. Ever since the first day I saw you!"

His hard young lips silenced her, his whole body possessed her. Because he had dissipated nothing of his manhood on other women, his rising passion consumed them. From now on, because the whole of her sweetness and her desire was his, nothing outside their love could ever really touch him. Never again could he know loneliness of spirit. Not while he could hold Anne to his heart and lose himself in the utter response of all her senses.

He pulled her down with him to the foot of the shadowed bed. For a while they sat there, talking a little between their kisses. But they spoke only in half sentences—too close in spirit to have need of them, too thrilled in body to care.

" To think I used to wonder if I should like you ! "

" Burley used to tell me about you." And then, with a little spurt of laughter, " I think he almost willed me to love you."

" And now all that matters is if I can be decent enough to *keep* your love."

Once Anne managed to free herself for a moment from the exciting urgency of his embrace. " What if Lizbeth comes—now ? "

" Even Gervase wouldn't be fool enough——"

" What will you tell her tomorrow, Richard ? "

" That I spent the night in prayer and meditation and have at last found her a suitable husband."

The room was filled with their mingled ecstasy of unsteady laughter, refuting life's venom with fond foolishness. Then Richard's deep, happy laugh, alone, as he raised himself a little to blow lustily at the nearest candles and drew her down and down into his arms.

CHAPTER XIX

"AMONG other things, Parliament is seething about your giving de Vere a dukedom. They say that before long he will persuade you to make him *King* of Ireland."

"Far from persuading, he doesn't even want to go there. And Gloucester was eager enough for Uncle John to clear out of England and make himself King of Castile."

Sir Simon Burley had never looked more bothered nor the King more bland. They were strolling, as they talked, in the gardens at Sheen. The dew was scarcely off the grass, and the Queen not yet dressed.

"I came early to warn you that there's an angry deputation on the way," added Burley, with a sidelong glance at his companion.

But nothing seemed to shake Richard this morning. "You are always welcome, however early, Simon," he said. Like his uncle of Lancaster, he was a charming host.

But after a night of sleepless worry his imperturbable detachment was more than the privileged old statesman could bear. "For once, and with regard to this particular foolishness, I agree with them," he broke out, with heat. "For years the gifts and lands you have loaded Oxford with have made your personal expenditure look even more extravagant than it is. And he's not good enough for you, Richard!"

Having eased his mind of the long felt words, Burley waited for the full spate of Plantagenet rage to break across his devoted head. But a smile still lurked at the corners of Richard's mouth as though his mind were centred on some happy reminiscence. "If only you'd tell me one thing——" went on Burley, emboldened by such unwonted mildness and trying to voice what half the nation wanted to know. "I don't often probe into your private concerns, do I, Richard?"

Richard plucked himself from his abstraction to pat him affectionately on the shoulder. " God bless you, Simon, no ! "

" Then tell me—what *is* it you hold so precious about de Vere ? "

They had come to a low wall dividing private gardens from public barge walk. And still Richard, recently so cruelly sensitive on the subject, showed neither self-consciousness nor resentment. " Oh, I don't know," he said, picking consideringly at a close-packed wad of lichen. " He's precious in grooming, looks and grace ; and even in the timing of those priceless remarks of his." There was a perfection of artistry in verse, vestment or architecture from which Richard wittingly drew great joy ; but in a person the quality was not so easy to define. " He's so—different from everybody else. He stands apart and laughs at them—dispassionately—like some Greek god."

" Is that such a good thing ? Or just selfishness ? "

" A thousand times better than snarling gregariously in the bear pit of our daily bread—or just raging impotently on the edge of it, like me ! Robert's always such good company——"

" But so undependable. Look at his poems, Richard. Pure gold in places—in others second-rate dross. It was the same with his tilting, you remember. . . ."

" To me he is always the same."

As he grew older Richard so often said quiet, unexpected things like that, which cast a new light on things, showing them from some reasonable angle which seemed in part to prove him right. " I believe he is," agreed Burley ungrudgingly.

Richard turned on him with his disarming smile. If only more of his Councillors would try to bridge a generation to meet him mentally sometimes ! " I have to conform my life to the ideas of so many uncongenial people," he took the trouble to explain. " They grate on my nerves excruciatingly at times. Robert de Vere, never."

He looked at this older man who never grated either. Whose

susceptibilities were so fine that he could garnish truth with kindness, and who made so dignified a picture with his grey hair, uncoarsened figure and long, belted houppelarde. How pleasant life would be, thought Richard, if one could stay always at Sheen with the kind of people one loved best! Years of deep understanding made it one of those moments when a man may speak his inmost thoughts without offence. Burley smiled back at him. " And the Queen? " he asked gently.

Richard looked really perturbed at last. " You mean—is she jealous? "

Burley put a hand on his arm to fend off resentment. " She might conceivably be *hurt*—— "

" How awful, Simon! She might have been." Richard seemed to speak only in the past tense. And then, to Burley's amazement, his grave concern gave place to laughter. Spontaneous, wholehearted laughter which made the suggestion sound ridiculous. But as Richard turned around the laughter stopped abruptly and the bits of grey-green lichen fell unheeded from his hands. He drew himself erect as any pikeman on parade. He didn't know that he did so, but Burley felt the stiffened arm fall from beneath the friendly pressure of his own fingers—felt the whole consciousness which had an instant before been contacting his—utterly and instantly withdrawn.

He looked up and saw Richard's face. His umblemished young face lit strongly by the sunshine of early morning. Watched happiness transfiguring him and the way he looked back towards the palace with all his soul in his eyes. And then Burley himself turned and saw the Queen.

She was coming down the garden path with something more glad than beauty about her. Something that had nothing to do with terrestrial grief or time. Yet she must have chosen each item of her toilette with special care. Her little buoyant shoes were grey, her gown a poem in dull pink; her long, white veil out behind her from her high headdress as she walked. And her cheeks, fragile as narcissi, were radiant with a shade just pinker than the gown.

Richard watched her come down the path as if by no movement could he bring himself to destroy a vision. A vision, it seemed, of something which he had scarcely hoped for this side of Heaven. Only when she had come quite close did he take a few steps to meet her, and seize her hands and kiss them with a sort of humble gratitude. Even then it was not so much as if they walked towards each other but as if they were drawn, each to each, by some attraction stronger than themselves, until their shadows merged in the most moving silhouette upon the flower-strewn grass. The silhouette of a young man and a girl held deeply, passionately, in the bonds and wonder of first love.

Simon Burley turned away and leaned upon the wall, as if absorbed in the unloading of a red sailed wherry that had come up with the tide. He was comprehending the nature of that new armour against calumny and adversity and thanking God for the fulfilment of a daily prayer. And at the same time he found himself murmuring a Nunc dimittis. Looking at their young rapture had suddenly made him feel old. He had an inkling that his task of king-making was nearly finished. It had not been easy and soon, perhaps, he could relinquish the exacting effort. Anne, whom he had influenced, would know how to carry on.

He would have slipped away, and left them alone a little longer in their sunlit garden, had not Anne disentangled herself from the King's embrace and come to him. Always, she greeted him with affection. But this morning she did a thing unusual for a queen. She reached up a-tiptoe on those mouse-grey shoes of hers and kissed him on either cheek. " Don't go away, dear Sir Simon. I want to thank you all over again for bringing me to such happiness," she said simply.

" He can't go away," explained Richard, watching their mutual pleasure with delight. " There's a deputation from the Commons arriving at any moment."

Anne's face fell. "Not *today*, Richard! I had hoped we could go riding. The broom is flaming in the deer park. . . ."

"Even today," he sighed. Clearly, for them, it was some very special day, and time spent on Parliamentary business like golden hours torn from a honeymoon. Normally, Burley might have tried to stave off the Commons with their everlasting mutterings, or have got de la Pole to deal with them. But this time the opposition lords were hand in glove with them and their treachery far more serious than Richard realized. Burley suspected that Richard did not realize by the carefree way in which he swung himself up onto the wall. "I've been thinking," he announced, swinging his feet as they dangled just above the clean, upturned faces of a spread of daisies.

"About the miserable Commons?" asked Anne, drooping a little and wondering why she had gone to all the trouble of putting on his favourite dress.

"No. About Lizbeth."

"Richard! After—last night?"

"Oh, not in that way, darling! I've just thought of a husband for her."

"Who?" his audience asked in eager unison. Anne looked inordinately pleased and Burley's quick sense of amusement was tickled by so swift a gesture of amendment.

"Sir Edward Dalyngrigge."

Even Anne, who bore the wench no love, wouldn't have done anything as drastic as that. "*That* ruffian!" she exclaimed.

"The man's something out of the last century. He still fights with a spiked mace," murmured Burley, stroking his little pointed beard to hide a smile.

"Positively pre-crusader," scoffed Anne, always ardently modern in her views against the subjection of her sex. "My women say that whenever he went away to sea he used to have the armourer padlock his last wife into her old-fashioned iron stays!"

Richard gave vent to a delighted guffaw. "Which just goes

to show my acumen! Isn't he the only man who's likely to keep my lovely ward in order? Not that I'd give her to him unless I really liked him," he added, a faint trail of Lizbeth's sweetness still troubling his senses. "But I've always owed him something for his help in the peasants' revolt and, given a lovely heiress, a man like that might come in very useful again."

Anne eyed him suspiciously. "Is that your only reason?" she inquired.

"Well, no——" Without meeting her gaze, Richard began whistling softly to the flippant prowlike points of his swinging shoes.

"I thought not," said Anne severely. She would have to be firm about this tendency towards commercial calculation. It must be something he had acquired from Brembre and his fellow tradesmen.

"You may as well tell her," urged Burley, highly diverted by the growing nimbleness of his erstwhile pupil's mind.

From his perch on the wall the King of England began to propound his nefarious scheme. "Well, Dalyngrigge has been pestering me for a permit to build a new castle. To defend the Sussex coast, he says. Hoping to get a grant towards the expenses as well, which I can ill afford. And Arundel, who has property there, backs him up. But I know very well it's because the incurable old pirate wants a handy jumping-off place for his own ships to raid the French. And I've promised Charles of Valois that this cruel, senseless sacking of seaport towns on either side shall stop."

"What's all that got to do with Lizbeth?" asked Anne.

"Her parents had a castle at Bodiam, hadn't they?" recalled Burley, beginning to see light.

Richard nodded. "It's in Sussex, and not *too* near the sea. Dalyngrigge can have that—and Lizbeth with it."

Secretly, Anne was more relieved than shocked. "Oh, Richard! And you talk about the low cunning of the Commons!"

"I've been taking lessons in statesmanship from de la Pole, my sweet. And I have a very retentive memory, haven't I, Simon? What is it Michael says?" Looking up into the summer blue, Richard aired some of his new Chancellor's axioms as if repeating a carefully conned lesson. "'When your enemies grow dangerous, watch for the first rift in their camp, and use it to drive a wedge between them. Sooner or later, opportunity will deliver them into your hands.' That's heartening, isn't it? And then again, 'Never forget individual requests. Hold them in your memory like the frayed ends of a rope until you can knot them together to your own advantage.'" Looking maddeningly pleased with himself he jumped lightly from the wall and went to Anne as if, fooling or serious, he could no longer bear to be separated from her. "Dalyngrigge asks for a castle, and my wife—admittedly not without reason—thinks it high time Lizbeth de Wardeaux got married. *Et voilà!*" he declaimed, waving a declamatory arm and then stooping to arrange a jewel at Anne's neck to better advantage.

"Idiot!" mocked Anne. "And am I to infer from that that my desires rank equally with a pirate's?"

"You can infer from it that you have me eating out of your hands!" Richard told her, turning up her small palms to kiss them. "I put it to you, Simon," he appealed, with plaintive solemnity. "If I were to go fluttering the dovecotes at Bodiam —king or no king, and quite apart from the little difficulty of the stays—shouldn't I get my brains bashed out with that horrible mace?"

Their laughter had scarcely died away before a servant came hurrying out from the palace. "The deputation," groaned Richard, letting go of Anne's hands. "Whom do you suppose they have sent *this* time, Simon?"

Burley looked at him pityingly. Extravagant and wayward he might have been, in the common manner of youth. But couldn't they ever let him alone and trust to that brilliant flair that was in him and the new steadying influence of a sensible wife? Must the shadow of a disapproving Parliament always fall across these two? "Gloucester and Arundel, I am afraid," he said.

Richard flung round on him. "Gloucester and Arundel! Since when have they constituted themselves the mouthpiece of the Commons' grievances?"

"It is probably they who stirred them up in the first place," said Anne indignantly.

In spite of serious foreboding, Richard managed to smile at her. "I'm sorry, my dear. You and Agnes will have to go riding alone," he said. "But don't forget to gather me a sprig of broom for luck, my love. Because it is June."

Reluctantly he nodded to the waiting servant, whistled to Mathe, and walked back to the palace with Burley. All pre-occupation with happiness was gone. "I wonder if I was a fool to listen to all these aspersions on Lancaster and let him go?" he said.

"It is difficult to know, Richard," answered Burley. "If it comes to a life and death struggle between two parties he would certainly have been powerful enough to tip the scales. And it is my personal belief that the aspersions were cast purposely because if he were here—and on your side—Parliament would never have dared to do this."

The King looked up sharply. "Do what, Simon?"

"They are threatening to impeach de la Pole. I couldn't tell you just now, in front of the Queen."

Richard quickened his pace, forgetting that it was hard on a man of sixty. But at the palace door he stopped. "You're not in any danger from these devils yourself, are you, Simon?" he asked earnestly.

Burley looked back over the way they had come—the rose-lined pathway and the longer pathway through the years. More than anything he had wanted to live to see this pupil of his make good. None knew better than he that this scion of the able Plantagenets, given wise handling and a fair chance, had gifts enough to make one of the best kings England had ever had. But what wise handling or fair chance would men like Gloucester and Arundel ever give him? And was that strange Aquitanian woman completely *eldritch* when she used to say that her nursling was "ill-beset"? Simon Burley thought it probable that he wouldn't be there to see, but he answered evasively so as not to distress a man who already had enough burden on his shoulders. "When people are frightened with a sort of mass hysteria—as they are frightened just now about this bogey of a French invasion—they can be made to applaud incredibly cruel things," he said slowly.

"Simon, you don't think——"

"Much depends on how cool you keep, and how reasonably you treat with them."

"*I*—treat with them! With that scum——"

Richard's flurry of scorn was fine to see. So might his father and grandfather have spoken. With a victorious army and a united nation at their backs. But their very prowess had left a painful legacy behind. A legacy of debts and maimed men, of ambitious war veterans and peasants who had begun to perceive their own value. Things were very different now. . . .

"I am afraid it will come to that," warned Simon Burley.

CHAPTER XX

Young Tom Holland was pouring wine for the King's uninvited guests in the great hall at Sheen. He was also trying to overhear what they said; but they talked in rumbling undertones, standing close together like conspirators. The tall, beak-nosed bishop and the dark, humourless duke. The duke was a sort of relation, but he never tipped a page a florin or two towards a new hawk or took the least interest in his advancement. Tom handed him his wine and hoped that it would choke him.

But before Gloucester could quench his thirst a door opened at the far end of the room and Richard himself came in, followed by Simon Burley. The conspiratorial undertones stopped abruptly and both men stood looking at him, their glasses in their hands.

"Good morning, Uncle. *Pax vobiscum*, milord Bishop. To what am I indebted for this—visit?" he asked pleasantly.

His very urbanity held them tongue-tied. Seen like that at the end of the hall, with his hound beside him and the light from a tall coloured window etherealizing his good looks, there was a dignity about him which at times abashed even Gloucester.

"There are certain questions, sir——" began Thomas Arundel, Bishop of Ely, and brother of Richard Arundel.

Richard was clever enough to appreciate that a certain material distance kept them in their place. "I will do my best to answer them," he said. "But I was under the impression that I had promised audience to forty members of the Commons."

"The Commons can ill afford to risk forty of their best members," broke in Gloucester rudely.

Richard's eyebrows shot up in genuine surprise. "You suspect a trap? The same sort of trap, perhaps, as you told me

Lancaster had prepared for me on the way home from Scotland?
It was stupid of me, but I really hadn't thought how easy it
would be for me to hold them as hostages. Particularly as I
had flattered myself the Commons were my loyal subjects."

Richard's voice was cool and mocking. For just so long as
he kept it so he would, he felt, have the whip hand over these
two. Even though they held all the cards. He had felt like that,
he remembered, facing Wat Tyler's men at Smithfield. As if
he were keeping wild beasts in check. And, although the
peasants had certainly held all the cards, he had fooled them!
He took his own wine from his page, keeping a friendly arm
about him as he drank. Tom Holland was growing almost as
tall as he, and looked more like a younger brother than a
nephew. Joan's fair beauty was stamped on each of them,
and Richard kept him there because he guessed hopefully that
any sort of duplication of himself must be an annoyance to
Gloucester. "Come, drink up your malvoisie," he urged
hospitably. " Or do you suspect that it is poisoned ? "

Gloucester bolted the strong vintage at a gulp. " I suppose
you know that the nation won't stand for this last absurdity
about de Vere ? " he spluttered, wiping the dregs from
moustache to sleeve. He was always at his worst at Court,
where his manners became a deliberate protest against the
niceties of Anne's and Richard's household.

" The dukedom, you mean ? " inquired Richard blandly.

" And all the lands—— Already, he, who is no blood relation, has more than I——"

" If I had known that you wanted them, dear Uncle——"

" What has he ever done to deserve them ? "

Richard appeared to meditate. " He has always been amiable
and amusing. Perhaps if you, too, had been able to find time
from all your violent activities to see a joke or write a sonnet
sometimes——"

To young Holland's intense joy, Gloucester nearly choked
indeed. "Except for that military promenade through
Scotland, the scented young fop has never even been to war,"

he shouted, advancing the only criterion he knew of for a young man's worth.

"No," agreed Richard, handing back his glass and coming to warm his hands at a fire burning in the middle of the hall. "But he is going now. I have sent him up to Cheshire to prepare an invasion force against Ireland. Although I hope it won't be necessary to kill many of those unfortunate people. My idea was rather to colonize——"

But the deputation was not interested in his ideas, only in their own. "Ireland!" they cried, almost in unison. "With the French at our gates!"

Richard had heard the parrot cry so often that he ignored it. "And you and milord Arundel will notice, perhaps, that Robert de Vere and I are not quite so inseparable as our foulest enemies make out," he added, looking straight at his uncle.

He had the satisfaction of seeing Thomas Plantagenet's hard-bitten hide go fiery red. "If you and he went to fight our enemies in France there'd be less need to persuade your enemies at home," he muttered.

As a churchman, Ely rushed in to keep the peace. "The people are naturally beginning to panic about the possibility of a French invasion," he twittered, because it was the only thing he could think of before a Plantagenet storm had time to burst.

"Very naturally, since they are never given a chance to stop thinking about it." Richard could still manage a casual voice, but Burley noticed that there was a brittle edge to it.

"They might panic with some cause if they knew that your agent, Chaucer, had been caught in Canterbury," said Gloucester.

"One scarcely speaks of a government official being 'caught' in the exercise of his duty," murmured Burley, trying to draw their fire and give the King time to compose himself.

The duke looked round as if only now aware of the elderly statesman's presence. "You don't deny, I suppose, that he was on his way to Calais?" he demanded, in that sharp way of his.

" Why should I ? " shrugged Burley.

" Nor that he was entrusted with power to make negotiations ? Negotiations to sell Calais ? "

" Negotiations to sell *wool*, my dear uncle," broke in Richard
wearily. " I am naturally interested in wool, since most of my
begrudged income comes from the wool taxes a more generous
Parliament once voted me. You seem to forget that, apart
from the upkeep of all my palaces, I have a wife to keep."

" And all her Bohemian friends ! " sneered Gloucester.

Even then, for Burley's sake, Richard bit back the hot retort
from his tongue. So that he shouldn't have to look at his
tormentors, he walked carefully to the window, Mathe moving
like a lean, stately lioness by his side.

" The matter of your Grace's income might have been
remedied," Ely was saying in that oily voice of his. " But once
the Commons heard about this latest honour heaped upon
Oxford and the expense of raising a force for Ireland——"

" Which I paid for myself."

"——even the Duke of York couldn't persuade them to
make any further grant. They say that you should live out of
your own——"

To keep his hands from hitting someone Richard began
violently plumping up the window cushions. He had lost all
grip on mockery. " Live out of my own ? " he cried, betrayed
into serious argument. " What have I but my own private
estates in Cheshire ? You know very well that the Duchy of
Lancaster should have gone with it—always *has* gone with it—
but that my grandfather was so fertile he had to leave something
to Uncle John. Had he guessed that my eldest uncle of Clarence
would die, he probably wouldn't have. But as it is, although I
am king, Henry Bolingbroke will inherit more private property
than I. The Commons don't expect me to go out into Cheapside each morning and run a chapman's stall, do they ? "

" I don't know what they expect, but they are setting up
a commission—now—to control all grants and taxation,"
answered Gloucester.

" *They* ! *You* are, you mean, using them as your cat's-paw ! " accused Richard.

" If they provide the money I suppose they've a right to see how it's spent."

" You didn't think that when you wanted grants for your own b-bloody wars ! "

" All these stalwart, well-trained soldiers staring at the sights of London, for instance."

" A handful of my own Cheshire archers—a mere body-guard—now that Lancaster has withdrawn his forces. You're not suggesting that I'm trying to terrorize Parliament with them, are you ? "

" In case you should, we have some excellent levies gathered in readiness at Waltham Cross, and the first thing Parliament will do will be to get rid of your plebeian Chancellor."

All histrionic caution forgotten, Richard flung round on them, furious and fighting back. " Get rid of de la Pole ! How can they ? What can they possibly find against him ? Except that he has striven for peace. Sacrificed cheap popularity in an effort to give this battered, blood-drained country a respite after fifty years. A chance to rebuild her cities and to reconstruct her trade. And what is wrong with that ? Except that it throws warmongers and profiteers like you out of commission."

" It is not I who will be out of commission," sneered Gloucester, perceiving that he had jolted Richard out of his quelling superiority. " Nor Richard Arundel nor Warwick nor Ely. It is friends of yours like Burley there, and that smirking tradesman Brembre——"

" Just because they *are* my friends ? "

" Yes, if you like. And lesser men like Chaucer, who creeps about on your secret missions—and Medford, your incorruptible secretary. And half your household . . ."

Gloucester was almost incoherent and, at sound of their raised voices, Mathe had begun to growl.

"This is unendurable—to speak so in the King's presence," protested Burley.

The bishop had already backed towards the outer door.

"So you would do that to me?" said Richard, his voice husky with fury. "Poke into my private household. Have me spied on in my own courtyards. When even the poorest country squire is master in his own manor!" Warm and beautiful before his mind came the contrasting picture of a tousled kitchen lad taken and forgiven in some forgotten fault, stooping to kiss his master's shadow. "Go back to Westminster, you traitors, and tell them I will not dismiss a single scullion at their bidding!" he shouted.

Mathe's growl had grown dangerous. Teeth snapped murderously between drawn back jowls. Knowing the deerhound's strength, Richard instinctively reached out and gripped him by the collar. He was aware that Tom Holland had come closer to him. That Ely's face was white as his episcopal robes. That Gloucester was beside himself with rage.

For once Gloucester had failed to intimidate. This was the Richard who had defied a mob and laughed in his face. All these years he had supposed the young whippet to be cowed by the lesson given him after the Revolt; but here he was asserting himself again and learning to stand up to his elders with a fury equal to their own. He must be brought to heel. Without taking his hating eyes off him, Thomas Plantagenet reached for the helmet which he wore even in peacetime. "Edward the Second was made less than a scullion!" he reminded him, gritting the words out between savage teeth.

But Richard had drawn new strength from somewhere. "Get out! God damn you, get *out*! Before I loose this hound," he shouted. Even while he was still pulling on the leather with all his might, Mathe was dragging him forward step by step, straining to be at the throat of any man who quarrelled with his master. Gloucester was no coward, but he had seen many a stag mangled in the chase and he read death in the eyes of both of them. He clamped his *casque* on his head and followed the decamping bishop.

Richard's straining muscles relaxed and the dog leaped. But the great oak door banged shut, cheating him by a second of his prey. Quivering and distraught, the creature ranged up and down, yelping and sniffing along the floor boards.

The deputation was over.

Richard drew a square of checkered silk from his close-fitting sleeve. Automatically, he began wiping some blood from his fingers where the iron studs of Mathe's collar had torn them. "I need not have lifted a hand to him—and it would have been accounted an accident," he muttered. He half turned towards Burley, as if to justify the thought. "I couldn't have held Mathe many seconds longer, Simon. You know I couldn't. . . ."

And then quite suddenly, he seemed to crumple onto the window seat. With almost human comprehension, Mathe padded back across the room to lick consolingly at his slack, stained hands.

"A pity you held him back so long, sir!" ventured Tom, patting Mathe approvingly.

Burley held his peace. He had been ageing perceptibly of late, and he, too, was shaken. And because it had been partly his own life Richard had been defending, it ill became him to criticize.

Presently, Richard pulled Mathe's head against him, fondling it with rough tenderness, and looked up. "Go on, say it, Simon!" he invited, with a poor attempt at a grin. "And for God's sake sit down. Tom will pour us another glass. Heaven knows we need it!"

Thankfully, Burley eased his joints onto the opposite seat to him in the raised embrasure. "They goaded you to it," he said. Then, twirling the freshly poured wine that Tom had brought him so solicitously, "I suppose it would have been wiser to submit tamely, but it wouldn't have been you."

Richard smiled at his page and dismissed him. He had no need to tell him not to chatter. The members of his household had learned loyalty from their master. "I was doing pretty well until the last round," he said ruminatively, when he and Burley were alone. "Somehow I often seem to go down in the last bout."

Burley was feeling better. He was sipping his wine and watching the Queen snipping off rosebuds down in the garden. "You won't now, Richard," he said quietly.

"No. Thank you for reminding me, Simon." Richard's gaze followed his, and all the sunlight about Anne seemed to wash into his darkling soul, sustaining him. "It's going to be a long wrestle, and it looks as if I'm in for some hard punishment. And the score's not too good," he calculated. "Back almost to where I started from. A bewildered boy in a gilded cage, it was then, with the odds on any one of the three uncles. Well, now the boy isn't there any more—and we know which one we're fighting." He settled the slim gold dagger belt more snugly round his middle and jerked down the nether pleats of his short tunic. "And fighting can be good fun when one wears a lady's favour!"

Burley's eyes were warm upon him. He himself had seen the inside of some good fights in his time, and he would have given much to see the end of this one. "I was wondering why you didn't try to make conditions about de la Pole instead of flying out about the servants," he asked. "Was it wise—or necessary?"

Richard looked up in bland surprise. "Of course it was necessary. Surely you of all men needn't ask me that? It was you who took me to my father the last time he sent for me—that day he lay dying."

Some measure of understanding came to Burley, with uncertain recollection. But Richard's next words painted the scene with all the vividness of detail that such a sombre occasion was likely to make, unguessed at by his elders, upon an impressionable boy of ten.

216

"Don't you remember that darkened room at Westminster —full of people? And those awful embroidered Saracens on the bed hangings? And my father's face, the colour of mouldy parchment, propped up on pillows? And the uncles and all of them having to kiss my hand and promise allegiance? And the solemn way the Prince said 'I recommend my son to you because he is but young and little'? I had to go down on my knees close to him while he gave me his blessing. His hands were like claws and the bedclothes smelled of mortal sickness. And he was saying between horrid gasps, 'Swear by the Book that you will never rid yourself of any of my servants, Richard'. I kept wishing my mother would stop crying and smile at me. But someone put a hand on my shoulder. . . . It must have been your hand, Simon. . . ."

"Yes, it was my hand," corroborated Burley. He remembered now. And Gloucester and Arundel ought to have remembered too. He had a shrewd idea that when the Black Prince had referred to servants he had meant people a good deal more important than scullions; but Richard's fertile mind had a flair for making his actions sound right. "Why didn't you say that just now, when your uncle and Ely were in the room? Why didn't you remind them of your promise—and of their own?" he asked.

"Remind Gloucester of promises?" scoffed Richard. "I shouldn't imagine he knows what the word means. Not after the so-called trials to clear up the peasants' revolt!"

He got up and wrenched at a bell-pull. "Tell Standish to bring me a map of the Western Marches," he said, when Tom appeared. "And I want the Captain of the Guard to have a company of men stand by as escort for a long journey."

"What are you going to do?" asked Burley, when they were alone again.

"Ride to Chester and bring back the rest of my archers," said Richard grimly.

"And leave de la Pole and Brembre and men like Chaucer to the machinations of these scheming murderers in London?"

Richard stood tapping his teeth in momentary indecision. "No, Simon. You're right. I can't do that."

"Nothing would please Gloucester better, of course. If this struggle for power ever came to a pitched battle—which God forbid!—whoever won or lost, he would make it his business to see that you were killed." Burley leaned forward earnestly. "Richard, *must* you resort to force?"

"Since Gloucester's crowd are already armed——" At sight of one so dear to him in so much peril, Richard came and slid boyishly along the window seat and threw an arm about him. "*Ne vois tu, mon brave, que c'est question de ta vie?*" he urged, slipping into French as he so often did in moments of tenderness.

But Burley was not thinking of his own life. "You will be no better than they—plunging England into civil war for the sake of power," he argued.

"But don't you see the difference? They are clutching at something which isn't theirs, while I should be fighting only to keep what is my own. One decisive battle, perhaps, Simon. I would see that our forces were big enough, as I did in Scotland."

"This comes oddly from you, Richard."

"I know. But you don't suppose I want victory just for my own glorification, do you? Why should I? What can I be that is higher than king? It would be truer to say that I want the right to serve. You remember my father's motto, '*Ich Dien*', which he took with the plume of feathers from Anne's blind grandfather? It always seemed a stupid motto for a king. But now I want with all my heart to make a civilized country where homes are not always being broken up and where people can go about their business and pleasure without this bogey of invasion. Where the arts can flourish and men can give their best endeavours to making beautiful and useful things instead of making armaments. I want them to reason and arbitrate instead of murdering each other with senseless violence. Oh, I'm not pretending that it's all altruistic, Simon.

. . . But it's so much more worth fighting for than silly, sadistic raids on France! And I've got the ability to rule like that, and either by reason or by force I mean to get the power."

" Doing evil that good may come, as the clergy say ? "

" I suppose so. But I promise you on all I hold most sacred that once I have fought this out with Gloucester I will sacrifice anything—anything—sooner than let such a thing ever happen in England again."

" Well, it is these fools who are forcing it upon you," sighed Burley. " But you *will* go and try persuasion at Westminster first ? "

" Yes. Only while I am there I will send Bolingbroke to get me the backing of my archers. It is only common sense, and he is the best strategist I know."

Burley drew the long skirt of his houppelarde about him and got up slowly from the window seat. " Wouldn't it be best to find out first which side he means to fight on ? " he suggested.

Richard's fair skin flushed as if someone had struck him. " You don't suppose——"

" No. I don't suppose. I *know*," said Burley, coming to lay a compassionate hand on his shoulder. " It is he who is mustering Gloucester's men at Waltham."

" Bolingbroke—*dans cette galère*! " Richard moved away to the hearth, trying to swallow the blow to his pride. And to his hopes. For Gloucester's forces would certainly be well mustered. For a few moments he played with the idea of abandoning his friends to their fate and leading his army himself. Henry was a far more experienced soldier than he, and physically stronger. But it would be exhilarating to fight against Henry at last. Henry, whom he had begun to hate.

But Burley had followed him and he saw by the man's face that there was worse to come. " Yes ? " he asked peremptorily.

" Richard—I know this will hurt more than all their treacheries. Tom Mowbray is with him. I couldn't tell you out there—when you were so happy——"

Richard stared at him. "But—but what have I ever *done* to him?" he faltered. "Why, even Mathe here shows him affection."

"Don't forget that he is Arundel's son-in-law now. Besides, he always *was* jealous of Robert, and probably this Irish title was the last straw."

"I suppose I was a fool about the title—and to mind so much what people said," admitted Richard, savagely kicking a fallen log back into the fire. "But these are men who practically ate out of my hand. Henry I can almost forgive. He had only my hospitality. But Tom had my friendship. Are they *all* Judases?" He turned back to Burley, forcing himself to get on with the matter in hand as if nothing had happened. "Then Ireland will have to wait and Robert must bring his levies down with mine," he decided. "After all, he is on the spot, and it will be the same thing as if I led them myself."

"I'm not so sure," murmured Burley.

"You're not going to suggest that *he*——?"

"Of *course* not, Richard. Only——"

Richard had always measured his friends' loyalty by his own, and that was often larger than his judgement. He had gone to spread the map Standish had brought him on the window seat and, standing with the river flowing placidly before him, he suddenly recalled how Robert had once stood by a similar window in the Tower, suggesting that it might be better if he went back to Oxford. Memory reconstructed the scene—the bed, the *priedieu*, the frightened pages. Surely from where Robert had stood he must have seen London beginning to burn, before exerting himself to pull the curtain. Inside Richard's mind some shutter seemed to fly open for a split second, admitting a shaft of shameful doubt. It shook him momentarily that this could happen and that he had caught himself dwelling on the fact that Oxford during the Revolt had been *safer*. And in order to dispel such hateful cynicism he turned hurriedly to contemplation of his own shortcomings. "I am afraid I must often be a sore disappointment to you, Simon—

landing you into such dangers and perplexities," he said, holding the map half unrolled between his hands. "Particularly after the way you admired my father."

"Admired, yes," said Burley slowly, looking into the redness of the fire. "But just in case you and I should ever be parted, Richard—I'd like you to know that I've come to care for you far more than I ever cared for him."

Richard went red with pleasure. Here was the commendation he had always craved. And it was like old Simon to reserve it for a moment when one's stock was so low—to offer it as a *quid pro quo* for the defection of Tom Mowbray. "T-thank you, sir," he stammered, like any schoolboy.

"I used to think military achievement mattered most," mused Burley, fingering the gold chain the Black Prince had given him after Poitiers. "But most of us learn more from our children and pupils than they can ever hope to learn from us. New ways—new values—a new kind of courage, perhaps . . ."

"Courage?"

"Perhaps after all, my dear Richard, it takes more courage to stay unromantically at home and take care of the things which the great Cœur de Lion neglected."

CHAPTER XXI

FOR THREE weeks Richard had fought for the freedom of his friends. He had been a fool, perhaps, to put his own safety in the noose by coming to London. For what had he—or they—gained by it ? Except Michael de la Pole. While the King argued at Westminster, de la Pole had had time to escape to the Continent. At least Richard had the satisfaction of knowing that he had saved his Chancellor. But he himself was more or less a prisoner in the Tower.

Feeling had run so high after the escape that, for the second time in his life, he had been forced to take refuge there. Back in the same rooms where he had spent those nightmare days of the Peasants' Revolt. The only difference seemed to be that now, instead of Wat Tyler's mob milling round St. Catherine's wharf, there was an armed force of Gloucester's men at Waltham Cross. The wretched peasants had been goaded by a dozen different injustices, but only ambition goaded Gloucester.

Outside the Tower a dank evening mist was rising from the river, wrapping the precincts into a world apart and muffling all sounds but the dreary, owl-like " Hoo ! " of passing watermen. Thick Norman walls and small, deep-set windows gave a sense of security, but they made a room infernally dark. Richard sat alone by a badly smoking fire, sunk dejectedly in his chair with his legs stretched out before him. He felt extraordinarily tired. It seemed to him that he must have been arguing for months. Using his wits to hold a Parliament packed with Gloucester's supporters—issuing writs—playing for time. Whenever he had retired to his own private apartments at Westminster he and Anne and Standish had pored over a map, calculating how far Robert must have come. All the while he was haranguing the appellant lords about their unconstitutional methods, or trying to prove that every public act of Burley's had been done in his service and with his sanction, it had seemed in his mind that the two kinds of effort were converging together—his own mental ingenuity and Robert's marching men. Even as he cajoled the clamorous Commons to spare their colleague, Brembre, it was seldom their vindictive faces he saw, but his own splendid archers winding like a silver snake down through the winding roads of England. Coming nearer and nearer until they took that Waltham force by surprise and routed them, and then marched triumphantly through some City gate and right to the doors of Westminster. For only then, with the weight of a proper army behind him, could a king turn the tables on his enemies and cease to speak them fair. The thought of it had been like a mirage, helping him to hold out until Robert came.

And now, at last, he knew that Robert wouldn't be coming. Now, quite suddenly, there was nothing to work or wait or hope for anymore. Not since Radcot Bridge.

But in the Tower, unfortunately, there was plenty of time to think. Richard slumped yet further into his chair, trying to evolve some fresh plan—to think about Burley and Salisbury and Brembre, and poor Chaucer, condemned to death for his sake—to consider his own impecunious state with even the wool tax appropriated by Parliament, and the humiliation of being under the thumb of this parsimonious commission. But his thoughts always came back to Radcot Bridge.

Although he had never in his life seen the place, it seemed that part of him had died there. All that was young and gay and proud. All that had reason to be proud. For Radcot Bridge had been Robert's undoing. It had stripped him of all his debonair splendour, his wit and cynical immunity, and exposed the meagreness they had hidden. Like the shocking nakedness of a cat without its fur.

Again and again Richard went over each account of this travesty of battle. But nowhere could he find any loophole for his friend's honour. However garbled, all accounts had agreed about the few bald facts which made each messenger afraid to tell him the truth. Forty thousand men, Robert had had. Richard himself knew that much without any telling. The King's own Cheshiremen, some Welsh troops and some of his own Oxfordshire levies. A brave sight they must have been. How their bows and pikes must have glistened in the sunlight! Robert was bringing them down from the Severn valley to cross the upper reaches of the Thames. Coming through Oxfordshire where he should have known every inch of the terrain, every river bend and wooded hillock suitable for an ambush. Where he had every advantage. That was the last hasty message Richard had received from him. That was how he had pictured their army. And at Radcot Bridge Robert had let himself be ambushed.

Henry Bolingbroke must have sent out scouts and got wind of his approach. With superb generalship he must have withdrawn his own men secretly from Waltham and gone by forced night marches to meet him. Henry, who never waited for his enemies to move first, must have set a trap for him.

And Robert de Vere had walked into it. Gaily singing one of his latest songs, no doubt, thought Richard savagely. And, finding himself surrounded, he had surrendered without so much as a shaft loosed from those bows or a thrust from one of those shining pikes. And—as if that were not enough—he had deserted his bewildered followers and saved his own skin by running away. Like John Holland on Hackney marshes.

Richard's whole body writhed at the thought of it. He got up and prowled about the darkening room because there are some mind pictures that the body cannot endure in stillness. "With forty thousand men!" was the constant burden of his thoughts.

Last night, after the news had come, he had lain tossing and turning on his bed, trying to find some possible explanation. Henry's men must have had some new weapon—one of Gloucester's new cannon perhaps, with a range which had rendered bows useless. Or a mist might have come up over the low-lying river country blotting out everything, just as here it was shrouding even moat and walls.

But, try as he would, there was nothing to be found but ridicule and shame. The comedy of an unfought battle which chroniclers like Froissart, writing of his reign, would record for all time. Apart from the ghastly consequences of defeat, he—Richard—and his cause had been hopelessly let down. " Gloucester was right. These are the kind of young men who pule for peace with France ! " people would be sure to say, pointing the finger of scorn. Couldn't Robert have seen, curse him, that the more one advocated peace the less one could afford to be a coward ?

In those first hours of bitter disappointment it seemed to matter so much more about Robert than about the battle. If the worst came to the worst and Burley and Brembre were executed, they would still have been real people, a living memory at which to warm one's heart. But although Robert might elude his enemies and live on, the friend Richard had loved best had never really lived at all, save in his own imagination. Only the familiar, attractive husk of him which was still so painfully dear.

With a life so set apart from other men's, it was largely through the strength of his affections that Richard had touched reality. And because all that inner gallantry that he had taken for granted had been proved an illusion, a sense of futile unreality gripped him too. Even the everyday furnishings about him seemed momentarily unreal, so that he found a voice in his consciousness affirming desperately, " It is I who am here, touching this table, enduring this hell. I really am I —here, now—and nothing can stop it." The very realization of his own present existence in the midst of all that seemed unreal beat upon his brain until his heart quickened suffocatingly in fear of he knew not what. And then the low arched door opened and Anne came into the room, and everything became real and normal again.

" Why, Richard, sitting alone in the dark ! " she reproached, and the very homeliness of her words was a comfort.

She went straight to him and he caught at her hand. " In outer darkness—ever since you left me," he admitted. " You've been gone a long time, Anne. What have you been doing ? "

" Trying to comfort Agnes," she told him quietly.

" It must be pretty awful for his wife, too," he said, ashamed that he had forgotten about Agnes.

Anne went to the door and called to the anxious servants. " Bring candles, Martin. The biggest you can find, and put them everywhere. And come, one of you, and heap up the fire." She came back bustling and shivering a little. " I am sure these rooms are damp. They never get any sun."

" That I should have brought you here—a daughter of the Caesars——" he began.

But she was making conversation as one does to cheer the sick, rather than grumbling. " Since you are here, my love——" she whispered, with a little secret smile that brightened life for him more than all the lights the servants brought. " I really came to tell you that we have a visitor. Your Uncle Edmund. I have just spoken to him outside the Lieutenant's lodgings."

" Uncle Edmund ? Here ? "

" You know how long he takes to puff up the stairs——"

Richard was all action immediately. " Go down, Martin, and light the Duke of York," he ordered.

But Edmund of York's round, red face was already visible at the top bend of the stairs, and soon his scarlet-clad girth was filling the doorway. Anxiety sat incongruously upon him and he was badly out of breath. " My—dear—nephew ! " he panted portentously.

Richard gripped his hand and settled him in the largest chair. " How kind of you to come ! " he exclaimed without ceremony.

" I'm afraid I've only bad news for you."

Richard and Anne hung on his heavy words. "What did they decide this morning?" they asked, almost simultaneously.

The Duke mopped his brow unashamedly with a handkerchief Anne had made for him. "It's the death sentence, Richard. For Salisbury, Brembre, Chaucer—and poor Simon Burley."

"God!" muttered Richard, walking away to the window.

"And Robert de Vere—if they can catch him," added York, trying to sound decently sorry.

Anne came and sat near him, laying pleading fingers on the arm of his chair. "But couldn't you—weren't there any members who——"

He covered her hand with his own white, podgy one. "I did what I could, my dear."

"They tell me you quarrelled with Uncle Thomas over it in Council," put in Richard appreciatively, from the window.

"There are some things that even an easy-going person like me can't stomach," admitted York, with rare sincerity. "But Gloucester and Arundel are on the crest of the wave just now. That French ship they captured in the Channel turned out to have her holds stuffed with good Chartreuse and——"

"Oh, don't tell me!" implored Richard bitterly. "And they were clever enough to refuse all profit on her, just to show up my extravagance, and now London is flooded with duty-free wine. Isn't that so? And isn't it the sort of thing that *would* happen at the right moment—for *them*?"

"I'm afraid you're right, Richard. Normally, there are scores of moderate, level-headed members and citizens who think these two go too far, and who would have been profoundly shocked at the idea of a man like Burley being hanged, drawn and——"

"Don't!" cried Anne, and in a moment Richard was standing beside her, pressing her cowering head against his side. "Not that, York! For God's sake, not that!" he protested. But no cruelty nor indignity was too great, it seemed, for any man who had been his friend. Across Anne's stricken head the Duke made an expressive gesture indicating that the same fate was in store for all four of the impeached.

Nobody moved for a minute or two. Only the licking flames on the hearth broke the silence. And then Richard's slow, sorrowful words. "Simon Burley was like a father to me. Sometimes I've wished to Heaven he *were* my father!" He began to pace up and down, beating fist to palm. "I'd do anything—anything . . ." he muttered.

"You've already done a good deal," York reminded him. And perhaps only he knew how near Richard had come to losing his crown over it.

Anne lifted her tear-drenched face to look at her husband. "Do you mean that, Richard? *Anything?*" she asked.

"Of course."

She got up slowly, almost like an old woman. "Then let me go to Arundel's house and beseech him——"

Richard stopped short and stared at her. "You must be crazed!" he said.

She went towards him steadfastly. "But you said just now——"

"I said *I* would do anything. But I can't go on bended knee and beseech my own subjects——"

"Everybody knows you can't. But I'm asking you to do something much harder, Richard. For Brembre and Salisbury, Geoffrey Chaucer and—Simon Burley." Seeing his face still adamantine, she clung to his arm. "Oh, Richard, remember that I love him too. And that I, too, want to do something—anything—to atone for the trouble I caused when I wrote to the Pope about granting Robert a divorce."

Richard caressed her absently. Although nothing ever could make him angry with her, he knew how much her ill-considered action must have enraged all Philippa's important relatives, who were mostly his enemies, and how often he had caught

Anne worrying about it. But this suggestion of hers was unthinkable. . . .

"There is nothing more any of *us* can do," York was saying. "And if the Queen sees Arundel privately there is just a chance . . ."

"Send my wife as suppliant to a soulless fiend like that? A man with a reputation for raping nuns——"

"I know how you feel, Richard. But Standish and some of her ladies can attend her. And if she should be able to save the life of any one of those four you'd both be glad all your lives."

Neither of them had ever seen the "middle" uncle behaving with such reasonable dignity, and because he sounded almost like Burley, Richard gave in. "I suppose you are right," he agreed reluctantly. "But will you arrange for some of your people to go with her? I don't want her—to encounter any unpleasantness—in the streets."

"Willingly," promised York.

To hide the hotness of his face, Richard bent over a chess-board on which the pieces stood just as he and Anne had left them, when trying to pass away the dragging hours of suspense. Experimentally, he moved a red pawn so that the white king was in check from a bishop and a knight. "It has come to something—when I have to ask that," he said.

Even Edmund Plantagenet, unimaginative as he was, regretted at that moment any part he had taken in his nephew's humiliation. "You are right," he said kindly. "And I am sure that Lancaster would agree."

Richard looked up and smiled at him. "Won't you stay to supper?" he asked, with genuine invitation in his voice. He must be sadly bereft of real friends, he reflected, to be really wanting him. But when York refused, Richard didn't press him. His own quick initiative told him that it had cost the man a great deal to come, and that beneath his well-fed unctuousness he was fidgeting to get away before the convenient mist cleared and any of his friends should see him. "I should take

Anne away to the West of England for a while until this blows over," he was advising, kissing her hand and fussing for his gloves. "After all, the next piece of luck may well be yours."

"It would be refreshing if you could think of any that's likely to be!" smiled Richard, with an attempt at normal insouciance.

York pursed his fat lips. "Lancaster might come home," he suggested. "John Holland says——"

"John Holland! I thought he was supposed to have gone on a crusade?"

"He's just back from Spain. Oh, it's all right, Richard. Even the opposition don't want him in the country. They've given him an appointment abroad—in Aquitaine, I believe."

"In my own Duchy! Without my consent!"

Having had a hand in the appointment, the Duke ignored the criticism. "It appears that Lancaster has failed to substantiate his claim to the throne of Castile," he said.

"Why, then, all those men and all the money the Commons voted him were wasted!" exclaimed Anne, seething because they would grant Richard nothing.

"But he has managed to marry one of those gawky daughters of his to the Castilian heir," added York, pulling on his gloves at last.

"How like him!" laughed Richard.

Anne turned to him eagerly. "Why don't you write to your uncle of Lancaster? Perhaps, if he came home now——"

Richard's face brightened. "It's an idea. But he wouldn't be in time to prevent——"

Anne caught at the departing Duke. "*You* don't believe Lancaster was treacherous, do you?" she demanded, with the disconcerting forthrightness of her sex. Caught off his guard like that, York forgot that a direct reply must of necessity incriminate either one brother or the other. "If he were, he wouldn't have taken all those men out of the country, would he?" he countered conclusively. "I should take the Queen's advice, Richard, if I were you. It might end this uncomfortable quarrelling and instability for us all." From the doorway, he added with gusty emotion, "It's a long time since I last saw John ! "

" And, quite understandably, the poor fellow's getting rather tired of having to look at Thomas," observed Richard, as soon as the door swung to behind him.

He leaned against it and took Anne in his arms, kissing her closed eyes and her sweet, responsive mouth. " I hate your going," he said, crushing her little body possessively against his own.

" I hate it terribly myself," she whispered. " But I will put on my most becoming dress——"

" Not the pink one. That is only for me ! "

" Of course not, imbecile ! But something a little bizarre that will give me confidence." Womanlike, she was already planning an alluring toilette ; but she dared not tell him that she would even try to enslave the senses of a notorious libertine to save him the pain of losing Simon Burley.

" I will give Standish special instructions to take care of you," said Richard. " And you will take Agnes ? "

Anne shook her head. " Agnes's eyes are red as winter berries, and she is afraid to leave the window overlooking the Byward gate in case Robert manages to send her some message."

" You think he will try to reach her ? " In spite of everything, a note of relief lightened Richard's voice.

" I am sure he will," Anne assured him. " Their love is very real, Richard."

He released Anne and went back to finger the chessmen, absently trying to get the white king out of check. " I suppose that in his own way Robert *did* love people," he mused, as if speaking of someone who was already dead. " I remember once when we were boys practising for a tournament, I had just made a worse exhibition of myself than usual, and he let himself be unhorsed in the dust to keep me company. He had on a new pink velvet coat, I remember. So he must have cared for me quite a good deal."

" *Please*, Richard, don't talk like that ! " remonstrated Anne. " You must *know* that, whatever his faults, Robert loved you. That he was always completely loyal to you——"

He shrugged and swept the ivory pieces back into their box. " Oh, what does it matter, one way or the other ? " he said.

" It matters to me that Agnes should be happy again."

Richard was all contrition at once. " Of course, my darling. What a selfish swine I am, puling about my own emotions ! And you doing all this for Burley ! " He took a thoughtful turn or two about the room, while she waited impatiently to be gone ; and presently, having hit upon an idea, he shot a question at her. "Agnes and Lizbeth were friends, weren't they ? "

" Up to a point, I suppose." Anne's surprise gave place to a humorous dig. " You see, they were both desperately in love with other women's husbands."

At any other time Richard would have smiled at her sophistry, but he was absorbed in a scheme which in his heart he knew to be really for Robert, more than for Agnes. " Then tell her—if her messenger should come—to say she will wait for him at Bodiam."

" Bodiam ? But that's a little inland place, isn't it ? "

" All the ports will be watched, my dear. But Edward Dalyngrigge has ships that steal down the Rother and might be after more French wine any dark night. So nobody is likely to try to stop him at Rye. And Lizbeth is still a bride, isn't she ? And a very bewitching one, I should think, when she wants something done—say, in Calais. . . ."

Anne had almost forgotten the Earl of Arundel. " But would Lizbeth help them ? She was always so jealous of Robert."

" Which only goes to prove how much she would still do for me," grinned Richard, " even though she is furious with me about her wedding."

Anne came closer, regarding him almost with awe. "Richard, you're a genius!" she breathed gratefully.

He tilted her adorable chin and kissed her adieu. "I look like one, don't I, cornered in one of my own castles?" he mocked.

Apparently his plan prospered, for Agnes had received her message and slipped away before the Queen's return. But Anne cried herself to sleep in his arms that night. Arundel had deliberately kept her waiting until some of York's men had protested, and when at last he had given her audience he had found her so delectable that he had been over-familiar. "You had better save your pretty prayers for that redeless husband of yours," he had said. The fate of Burley, Salisbury and Brembre was firmly sealed and out of his hands, he declared; but for the sake of her patient persistence he would spare her Chaucer. Secretly, he and Gloucester had been uneasy about having Chaucer executed in London because he was, in his quiet way, so popular with the people. Besides, a mere rhyming Customs official wasn't important enough to bother about either way, and being rather overawed by the Queen's imperial connections, Arundel decided that it might be as well to make some show of mercy. And when she went down on her knees to him, for very shame he had promised gruffly that Burley should be beheaded as befitted his rank.

"Simon will bless you for that, Anne," Richard told her, holding her against his heart in the healing darkness. "A man could go very proudly to his death, I think, knowing that his Queen had cared so much."

"If only I could have saved them all!" sobbed Anne.

"Life must be very sweet to Geoffrey Chaucer, with his golden gift and his friendly nature," he reminded her. "Salisbury and Burley are both old men, and Brembre will go out with a jest on his lips. But probably some of Chaucer's best poems are yet to be written. And the world will have you, my love, to thank for them."

It was good for Richard, having her to comfort. It gave him less time to think of his own grief, and made him, for the time being, lay aside his consuming fury against the men who had insulted his wife and killed his friends. But nothing that Gloucester or Arundel had ever done to *him*, or ever could, would call so loudly for revenge.

CHAPTER XXII

RICHARD began the day by singing in his bath. It was a long time since he had done that. Almost a year. There had been those awful weeks in the Tower when Mowbray and Bolingbroke had deserted him, and when he had had to endure the humiliation of being seen almost beaten to earth and helpless by the woman to whom he would have given the whole world. There had been the black day of his friends' execution. And then a sort of semi-exile in Bristol, with plenty of time for remembering the price they had paid for him and feeling ashamed of being alive.

Parliament had soon relented, and on the backward swing of the pendulum several members had felt sneaking shame for their outburst of savagery. There had been no French invasion and the stocks of French wine had run out. With their brains cleared from the fumes of Chartreuse and subversive oratory, people regained some sense of balance. And the heads of three good men stuck on London Bridge sobered them still more. Men began to speak of it as the Merciless Parliament.

Richard and Anne had come back to Sheen. But it had taken a lot of persuasion to make the King promise to re-enter London. When he appealed to the rich City Guilds to lend him a thousand pounds they had refused, and had torn to pieces an Italian merchant who, benefiting from his peace policy in Europe, had been willing to do so. Such senseless cruelty always enraged Richard. So he had promptly pawned his Aquitanian coronet and retaliated by taking away their charters.

On the proceeds of the coronet he had kept open house. All winter he had hunted hard, putting Barbary at the highest hedges, not seeming to care whether he broke his own neck or not. And at Christmas time he had plunged into an orgy of revelry, so that guests gorging themselves at his board reported that he cared for nothing but pleasure. But even in the midst of masks and mummeries, waves of bitterness and grief swept over him, and it seemed as if only Anne's comfort kept him sane.

But now it was summer again. And he was young and resilient and ardently in love. And so he leaned luxuriously against the tall, pulpit-like back of his wooden tub and sang. Although it was scarcely six o'clock of an August morning, sunlight lay in golden shafts across the floor rushes, mingling pleasantly with the steam that enclouded his naked body and drew pungent sweetness from a huge bunch of herbs hung from a rafter above his head. Over by the door the servants were rolling out the empty water tubs, and nearer at hand Jacot himself was laying out his latest creations on a carved hutch at the bottom of the bed.

Richard stepped from the foamy fragrance onto an Eastern rug a page had set for him, and allowed Standish to rub him down and his barber to shave him. It was fun putting on well-cut clothing when one had the figure. He hoped fervently that he would never grow fat. How devastating to grow a belly like Uncle Edmund's, or fleshy hands that would make an obscenity of the tenderest caress !

" The striped *ray* is the *dernier cri* from Paris, sir. So youth-ful, so *légère* ! They say King Charles of France had one made for Candlemas," chattered Jacot.

" They say too that he has at last shaken off the outworn regency of his uncles," murmured Richard, through the trickle of rose water being sprayed on his freshly shaven cheeks. The multi-coloured gaudiness of the *ray* was certainly tempting ; just the thing for a river party or a *bal masque*. But today he wanted to look his age, so he chose the fawn *lame* with the gold lined over-sleeves.

" You've certainly surpassed yourself in the cut, Jacot ! " he commended, when they had buttoned him into it. Clasping the narrow gold belt, he pivoted round to survey straight shoulder and slender flank in the burnished Saracen shield young Tom Holland held for him. Not a crease anywhere. The quiet, expensive material and up-standing collar gave him dignity ; and the narrow line of white linen at neck and wrist added that touch of modishness which so became him.

The little French tailor skipped round him, smoothing here and tweaking there, and giving vent to staccato superlatives.

" Stop behaving like an ecstatic monkey, and go home and give my love to Mundina ! " laughed Richard. " Tell her that Chaucer has written a marvellous allegorical fantasy about the Queen. It is called ' The Legend of Good Women,' and he reads it to us all among the roses in the garden. In it he says God made her like a daisy, fair to see. And everybody is so enchanted with it that my wife is badgering me to have the whole scene painted—to remind us of happiness when we are old or sad, she says. So I specially want Mundina to be sitting among her women in the foreground."

While Richard was still sipping his morning cup of hot spiced wine, Medford came to read him a list of the day's engagements in London. In spite of the royal dudgeon, they sounded pleasant enough, and Richard had promised himself an unscheduled and chancy adventure to which he looked forward with keen excitement. He gave orders for all the most important members of his household to accompany him. But first he must go and bid the Queen good morning.

He found her still abed; and shooed the tiring women from her room.

" Lazy wench ! " he remarked pleasantly, looking down at the sleepy weight of curled lashes on her unpainted face.

" Whose fault ? " she countered, turning on her pillow in delicious drowsiness.

He sat on the edge of the bed and pulled her up against his shoulder, so that her long dark hair made a curtain over his possessive hands. " Nice ! " murmured Anne, nuzzling appreciatively at the smooth fawn cloth. " How do you

237

manage to look so vigorous and smell so nice at this hour in the morning?"

"By taking a herb bath at the crack of dawn," he told her.

"You're like a child," she complained adoringly. "Waking instantly, clear-eyed, and sparkling irritatingly before anybody else can bear to be funny."

"Well, we've quite a lot of things to do today."

"What sort of things, Richard?"

"Since you insist that I go to London, I am taking the opportunity of meeting the architect about the new roof I want to put into Westminster hall. The proportions of the place are so perfect that it deserves something really beautiful, and Chaucer seems to think that we can take down those supporting Norman pillars and span the whole roof space with oak. He seems to know quite a lot about architecture as well as poetry, Anne."

"You will have to make him Clerk of the Works," laughed Anne, who always felt specially responsible for his career now that she had been instrumental in saving his life. "What next?"

"The College of Heraldry experts will be meeting me there with the designs they've been getting out for livery badges. All sorts of suggestions for people to choose from, and taken mostly from our coats-of-arms."

Anne settled herself more snugly in his arms. "Why are you so anxious for everybody's followers, as well as ordinary household servants, to be labelled?" she asked.

"Because it will make a lot of people come out into the open, and we shall know where we stand. And I rather think the Gloucester-Arundel faction are in for some surprises. Specially now that Lancaster is coming home. I want you to be there, Anne. It should be rather amusing. Some of the barons may sneer and say it's one of my fantastic ideas, but they'd hate to be left out."

"I wonder what your uncle Thomas and Arundel will choose," gurgled Anne.

"Oh, a couple of belching dragons rampant, I should imagine."

"And after that?"

Richard got up and smoothed down his new tunic. "After that," he told her with dignity, "I have some state business to attend to."

"Oh!"

The dignity crumbled very quickly. "But first there is this state entry," he complained. "Our stock seems to have gone up with the civic corporation. Probably it shook them, my pawning the Aquitanian regalia. Anyway, they're feeding us lavishly at the Guild Hall. Peacock and roast boar, I understand. And I suppose Richard Whittington or someone will sit in Brembre's place and expect me not to notice. And to have a good appetite."

"My dear! But I suppose it is their way of trying to win your forgiveness."

"I can't forgive them. But I can ride through the streets loathing them if it will please you."

"Not to please me, Richard, but because we can't afford to quarrel with them. I am *sure* Simon would have thought it best." It was difficult giving advice in a strange country. Anne frowned in perplexity, sitting bolt upright braiding her hair into two glossy ropes. "What I can't understand is why the Londoners betrayed you, when you and Robert and Brembre were always planning things for their good."

"Because, long before you came, Gloucester destroyed their trust in me. And trust doesn't grow a second time," Richard explained sadly. "But they loved me once, Anne. You should have heard the bells ringing after I'd saved their city from Wat Tyler's men!"

Anne knew how much Chaucer's "flower of cities all" meant to Richard. She slid down from the great four-poster and ran barefoot to where he stood, putting warm, bare arms about his neck. "I will make them love you again, Richard," she promised.

He held her tight, remembering how uncomplainingly she had shared his misfortunes. "And I will give you a lovely, peaceful England. A place fit for a wonderful queen to reign over," he swore. "Sooner than you think, perhaps." His face kindled as it always did in his enthusiasms, and he held her at arm's length, all the artist in him considering the porphyry loveliness of her nude body almost as impersonally as he might have studied the perfection of a statue. "Anne, I want you to look queenly today," he said urgently. "I want you to put on that silver dress stitched over with pearls."

"I can't put on *anything* unless you go away and let my women come in," pointed out Anne.

Richard let her go. "They can come in now," he said, obligingly clapping his hands for them.

"But darling, you know how shocked old Mother Techsen is because you *will* wander about my bedroom while they're dressing me," objected Anne, reaching hurriedly for her wrap.

"Shocked? The prim old Hussite! But I sleep here, don't I?"

"That's different," explained Anne, furling the extravagant garment about her slender hips. "They're not here then."

"Good God, I should hope not!" ejaculated Richard, scowling horribly as they all trooped into the room bearing towels and perfumes and stacks of feminine gear. He bowed frigidly to the hawk-eyed duenna in charge of them. But by the time he had reached the door a happy thought had restored his good humour. "Landgravine Techsin, the Queen and I invite you and the other Bohemian ladies to come to London with us this morning—in your best dresses," he said graciously. "My late mother's state charette will be at your disposal."

They all looked much elated at the honour, and even the landgravine preened herself at the thought of riding in the grandest equipage in the stables.

To Anne, Richard kissed his fingertips, adding in very bad Latin, "The scarlet hangings are moth-eaten and it jolts like a pack horse!"

So they rode out from Sheen, all in the summer weather—Anne radiant in a gown studded with precious stones and Richard wearing the floreated ducal coronet which he had redeemed from the moneylenders for the occasion. And by the bridge gate at Southwark was Whittington, the Lord Mayor, waiting for them with a splendid gift of two white horses for the King and a little white palfrey for the Queen. Richard loved the horses, of course, but was not placated. Like a good wife, Anne tried to cover the stiffness of his thanks with her own genuine enthusiasm, and watched the sulky set of his lips with foreboding. Unfortunately, the worthy Whittington saw fit to accompany the gifts with a long, boring speech sprinkled with hints about the return of his City's charters and the influence of gentle wives.

"It was clever of you to think of the horses; he loves them so. And I will do what I can to persuade him," whispered Anne, pleasing the perspiring Lord Mayor immensely by riding beside him.

And on London Bridge the fates were kind to their collusion. Crowds followed them from Southwark and crowds swept forward from London to meet them, and close behind them pranced the startled white horses. And in all the confusion and press of people the brightly painted charette full of Anne's women wobbled on its worn wheels and overturned. Bohemian ladies rolled out of it, best dresses, horned headdresses and all. Prentice boys jeered and cheered and worthy citizens, hurrying to their assistance, found themselves too shaken with laughter to help. And Richard and Anne, hearing shrieks and foreign voices raised above the pandemonium, looked back to see the narrow roadway strewn with scarlet upholstery and inebriated-looking ladies.

"Oh, my poor dears!" cried Anne, thinking of the river racing through the narrow arches below.

"I'm sorry! I'd no idea the old hen cart was as rickety as that!" spluttered Richard, trying to look repentant. But the sight of Old Mother Techsen's skinny legs sticking through the side window was too much for him. "Tell her how shocked I am," he tried to say severely. "Bare to the thigh, and *not* in the privacy of her bedroom!" But at sight of his wife's anxious face he stopped grinning and turned to the Lord Mayor behind him. "For God's sake, Whittington, go and see them properly packed in again," he ordered. And there on London Bridge he forgot all about his royal dudgeon, and made his entry into London, enjoying himself enormously in the middle of a laughing crowd. And if Anne were hurt because her countrywomen were the target of their ribald mirth, she was too wise to show resentment. Her love for Richard was such that she would have been glad of any event that seemed so happy an augury for him.

They feasted in the Guild Hall. The Cheapside conduit ran red wine, and bands of musicians made harmonies about St. Paul's. Down Ludgate Hill the royal party rode, between tall houses hung with gold and silver tapestries; and out from the Wardrobe gatehouse came Mundina to kiss their hands. As they passed under Ludgate and clattered over the Fleet, bevies of golden-haired girls dressed as angels showered them with scented flowers, and at the Temple barrier they drew rein to watch a pageant which included lions and dragons and even a Garden of Eden serpent, and must have cost the repentant magnates hundreds of pounds.

"Peace be to this city; for the sake of Christ, His mother, and my patron St. John," said Richard, kissing the gemmed crucifix they gave him. And because he was obviously moved, others besides Anne saw that light of inner grace about him.

The apartness of his kinghood was still upon him as he ascended his throne in Westminster Hall. But he led Anne to the throne beside his own and, still sitting, addressed his people. Richard never made long speeches and what he said was always spontaneous, his beautifully modulated voice carrying even to the crowds standing in the sunlight outside the great open doors. "I will restore to you my royal favour as in former days," he promised, "for I duly prize the expense you have incurred, the presents you have made me, and the prayers of the Queen." He knew that their tumultuous cheers were even more for her than for himself, and gave them time to exhaust themselves. " Take back the key and the sword," he said, taking the symbols of their freedom from his squires and handing them to the kneeling Lord Mayor. " Henceforth avoid offence to your sovereign and preserve the ancient faith. Keep my peace in your city," he added sternly, " and be *my* representatives among the people."

Anne was eaten with pride in him. In that rich setting, with the gorgeous banners of his knights and ancestors as background, he bore himself so much a Plantagenet. But beneath all the romantic ritual of his public personality he was still her own, everyday Richard, and as the scarlet-clad aldermen filed out she heard him say to York with irritable realism, " To-day's show must have cost them every groat of a thousand pounds. Why, in the name of common sense, couldn't they have lent it to me in the first place ? "

A few minutes later he was immersed in plans for the new roof, poring over parchments, listening to architects' opinions, and walking about the hall with unflagging energy to view the possibilities from all angles.

But when the experts from the College of Heraldry were admitted he rejoined Anne on the dais. " One gets a better view from here," he whispered, preparing to enjoy himself.

The body of the hall was all animation at once. Nobles and knights—anybody who was anybody at all—crowded round the long refectory tables upon which the designs of proposed badges were being spread. Obviously, their *amour propre* was very deeply involved.

" Let Thomas Holland choose first. He is a sick man," Richard ordered, across the rising din of their contentious voices. And his elder half-brother, who hadn't long to live, chose—as everyone had expected—the hind from his mother's quartering.

"Which heraldic beast are you going to have for yourself, Dickon?" he asked, from the chair in which his servants had brought him.

"Something fierce, symbolic of his bloodthirsty Cheshire archers?" snickered Gloucester.

"Forty thousand of them, weren't there?" grinned Henry Bolingbroke, behind his hand.

"Presumably, you will choose the lion, sir," York hastened to suggest. Since Radcot Bridge, he considered young Bolingbroke was growing too big for his boots.

"No, I am leaving that for Uncle John," said Richard, flicking them with a reminder that the mighty Lancaster was on his way home. "I will think for a while, while the rest of you choose."

Tigers, panthers, foxes, bears, fierce cockatrices, wild boars —they parted the whole menagerie among them. Fiery cressets were hot favourites. Lions rampant and lions couchant they haggled over. They were quite unaware that their young king and queen were laying bets on them with suppressed laughter. And presently Richard strolled down to the table. They made way for him and he stood among them, lifting first one design and then another, looking at each consideringly. Anne felt certain that all the time he knew exactly what he meant to have, and that he was only amusing himself keeping them standing there, watching him. "I think I will choose this," he decided at length, holding up an exquisite drawing of a little white hart.

Obviously some of them thought he was joking.

"A white hart—for the King of England!" exploded Gloucester. "Have you no pride, Richard?"

"After Crécy! And with the three leopards of the first Richard on your shield!" snarled Arundel.

"A *chained* white hart, I think," went on Richard, as if they had not spoken. "You could easily add a collar, couldn't you?" he asked, turning to the hovering draughtsman.

Even Edmund of York, who had chosen an inoffensive

falcon, was vaguely shocked. "My dear Richard, at least add a sunburst or a broomscod or something," he remonstrated.

"You think so? Well, perhaps the collar can be turned into a crown—worn round the poor creature's neck. And I think *two* chains," he added, staring gently at Gloucester and Arundel, "to lead it by."

None of them knew how to take him, and their discomfited glances followed him as he turned aside to arrange about a coat-of-arms for Chaucer. Really, when he looked round the hall, Geoffrey Chaucer seemed to be the only friend left out of his old life. And, after all, Philippa Chaucer's family had borne arms and her sister, Katherine, was Lancaster's mistress. "Trace it through Mistress Chaucer's father, Sir Payne Roet," he told Surroy King-of-Arms.

Anne, of course, was delighted. But before he went to attend a full Council meeting she drew him apart to scold him gently. "You just try to provoke them!" she whispered, straightening the buckle of his belt.

"Did you see Warwick oozing disgust, and Henry's popping eyes!" Richard chuckled reminiscently.

"But why did you have to choose a white hart? Was it just a joke?"

"No. There are some things one doesn't jest about." He was suddenly serious and, seeing his squires waiting to conduct him to the Council Chamber, he explained in low, hurried tones, "Just before the peasants revolted my mother tried to keep me with her in Canterbury. I know now that she must have been worried about my going to London. She tried to persuade me. . . . She had even had some stuff specially woven for me for a new hunting coat. It was covered with little white harts. I never had that coat. It seems so churlish now. . . ."

Anne was pressing his hand in hers, unobtrusively because of the waiting squires. Her eyes were wet. "She must be pleased," she whispered hurriedly, by way of atonement. "And I believe Gloucester and Arundel and Henry are half

245

afraid of you when they're not sure if you're making fun of them or not."

"Splendid! Perhaps that's another good augury," he said. "Wait for me here. Please, Anne! Don't go home to Sheen until I come."

When she looked up his eyes were bright with excitement like a man going into battle, and he strode away hurriedly to his meeting.

His uncles and the rest had gone before him to take up their places. The scarlet of the Lords Appellants' cloaks was like a strident field of poppies against a paler cloud of bishops. For once their babble of argument was hushed completely when he came in. He went swiftly to the state chair at the head of the table and motioned to them to be seated. But he himself did not sit down. He just stood there absently shifting the pile of documents awaiting his signature, and smiling a little to himself.

"Are you still thinking about that ridiculous contretemps on London Bridge?" ventured York, his own lips quivering at the recollection.

"Well, no. As a matter of fact I was thinking of my very good friend, Charles of Valois. . . ."

"Your *friend*!" exploded Gloucester. "Are we not at war with France?"

"We *were*," agreed Richard mildly. "But now I have had a reasonable peace treaty drawn up for Charles's consideration, and I think that the French will be as glad of it as ourselves."

The Earl of Arundel rose in wrath. "You mean you have had a peace treaty drawn up without consulting Parliament?" he demanded.

Richard ignored him and, putting down the sheaf of parchments, looked straight at his youngest uncle. "How old am I?" he asked, shooting the question at him with apparent irrelevance.

Gloucester, never much interested in family matters, glanced at his elder brother for enlightenment. But Edmund of York

246

appeared to be smiling at something rather pleasing. And, for the matter of that, so did a number of other people: "Twenty-two, I suppose," replied Gloucester sulkily, after a few moments' consultation.

"Just so," agreed Richard. "And therefore, like the meanest of my subjects, I am old enough to claim my inheritance and to take up the reins of government."

The scarlet mass of Lords Appellants was taken aback. Men who had traded on his youth ever since the late king died, stirred angrily in their seats. Many of them began to protest. But they found they hadn't the backing they expected. Looking around them, they perceived that the place was packed with Richard's followers, just as the Merciless Parliament had been packed with Gloucester's. And that many a waverer had come out into the open and was wearing a hastily improvised white hart on his sleeve. They perceived, too, that they had been cleverly rushed into this unexpected moment, ill prepared, at the end of a day's junketing, and that the King's dramatic sense had worsted them. Never had they intended to give him a chance to press his rights in full Council like this. And the very fact that he looked so coolly responsible with nothing frivolous about him, added to their discomfiture.

"You know well that for the twelve years of my reign I and my realm have been ruled by others, and my people oppressed year by year with grievous taxes," he went on, flicking his enemies with a glance. "Henceforth, with God's help, I shall labour assiduously to bring my realm to greater peace and prosperity." No one could doubt his sincerity, and a deep rumble of applause began to gather beneath his words, lending them strength.

He was succeeding. And the power of success swept him along. In freeing himself from all blame for the past, he laid it where it belonged. "Up to now I have been allowed to do nothing without my—protectors." For the first time he allowed himself that free joy of contemplating the starting eyes and dropped jaws of men who had murdered his friends and tormented his soul. "Now I will remove all of these men from my Council, summon to advise me whomsoever I will, and transact all my business myself," he said, with the drawn-out pleasure of uttering words he had been aching to say for years. "And as a first step I will trouble you, Richard Arundel, for the Chancellor's seal."

He swung round with outstretched hand, and Arundel handed it over without a word. Having won, Richard was far too clever to prolong the proceedings, and turned on his heel. In actual fact, all that was boy and lover in him had suddenly taken impatient control, so that he could scarcely wait to show the symbolic thing to Anne.

One or two of the older Councillors made muttered protests, and Edmund of York flurried after him. He was delighted that Gloucester had been put in his place, of course, and that Richard had had the spirit to bring off his *coup d'état* without waiting for Lancaster to come home. But to his conventional mind, things should be done decently and in order. "Milord Arundel's successor——" he quavered anxiously.

"I will let you know by noon tomorrow," promised Richard.

"But consider, sir. For twenty-four hours there will be no Chancellor of England——"

Richard turned and treated him to a radiant smile. "No, my dear uncle," he agreed, "but there will be a king!"

CHAPTER XXIII

"IT'S SUCH fun, being married to Richard," confided Anne, with a low happy laugh.

John of Gaunt, Duke of Lancaster, looked down at her appraisingly. At the piquant, wimple-framed features, the sparkling eyes and the whole immaculate daintiness of her. Eight years ago, before he left for Spain, she had been a captivating little bride; but he had never supposed that she would mature into anything so poised and charming at thirty. When a woman was made glamorous by being so passionately loved it didn't really matter whether she were actually beautiful or not, he decided; and Lancaster was a judge of women. "It can't always have been much fun at first," he remarked, in that unhurried, cultured voice of his that was so like Richard's.

"No," admitted Anne, seriousness passing like a summer cloud across her laughter. "But all that seems so long ago now, so that one can almost forget it."

"I doubt if Richard can," said Lancaster.

They were standing near the doors of Westminster Hall waiting for him to ride with them to watch two champions tilt. Because they were entertaining some distinguished visitors from Scotland, there had been lavish distractions all the week, culminating in a huge tournament at Smithfield; and Anne, who was a little exhausted, was not sorry for a few minutes' breathing space. It was quiet and cool in the spacious hall, and the crowning glory of Richard's hammerbeam roof was a dream come true, so that she knew what he meant when he spoke of the sense of light and space being so breathtaking that it always made him feel he was stepping into Heaven.

While she and Lancaster waited they watched him talking to a group of gesticulating bishops on the dais at the other end of the hall. They could not hear what he was saying but there was a quiet air of authority about him; and if he had lost some of his boyishness he had certainly kept his figure. "In fact," thought Anne, "he looks taller and more slender now that he has taken to wearing those long, belted houppelardes so fashionable among the older men." Though whether or not she liked the small, pointed gold beard and moustache he had grown, she never could decide. It certainly suited him and made his kisses all the more exciting, but then she had fallen in love with a clean-shaven Richard and no later edition could remove that image from her heart. "He always seems so content these days," she said doubtfully, hoping he didn't often think of all those tragic griefs and frustrations that had darkened the beginning of their married life.

"All the same, Richard has a long memory," argued his eldest uncle. "And I often feel he is like two separate people. The gay, charming one he shows to us, and some more sombre personality he keeps chained somewhere deep down below the surface."

Lancaster was too much a man of the world ever to have believed in Richard's fundamental naïveté or to understand, as Burley had, what Gloucester's cruelties could do to it; but at least he had known her husband since he was a child. "You're not suggesting that he isn't normal, I hope?" Anne asked anxiously, her gaze still brooding over the man who was all the world to her.

Lancaster moved a little nearer the door so that he could see their horses being walked up and down in the sunshine. "Delightfully normal, I should think—as long as life will let him be," he answered, a little absently. It was the first time he had brought Katherine Swinford with him to a public function, and now that he was a widower again he was hoping to legitimatize her children; so naturally his mind strayed occasionally to the gaily dressed group of courtiers waiting outside. But he was quick to smile down at Anne in apology. "That is why you are so good for him, my dear."

Because Richard was gradually tightening the reins of government, there always seemed business to attend to before pleasure these days. But the moment he had dismissed his secretary and got rid of the importunate clerics, he came hurrying towards them, taking the shallow steps from the dais at a run and crossing the hall with those quick, light strides of his which made the dignified purple velvet houppelarde almost an anomaly. "My dear, I'm so sorry to keep you waiting! And you, Uncle," he apologized charmingly. "Those bishops will be the death of me!"

Anne forgot that she had been feeling tired and laughed at the way he flicked a gaudy square of silk from the tightness of his buttoned sleeve and dabbed it melodramatically across his forehead. "What's the matter with them this time?" she asked, playing up to his infectious gaiety.

"Oh, they seem to suspect us of being Lollards because I won't have Wycliffe's followers burned as heretics. Surely one can be an orthodox Christian without wanting to burn people alive! Just as one can want the peasants' children to have some sort of education without favouring another revolt. I'm sure some of the peasants are as intelligent as most of the bishops!"

"And what were those laymen wanting?" asked Lancaster.

"Oh, the usual thing. Permits to build new castles," said Richard wearily. "As if England weren't far too full of castles with dungeons where people can be quietly done away with! You know, Uncle, now Tom Mowbray's Governor of Calais, he tells me that that old pirate Dalyngrigge is snooping off the French coast again. It appears that instead of repairing the Wardeaux's castle at Bodiam, he's built himself a brand new one with Lizbeth's money. Further down the Rother. I shall have to get Chaucer to send someone down there from the Office of Works to-morrow."

A horse whinnied outside and they could hear Mathe barking excitedly. "Ah, well, now we can go out and enjoy ourselves," said Richard, shaking off his cares of state. As usual, after they had been parted, he turned to Anne as if seeing her for the first time. Taking in every detail of her toilette and making quite an occasion of their reunion. "I love you best in that dull pink, but you look pale this morning, my sweet," he observed, brushing a minute blob of mascara from beneath her lashes with as much concern as if he were signing a death warrant.

"Ill painted, you mean," grimaced Anne.

Having settled her appearance to his satisfaction, he kissed the tip of her adorable nose and turned eagerly towards the open door. "They should be quite well matched, Lord Welles and this Scottish knight," he said to Lancaster.

Anne slipped a hand through his arm. "Didn't they have enough tilting in all that heat at Smithfield yesterday?" she asked, a little pettishly.

He stopped short immediately, not caring that he almost cannoned into his uncle, who was close behind. "You *are* tired! We'll have it put off until tomorrow," he declared.

In spite of the crowds and the preparations, Anne knew that he was perfectly capable of doing so for her sake. "Oh, please, Richard! I'm perfectly all right. It's only that we *have* had rather a hectic week, though I've loved every minute of it. But tell me, why do they have to tilt on London Bridge?"

"Oh, for the novelty of the thing, I suppose." She had coaxed him through the doorway and, finding some of their Scottish guests within earshot, neither he nor Lancaster mentioned that the fantastic idea had originated because one or two cases of plague had been reported at Smithfield.

"But surely it's too narrow?" said Anne.

"The Queen has never forgotten the day when her ladies' equipage overturned on the Bridge," he explained gravely to some Scots who had been whiling away the time watching Tom Mowbray put Mathe through his tricks. Before mounting, Richard and Anne and Lancaster paused to watch too. "Like the rest of us, Mathe is glad to have you at court more often, Tom," said Richard. But after a moment or two he snapped his fingers and Mathe bounded across the courtyard to stand on his hind legs with a forepaw on either of his master's shoulders—a greeting he had learned in puppyhood when neither of them was full-grown, and which he vouchsafed to no one else.

Mowbray had become an important personage. Besides being Governor of Calais, he had inherited the dukedom of Norfolk and all the rich Bigod estates; and he sought assiduously to regain the King's favour. Richard was invariably pleasant to him. Indeed, there were moments when their mutual love of animals made it difficult not to forgive him. But before Radcot Bridge Richard wouldn't have called off the hound like that, leaving Mowbray looking rather a fool in front of so many people.

Everyone seemed in holiday mood and crowded round the King and Queen as they mounted. Richard was charming to Sir David Lindsay and Lord Welles, the protagonists, whose international challenge was to provide the culminating feature of the week, and he made a special point of speaking to Lancaster's mistress. He had disliked his Castilian aunt and was glad that Katherine Swinford had some chance of becoming a duchess at last. "How's that famous brother-in-law of yours, Kate?" he asked genially.

Lancaster appreciated the gesture. "Chaucer was set upon by footpads last night, you know," he explained to Anne. "Now that Richard has made him Clerk of the Works he takes the wages every week to the men working on the repairs at Windsor."

"Oh, I hope he wasn't hurt?" The Queen was all concern at once.

"More shaken in conscience than in body, I should imagine," answered Richard, as they started out along the Charing road. "He was in a grievous pother because he had lost all that money."

"And I expect you made it up out of your privy purse," laughed Anne. She loved Richard for his reckless generosity, but she was well aware that an exasperated Parliament called it extravagance. A gaudy week like this, for instance, was sure to upset them, and they couldn't see how much cheaper it was than another Scottish war. She wondered if they knew that every time Richard fed three hundred guests at his table he fed three hundred beggars at his back door. And that he had never sent them away empty, even that bitter winter after the crops had been so bad. The people themselves must know it, she supposed, for they set up a tremendous cheer as soon as he appeared in Charing village. " I told you they would love you again," she couldn't help whispering, guiding her palfrey close against the stately Barbary.

" It's probably you they're cheering. Or Lindsay, after the splendid tilting showed them at Smithfield yesterday," smiled Richard.

But Anne could see that he was happy. " I'm quite sure all the women's cheers are blessings on you for saving their sons and husbands from war," she persisted, purposely raising her voice a little because Gloucester happened to be riding near her.

Even Gloucester was in good mood this lovely blue and gold day. " Don't flatter him ! " he expostulated, with a cumbersome attempt at facetiousness. " He always *did* know better than his uncles ! "

" And Uncle Thomas knows better than his Bible, wherein it is written, ' Blessed are the peacemakers for they shall be called the children of God,' " said Richard, who could afford to poke fun at him.

Richard had ruled England for eight years now. And ruled her well. These were the years that Froissart and other chroniclers would probably pass over with a sentence or two, as all prosperous times and happy marriages get passed over. But they were the *raison d'être* of his reign and the true expression of himself. And they gave England that respite which she so much needed in order to re-establish herself, and give her population a chance to partake in the cultural renaissance which was spreading over the Continent.

Richard had long ago signed a peace treaty with France, here he was offering lavish hospitality to the Scots, and he had even settled the ever recurring problem of Ireland. He had not only seen Ireland as a potential colony, as his grandfather had done, but also as a potential danger if used by invading troops ; and so he had led a campaign there himself. After an initial show of force, he had treated the barbaric chieftains so reasonably and humanely that they had sworn friendly allegiance and ceased harrying the English within the settlers' Pale. And he had left young Roger Mortimer, his heir, as Governor.

At home he had given Anne the kind of kingdom he had promised her. When he took over his inheritance he had been wise enough to retain experienced men who had served under his grandfather, and tolerant enough to take no revenge upon men like Gloucester and Arundel. And—to everyone's surprise—he had not endangered the hard-won tranquillity by attempting to recall Michael de la Pole and Robert de Vere. But the violence of baronial families was now being held in check, and cheating tradesmen brought to justice. Beautiful merchandise poured into the country, Gothic churches raised their graceful spires, colleges were founded and infirmaries built. And learning flourished so that the clerks could not copy all the books quickly enough, and began to experiment with mechanical devices for doing so.

"I suppose England is too quiet for Henry these days," Richard remarked to his eldest uncle. "I hear he has gone abroad again."

"I rather think he is the loser," smiled Lancaster. His own adventuring days were done, and all the connoisseur in him appreciated Richard's England.

As they passed along the Strand and up Ludgate Hill he noticed improvements everywhere. A toll had been levied to lay cobstones along that particularly vile bit of road so that one need not dismount and go by boat on muddy days to avoid splashing one's best hose. The new Clerk of the Works had been ordered to straighten the river bank and repair the sewers. Butchers no longer flung offal in the gutters, but had to do their slaughtering outside the city at villages like Knightsbridge or Stratford-le-Bow; and the public privies that had polluted the moat of the Fleet prison had been pulled down. There were far fewer maimed beggars by the roadside, and—best of all, perhaps—the warning bells of lepers were seldom heard. Richard had had proper lazar houses built for them across the water on Bankside.

London had never looked more lovely. An early shower of rain had washed the gleaming spire of St. Paul's and made the Temple gardens verdant. And now the sun shimmered on a full, majestic river, making a bright parterre of warm brown sails and boatloads of sightseers in holiday garments. It garnished gay little tavern bushes and barbers' flamboyant poles, and twinkled on wrought-iron signs above the shops.

"Let us linger a little while and look at it all," begged Anne. "I love it even better than Prague."

Richard laughed at her indulgently and signed to his cavalcade to stop, and she reined in the white palfrey the Londoners had given her and sat on the top of Ludgate Hill drinking in her fill of their city.

"No need to devour it as though you'd never see it again," teased Richard.

She raised puzzled eyes to his adoring ones. "Why is it so specially beautiful today?" she asked.

"Because it is June," he told her.

"I wonder what will happen *this* June," she speculated, as they moved on again.

"An unexpected visitor, perhaps," suggested Edmund of York comfortably.

"Whom would you choose, milord?" asked Ralph Standish, who was in attendance.

York thought it would be nice if the Queen could see her brother, the Emperor; and Lancaster tactfully chose the King of Scotland.

They all made a game of it, idly, as they passed along Cheapside.

"And you, Richard?" asked Mowbray.

"Oh, Jehan Froissart, I think. He was chronicler for my father's wars, and must have known my parents when they were young because I am told he was at my christening. Besides, I've often thought how amusing it would be if he and Geoffrey Chaucer could meet."

They crossed the bridge to the Southwark end, where a gaily decked stand had been erected for them. The Bridge gate guard sprang to attention and the watchman up on the battlements blew a fanfare on the huge horn which had been issued for calling reinforcements ever since Tyler's men had rushed the drawbridge in 1381. Along the dusty road beyond the closed gate as far as eye could see, all manner of laden country carts were held up, waiting till the tilting was over to pay their farthing toll to come in and feed the insatiable city.

"Who is the venerable man in red with all the official buttons?" asked Anne.

"The Bridge doctor," explained Richard. "He's supposed to examine everyone who passes through and turn back all the lepers and plague suspects. It's extraordinary, though, no matter what arrangements we make for them to be fed on the other side, they always try to slip past and come back into London somehow!"

"I should think he found it difficult with all those crowds pouring in for the tournament yesterday," said Standish.

Tom Mowbray was busy clearing the roadway and instructing the heralds. And soon Lord Welles and Sir David Lindsay were charging across the strange lists with couched lances, each using his utmost skill to uphold the prowess of his own country. The bridge shook beneath the pounding of their horses' hoofs so that York, whose weight was considerable, feared that the stand might collapse as had once happened in the time of his mother, Queen Philippa. Cheers and shrilling

257

of trumpets filled the air, broken from time to time by Mowbray's crisp orders, or the shriek of some silly women in the packed boats below. The bouts grew more and more fierce, and the sun rose higher in the summer sky.

Presently Richard felt Anne's head come to rest against his shoulder. " Tired, my love ? " he asked, withdrawing his gaze from a particularly exciting thrust to glance down at her. It was so unlike Anne to make demonstrations of affection in public.

" It is so hot ! " she murmured.

He sent a page for a cooling drink and took one of her hot hands in his, holding it on his knee. And she said no more, fearing to spoil his pleasure. If he knew how awful she really felt he would throw down the gold baton Mowbray had handed him and stop the combat—and it was the final championship combat of the whole week upon which everyone had laid their bets.

But at last the contest was over. A roar of cheering roused her and Richard sprang to his feet, almost forgetting that she was leaning against him. Lindsay was the victor. Scotland forever ! Red-bearded Highlanders and London prentices yelled in unison, Richard presented Sir David with a cup the Goldsmiths' company had made, and men began to take up their bets. Anne sat very still, resting her head against the tall back of her crimson-painted chair and gripping the lions'-head arms. It was not until the shouting died down and the crowds were preparing to depart that Richard noticed how white she looked.

Her eyes were closed, but she felt him bending over her and smelled the pleasant perfume of his clothes. " Anne, darling, you really *are* tired. We'll go back to Westminster at once," he was saying; but somehow his voice sounded as if it came from a long way off. And when she opened her eyes the shimmering light on the water made her feel giddy.

" Not to Westminster. Home to Sheen," she managed to say, through lips that felt stiff and swollen.

"But, my darling, our guests . . ."

She caught at his hands, and her own were burning.
"Please, Richard . . ." She was aware of the two elder uncles
looking at her anxiously—of her women loosening her dress.
She hated making a fuss. But just as an hour or so ago she had
wanted to drink in the happy look of London, so now her whole
being yearned to be at Sheen.

She felt too ill to notice how they got her there, except that
she lay on cushions in a closed litter. And that Richard walked
the whole way beside her, easing the stretcher with his own
hands and cursing softly every time the grooms encountered
a rough bit of road. And then at last she was being carried
upstairs into her own dear, familiar room, and Richard himself
was laying her on her bed. Her women were putting hot bricks
to her feet and two of the King's physicians seemed to have
appeared as if by magic out of the blackness that kept
threatening to submerge her.

The Queen was ill. Agitated servants ran up and down stairs
with hot water, or huddled in whispering groups. The uncles
stood respectfully in the ante-room, and her husband paced
up and down outside her door. He had never seen her look like
that. Suppose she were going to be ill all the summer? Illness
had never touched them. He had never even been called upon
to wait while she bore the agony of childbirth. But that would
have been sharp and over in a few hours—and then such joy
for both of them!

Surely the doctors must have finished their examination.
Why couldn't old Waldby come out and tell him if it were
really serious? He went to the door and listened. The stillness
in the room got on his nerves so that he bit his lip and was
surprised to find it bleeding. Ah, at last someone was moving.
He heard the murmur of professional voices. They would
come out in a moment and tell him that Anne had caught a
sunstroke or a chill. And then suddenly a woman screamed.
Not in pain, but terror. The door was wrenched open from
within and a very young, distraught lady-in-waiting appeared,

banging it behind her as if she had escaped from something unspeakable.

"It's the plague!" she croaked, staring straight into Richard's face with frightened, bulging eyes.

Richard seized her by a wrist. "Keep quiet, you fool!" he whispered, flinging her aside. And then the door opened again, more decorously, and Robert Waldby, the senior physician, stood there, both arms queerly outstretched. "It is true, sir," he said.

Richard stared at him stupidly. He was vaguely aware of shocked exclamations from the uncles behind him. "You lying old goat!" he said, with a crazy sort of laugh which cracked in the middle because he could see now by the man's face that he wasn't lying.

He threw himself upon the physician and forced his way back into the room. He could see his wife lying motionless where he had left her, her long, unbound hair and one open palm trailing pitifully over the side of the bed, and her face turned from him. "Anne!" he cried desperately. But she did not answer. And then a dozen hands seemed to seize him, and a barrier of bodies was pushing him from his beloved. "You can't, sir . . . Consider England . . . My dear Richard, it isn't as if you had a *son* . . ." Bits of their agitated arguments penetrated his stunned brain. He knew that they were right. But it made no difference until, in his struggles, he found himself wedged against Gloucester. Gloucester, who raised no hand to stop him—whose mocking eyes said as plainly as words, "Go on in and be damned to you!" And because he knew that Gloucester hoped he'd catch the plague and die, perversely he stopped struggling and let them lead him away.

Clearly, Anne's own women were useless. Richard sent Ralph Standish for Mundina. He knew that Mundina, in the strange way of women, did not love Anne, although her dearest hope had been to nurse Anne's child. But he knew beyond all doubt that anything that was dear to him Mundina Danos would fight for with all the strange strength that was in her.

All afternoon he paced his room or flung himself down in prayer, bargaining desperately with the Almighty. He neither spoke nor ate, and suffered no one but Mathe to be with him. Only the dog's dumb sympathy was tolerable. But when the unending day dragged towards dusk Richard went out into the gallery and called for Tom Holland, telling him to have the cooks prepare some of the Queen's favourite frumenty, and to come back for a message before carrying it to her room. He and his squire were both of a height now, and still very much alike. Richard gave the order loudly so that several people should hear him, and purposely forebore to rate the servants because they had forgotten to light the torches.

When Tom came with the stuff Richard changed clothes with him, putting on the plain green livery with the white hart badge. He told the young man to lie on the bed in the shadow of the hangings so that anyone entering would say, " The King sleeps. In the name of charity don't disturb him ! " And then he took the bowl of steaming frumenty and went hurrying with it through the darkening passages to his wife's room.

Mundina herself unbarred the door, as if she had been expecting him. His eyes searched hers and found no trace of hope ; only a fathomless pity. " The Queen has been calling for you," she told him. She took the bowl from him and set it aside. They both knew that Anne would never taste frumenty again.

Mundina had long since sent the frightened women away and eased Anne's pain with her own herbal remedies. And somehow, with her tall gaunt frame and glittering dark eyes, she had managed to intimidate the doctors so that they let Richard stay.

" How long ? " he asked them tersely.

" A few hours, perhaps," they told him, and moved away.

In the midst of her delirium Anne sensed his presence. " Richard ! " she cried joyfully, holding out shaking arms to him as if he were an angel from Heaven.

He sat on the bed and gathered her into his arms. It seemed incredible that only that morning she had set forth with him, laughing and radiant. All the strength and youth seemed to have been burned out of her. " My heart's resting place ! " she murmured, great tears welling up into her lovely eyes.

All night long he held her. They had so little time left. The plague was like that. It had carried off his grandmother, the beloved Queen Philippa, before he was born.

At first Anne talked a little in happy, broken sentences. Why had all her women gone away ? All except Mundina, who knew just where the pain was and put hot poultices. Not that she minded their going, really—except that she had wanted Agnes. " I prayed to the sweet Mother of Christ that you would come. And now that I am in your arms again nothing else matters. . . . It's been such fun, Richard, being married to you ! " An echo of all the laughter they had shared throbbed weakly through her lovely voice. " Do you remember the little French song you used to sing ?

> " *My candle burns at both its ends*
> *It gives a lovely light !*
> *But oh, my friends, and ah, my friends,*
> *It will not last the night !* "

Anne was growing light-headed again. " You and Robert could make a party out of a bottle of Bordeaux and a couple of candles, couldn't you ? " The foolish question broke on a small sob, as if for the first time she realized that the fun was nearly over and the candles burning out. " Do you suppose that Robert and Agnes have been as happy as you and I ? "

Regardless of the dread disease, Richard crushed passionate lips to hers. " Nobody *could* have been . . ." he said brokenly, knowing that never again would her senses respond deliciously to his kisses.

" It seems odd—how I used to envy them. Before you really cared. . . ."

"Don't Anne! God knows I did too! And now—to think of all the precious, wasted weeks . . ."

Anne's flicker of strength was spent. Her lashes fluttered down again. "Nothing—is ever—wasted, Richard. . . ." Her tired voice trailed away.

There were ugly blotches on her bare arms and several times she retched horribly. As the night wore on, he was aware of Mundina and the doctors doing things for her. The ugly, necessary things of sickness. Once he laid her down while a priest came and gave her Extreme Unction. And soon afterwards she brought up blood.

After that they left him alone with her. He could not see beyond the haze of tapers at the foot of the bed, and no one moved any more in the shadowed room. Anne was jasmine white and could no longer speak. He knew now that their unexpected June visitor had come. That he was neither Jehan Froissart nor any of the pleasant people they had discussed so gaily a million hours ago, but uninvited Death. And that he had come only to see the Queen. With all his will Richard wrestled with him. He was learning the extremity of love. The love that lasts, with the sweets of passion shorn away. Beginning to understand that this kind of love was the only weapon with which he could in the end cheat Death. "Give her to me, God! With nothing for myself, if only I may keep and see and serve her," he implored, the sweat running down his face. But as the sands ran inexorably through the hour glass, so the dark, hooded figure approached nearer and nearer until his stagnant breath extinguished all their lovely youth and happiness.

The long night wore away at last. The tapers burned themselves out at dawn. Mundina moved quietly to open a casement. Out in the garden the birds were beginning their drowsy twittering. A faint pink flush in the east painted the beginning of a new June day. An earthly pageant that must inevitably flame to decay. But as yet the first quiet peace of early morning held some spectrum of a timeless world, and the dew-drenched virgin grass waited, expectant, for the touch of Heavenly feet.

Richard felt the faintest sign flutter from the cold lips against his cheek. In his arms he still held the beloved body that had wept and danced with him through the transient years; but the soul of Anne had escaped him.

Nothing that happened in June could ever matter any more.

CHAPTER XXIV

" *SUB PETRA lata mana Anna jacet tumulata——*"

The king's quill moved slowly over the parchment, and every now and then the words ran into each other, smudged by his tears. He was writing his wife's epitaph, and part of him seemed to be standing outside himself watching in unbelieving amazement.

Chaucer had humbly offered to do it. Chaucer, who could have done it so much better. For Richard was no poet. He could only feel poetry, as he had once explained to Robert de Vere. But he must do this for Anne. Because there was so little left that he could do for her. And he felt tough enough to live for years. Each night either Mundina or Standish had insisted upon his drinking a hot posset and he had fallen into a sound sleep. Some of the fond woman's witchery, no doubt ; but he had been more grateful for those hours of oblivion than for any spoken sympathy.

Laboriously, he construed each spontaneous English thought into metrical Latin.

> " *Under this stone lies Anna, here entombed,*
> *Wedded in this life to the second Richard . . .*
> *Christ's poor she freely fed from her treasures ;*
> *Strife she assuaged, and swelling feuds appeased . . .*"

" God, how often she kept me from hitting Henry ! " he recalled. And how she had held in check his smouldering hatred of Gloucester and Arundel ! The quill scratched on again.

> " *Beauteous her form, her face surpassing fair.*"

Her face surpassing fair . . . Richard Plantagenet laid his own face on his arms and sobbed, smudging the parchment still more. But he must hurry. In an hour's time the cortège was to assemble outside the palace of Westminster, where he sat writing. And he wanted his words to go with Anne to her last resting place in the Abbey, so that all should know how wonderful she was. Later they would be carved upon her tomb. " She passed away into eternal joys," he concluded, and laid down his pen.

" Oh, Anne, my darling Anne, God give you eternal joy ! But how can you be happy while I, the other part of you——"

He rose hastily, called to Richard Medford to take the thing, and strode through the still passages to his bedroom that they might dress him for his wife's funeral. The new mourning Jacot had made for him was already laid out. His pages and squires waited with downcast eyes so that they might not seem to look upon his ravaged face. They washed and shaved him in heavy silence.

Never had Richard dressed more carefully. Anne had always been so interested in what he wore. He fastened the silver belt himself because it had been her birthday gift last Twelfth Day. " Yes, my love, occupy your fingers with such foolish trifles," she must be saying compassionately, " so that your heart has time to grow gradually into its loneliness."

When he was ready he looked himself over critically in the metal mirror as he always had done, to see if he were well-groomed enough to meet her. The black brocaded houppe-larde suited him, with his fair skin and red-gold hair and beard. But he was almost shocked to see how young it made him look. Only thirty, like many a gallant going a-wooing. And all happiness behind him.

He went to a window and looked down at the great concourse of people gathered to do honour to his Queen. He had summoned them, knights and wives, out of every county. It seemed so short a time ago since he had dictated the words to Medford. " Inasmuch as our beloved companion, the Queen, will be buried at Westminster, on Monday, the third of August next, we earnestly entreat that you (setting aside all excuses) will repair to our city of London. . . . We desire that you will, the preceding day, accompany the corpse of our dear consort from our manor of Sheen ; and for this we trust we may rely on you, as you desire our honour. . . . Given under our privy seal at Westminster, the 10th day of June, 1394."

His invitation had been a command. Such wording had brought them all. He went down to join them, and their respectful silence greeted him. Only the occasional whinny of a horse or the impatient clink of a bit broke the silence as he took up his place in a procession which began to move, like an endless black serpent, towards the age-old Abbey where Anne's embalmed body had lain in state for weeks.

Richard was conscious of the warm summer sun on his face —the mocking summer sun which once he had so blithely loved. Of the deep bell tolling. Of the sad dirge of priests and the uncontrollable sobbing of. London women. And then the maw of the great monastic building swallowed him up and the chill of it smote into his soul. Here he had come each evening to kneel beside her. Here for both of them was the end of mortal life. For here, during the long cold centuries, their speechless effigies must lie among the dusty violet shadows, staring unseeingly at time as yet unborn. Other lovers would stare at them, wonder about them a little, perhaps. For their enlightenment he would see that he and Anne lay hand in hand. Already he had spoken to Lote and Yevele, the masons —and to an expert brass worker—about it. And how shocked the uncles had been ! So human a touch had never been wrought—and on a royal tomb. and during the lifetime of one of them ! But then his own life was finished too, and never had a royal marriage been like theirs.

He was walking slowly up the aisle, just as he had walked on their wedding day. Only then Anne had been beside him, instead of lying beneath the great raised catafalque around which the priests and singing boys were gathered. Just as then, the Abbey was ablaze with candles. He had sent for wax specially out of Flanders. There must be nothing gloomy or niggardly about Anne's funeral. They shone like stars from the high altar, and made tall lakes of soft light about her little coffin.

And then, as the shifting haze of incense swung by a score of thurifers cleared a little, Richard saw the yawning gap of the vault beneath the stone-flagged floor. He came upon it so suddenly that Standish put out a hand to stay him; and with it came realization. He and Anne had come to the end of their road together. It took all his kingly training not to cry out. To tell all these solemn priests and officials that he would not let them put her beloved body down there. The beloved body that he had burned with passion—the tender fingertips he had so often kissed lest they be nipped in wintertime. Alone, in the cold dark, waiting for him to come.

"*Libera me, Domine, de morte aeterna, in die illa tremenda . . .*" intoned Archbishop Arundel, as colourless as Simon Sudbury had been vibrant.

In a detached sort of way, Richard measured the depth of the vault. Grave-diggers' ropes trailed gruesomely on either side down to the level of the crypt. It should be deep enough to break a man's neck. If he took a step or two forward—now— there would be for Anne no waiting alone . . .

But it was one thing to meet death violently, as Stafford had done. To go unshrived and unhouselled to one's Maker through no fault of one's own. But to take one's own life? So that men buried you at the crossroads with a knife through your body to keep your lost soul from wailing over the heath o'nights. That would be to lose Anne forever. . . .

"*Deus, cui proprium est misereri semper et parcere, te supplices exoramus pro animaet famulae tuae Anna . . .*"

But of course the words had nothing to do with Anne. Anne was a living spirit. A joyful, tender essence which could neither be entombed in cold marble nor barred behind the gates of Purgatory. Something beautiful that would always be about him. Something that even in the midst of the most ordinary occupations he must always catch at, and listen for and hold.

268

So that never could she try to make contact and find no one there, at the listening place of his soul.

"*Sanctus, Sanctus, Sanctus Dominus Deus Sabaoth. Pleni sunt coeli et terra gloria tua. Hosanna in excelsis. Benidictus qui venit in nomine Domini. Hosanna in excelsis.*"

A sort of spiritual ecstasy upheld him, as if she had been spared from Heaven to comfort him in this most mutilating moment of his life. Never again could they two be separated as when he had been in Scotland or Ireland, and she at Sheen. Whenever he was tired or disillusioned, or wanted to tell her something funny, she would be there—closer than his eyes or hands. She would laugh through his brain and linger in his senses, wrapping him round with the tenderness of her love. And she would be more utterly his than ever, because no one else would see or hear her or know that she was there.

But that was a selfish thought. One that she, of all people, would deplore. There were so many others who loved her. Not in the way that finishes life—but to the point of tears. Geoffrey Chaucer, who had perceived the beauty of her soul— and young Tom Holland, whose eyes had been red for days. He must bestir himself out of this introverted melancholy and try to comfort them for Anne's sake.

Richard looked about him for the first time with seeing eyes. At Mowbray, leaning on his sword, motionless and reverent as a crusader—at Lancaster and York, looking as if they had lost some cherished daughter of their own—at Gloucester, expressionless, standing a little apart. He saw household servants weeping unashamedly as bearers wearing the white hart badge began to lower the coffin, and looking to the humbler places in the nave, he made his usual unobtrusive sign to Mundina whose keen eyes probed only at the sorrow in his soul.

The priests had ceased intoning, monks and choristers no longer sang. There was only the slither of ropes and the straining of the bearers. And then the sad silence was broken by a dull banging of the great West door, and footsteps coming louder and louder up the aisle. Spurred footsteps that began to grate across Richard's consciousness before his ears had really heard them. Even at that solemn moment, heads turned furtively. Priests stood arrested in the performance of their office. Archbishop Thomas Arundel, standing on the altar steps, looked down the pillared length of aisle, and because he was blood relation of the intruder his hand trembled on the illuminated missal which a kneeling acolyte held for him.

There was a moving aside of crowded people, a murmured protest and a thrusting. The King watched and waited, his brow black with Plantagenet rage. Opposite to him, across the open vault, appeared Richard Arundel, shoving his way into the place left for him beside Gloucester. Arundel, carelessly dressed and mud-splashed, with Richard's carefully worded invitation in his hand. Arundel, clattering in half an hour late for the Queen's funeral. The insensate brute who had dared to keep her waiting in her lifetime, and had let her kneel to him.

John of Lancaster glared at him. Chaucer, whose life she had saved that day, stepped forward to bar his way. Even Edmund of York said " Hush !" and waved shocked hands.

But something snapped suddenly in the King's overwrought brain. The imposing scene lost reality and all the tall candles ran together into one piercing swordpoint of light. All he saw clearly was the dark vault yawning before him and Arundel's hawk-nosed face on the other side.

Joy—that forgotten thing—surged up in him. The joy of some leashed beast within him breaking its bonds. To the horror of all beholders, he leapt the grave and caught Arundel a stinging blow on the mouth, so that the blood flowed. All the savagery of his ancestors momentarily possessed him, and Richard was so much stronger than he looked. The earl reeled backwards, striking his skull on consecrated flagstones.

Richard was vaguely aware of the gasp that went up, of people running and the sharp echo of overturned faldstools.

Of Arundel's groans, and Gloucester bending over him, the anticipatory smirk wiped from his face.

"One day I will kill you both," Richard vowed. "But this is not the time or place."

Aloud he said nothing. There was nothing to be said. He strode out of the Abbey alone, by some side door, to face the perpetual darkness of his joyless life.

PART
3

" Through Death men come unto the Well of Grace,
Where green and lusty May doth ever endure."
—Chaucer.

" Je te salue, heureuse et profitable Mort ! "
—Ronsard.

CHAPTER XXV

" **I**T IS HIGH time you married again ! "

The words had hammered on Richard's brain all day. And the raucous voice of his Uncle Thomas, saying them. Saying them in full Council, of course, with Arundel and Warwick to back him. Where everyone took it for granted that a king owed it to his State, and even York jibbered about the necessity of getting an heir. Whatever Lancaster had felt, he had declined to enter into the debate. Richard had been thankful for his silence, although he knew that most people cynically attributed it to the fact that his own son, Henry Bolingbroke, stood second in succession to the throne.

The matter had been bound to crop up. Richard himself was well aware that Parliament had been wanting—and not daring —to broach the subject for months. He had been a widower for two years and whenever he rode abroad he saw the same dictum reflected more humanely in his subjects' eyes.

What did they take him to be, he wondered furiously. A pawn to be bartered irrespective of feeling for some foreign alliance ? Did they see him in their bovine minds as a bull or a stallion, to be mated solely for the purpose of producing high-bred stock ? And in any case, what did it matter about an heir apparent, with Roger Mortimer, whom he liked and trusted, doing so well in Ireland ? Of course, if it had been a question of the succession passing to *Henry*, who could be relied upon to plunge England into war within a few weeks . . .

Richard rose impatiently from his half-finished dinner at Westminster and called for his barge to be brought to the landing stage. When he gave an order these days he gave it without a smile, and men ran to do his bidding. They loved him still, their hearts still bled for him—for had they not known the Queen, and been privileged to see the happiness of his private life? But there was none of that good-humoured badinage which had once made them feel part of some delightful pageant. The King seldom troubled to explain to them the why or whither of a journey. His voice had a clipped authority; and although he laughed and said the polite things in public, his eyes never smiled. He never mentioned Anne's name.

He spared no time on masques and tournaments but went about with a quiet, calculating look, as if he were planning something bigger and biding his time. All the people he had loved so loyally were dead except Mundina, who had left the Wardrobe house in Carter Lane to be with him. He played chess with her of an evening, and applied the same technique to statecraft during the day time. One game was as fascinating as the other to a man who had only his brains left to live upon. And as long as he lived Richard meant to be a move ahead of his opponents' knights and to keep the king out of check. It pleased him that he no longer had need to explain even his most startling movements to anybody. He held England in the hollow of his hand.

" To Sheen," he ordered curtly, as soon as he had stepped aboard.

He saw Standish and young Holland exchange glances. It was two years since any of them had been to Sheen. Two years since he had held his dying wife in his arms through the long June night. Two years to the day. Probably that was what had prompted Gloucester to probe the wound.

Although Richard's mind worked inwardly, his unsmiling eyes were extraordinarily observant. As he sat under the silken awning, sped forward by the rhythmic muscles of his watermen, he noted everything going on on either bank and stored it up, subconsciously, for future use. It was a habit acquired early from Michael de la Pole. He remembered what meadows looked prosperous and which of the landowners, living in their stately riverside mansions, had sided with the Merciless Parliament. It wasn't that he intended to harm them, but so that he could hold it over them. He wanted power to render his enemies impotent. To reverse the humiliating position of his youth. The acquisition of power had become almost an obsession. And now that love was denied him, and pleasures palled, his mind had room to play with hatred.

He left his escort by the Sheen water gate and strode up alone through the neglected gardens. Anne's unpruned roses bloomed in wild profusion. Because their sweetness tore at his heart he brushed brusquely past them, scattering their loosened petals with his swinging sleeves. The smooth lawns where Chaucer had been wont to read to them stood high with tottle grass, and cobwebs spanned the richly glazed windows. Inside the palace all was shuttered and desolate. The few remaining servants, caught in their undirected sloth, stared at him unbelievingly as though he were a ghost.

Either their wits were slow, he supposed, or they had grown used to ghosts. But the way they stared sent his thoughts back to the bustle there had been that other June, when he had arrived unexpectedly, mudstained and sore with slander, and Anne had healed him. And to Robert de Vere, an expensive, tinkling echo out of the carefree past. Robert, whom he had allowed to die on foreign soil, but whose body he had had honourably brought home because of the numbed sort of love he still bore him.

Richard went straight to his wife's room.

Though bathed in the clear light of a summer's evening, it looked cheerless and bereft. But he had had to come here once again to sort out his mind before settling this question of re-marriage which was being forced upon him.

He stood just inside the door and rammed home the bolt behind him. His nostrils dilated, hunting some lost scent ; but only the impersonal dankness of a scrubbed and unused room came back to him. Instinctively, as one dodges a lacerating swordpoint, his eyes avoided the bed. After one quick comprehensive glance at the rest of the room, he went slowly to a cunningly carved armoire between the two tall windows. Mundina had told him there were papers there. Papers

277

belonging to Anne. Things treasured by her, perhaps. Trifles that no one had dared to touch because of the plague.

With the westering sunlight emphasizing the new faint lines about eyes and mouth, Richard drew a key from his wallet and opened the armoire. And here was the alchemy he sought. Faintly, yet more poignantly than sight or sound, the subtle perfume that had hung about Anne's clothes drifted out to him, transmuting time. Avidly, his whole being rushed out to meet it ; but after that first heady whiff it had no more power to intoxicate his senses with the past. The long line of lifeless dresses were just dresses. Even the faded pink one against which he pressed his cheek. Steadying himself, he jerked open an inner drawer. He lifted out the contents one by one. The heavy necklace he had loosened from her neck the last night he had been here ; the faded sprigs of broom he had given her —and forgotten he had given—all those years ago before he went to Scotland. A roll of his letters from Ireland—the love letters she had wanted, tied with a gay ribbon, and already yellowing. The original of a poem in Geoffrey Chaucer's fine script.

> " So passeth al my lady sovereyne,
> That is so good, so faire, so debonayre,
> I pray to God that ever fall she fayre ;
> For had no comfort been of her presence
> I had been dead withouten one defence
> For want of Love's wordes and his chere."

Yes, by her kindness and humility Anne had saved Chaucer's life—saved him to write this delightful series of Canterbury tales he was giving to the world. If only she had been able to save Simon Burley too ! Burley who would have said to him, " Be glad, my son, through all your suffering, that at least you are bearing it instead of her."

With reverent fingers, Richard untied the ribbon and unrolled his letters. He sat down on Anne's dressing stool and read them through. He was glad of their tenderness. Fleetingly, he recaptured the feel of that lost thing—happiness. But when he could read no more because of the waning light, illusion lingered.

He turned towards their shadowed bed. The familiar hangings were half drawn and, with the spell of the past hour upon him, he could almost believe that Anne lay there—just out of his sight, in the shadow of the rosy tapestry. That she would stir presently and call to him and stretch out warm arms. That the frozen bitterness holding him in thrall would be all broken up, and his heart warmed again with the love that other men enjoyed.

But reality lay in wait and he could hear no more. With a strangled cry he tore aside the hangings and threw himself across the empty bed, his face breaking into unspeakable grief. "Anne! Anne, my beloved! Never, never will I hold another woman in my arms," he vowed. "Never will I love with my body some new queen whom my spirit rejects as wife. No matter how they badger me . . . Not even for England . . ."

He lay there, where night after night they had lain together, sobbing against her pillow. The hard, rare sobs of manhood.

"What does it matter about sons, if they be not ours? We were complete—too young and too desperately in love to care. How were we to know this would happen? Thank God, we didn't know . . ." he whispered brokenly. And then, when his sobbing had subsided, "I suppose, if you had left me a son, my heart's love—if he had looked like you and spoken with my voice—he might have done the things we dreamed of for my country. Unhampered from the start. Lifting her above the common, warmongering, unreasoning rut. Making her a pattern state for all Christendom."

The dam of his restraint was broken. "Oh, Anne, my sweet, it is so long—so terribly long—since I saw you! Your dear kind hands, your funny little plucked brows and your smile. Dear Christ, do I have to go on living for years, bearing this daily desolation?"

279

Presently, he raised himself on straightened arms, still talking softly as if Anne lay back on the pillows between them. "I know what I will do. So that they don't drive even this wedge of physical infidelity between us." At the thought of Gloucester and Arundel something of that closed, crafty manner came back to him. "Even in this I will outwit them, using their very importunities to further my own purposes. I will marry the French king's daughter." He sat up and laughed, a little wildly. "She is eight years old. I don't remember her name. It should cement the alliance so that there is peace with France so long as I live."

He was surprised to see how dark it was. His sharp ears caught the sound of approaching footsteps. Someone knocked at the door. He passed a handkerchief over his face and pushed back his hair. When he strode to the door and threw it open, a loutish country servant stood there, bearing a torch.

"Well ? " demanded Richard, furious at the intrusion.

"It be growin' mortal dark," the man mumbled.

"It's been mortal dark for two years," retorted Richard.

The old man stared, gap-toothed, at the King's disordered hair and ravaged face. "Oi thought maybe you'd be wantin' a light, sir."

Richard banged the door in his face. What should he and Anne be wanting with lights—here, in this room, where they knew every stick of furniture. Where there had always been light to lighten their darkness. In this room where no lesser lovers must ever sleep.

With a hand still on the bolt, a thought came to him. He changed his mind and opened the door again. "Here, bring back your torch," he called.

Already the man had descended half a dozen stone steps. As he turned in surprise his shadow mimicked every clumsy movement on the wall behind him.

"The torch, fool ! " shouted Richard, stretching out an impatient hand. His voice echoed weirdly down the turret stair and he had no idea how crazed he looked in the shifting light.

With maddening slowness, still staring uncomprehendingly, the old man clambered up again and gave it to him.

"Go with the other servants to the gatehouse, and tell the grooms to loosen whatever horses you have left and turn them into the tilt yard," Richard ordered. "Go now, dolt, and do just as I say, or it may be too late."

He heard the man fumbling his way down in the dark. Heard him say to someone at the bottom, "The King be crazed with grief. For the blessed Martyr's sake, bring me a stable lantern!" And then their confused footsteps dying away.

Richard held the torch high above his head and hurled it into the middle of the great four-poster. The scorching smell reminded him momentarily of Wat Tyler's forge. Flames began to lick their way up a curtain to the embroidered tester where his leopards and Anne's ostrich were entwined. Soon sheets and pillows, love letters and poems—all would be consumed. He left door and windows wide. "Good-bye, my little love," he whispered through the drifting smoke. "Pray the compassionate Mother of God that we may find some more abiding trysting place!"

He went slowly down the stairs and through the deserted hall where they had been wont to feast in the heyday of their lives, laughing at the wits of a cultured world and listening to the poets and musicians they had gathered into the most civilized court in Europe. Out in the cool of the garden Richard paused, contritely, to pluck a red rose from Anne's favourite bush. Once, he looked back. Smoke and flames belched from their windows into the sweet June night. Soon the whole conflagration would be reflected, blood red, in the river below. Soon, soon, the lovely palace of Sheen would be only a memory in men's minds.

CHAPTER XXVI

Aᴜᴛᴜᴍɴ lay like a russet carpet along the Rother valley, and inside Bodiam castle fires were lighted of an evening on hearth and brazier. All along the kitchen side of the open courtyard cooks and scullions bustled over the final supper dish, while pages scuttled back and forth through the serving screens bearing nuts from Spain and rare Venetian flagons of their master's choicest contraband wines. Never had these seafaring Sussex folk thought to serve such distinguished guests.

Richard the Second had come unexpectedly. Moreover, he had brought with him a brace of dukes. Thomas Plantagenet of Gloucester and Thomas Mowbray of Norfolk; to say nothing of a tall witch of a woman who the royal squires said had been the King's nurse. Only a month ago a man had been snooping on behalf of the Clerk of the Works, whoever he might be. And Sir Edward had stopped work on the new harbour he was building between moat and river, and milady Lizbeth's temper had been sharper than ever. And now the King himself had come. It was all to do with Sir Edward building a brand new castle instead of fortifying his wife's old home, further inland, where the Rother was but an unnavigable stream. And people who built castles without a permit could be put in prison.

So the plumpest pigeons must be brought from the dovecots over the well tower and the tenderest venison stuffed and spiced to placate King Richard. Or else, the steward had warned, they would lose their service with an open-handed master and all the fun of occasional raids, and get the castle pulled down again about their ears.

As often as they dared, grooms and maidservants who were not privileged to wait upon the company would slip along the buttery passage to peep at this powerful king through the carved wood of the screens. But he was youngish and fair and easily the most attractive-looking man on the dais, the maids reported; and he didn't look at all angry. In fact, he had set his abashed host at ease and was laughing outright at Dalyngrigge's tales of nefarious adventure, and exchanging reminiscences with his hostess who, it seemed, had been in his mother's household. And Milady—proud piece as she was—seemed all bemused by him. And small wonder!

Richard himself was perfectly aware of the household anxiety, and was playing on it quite successfully to get his uncle quietly conveyed to Calais. Mowbray, as Governor of the place, would normally have crossed from Sandwich or Dover, of course. But Gloucester needed a little persuasion; and it would be as well, perhaps, if the two of them were not seen leaving England together.

" Judging by Dalyngrigge's yarns and the taste of his Malvoisie, you should have plenty of sport with French ships in the Channel, Uncle Thomas," Richard said encouragingly. " It'll be quite like old times. Do you remember the French wine you and Arundel charmed the Londoners with when you wanted Simon and Michael out of the way ? "

Gloucester stirred uneasily in spite of the excellent wine. He never knew quite how to take Richard when he spoke in that silky sort of voice. It had all been so much easier when he used to rage and stammer.

" Besides, a change of air will do you good," urged Mowbray.

" Hasn't the poor Duke been well ? " inquired Lizbeth, putting all her charm into playing the perfect hostess.

" A little queasy, Lady Dalyngrigge," Richard explained, without giving Gloucester a chance to protest. " That's why I'm bothering your husband to take him abroad. Only last week Doctor Waldby—you remember old Waldby, my dear—remarked to me, ' The Duke looks rather like your poor brother Thomas before he died.' But he's been grieving for Richard Arundel, no doubt. They were always such friends, you know." Presented with the cook's elaborate confection of sugared marzipan, he obligingly waved away the best portion to his uncle on the chivalric principle of feeding a condemned man well. "My kinsman of Norfolk, on the contrary, stands up very well to the execution of his father-in-law, don't you, Tom?"

Richard folded back his gold-lined over-sleeve fastidiously so that it shouldn't get in the way of the sweet, and admired the chasing on the goblet set before him, which he strongly suspected had been stolen from some sacked Continental church. "Oh, and by the way, Tom," he ordered with his usual generosity. "Be sure to give Uncle Thomas my own apartments in the Citadelle. Very commodious I found them when I stayed there on my way to Paris last month. And such fine views over the harbour!"

"Is it true that you are going to be married again, sir?" asked Lizbeth, greatly daring.

"To the Princess Isabel of France. Hadn't you heard?" answered Richard affably. "But then of course, you've been so long away from Court. Ten years, isn't it? And you look lovelier than ever!" He smiled at her devastatingly over the golden goblet, and raised it politely to his host. "Let me congratulate you, Dalyngrigge. A bewitching wife and a strongly embattled castle. Three portcullises and a barbican. Let me see, who did you say was your architect?"

Richard was never drunk, but tonight he was scarcely sober. There was a pleasant haze over everything—candles and heaped dishes on the long table, Lizbeth's warm eyes, her husband's castle which was his for the taking, and the obvious discomfiture of Gloucester and Mowbray, the two red-clad knights whose fortunes he was playing with at the moment. Yes, clearly the white King was out of check and it was his move next. Mundina, sitting silently at the far end of the table, was aware of the undercurrent of excitement animating him into a sinister semblance of his former self. Tonight for him was evidently an occasion.

Dalyngrigge, who had no wish to discuss architecture, rose hurriedly with some mumbled excuse about arranging accommodation amidships since at the last minute the King had asked him to take Mundina Danos. Already he had seaboots on his feet and an ugly looking mace hanging from his belt. "We must weigh anchor almost immediately, sir, or I shall miss the tide," he warned.

"Then you and Gloucester will be wanting to get along, Tom." Richard leaned back comfortably in his chair and looked straight at Gloucester. "Don't let me detain you, dear Uncle, if you've any last-minute affairs to attend to. There's always so much to think of, isn't there, before one sets out on a long journey?"

This time the inflexible note beneath the smoothness of Richard's voice frightened Gloucester. He sat for a moment or two, regarding him in a baffled sort of way from beneath bushy brows. Richard's beauty was untarnished, his manner self-assured; and Gloucester had an idea that this nephew he always hated was playing on his fears just as he himself had so often tortured a boy's sensitive nerves, by harping on the horrid motif of Berkeley castle. Gloucester was a Plantagenet and above the law, of course. But the sharp fate of Arundel had shaken him, warning him that it would be as well to be out of England for a while. And as Mowbray had been good enough to invite him. . . . Besides, it was true—he *had* been feeling queasy of late. Even his brother Edmund had noticed it and started fussing and telling him he needed a change. And Edmund wouldn't be a party to any sort of plot. . . .

So Gloucester rose sulkily and went out, and Lizbeth, like a perfect chatelaine, excused herself and went with him to give orders for the comfort of her departing lord.

"Should you say that Calais *is* particularly healthy?" asked Richard, detaining his host for a moment after the other two had gone.

"It stinks," grinned Dalyngrigge, without euphemism.

"Quite," agreed Richard. "And I suppose quite a lot of

people die of fever there from time to time. There'd be nothing surprising about it, I mean?" He got up as the servants began to clear, and his manner became more informal. He picked up a handful of nuts from the littered table and began cracking them between excellent teeth. "Oh, and another thing, Tom," he went on, spitting out the shells. "Besides having a fine view, the royal apartments in the Citadelle have a backstair. Did you know? I noticed particularly. There was a time when I found it safer to notice that sort of thing whenever I stayed in strange houses. It appears to lead into a kind of closet behind the arras at the back of the bed. Very handy, I thought, for some of my disreputable ancestors' amours."

Richard hadn't troubled to lower his voice and Mowbray glanced nervously at the place where Mundina was still sitting after the departure of the dais party. Dalyngrigge's mind was on more personal matters. "My castle and everything in it is at your disposal, sir," he said warily, preparing to depart.

"Thank you. Everything except your wife, I take it?" smiled Richard. "But I shall be leaving early tomorrow morning."

Dalyngrigge was painfully aware of just how much his castle *was* at the King's disposal. Too painfully aware to dissimulate. "And the—er—little matter of the surveyor you sent?" he stammered.

The King stroked his pointed, golden beard. It was wonderful the power a good memory combined with de la Pole's advice gave one over people. "His report will probably come before me during the course of the next few weeks. And by that time, given fair wind and no contretemps, no doubt we shall all have something more important to think about," he prophesied cheerfully.

The old campaigner's weatherbeaten face was almost comic in its expression of relief. He had put years into building Bodiam and knew it to be the last word in domesticated defence. He bent gratefully to kiss the King's hand.

"Only remember, my dear Dalyngrigge," warned Richard, "there are some adventures it is wiser not to be amusing about—even at your own supper table!"

Dalyngrigge had no illusions about the inflexibility beneath Richard's pleasant voice. A long time ago he had seen him tackle a dangerous mob singlehanded, and he had been sorry when Gloucester and Arundel had cancelled out his courage afterwards. To his simple mind it seemed natural enough that the King should want to get his own back. They understood each other perfectly.

When their host had gone Mundina, who had no unmethodical last-minute packing to do, went to warm herself at the logs burning in the centre of the hall, and Mowbray lingered to face Richard uneasily across the deserted supper table. "Are you sure you want this—thing—done, Richard?" he asked, in a low voice.

Richard knew that a man with such divided loyalties must want to regain his friendship or his favour very badly to allow himself to get mixed up in such a scheme at all. "Why not?" he asked lightly, letting his handful of empty shells cascade onto a silver platter.

Physically Mowbray was brave as a lion; but the instinct of a gambler was not in him. Even when staying loyal to the King might have turned the tide before Radcot Bridge, he hadn't relished taking the risk. As a youth he had been gullible, and always he had hated being on the losing side. "Mightn't it—I mean, with your uncle's blood on your hands—mightn't it come between you and *her*—God rest her sweet soul?" he stammered, crossing himself and venturing upon the only argument which he supposed would bear any weight at this eleventh hour.

Only a slow thinker like Mowbray could fail to know that the question must have been in Richard's mind for months, or to deduce that otherwise Gloucester would long since have been dead. Richard didn't answer at once. One of his fine hands was playing absently with a knife lying on the laced

287

napery. "God will understand," he murmured after a moment or two, as if trying to reassure himself. And then—perhaps because Tom Mowbray was like a bit left over out of his old life—he actually tried to explain, rather desperately. "He must know there are worse things than killing the body, Tom, Sudbury, Burley, Brembre—it's over for them now, and they're with her. But what have those two done to me?" He found himself looking at Mowbray almost appealingly. "You remember me, don't you, when I was eager, generous, full of fine enthusiasms? They thwarted me here and betrayed me there. They poisoned my people against me. Blurred my intelligence with cunning, and destroyed my soul. I tell you, if ever it were true what the Book says about its being better for a millstone to be hanged about a man's neck, it's true about them! In the sight of God they must be Evil incarnate."

His hand on the knife shaft shook. "If only I could do it myself!" he said.

"You got Arundel impeached and executed," Mowbray reminded him. "Oh, I know it was all legal. You never lifted a finger. Only gave him rope enough to hang himself. And although he was my own father-in-law, I believed every bit of evidence you had brought against him."

"Yes," agreed Richard, as if the carefully built up evidence had had nothing much to do with it. "He was late for the Queen's funeral."

They both stopped talking as Gloucester's voice was heard bellowing out in the courtyard about the bestowal of his baggage. Mowbray went to join him and Richard strolled with him as far as the outer door, where he stood laughing and chatting and saying good-bye. It was a crisp moonlight night, with a touch of frost in the air.

"Don't stand there without a cloak, sir. The evenings grow chilly," Mundina called after him.

"Oh, I must just see the last of Uncle Thomas," he called back so naturally that it was hard to believe he meant the words quite literally.

From where he stood he could hear the creak of chain and windlass and an echoing splash of water. And presently two maidservants emerged from the dark archway of the well tower, giggling and slipping on a patch of water spilled on the smooth flagstones, as they bore their slopping buckets towards the busy kitchen. In the deep shadow just outside the archway Gloucester was bending to adjust a buckle. Richard strolled in his direction. The soft kid of his indoor shoes made no sound. An accidental stumble in the darkness, a strong push on the wet patch, perhaps. . . . But poor Dalyngrigge had probably spent much time and labour on his water supply ; and it was always better to do things decently and in order. . . . When Gloucester looked up again, Richard was leaning against the wall, whistling between his teeth to keep out the cold. And presently that minx Lizbeth had left her wifely duties and was making eyes at him again. " What is Princess Isabel like ? " she was asking, womanlike.

" Very charming, I thought. An elfin combination of light brown hair and hazel eyes, and a touch of that pale delicacy which so often makes French girls look delicate when they're not." The prospective bridegroom's dispassionate voice carried clearly to all who cared to hear, and he glanced down amusedly at the jealous fury in his companion's eyes. " She is just eight years old," he added.

Lizbeth let out a little laugh of sheer joy. " Aren't you coming down to the harbour with us, sir ? " she coaxed, slipping a persuasive hand through his arm. " It's such a lovely night."

" I'll come presently," promised Richard. " I must just say good-bye to Mundina Danos."

" Why do you have to waste so much time on that ugly old woman ? " pouted Lizbeth.

" Is she ugly ? I expect I'm too used to her to notice," he answered, with exasperating nonchalance.

Lizbeth lifted her own enchanting face framed in a becoming white fur hood. " Oh, Richard, you used not to be so blind about a woman's looks ! " she whispered.

Beneath the rising moon courtyard and castle were barred in sable and silver like a shield. Richard could see Edward Dalyngrigge watching them. Clearly the great ruffian, who could have broken his wife's neck with a twist of his fingers, lived only for her contemptuously given favours. "You see, Mundina happens to be the only woman on earth I still love," he said firmly, and turned back up the steps into the great hall.

The servants had finished clearing the dishes and the trestles had been pushed back against the richly tapestried walls. Mundina still sat where he had left her, as if she knew that he would come.

"Why didst thou suddenly decide to go with them?" he asked, in the warm patois of Aquitaine.

"I told thee, *mon cher*," she answered comfortably. "I have business to see to in Bordeaux. About my late brother's vineyards."

"Couldn't Jacot have gone?"

"No. Jacot may be able to make you marvellous clothes, but he couldn't do what I am going to do."

It was true enough. Like many men of genius, the little tailor had no head for business. Probably Mundina even made up his exorbitant accounts. Richard swung around to her, with one of his old impulsive gestures. "Mundy—I've always wanted to ask you. Your people were big landowners, weren't they? Why did you marry Jacot?"

The old woman looked up at him, her eyes bright with affection. "So as to be near you," she told him, without subterfuge.

Richard went and leaned over the back of her chair, with a hand gripping each of her gaunt shoulders. "I think I have always known it," he said. But he realized better now what it must mean to a woman to give herself to a man she didn't love.

"You didn't mind my asking you to arrange for them to take me, Dickon? I'm getting old, you know . . ." With rare demonstrativeness she raised a bony hand to cover one of his.

"I've told Mowbray to look after you. And you'll be sure to rest at Calais?"

"Yes, my dear. I will rest at Calais."

"I shall miss you horribly—and our games of chess," he said, helping her to rise.

"I think you're getting too good a player," she chuckled. "You always seem to win."

"Well, anyhow, you must come back soon because I'm soon going to fetch my new little Queen home from France and I shall want you to look after her."

Mundina did not answer, and they walked the length of the empty hall together. But because she had nursed him through sickness and made puppet shows for him when he was small, she could almost read the inner workings of his mind. "*Quand cette pauvre gosse soit arrivée à l'âge de puberté, qu'est ce que tu va faire, Richard?*" she asked anxiously.

He did not deny her foresight of his intentions. "I've been wondering . . . If the Pope knew that the marriage hadn't been consummated, perhaps she and Roger's son . . ."

"It could be, Richard. But if you can't be happy in this world I want you to be happy in the next. That's why— without condemning you—I wish——"

Half sentences were enough for them. Richard stopped on the threshold to look searchingly at the lined, wise old face that Lizbeth had called ugly. "You know, then?" he asked sharply.

"I'm not a fool. I've guessed for days. And I've always known that you would have to kill him sooner or later."

"And you're worrying about what Mowbray said—about it coming between me and—her?"

Mundina sniffed contemptuously. "I'd thought of it long before Thomas Mowbray!"

"He only said it because he didn't relish being made a tool of. Besides, as Robert de Vere used to tell us, 'Mowbray is very religious.'"

Mundina looked at him shrewdly as they crossed the

courtyard. "So are you, Richard Plantagenet—in a different sort of way," she said. "Only you've suffered so much that just now you're in a dangerously callous mood."

Richard didn't answer. He was thinking of that odd moment of temptation by the well tower. All his days he had been wont to spare life.

They passed beneath the three iron-toothed portcullises and out under the massive gate-house tower, with the arms of Dalyngrigge and Wardeaux and the martlets of Sussex carved in stone above the impregnable door. Richard slipped an arm through hers to guide her along the narrow, sharply angled causeway across the moat. At the Barbican, Dalyngrigge's guard sprang to the salute. Mundina should have felt like a queen, not like a heart-torn Rachel weeping for her children.

They could see lanterns bobbing about down by the river, and the riding light of the *Laughing Lizbeth* like a red star entangled in the trees. Halfway across the short meadow path Mundina paused to look back at the lovely lighted castle. A good deal of her life had been spent in castles. In them there had been birth and death, gaiety and danger—and always, for her, the homecoming of Richard Plantagenet's smile. "As you know, I'm an idolatrous old woman. I have served my idols on this earth, and probably God will punish me." She spoke slowly, and her eyes came back to him, standing bareheaded beside her in the moonlight. "But because I believe in Heaven for people like you—because I've seen it shining about you, as milady Anne did—nothing in this world or the next must ever come between you two."

The last word was said between them—the last intimate thought touched upon. The anchor of the *Laughing Lizbeth* was being weighed. Her stately, castellated stern and crimson sails seemed to fill the narrow river. Gloucester and Mowbray were leaning on the rail. Dalyngrigge had snatched a last moment ashore to bid farewell to his lady, who was standing on the little quay surrounded by her women.

When Richard came to the gangplank he felt Mundina

trembling. She thrust out a hand from the sombre folds of her cloak and caught fiercely at his own. "Dickon!" she whispered, and for the first time he saw tears in her eyes.

"Why, Mundy!" he protested. The wind was set fair and it was so short a way to France. He took her in his arms and kissed her tenderly before them all.

"Take care of her!" he shouted up the ship's side to Mowbray. "She is all I have."

CHAPTER XXVII

RICHARD had had a long day. He yawned as he climbed the short stair to the Dalyngrigges' guest room above the postern gate. He was glad they had put him here and not in the west wing near the priest's room and the chattering of the ladies' bower. Nor in the family apartments where he would probably have felt he must sit up late and be polite to Lizbeth. He had brought only his two most trusted squires, and he dismissed them both. He had plenty to think about and he wanted to be alone.

After the formality of palaces, the comfortable little room was a pleasant surprise. A good fire burned on the low arched hearth and a modern garderobe recess was built in the wall. The floor rushes had a sweet, countrified smell, and quaint, surprised-looking unicorns were embroidered on the bed hangings. Small cousins, surely, to the unicorn rampant on Dalyngrigge's shield. Anne would have loved them.

Richard unbuttoned his brocaded houppelarde and threw it over a carved chest. He went to the window overlooking the postern drawbridge. Moonlight had transmuted the russet of the countryside into silver. The half-finished quay was deserted. How quiet everything was after Westminster! How still the absurd little river! Dalyngrigge would be slipping out from Rye into the open sea by now, setting his course for Calais. Richard said a hurried *Ave* for Mundina, hoping she wouldn't be seasick. But the Channel could be as rough as it liked for Gloucester, who'd made such a hog of himself over that spiced venison. Gloucester who wouldn't need many more suppers. . . . But it didn't do to think about that. One didn't sleep.

Someone came quietly into the room behind him. Standish, no doubt, with that nightly concoction Mundina insisted upon. " I thought I told you I shouldn't want you any more," he reprimanded sternly. But after all, if one had been sleeping badly, perhaps it would be better to have company for a while. " Well, since you *are* here, get out the dice, Ralph," he ordered, without turning around. " I'll play you for that new wench of yours until our Epicurean suppers have gone down."

No one answered, and Richard turned swiftly, warned by some exotic scent.

Lizbeth stood there, laughing at him.

" By all the Saints——" he began, staring at her.

" I didn't come here to dice," she told him. She was more bewitching than ever by candlelight, with the soft fur cloak she had worn on the quay held sketchily around some flimsy kind of bed-wrap, and her raven hair all unbound about her shoulders. " Ralph Standish has gone to bed. And so have all our own servants," she added coolly, setting down the lantern that had lighted her way from the southeast tower.

" I see."

" I came to see if they had made you comfortable," she lied, losing face a little before his unresponsiveness and perfunctorily looking over the appointments of his room.

" Haven't you a steward or any chamber grooms ? " he inquired sarcastically.

" Oh, don't be cross, Richard ! It's so long since I saw you." She prowled about him, touching his jewelled belt and the silk of his shirt sleeve, with all the sensuous pleasure of a home-coming cat. " *You* haven't changed much either, you know. Except for the little beard. And I like it. It's exciting, some-how. Perhaps because it makes you look as if you could be dangerous. You kept them all deliciously afraid of you at supper time, didn't you ? " She went to the fire to warm her toes, shrugging the cloak from her shoulders and looking back at him with an enticing smile. " It was lovely of you to come at last, Richard ! And so clever to choose that child for a bride. And now that you will be going back and forth to France you can often come this way."

He scarcely appeared to be listening, but his grimness had given place to a wide grin. "He didn't lock you into your stays, then?" he remarked, looking at the alluring outline of her body silhouetted through rosy damascene against the flames.

"What do you mean?" Lizbeth hated being made fun of. She turned, affronted. And Richard remembered his manners. However wanton his hostess, he didn't have to stand there insulting her. "Oh, nothing," he said, turning away negligently. "Just something somebody once said."

This was scarcely the reception Lizbeth had expected. Doubt assailed her complacency. She raised widely flared nostrils, like some startled animal. "You wanted me, didn't you? That's why you came, isn't it? And sent Edward away."

The sharp contempt in Richard's voice whipped across the intimacy of the firelit room. "God, Lizbeth, you don't seriously suppose I'd deliberately send my host away and seduce his wife, do you?"

"Then why *did* you come?"

He perceived that he had given her wantonness some cause. Dalyngrigge was not the man to have betrayed the nature of their business. And to a woman whose beauty was notorious, and whose vanity was fed by a husband's undiminished and unrequited passion, the almost furtive nature of his visit might well have looked like that.

He offered her a chair, but she preferred the foot of the bed. Kicking off her ermine slippers, she sat there provocatively framed by her husband's prancing unicorns—giving them, as some ribald imp in Richard's mind observed, something to look surprised about.

"You won't be seducing me," she said softly, her eyes a smouldering invitation beneath up-curled lashes. "I've always been yours—in desire. And you know it. The violation was when you made me marry *him*. A great clumsy devil who cages me in this God-forsaken place and comes to bed with his blood-stained boots on! Who'd strangle me if I smiled out of sheer boredom at that shaven priest down there, and yet can't keep faith with me if he goes on a three days' foray!"

"Oh, come, Lizbeth! He isn't as bad as that," protested Richard, with compunction. "Look how he trusts you—tonight, for instance."

"It's you he trusts—not me!" she spat at him, and could have bitten her tongue out as soon as the words were spoken. For she, of all people, ought to have known Richard long enough to take into account his loyalty.

"Oh, what does it matter anyway?" she hurried on, trying to cover her mistake. "I know why you made me marry him, and because of that I've tried to forgive you."

"Forgive me?" As a king, Richard had to laugh at her brazen impudence. "I'd be interested to know what reason you ascribe to me—other than the normal one of having a marriageable ward and wanting his money?"

Life had made Lizbeth too sure that with all men the delight of her body excused the sharpness of her tongue. "It's obvious isn't it?" she shrugged. "Because you yourself had to marry. A girl you'd never seen. To beget an heir. You weren't in love with her and——"

Richard dragged her off his bed and shook her until the damascene slipped from her pointed breasts. She had roused him from his nonchalance at last. "Be quiet, will you, you jade?" he shouted at her, his face white with anger.

But no Wardeaux had ever wanted courage. "You weren't! You know you weren't!" she snarled back. "And yet you were too fastidious to offend your wife with an affair like any other man. But when Robert de Vere was making love to Agnes, you were so nearly in love with me—you thought you'd better find me a husband!"

"You were always singularly intelligent, Lady Dalyngrigge," he mocked, trying to keep a hold on himself.

Nothing had been denied to Lizbeth de Wardeaux as a child, and now, at thirty, she was grasping for the only thing she had ever really wanted. Something that money couldn't buy. " That day you kissed me by the pool at Westminster——"

" Don't tell me I loved you! I never in my life came within miles of loving you! " broke in Richard. " For an hour or two I may have lusted after you. I suppose most young men about the Court did at that time."

" Yet you sent me a message that you were at Sheen——"

" As far as I remember, Robert and I had a bet about it."

Lizbeth threw back the heavy strands of her hair. Her eyes were angry as a tiger's. She went back to the hearth and beat with clenched fists upon the stone canopy. " And when I got to Sheen—they told me you were with the Queen! " she cried, in a strangled sort of voice. She stood for a while resting her forehead against the stone. By some sort of just reckoning it seemed that she, who nightly tormented Edward Dalyngrigge, must be driven suppliant to Richard Plantagenet. She turned to him with a sort of wistful, impassioned earnestness. " Oh, I don't deceive myself. I know that no other woman ever existed for you afterwards. But I'm not asking for that stained-glass sort of love. I shouldn't know what to do with it." She came and sat on the edge of the hutch where his houppelarde lay, beseeching him. " I only want your kisses, Richard, and to feel that coldness in you run to flame. Not because you're a king . . ."

" I know that."

" Richard, I've waited ten years for you to come——"

Between pity and his driven senses, he turned to her almost savagely. " Why must you make me hate myself? I don't forget that you saved my mother's life. Nor the fun we all had before—Radcot Bridge. But a man doesn't want cheap tavern stuff once he has drunk good wine——"

A new look of amazement came into her beautifully chiselled face. It was as if she were really thinking about him for the first time. " But now that your life is dust and ashes, Richard? You must long sometimes to forget."

He leaned wearily against one of the carved bedposts. "There is nothing I want to forget. I treasure every moment," he said.

"And you seriously mean that all these months—with all the girls who must be enamoured of you—there's never been another woman?"

"Since you are impertinent enough to ask—no, there hasn't."

It seemed incredible to Lizbeth. "And you mean to go on trying to live like that for the rest of your life?"

She approached him gradually, almost gaping at him as she came. "You make me wonder—is it true what people say about you—that you were sired by one of the priests in the Bordeaux abbey where you were born? Are you a saint or something?"

Richard laughed harshly. "On the contrary, I'm a very thorough-going sinner. My conscience is black as hell. So black that I can't sleep o' nights. If you could see into my mind, my dear Lizbeth, strumpet as you are—you'd shrink from me!"

She was too accustomed to living with men of violence to shrink from evil consciences, and his very indifference excited her. She slipped bare arms about his neck. "Then what further harm can it do to sin or sleep if I stay with you to-night?" she pleaded.

He still stood unresponsive. "You pretty fool! It has nothing to do with goodness. Can't you understand that when Anne died all that part of me died too? For ever."

She drew away then, half incredulous, half fearful. Almost as if he were something inhuman. And as if to prove the thing he said, both to her and to himself, he suddenly reached out and pulled her half naked body close against his own, kissing her roughly till he bruised her. Those moist, seductive lips that so many other men had thirsted for. Lizbeth closed her eyes in ecstasy. But after a moment or two he released her, and struck her open, avid mouth lightly with the back of his hand. And somehow he managed to make the blow less offensive than the kiss.

She recoiled from him as though he had stripped the lure of her warm flesh to the repulsive bone. "I would sooner you had beaten me," she breathed.

But he only laughed, a little insanely, glad for the proved triumph of his constancy. People shouldn't tempt him to half the sins in the decalogue all in one day like this.

"It's not being a strumpet, to desire one man all one's life —so that even until one grows old and passion passes one can find joy with none other," she protested presently. All the proud, laughing fire had gone out of her voice, and she was half crouching against the bed hangings.

He turned and looked at her with understanding compassion. "My poor Lizbeth," he said.

When she gathered herself up, her movements were no longer lithe and young. She had learned so much in so short a time. "Just occasionally, I suppose, only one insatiable love is given to a woman——" she whimpered.

Richard picked up her cloak and put it across her shoulder. "And—more occasionally still—to a man," he agreed.

He wandered to the window and stood there with his back to her, trying not to hear her sobs of self-pity. After a while he heard her whimper her way towards the door and down the winding stair. Although he did not see the actual moment of her going, at some point he knew himself to be alone, and eased his strained emotions with a deep sigh. In a few moments, as far as he was concerned, it was as if she had never been.

The moon had risen high above his vision, shedding a gentle silver radiance on the smooth turf of the tilt yard and on the lush river meadows beyond. Somewhere in the beech trees an owl hooted. The water of the moat looked black and fathomless in the shadow of the castle wall, and on its surface, cupped by a darker bed of floating pads, glimmered a single water lily left over from summer. To Richard's longing eyes it looked like the little white soul of Anne.

As always, the perfection of the night's beauty was like a sword, stabbing at his loneliness.

"Anne! Anne!" he whispered softly. And instantly the reassurance of her abiding love came back to him.

He leaned against the stone embrasure with closed eyes, letting her tenderness enfold him. For a few blessed moments all the frets and plottings of the day were blotted out. But to-night he could not keep his mind blank enough. Other thoughts kept crowding in. Suppose Mowbray's warning were true? Already this thing he planned to do in Calais was intruding upon Anne's influence. Coming between them. What was the good of pretending to Mundina that it wasn't so? Of brazening it out? Deep in his soul he knew that if Anne had lived she would never have let him become a murderer. That he was sacrificing some part of his love for her to his hatred of Gloucester. That if he did this thing, the unappeased Christ must always come between her white soul and his guilt.

"Everything that I have or am that man has spoiled, dear God!" he moaned. "All my life he has been goading me to this hour, and if it be accounted mortal sin to kill such vermin why, why should the punishment be mine?"

He turned, shivering, to his cold bed. The fire had burned low and the servants were long since asleep. He kicked the door shut and closed the casement. The following wind had freshened. Running before it, Dalyngrigge's ship must be halfway to France by now.

CHAPTER XXVIII

WESTMINSTER PALACE was in a turmoil of preparation for the state visit to France. The regalia was brought from the Jewel Tower, and courtiers were getting out their best furs. Servants must have new liveries and horses new trappings. And even Mathe, a new collar. The ladies who were invited were either vying with each other over the height of their headdresses, or deep in dudgeon because "that governess of the Lancasters" was now a duchess and—until the new Queen came—the first lady in the land.

In his private apartments the King was trying on his resplendent new clothes. Bed and chairs were strewn with them. Pages bumped into each other, running back and forth with coloured leather shoes and scented gloves and other modish accessories. Squires and gallants who prided themselves on being dressed in the *dernier cri* were struck dumb with admiration for such sartorial genius.

This was Jacot's hour.

He was fitting the cloth of gold houppelarde his master was to wear to his meeting with the King of France. And Richard Plantagenet, that super-critic of beautiful fashions, was regarding his reflection with satisfaction in the long metal mirror. Jacot's dark hair was winged with grey, but he bobbed round his royal client with the same ecstatic, simian movements as of yore.

"Well, Jacot, any news of Mundina?" asked Richard leisurely, when the more breathless moments of suspense were over.

"News, sir?" repeated Jacot absently, marking an alteration of the fraction of an inch in a seam.

"From France."

The little tailor looked up, more like a puzzled monkey than ever. " I don't understand, sir, I thought she was here with you. I was going to see her presently——"

" But surely, Jacot, you knew she asked me to arrange for her to cross to Calais with the Duke of Norfolk ? On her way overland to Bordeaux ? "

Jacot laid down his chalk and blinked. " To Bordeaux, sir ? "

" To settle up her brother's estate or something."

Richard was holding up to the light a selection of rings a page had handed him, and he had put them all back on their black velvet cushion before he noticed her husband's curious reactions.

" Mundina never had a brother," Jacot said.

Their eyes met in the reflecting mirror. They had both forgotten about the houppelarde. " I thought it strange at the time that she had never mentioned him. But Mundina is like that," said Richard slowly.

When a couple of his gentlemen had eased the gorgeous garment from his shoulders, he walked over to a window recess and beckoned Jacot to follow him. " You had better come with me to Calais," he said. " I told her to rest when she got there. And the Governor sent a message by Sir Edward Dalyngrigge to say that she seemed none the worse for the journey and left the Citadelle a week later with two of his own servants."

" Since milord of Norfolk says she is on her way to Bordeaux——"

But all Richard's sense of security as a child had been staked on Mundina. Never once had she deceived him. Why should she lie to him now ? " All the same, you had better question the servants. And make inquiries in the streets. You're a Frenchman. They'll tell you things." Come to think of it, there were quite a number of things one would like to know. " And while you go about it, unpick my badge from your cloak," Richard added.

The word " Calais " was on everybody's lips that winter—and on their minds. The King was going to France to fetch his new bride. How strange to have a child for a queen! Though better by far than having a bad queen out of France like the second Edward. And if King Richard had chosen anyone grown up she'd need to be an angel, God help her, after their beloved Bohemian one!

People lingered about the palace, watching all the going and coming by day, and then looking up at the lighted windows. For what was going on in there concerned them intimately. The King was not only going to get married. He was going to sign a peace treaty. Something to last for years, this time. Well, perhaps it really *would* last now that Gloucester was out of the way. Men lowered their voices when they said " out of the way." The words had a sinister sound and they weren't clear what had really happened to him. He had gone to stay in Calais because of his health, and news had leaked through that he was dead. Nobody knew quite how or when. Some said he had died of fever, others that he had been murdered. Probably by the King's orders. Anyway, it had come at a mighty convenient time.

Thomas of Gloucester, with his everlasting warmongering, wasn't such a popular figure that he'd be greatly missed. And relaxation from this ever-recurring fear of invasion would be a relief. Young married men would be able to till their fields or go about their business without the nagging feeling that any year they might be called away to war. But it was to be hoped the King in his zeal for peace wouldn't sign away Calais! England without Calais would be like a house without a front door. The very word Calais touched an Englishman's pride.

Richard himself was mindful of it when it came to leaving Calais for St. Omer. " God knows I'll have finessed and fought for this peace as hard as ever my father fought in battle," he said, while Standish and Tom Holland were putting the finishing touches to his grandeur before meeting King Charles.

Young Holland was Duke of Kent now and went with him everywhere. " Do you remember, sir, how implacable Gloucester was when we came before ? Even when the French lords loaded him with gifts ? " he asked, kneeling to fasten the Garter above his uncle's knee. " And how you had to bribe him to take himself and his ill manners home again before he started another war ? "

" It cost me as much as a dozen of the dinners he was always grumbling about," laughed Richard reminiscently. He could afford to laugh now.

" Well, thank God, he won't be here to spike everything this time ! " said Standish, arranging the ermine cloak.

Richard said nothing. A fortnight after Mowbray had sailed from Bodiam, Dalyngrigge had brought back news that Gloucester was dead. The two other uncles had gone into mourning, and he fancied that they had looked askance at him. And if, during the long conscience-ridden nights, he often wished the deed undone, he had persuaded himself that it was part of the price he must pay for peace.

On the whole he was in better spirits. His life's policy was about to be crowned with success. Simon Burley and Michael de la Pole seemed very close to him as he rode forth to St. Omer. The whole journey seemed propitious. He got on well with Frenchmen, speaking their language and often thinking their thoughts ; and he always had had much in common with his future father-in-law, who wasn't much older than himself. Each of them had managed to throw off the yoke of avuncular control. Each of them had made his Court a cultural centre. They had books and architecture and the chase to talk about—and neither of them had really wanted war. True, the French Queen hinted that poor Charles was as mad as a maypole at times. " And perhaps we even have that in common, too ! " thought Richard, remembering the grief-crazed hours in which he envisaged an eternity spent apart from Anne.

There was all the usual ceremonial feasting and display, but within the golden tent prepared for them, he and Charles and

Lancaster, with the powerful Dukes of Burgundy and Orleans, managed to talk some sound sense as well. With the same good will on both sides which Richard seemed able to inspire whenever he set foot in Ireland, they came to an agreement whereby the English retained Calais and he promised to renounce all claim through his wife to the French throne. A light enough promise, in reality, seeing that Charles had three sons, but one which he felt sure his ambitious cousin Bolingbroke would bring up against him.

As soon as all these solemn conclaves were ended and the documents signed, the two kings and their retinues had dined in a still larger tent, strewn with priceless rugs and warmed by glowing braziers. And towards the conclusion of the feast, Richard's little bride had been brought in—rather as if she were a sort of postscript to the wines and spices.

And a very charming postscript she was, with her mother's beauty shorn of malevolence, and her father's friendliness tempered by shyness. The English ladies were delighted with her, and the French ladies responsible for her deportment need have known no qualms.

Richard had a happy way with children. " How will you like being Queen of England ? " he asked, when Charles had formally given her to him.

" If it please my lord and father, I shall like it very much," she had answered with quaint solemnity. " For, being your queen, I shall be a very great lady."

Everyone had smiled indulgently, but interest in her had soon given place to their still more burning interest in her dowry. After the napery was drawn and the servants had retired, Medford and the French clerks brought out long, legal-looking parchments, and tongues blurred a little by good wine grew sharp as swords on the question of finance. Medford was an important person these days, as Richard had rewarded his able loyalty by making him Bishop of Salisbury. As the dull discussion dragged on, Richard was aware of a small hand creeping into his. The same hand that he had kissed so formally a while ago. Only now it felt a little limp and moist. He squeezed it encouragingly and, although he had to watch his own interests with these shrewd French lawyers, he found time to look down at the stiffly dressed small figure at his side and caught her stifling a yawn. Poor little Isabel! He remembered so well how it felt to sit through tedious ceremonies when one was small. And this was Isabel of Valois' first sally from the schoolroom!

And somehow the feel of that little hand in his had been a warmth at his heart for hours afterwards. Something helpless to be cared for—an appeal to his essential kindness. Something to crack the ice forming so hopelessly about his whole nature.

And later in the day, when state affairs had given place to pleasure, another small incident seemed of good omen. Richard was listening appreciatively to the King's minstrels when he noticed a look of anxiety on Charles's face. Following the direction of his gaze, he saw his little princess and the Duke of Orleans' small son playing quietly with Mathe. Tired of her official role, Isabel had been decking the hound with a rose garland from the table. She had climbed on to a stool and the small boy, who was evidently her adoring slave, was holding Mathe's collar and pretending to be her groom. While the ladies in charge of her were momentarily distracted by the music, she had gathered the ends of the garland as reins and was trying to mount the tall hound as though he were a horse.

It was an ordinary child's game but Mathe was getting old. His temper was uncertain these days and he wasn't used to children. Charles of Valois half rose, and called something to his squires. Isabel was the apple of his eye. But Richard Plantagenet was quicker than any of them. Like a whirlwind of crimson and gold he had crossed the richly covered floor, swept past the astonished ladies and picked up his promised bride.

He found her light as thistledown, surprised and not a little indignant. "But I want to ride him and he likes me!" she protested.

"I was only afraid that he might bite you, little one," explained Richard. "Usually, he does things only for me."

He set her gently on the coveted steed, whispering something to Mathe as he did so. Proudly and carefully, the sagacious old deerhound bore his precious burden across the tent to her father's throne, with Richard walking on one side and the small Orleans boy on the other. French and English were delighted at the impromptu pageant. And when Richard lifted Isabel down she ran and kissed Mathe's forehead while he nuzzled against her fearless hand. "What tricks does he do for you, my lord?" she wanted to know, between shrieks of delicious childish laughter.

Richard snapped his fingers and the handsome creature rose on his hind legs to place a paw on each of his shoulders, regardless of cloth of gold and ermine.

Both children watched with shining eyes. "One day will he do that for Isabel, sir? When she is Queen of England?" inquired little Charles of Orleans.

"I hope not, or he will certainly knock her over!" laughed Richard, envying the Duke so delightful a son.

The spontaneous interlude had broken up formality, and when it came time for parting the two children kissed with tears. Richard tactfully withdrew to discuss some minor point with Lancaster while Isabel made her adieux to her parents, and for her sake they were cut as short as possible.

"You will see them again," Richard comforted her, when the horses were ready.

"I know I can trust her to you, my son," said Charles.

"My own cousin, Philippa de Courcy, will look after her at Windsor," promised Richard. "And my own old nurse, when she comes back from Bordeaux."

So they rode briskly back to Calais. Isabel had been up betimes to be dressed and the next day would be her wedding day. When they lifted her from her litter she was fast asleep.

Richard went to his own room in the Citadelle. The room in which Gloucester had died. He knew that people were watching to see if he would avoid doing so, and that they would judge his conscience accordingly. When his body squires had divested him of the cloth of gold and all the royal insignia he stood looking at the bed. Especially he noticed the high down pillows in cases of fine linen, each embroidered with a chained, crowned hart. The very pillows, probably, with which Mowbray had had Gloucester smothered. Not unnaturally, he decided to sit by the fire for a while. And also he bethought him of a piece of pearled braid that didn't set properly on his wedding tunic. Jacot had better come and see to it, against the morrow.

Weary as he looked, Jacot came obediently. " Only he and the King could possibly find a fault in the cut of that white velvet ! " the squires exclaimed, once they were outside the door.

" Well, what did you find out ? " asked Richard, as soon as he and his tailor were alone.

" It is true, what milord of Norfolk told your Grace," corroborated Jacot, beginning to refold the faultless garment. " Mundina left Calais at the end of the week."

" Which way did she go ? "

" By what they tell me, I think she took the road home."

Jacot was still bending over the hymeneal velvet and his voice dragged uncertainly. He had always feared Mundina more than he had loved her. And he wasn't at all certain what Mundina would want him to say.

" You gathered nothing more about—my uncle ? "

" No, sir. Some say that he was smothered, some that he was poisoned, and others that he died in his sleep."

The King sighed, " You sound tired, Jacot," he said. " All this spate of wedding garments must have been a strain on you. You'd better go to bed, and start for Bordeaux in the morning."

He had no idea that Jacot knew the journey to be useless, and had no desire to go.

CHAPTER XXIX

STRENGTHENED by a French alliance, and with a Council of eighteen supporters overriding Parliament, Richard became more and more absolute. Isabel's dowry and the subsidy on wool which he had wrung from the Commons went far towards resolving his ever pressing financial problems. And before the year was out a private quarrel had delivered Bolingbroke and Mowbray into his hands.

But their quarrel, blowing up so suddenly, had shown what dangerous rifts lay unsuspected beneath the smooth surface of his autocracy. It should have taught him that men do not dare to tell things to a despot and that because his ear was less accessible he was losing touch with the pulse of his people. Losing that gift of imaginative insight by which he had ruled so instinctively and so brilliantly. But he did not want to look back to any element of that other life, nor realize, while there was yet time, the unreal security in which he lived. By a series of monstrous blows, all those whom he had loved so devotedly had been taken from him. Ill-beset indeed he was. Even Mundina, who had first said it, seemed to have walked out of his life. And nothing seemed left but the making of a new, cold world of his own, building further and further away from warm reality.

At times his mind was still informed by Anne. But his sense of humour was drying up within him, and without that to keep him sane he was beginning to believe that because he was a murderer—no matter what the provocation, no matter how often other men killed—God would not let him find her again. And that being so, his restless mentality impelled him to fill his days with some sort of effort, of which the ethics scarcely mattered.

Bolingbroke and Mowbray had each accused the other of

treason. Searching for some cause, Richard saw ambition on the one side and fear on the other. It touched his pride that two of his contemporary associates should be wrangling in public about an alleged plot to take his life. At first he joined with Lancaster in trying to reconcile them and hush the matter up. But the quarrel was too savage, the honour and safety of each too deeply involved. Bolingbroke had even accused Mowbray of embezzling money granted for the upkeep of Calais. Finally, they had thrown down their gauntlets at each other's feet. By all the laws of chivalry there was but one inexorable solution : single combat to the death.

So Richard found himself sitting in the royal pavilion overlooking the lists at Coventry. The proud old Midland city had been chosen for convenience sake, because one protagonist had estates in the north and the other in the east, and every man who called himself a sportsman wanted to see England's two foremost champions fight. They came flocking from every county, but few of them brought their wives. Since the combat was *a l'outrance*, the culmination would scarcely be a pretty sight for women.

Richard said a few words to hearten the anxiety of Lancaster, who sat at his right hand, and then allowed his jaded gaze to wander over the familiar trappings of a tournament which once had seemed so fair. The place was packed, and people looked down from the battlements of the city walls. Because comparatively few feminine head-dresses were seen to rise among the more sober velvet caps of the men, he was all the quicker to notice Dalyngrigge and Lizbeth seated in the enclosure immediately below him. How like Dalyngrigge to bring his women up tough, thought Richard, with a smile. Or could it be that even after that night at Bodiam Lizbeth still sought every opportunity to come to Court ? But when the heralds had blared his arrival and everyone had stood and shouted, he was sure she had not turned around. And although she sat immediately below him, she went on calmly eating comfits from an ornamental box.

312

During a pause while the combatants were being shriven before their entry, Richard's attention settled on the box. It was a small, exquisitely worked affair cased in mother-of-pearl. He leaned forward and told an official to attract the lady's attention.

Lizbeth and her husband rose immediately and made obeisance, while Richard greeted them as if he had not seen them for many months. " A lovely comfit box you have there, Lady Dalyngrigge," he commented conversationally.

" My husband brought it back for me from his last voyage, sir," she answered.

" I see," smiled Richard. " One of those tactful gifts a man buys his wife after a three days' foray ? "

" Just a little trifle I picked up in Calais," explained Edward Dalyngrigge, who seldom bought anything if he could acquire it more adventurously. And since both the King and the Duke, his uncle, were known to be amateurs of good craftsmanship, he handed it up for closer inspection.

Richard passed the familiar box to Lancaster, as much to distract his anxious thoughts as for any other reason. " Do you remember this, Uncle ? " he asked.

Lancaster took it with unsteady fingers. " Why, yes, Richard. I brought it to you from Aquitaine that first winter you came to England." He laughed with the nervousness of a man undergoing great strain. " A present from Bordeaux to cheer you ! "

" I thought I couldn't be mistaken," mused Richard. " I used to play with it when I was sick with the cold."

" What became of it ? "

" The last time I saw it was in a room at the Wardrobe," said Richard slowly.

Dalyngrigge looked badly flustered. " I had no idea. But since it appears to belong to your Grace, I am sure my wife will forgo——" he began.

But the King wouldn't hear of it. " You know what the Book says, my dear Dalyngrigge—' a faithful wife is above rubies ! ' " Before handing it back, he snapped open the familiar clasp and helped himself to a comfit. " Let me see, where did you say you—er—picked it up ? " he inquired negligently.

" Somewhere near the Citadelle, I think. Ports like Calais are so full of curio shops . . . I really forget . . ." stammered Dalyngrigge.

" Perhaps by the time we meet again you will be able to remember," suggested Richard meaningly.

As he handed the box back to Lizbeth their eyes met. And something in the look she gave him made him remember that she and his mother had been present when Lancaster had given it to him, and that she, too, might have recognized it. He understood why she had sat just there, and why she had not thought it necessary to turn around. Pride would never prevent a woman of Lizbeth's passionate temperament from seizing every opportunity of seeing the man she loved.

Richard's attention was claimed from the Dalyngrigges by a preliminary fanfare of trumpets. He took the ceremonial baton from young Holland, who was acting as Marshal in Mowbray's place. The barriers at either end of the lists were being opened to admit the combatants and their attendant squires. Hundreds of heads turned first this way and then that like a field of coloured flowers blown by a variable wind ; and then the expectant crowd settled down into a silence so tense that it might have presaged an execution rather than a sport.

" Bolingbroke is the favourite——" A spectator's voice trailed belatedly into the silence as men passed along the benches making up last minute bets. Unsoothed by happiness, Richard knew a sharp prick of jealousy for his cousin's popularity and prowess. But, having practised with both protagonists from boyhood, he knew their thrusts as well as his own. He knew that Norfolk, hoping one day to distinguish himself on some holy crusade, rose early and practised daily. And that while Henry Bolingbroke was by far the finer general and strategist, he stood little chance against Mowbray in the

314

lists, where surprise tactics were ruled out by chivalric convention. But he waved aside all proffered wagers. This was too personal an affair for either him or Lancaster to bet on.

The Duke's face was ashen. How cruel that an old man should have to come to see his son killed! But Lancaster had been reared in a sterner age and scorned to stay away. Yet apparently he, too, foresaw the issue. "Tom will kill him . . ." he muttered, while trying to show a brave front to his world.

Richard felt profoundly sorry for him. Suspicion had long ago died down between them, they had many interests in common and had drawn much closer together during the years when Henry had been so much abroad. Richard turned aside while his cousin knelt to receive a father's blessing.

When both Bolingbroke and Mowbray had sworn to the truth of their accusations and clanked to the barrier to bend a knee formally before their king, they might have been strangers. Encased cap à pie in plated armour, they were unrecognizable save for the arms emblazoned on shield and jupon. Only their eyes showed through their open visors. And yet they and he had played together as boys. As they strode away to their waiting chargers the smell of freshly thrown sand, stirred in the heat by their mailed heels, assailed Richard's nostrils, carrying him back through the years. Back to that summer's day at Eltham which, by reason of an abrupt plunge into tragedy, would epitomize for ever the carefree essence of lost youth. The battered quintain, the roses on the garden wall, Simon's dear face and Robert's laughing friendship. The thump he himself had caught from a muffed thrust, and even the faint feeling of nausea. He had only to shut his eyes to see Henry and Tom as two stocky youths arguing with old Bartholomew about the score. . . . It had all been friendly rivalry then. And now they were trying to kill each other. Richard felt so much older than either of them. And death was so irrevocable. So much more irrevocable than young men realized until it had struck at some loved one and shorn all life of meaning.

More trumpets sounded. One at either end of the lists, the opponents sat still and tall upon their chargers. Bolingbroke's, in blue and green trappings, was held by his squire, Sir Piers Exton, himself no mean exponent in the lists. The sun, glinting on Mowbray's shield, picked out some of the noblest quarterings in England. Their great lances were being handed up to them. Another fanfare, and before long one of them would be lying dead beneath the uncaring sun. One thought was in a thousand minds. Which of them would it be? To John of Lancaster it meant everything. To Richard—personally—so little. To him, it would be the man who was left alive who would matter. Supremely, perhaps. Henry, flushed with triumph, a new idol for the nation? A menace growing cancerously in Gloucester's place. Or Tom Mowbray, who knew the secret of his king's guilt? Mowbray, who spun from winning side to winning side like a gilded weather-vane. One would never feel safe with such a man in the realm. . . .

" In the realm . . ." At that moment the idea came to birth in Richard's brain. How stupid of him not to have seen that this was the moment he had been waiting for for years! They had deserted him at Radcot Bridge. But for them Burley would never have been butchered, nor Robert de Vere exiled. Death was too good for both of them. What was it Chaucer had written about death? " Through me men come unto the Well of Grace, where green and lusty May doth ever endure." A delectable place, which Richard longed for. Surely, it was the living who were to be pitied? . . .

He glanced down and saw Lancaster's hand tensed against the dark velvet on his knee. The fine sword hand of a man who had once been strong and lusty. And the sight of an old man's veined hand mingled pity with Richard's motive of revenge. It moved him to action. He sprang to his feet and flung the baton he had been holding into the lists. It struck against a stanchion and rolled glittering to the centre of the barricades.

316

The effect was magical. Even at that moment, some base part of him found pleasure in the instant reaction to his power. Heralds, sounding the charge, stopped in mid-blast, their cheeks still absurdly inflated. "Hold! The King has stopped the combat!" yelled the untried Marshal, rushing between the combatants to confront an almost unheard-of contingency. Lancaster seemed to crumple with relief, a smothered thanksgiving on his lips. The crowd rose to a man, in staring silence. The two champions, already crouched like tigers for the attack, relaxed dumbfounded.

And then, almost as much to his surprise as theirs, Richard heard his own voice, trailed by an impersonal echo coming back from the high city wall, solemnly pronouncing sentence of banishment upon them both. Henry Bolingbroke, Earl of Nottingham and Derby he banished for ten years; Thomas Mowbray, Duke of Norfolk, for life.

CHAPTER XXX

As the months passed, Richard began to realize that his popularity had begun to wane when a crowd of English sportsmen were cheated at the last moment of the stirring contest they had travelled so many miles to see. There had been no reparation, no sop to their disappointment in the shape of a secondary event. As for Bolingbroke and Mowbray themselves, just as a felon often prefers a flogging to imprisonment, so banishment seemed to each of them a harder sentence than his fifty-fifty chance of death.

Richard had tried to be as fair as possible about it. Both had disturbed the peace of his realm, but because treason had not been proved he refrained from confiscating their estates, although—since one or other of them must be lying—one inheritance at least was legally forfeit to the crown. Rather than send forth a guiltless man penniless, he allowed each of them to appoint an agent to manage his affairs and send abroad the profits. And, as usual, he was mindful of the underdog, taking care to see that none of their dependants or tenant farmers suffered. But he could not explain all this to the man in the street; whereas Sir Piers Exton, who had been left in charge of the Hereford lands, started such lying rumours that the county sheriffs were given orders to report on all things spoken against the King.

Lancaster aged sadly after his son's banishment. "When you made it ten years, Richard, were you thinking that by that time the little Queen will have grown up and you may have sons of your own? So that Henry wouldn't be so dangerously near the succession," he had asked, the last time Richard had gone to visit him.

And Richard had answered carefully, "I promise you, dear

uncle, that as soon as I have a son of my own Henry may come home—whether the ten years be up or not."

But his uncle had lived only until Isabel was eleven. He slipped away quietly with the close of the century. The death of John of Gaunt, Duke of Lancaster—whose name had been a household word in many lands—was the great event of 1399. The King had him laid to rest in St. Paul's Cathedral, with his great lance and shield beside him.

And now Richard was truly alone. New men sprang up—lordlings like Bushey Green and Baggot—but after the great barons of the fourteenth century they had little power, and less personality. For Richard the rooms and passages of Westminster were empty. Mundina had never come back from Calais and Jacot had searched Bordeaux in vain.

And then came disquieting news from Ireland. One autumn morning Richard received a letter from his heir, Roger Mortimer. The last time he wrote, English and Irish had been on good terms and even intermarrying. But now it seemed some sudden ferment of unrest had moved the chieftains to revert to their old ways, plundering, raping and murdering colonists within the supposed safety of the Pale. Long after the torches were lit, Richard sat with his Council, planning to send military reinforcements and dictating instructions and advice for Mortimer.

But the next day, soon after breaking his fast, he laid aside state papers. Having once enjoyed such happy family life, he knew better than most that a ruler must sometimes relax with his equals. He held his clerks and squires in affection, but had never been such a fool as to make intimate confidants of any of them. "I am going to Windsor," he said.

It was a long time since he had included people pleasantly in such projects. He just said he was going to a place, and his household servants exerted themselves to have everything ready punctually as he wished. They knew that he did not suffer fools gladly. Even Standish did not dare to suggest that he should wait until the rain ceased.

Richard rode to Windsor in silence—a little ahead of the small, unofficial retinue he took, his face a set mask in the shadow of his hooded cloak. As he passed through Hounslow and a score of other villages there was little cheering. And as he rode he thought the hard, cunning thoughts of a man fighting a lone hand.

But once within the walls of Windsor he shed his surliness with his sodden cloak. Swift, graceful, agile—immaculate as ever—he strode along the galleries to the little Queen's apartments. As usual when he visited her, he forbade anyone to announce him. He wanted to assure himself that she was well cared for whether he came or not. He even stood listening for a moment or two outside her door—and at sound of her voice coming thinly through the heavy oak his firm lips relaxed into a smile. He pushed the door open softly and stood just inside, and presently, when her two French waiting-maids looked round, he laid a warning finger on his lips. Marianna and Simonette were quick of wit and—like many women about the French court—imagined themselves enamoured of the handsome English king. They glided from their mistress's side and out of the room, his smile amply rewarding them as they passed.

Isabel was seated on a stool before a tall, rain-washed window, and Richard thought she looked like one of the fair-haired angels on the bedhangings at Carter Lane come to life. She was bending over her needlework box, patting down the fruits of her labours. " Do you think the King will like it ? " she asked earnestly, unaware that Marianna and Simonette were gone.

When no answer came she looked round with a funny little air of bewilderment.

" Isabel ! " he called softly, laughingly, from the doorway.

He saw her start and quiver like a thoroughbred hound. The stool was scraped back—silks flew in all directions. There was a slither of satin slippers as she ran the length of the room towards him. She might have been hurrying to reach the closing gates of Heaven.

"Richard! Richard, *mon cher mari!*"

The words were a whisper of joy—poignant as only a child's can be—as she hurled herself into his arms. Her head reached only to his breast, but she was pressing it against the peacock velvet as if listening for his very heartbeats.

He lifted her gently so that her glowing face was level with his own. "*Doucement! Doucement, ma petite!*" he chided tenderly, half frightened she would harm herself by such ardour, and wholly touched.

The soft gold of his moustache brushed her cheek. When he set her down he could see the quick rise and fall of her immature breasts beneath the pearled roses on her gown. "My little one, if you are so *very* glad to see me I shall be wretched, concluding that all your other days are unhappy!" he protested.

"All the other days are dead," she said, her hazel eyes dark with childish tragedy.

"But poppet, you have Madame de Courcy."

"Yes."

"And those two charming creatures who went out just now. Though I hope you're not always chattering French with them." He knew quite well she had been, and tried to speak sternly. "You're supposed to be learning English, you know."

"It's so difficult not to," admitted Isabel.

"I know." Richard took her hand and walked with her towards the window, guiltily aware that he usually forgot and talked French with her himself. "Well, where is this *chef d'œuvre* which it seems important that the King should like?"

A sunny child again, she pulled him to her governess's high-backed chair. "Sit there, please, and shut your eyes," she ordered.

Richard grinned, but was too sensible of the seriousness of the moment to peep. "Suppose you show it to me so that I may open my eyes and enjoy looking at you," he suggested.

It was the old Richard speaking, whose voice and smile charmed people's hearts out of their bodies.

Isabel came and leaned against him, taking a last critical survey of her gift and smoothing it out on his knee. "You may look now, Richard," she said. "And if it isn't quite as your mother and your—first wife—used to sew, at least it is with all my love."

Richard found himself staring down at a little green purse painstakingly embroidered with a white hart. The poor beast had a distressing squint and one of his curiously shaped legs was a bit grubby. Presumably the French king's daughter had been allowed to spend more time playing with her palfrey than at her embroidery frame. But after a moment or two Richard found that he couldn't see the defects very well although his eyes were open, because they were wet with tears.

"D—don't you like it?" asked Isabel anxiously, because it seemed so long before he said anything.

Richard detached the leather wallet from the girdle of his tunic and carefully fixed the purse in its place, allowing her to transfer the fascinating contents from one to the other. "It is the loveliest gift I ever had and I shall keep it until I die," he said.

Isabel gave a little squeal of delighted laughter. "But it will be worn out long before then!" she said. "And I will make you lots more purses—as many as you want. Only as I grow older I will learn to make them better and better."

Already the woman she was to become showed through the child she was. "What a queer little thing you are!" he said, drawing her onto his knee.

She sighed prodigiously and leaned back against his shoulder. "I am so lonely when you are at Westminster," she confided.

It was peaceful in the little queen's room, shut away from regal worries and the rain. Richard was well content to sit physically and mentally relaxed, stroking her hair. "They are kind to you, my poppet?"

" Oh yes."

Some lack of warmth in her response left him unassured " Don't be afraid to tell me. No one shall suffer for it," he urged.

She sat up and answered him with troubled gravity. " Richard, I don't very much like Madame de Courcy. She isn't unkind—only cold and haughty. I know I am only a child, but sometimes one would think it is she who is the queen. And once she spoke against you, hinting that you had let someone spoil her marriage. I didn't quite understand, but it made me very angry."

He laughed indulgently. " Then I will find you someone you *do* like, if I have to scour England. Someone who will fall under your spell, little witch, and stand like a dragon between you and the slightest thing which might hurt you. Someone who will love you as devotedly as my old nurse loved me."

" That would be lovely. Did your nurse die, Richard ? "

" I don't know, Isabel. She went on a journey and neither her husband nor I have ever been able to trace her."

" I will light a candle to St. Christopher for her every day."

He was so moved by her sweet naïveté that he suggested something which he had never offered even to Anne. " Isabel, would you like me to leave Mathe with you sometimes ? "

" Oh, would you ? "

After all these years it would seem like leaving a part of himself, but the feel of the little purse at his belt warmed all his pent up generosity. " For you I would, sweetheart. But I couldn't bring him today. It's too far for him and it's raining. He grows blind, I'm afraid."

" Oh, Richard ! But he still comes and puts his paws on your shoulders, doesn't he ? "

" Mostly by sense of smell, I think. Sometimes, if Tom or Ralph leaves a garment of mine about, he'll go and rest against it instead of sitting with me."

Even the pathos of a dog's old age was very real to this princess of France. " Then I don't think I will have him, thank you," she decided. " You see, you've had him so much longer than you've had me. And he might pine, mightn't he ? "

" I'm afraid so."

" Besides," she added, as if the idea had only just occurred to her, " perhaps *you* are lonely sometimes, too."

" Very lonely," admitted Richard.

Isabel knitted puzzled brows. She had supposed that wherever the object of her affection was, there the atmosphere must always be bright and rarefied as it was when he came to see her. " But you have all England—everything——"

The lines of a man who has lived and suffered seemed to deepen at the corners of Richard's mouth and eyes—or perhaps it was only the strong light from the window, for when he was playing with her or teasing her Isabel never noticed them. " That is only an illusion, my child. Inwardly, I have nothing —now. . . . Except you," he added, seeing the stricken look on her face.

She slipped from his knee, all practical energy at once. " Then, Richard, let me come and live with you at Court. You do want me, don't you ? Surely with Mathe and me there——"

" Chérie, we have been all over that before——"

" Oh, please, please, Richard ! " She was standing between his knees, twisting at the knobbly buttons of his tunic in a frenzy of supplication. To her it all seemed so simple. She understood nothing of the passion she was striving to supplant. She could not see the ugly picture in Richard's mind of Henry Bolingbroke grasping at a child wife because she was an heiress, nor know that Mary Bohun had given him their strapping son Harry before she was thirteen, and then a string of other children, and that now—before the bloom of womanhood—she was dead.

Richard caught her little hands and held them firmly. " Listen, Isabel. When your father used to tell you you couldn't do something you wanted, you always obeyed him, didn't you ? "

Her excited hands lay still. "Yes, Richard," she agreed in a small voice.

"Even when, in his wisdom, he decided that you were too young to understand the reasons why?"

She nodded, her adoring eyes on his.

Richard sighed, wondering what he should do when she *was* old enough. She was tall for her age, and maturing every day. "Very well, then. I'm not always as wise as he, I'm afraid. But you'll have to obey me just the same," he told her, rather inadequately.

Reminded by mention of her father, he drew from his belt a slender roll of parchment with a vastly important-looking seal.

"From France!" cried Isabel, recognizing the dangling fleur-de-lis.

"And full of messages for you," smiled Richard. "Would you like to hear them?"

While he read out all the bits that were not about state affairs, Isabel stood leaning against his chair, the unbound chestnut of her hair mingling with the copper of his. Being there with her had soothed all the evil out of him, as it always did. "It's a pleasant novelty exchanging letters instead of arrows with France, though it seems to have taken me a lifetime to achieve it," he said.

"Then help me write a reply in perfect English to please my parents—which will take you only half an hour," coaxed Isabel, perceiving an opportunity of avoiding a dull session with her governess.

Richard sent for pen and parchment and patiently helped her to concoct a missive which must have amazed them very much. "Though I simply can't go on acting as your clerk if you keep saying such extravagantly nice things about me!" he protested.

As soon as the letter was signed and sealed they went into the hall to dine. A large cushion was put for Isabel so that she could sit at the King's right hand, while Madame de Courcy sat at his left. It was a merry meal, with minstrels and some acrobats the King had sent for specially to amuse her. And when it was over, Tom Holland brought in the little white puppy he had carried all the way from the royal kennels under his cloak. " Don't think we forgot you altogether because we couldn't bring Mathe ! " laughed Richard, watching her surprised delight.

All the happy afternoon Richard of England and Isabel of Valois, with Ralph and Tom and Marianna and Simonette, romped with the leggy little creature and sang ballads in bilingual abandon. To Ralph and Tom it was like a piece out of the good old days to watch the King fooling. At any moment, they felt, Anne—the real queen—might open the door and stand there laughing at them as she used to do at Sheen. They could almost hear her saying in her inimitable way, " My sweet Richard, do remember you are getting on for thirty-three ! "

Towards evening, seeing that Isabel was flagging through so much happy excitement, Richard had the fire lit, and while the horses were being saddled he sat facing her contentedly across the hearth. " Just as if we were really married ! " she remarked, rather pathetically.

The days when he came to Windsor were never long enough, and because the shadow of approaching parting was saddening her, he tried to distract her thoughts. " I had a letter from Roger Mortimer, as well as from your father, this morning," he told her, with apparent irrelevance.

" Why do we never see him ? " asked Isabel, a little listlessly.

" Partly because he is one of those rare, retiring sort of persons, I imagine. And because at the moment he is away keeping the Irish in order for me," answered Richard. " But he has a son about your age. I must arrange for you two to meet."

" Would he play with me like Charles of Orleans ? " asked Isabel.

" I am sure he would."

"What is this Roger Mortimer, whom you think so highly of? What is he like?"

Richard considered. So few people knew the Mortimers because they never pushed themselves at Court. "Not unlike Mowbray, perhaps, in his love of outdoor life. But more dependable. Would you like me to tell you a story about him?"

"Has it a happy ending?"

"Well, yes—for me. Once, long before you came to England, the late Duke of Gloucester invited Roger to dine at his manor of Pleshy. And after dinner when they were quite alone, as we are now, Gloucester suggested that they two should murder me. Then Roger would get the throne, he said, and they could share the power between them. I suppose he thought Roger would be more obliging and docile to manage."

"And what did Roger do?" asked Isabel, her attention weaned at last from the clatter of horses down below.

"Oh, he listened quite politely. He was never one to make trouble. Besides, he was probably rather afraid of his uncle, as I was. He even promised not to repeat anything he had heard. And he never did. But he declined to co-operate, and went back to his affairs in Ireland, leaving our respected uncle feeling very insecure indeed. Roger could have come favour-seeking to me, of course, with all the pother of an unmasked plot, the same as the others were always doing. But he didn't bother me. There was a quiet sort of loyalty about his behaviour which I appreciated."

"Then how did you ever get to know?" asked Isabel.

"Some friends of mine persuaded Gloucester to write a kind of confession before he died."

"And how did the horrid wretch die?"

"Oh, much as he deserved," answered Richard lightly. But he started more than a guiltless man should when Ralph Standish happened to appear at that moment at his elbow.

"Well, what is it?" he asked sharply.

"Your Grace's Councillors—Bushey, Baggot and Green,

sir. They've ridden from London. It's urgent, sir, or I wouldn't intrude."

Richard was not sorry for Isabel's sake that their adieux should be cut short. "You see, my little one, how they plague me even when I am by my own fireside with you!" he complained jestingly. He kissed her good night, bade her maids put her to bed, and promised to come again soon.

Standish loitered a little in opening the door for him. "It is bad news, I fear," he warned.

Richard laid a friendly hand on his shoulder. The hours spent with Isabel had lowered the guard of his loneliness. "What else has life trained me to expect, Ralph?" he countered.

So often he had been called from happiness to sudden deputations such as this. But instead of the three distinctive Plantagenet uncles who had awaited him in the past, he now found three respectful, ineffective knights.

"Well, my friends?" he asked, disliking their nondescript faces.

"Roger Mortimer, Earl of March——" began Bushey.

"Your heir, sir——" added Baggot, trying to underline his colleague's preface with unnecessary information.

"Well?" snapped Richard a second time, supposing that another worrying letter had arrived.

"He has been ambushed by the Irish, and killed," concluded Green.

CHAPTER XXXI

JEHAN FROISSART came to England just as the whole nation was clamouring for reprisals against Ireland, and for once in his life Richard was too busy to show suitable hospitality and appreciation of the arts. He had been obliged to receive the celebrated French chronicler hurriedly, having his beautifully bound gift of love poems carried to his bedroom that he might scan it before sleeping, and then turning his guest over to the care of a kindly old knight while he himself prepared to lead the expedition to Ireland. There had been no chance to enjoy long, leisurely talks with one of the best informed men of the day, nor to glean some of those revealing little stories about his parents' youth which do not enliven official recordings. He would always regret that Froissart could not have come a few years earlier and seen England in the heyday of her peaceful culture which was his achievement —and above all that he should not have seen Anne!

And now, just as everybody was busy with levies and shipping and victualling, Geoffrey Chaucer must needs be affected by the same spring urge, and choose this moment to send his latest crop of verses to his royal patron! The best thing to do, Richard supposed, would be to put the two men of letters together while one got on with the war.

"Read the new poem aloud while I look through this armour," he bade Medford—loath as he was to forgo the first joyful impact of Chaucer's golden words.

He went on indicating to a brace of squires which pieces of personal equipment he would take. But after a minute or two it dawned upon his absorption that nobody was reading anything. And, glancing up, he noticed that his secretary was staring at the unrolled parchment, looking very red about the tonsure and very white about the gills.

"What has struck you so dumb, Medford?" he demanded, pausing with a pair of spurs in one hand and a jupon bedizened with leopards dangling from the other.

"It's—it's not the sort of verse Master Chaucer usually writes," stammered the embarrassed bishop, whose Court life had accustomed him to flattery.

Richard looked round the crowded room with irritation. York, who was sitting near him, was lamentably wheezy; and his son, young Edward of Aumerle, read verse with about as much expression as if he were crying the curfew. "Here, give the thing to me," he said, bundling spurs and jupon into the arms of his new French squire, Creton, who had come back with him from St. Omer.

Richard took the verses to the window, beginning to scan them over as he mounted the shallow steps. Brief and pointful as they were, he found the subject matter scarcely credible. Forgetful of the roomful of people watching him, he read them over twice. And as he read his face flamed with anger—and with the tardy shame which the author must have meant to stir in him. Having yielded to temptation and seized John of Gaunt's estates instead of handing them over to Henry, he had tried to stifle his conscience with plausible excuses and think no more about it. And here was a mere vintner's son daring to criticize!

> "Oh, prince, desire to be honourable;
>   Cherish thy folk, and hate extorcion!
> Suffre no thing that may be reprevable
>   To thine estate, done in thy regioun.
> Show forth thy sword of castigacion.
>   Dred God; do law; love trouthe and worthinesse
> And wed thy folk again to stedfastnesse."

Reading such blunt reproof from so unexpected a quarter, Richard felt much as he had done on receiving a well-earned thwack from the quintain.

No wonder Chaucer hadn't waited upon him in person! From what source had he drawn courage to write the impertinent stuff at all? Recalling his other poems written on happier themes, one could not but realize how deeply they were imbued with the very essense of England. Had he not braved exotic ideas of culture by making a medium of his own tongue? Richard had the grace to be glad that there would always be Englishmen to take up pen or sword, not only against danger from abroad, but against tyranny at home. And that it would always be the gentle, law-abiding citizens who would be the first to fight.

But that touched his conscience all the more. For he himself had been that kind of man. He crumpled the parchment in his hand and let it fall to the floor. Chaucer was only putting into telling words what a lot of shrewd Londoners said of him. Yet what did they know, any of them, about the difficulties that beset a king?

"Desire to be honourable . . ." How could one deal honourably with men like Gloucester? Or lead an expedition to Ireland without money? And mightn't his pledged word have applied only to Henry's Hereford and Derby estates, which were all he had at the time of exile? It was all very well for shopkeepers with no knowledge of statecraft to condemn him as if he had robbed their idol of his money like a common thief; but it was more a question of power. How could a sovereign rule England while a third of it belonged to someone else? Lancaster had had the power, but had used it to feed his ambition in Spain. With Henry there was no knowing. One remembered only which side he had been on at Radcot Bridge. . . .

And then again—"hate extorcion." That would be a dig at fines levied on counties for half-forgotten risings, and for the promises of blank loans he had forced his wealthier subjects to sign. Of course, it had all looked very high-handed. But he had no intention of making his people pay up, any more than he had insisted upon the sheriffs reporting their grumbles. Couldn't the fools see that? When had he ever been ungenerous, or ground down his subjects? It was only that he wanted to hold the whole land in leash—particularly now that he was going away. So that as long as he lived there should be but one ruler —a benevolent one who saw to it that they had peace and prosperity—instead of a hydra-headed growth of self-seekers who would waste their substance in violence.

Back and forth swayed Richard's thoughts, like the good and the bad wrestling within him. In spite of all his plausible reasoning, he knew that he had been behaving outrageously. The ill-controlled forces of his baser self had been gathering momentum with the mounting sum of his misfortunes. A man needs love and laughter to keep him sane. And he had only to love a thing, it seemed, to have it taken from him.

Even the love of his people was rapidly turning into fear. Well, let them whine like whipped dogs, fearing and mistrusting him, if they wanted to! Hadn't he himself been bludgeoned into subjection as a boy? There were times when all that was bad in him took a savage delight in being feared.

But fear makes men do strange things. And it was this unrest against which Chaucer was presuming to warn him. " Wed thy folk again to stedfastnesse," he had implored, evidently torn between anxiety for him and for England. Presumably, the man knew himself safe from royal displeasure because the same pen had written such lovely things about Anne. Perhaps he was saying things now, in the only way he knew, *for* Anne. If Anne were here she, too, would say " Love truth and worthiness, dear Richard ". And perhaps one wasn't being too truthful, even with oneself. . . . But then, of course, if Anne were here everything would be different..

Richard stooped to pick up the crumpled ball of parchment, absently smoothing it out as he came down slowly from the window seat. Not one of the men in the room so busily engaged in preparations for battle had any idea that a spiritual skirmish, far more important to their future, had already been fought silently in their midst—and partially lost.

"What a mercy the King signed a long-term peace with France before all this trouble started in Ireland!" the Duke of York was saying to nobody in particular. Poor York! Trying, as ever, to gloss over some passionate complexity in a nephew he couldn't even begin to understand.

"So people are just beginning to realize it!" remarked Richard caustically, coming to join him.

"Now you've to go and avenge Roger they must be thankful you're not leaving our shores open to a threat of invasion," minced Edward of Aumerle.

But fear of a very different kind of invasion lurked at the back of Richard's mind. Charles of Valois was sound enough, with his daughter Queen of England. But the whole coast lay open to Henry. And Henry was a potential danger now, with only Roger's youngster balking his way to the succession. Probably the Yorks were too stupid to think of that. Or were they? Richard's gaze dwelt appraisingly on his cousin, while he himself did some quick thinking. He wasn't yearning for Edward's company in Ireland, but there was plenty of mischief a conceited young scion of the family might get up to in England. . . .

"I shall want you to act as Regent for me while I'm gone," he told his uncle. "I will see to it officially tomorrow."

York rose formally. "I will do my best, Richard, since you so honour me. But I am getting to be an old man——"

"And never amounted to much anyway!" thought Richard. But there was no one else of sufficient standing whom he could trust, except perhaps the able Bishop of Carlisle. And one couldn't very well pass over an uncle. He turned with intentional abruptness to Aumerle. "You, Edward, will come with me," he ordered.

Aumerle's effeminate features flustered with confusion, and in that moment Richard was sure that his command had clashed inconveniently with some previous plan. Though probably the foppish sycophant wouldn't be much of an asset to any party. Replicas of trusty leaders like Knollys and Stafford weren't two a groat nowadays.

"And Bolingbroke's young son, Harry, can come along too," he added, looking with disconcerting directness into Aumerle's startled eyes. "It'll be useful experience for his future wars with France—if his father should ever succeed me."

"My dear Richard!" protested Edmund of York. "Everyone says he is a promising, upstanding boy—but surely too young to fight!"

To his uncle's annoyance Richard burst out laughing. "Funny, how familiar that sounds! Burley used to say those very words, surely? When you and the other uncles were trying to hound him into sending me on some campaign before I could couch a lance. And do you remember how shocked your bloodthirsty brother Thomas was because the Black Prince's son had never even seen a man killed? Well, he's seen plenty now! The trouble is that so few of the decent ones are left alive." Richard broke off in mid-tirade. Now that he was a widower, laughter so often degenerated into bitterness. "Oh, don't worry," he soothed, seeing that York's affronted face had taken on a yet more florid hue. "There will be no need for young Harry to fight. He may come in quite useful in other ways."

Aumerle said nothing. He knew well enough that Richard wanted Henry's son as a hostage. Richard was so damnably clever like that. You thought you'd got him in check, and he was always a move ahead of you. Life seemed to have taught him more expediency in thirty-three years than most grey-beards assimilate in a lifetime. "This expedition is going to cost coffers of money," he grumbled, picking up a long list of levies.

"Yes," agreed Richard, returning briskly to the work in hand. "And without the Lancaster estates we couldn't restore law and order in Ireland at all."

York had been too profoundly shocked by their seizure to discuss the matter. "If you were to call a Parliament I am sure they wouldn't be unreasonable about a grant," he suggested, without much conviction.

But to reassemble Parliament was to hand over the power when Richard wanted it most. Better to gamble with the pieces one held and get this necessary Irish business over and done with, and return to England as soon as possible. "There isn't time, Uncle. When I come back," he evaded, making a note to send for Henry's son before Edward could spirit him away.

Later in the day, when York and Aumerle had gone back to Langley, Richard had the royal coffers opened. Something furtive in his cousin's manner had made him decide to take all his plate and money with him. And—more important still, perhaps—the crown. Holding the hollow, shining thing in his hands, he thought back upon the long train of his ancestors who had worn it, and wondered who would wear it next. "If one of my cousins had to be murdered, why couldn't it have been Henry Bolingbroke and not Roger Mortimer?" he wondered, for the hundredth time.

Not until everything was in readiness for the expedition did he go again to Windsor. Isabel must have been counting the days, but he simply hadn't had time. And when he went it was May. Maytime in England, wiping out all her sullen winter greyness with the perfection of a single smiling hour. Hawthorn bushes flung a froth of pink and red and white against the darker trees of the forest, and the Thames meadows were just that hopeful shade of green which wilts so soon before the summer heat. Cooling his horse's feet in the silver shallows at Runnymead, Richard lingered to look and look, and store the loveliness—just as Anne had done that day before she died, by London Bridge.

But there was no time to dally by the Thames. This was a much more official visit than his last. He was received into the vast castle in state. Isabel welcomed him in the wonderful dress the Paris goldsmiths had trimmed for her with golden birds sitting upon branches of pearls and emeralds. Her very grandest dress of all.

"I have to go across to Ireland," he told her, "and I have brought the Earl of March's widow to look after you while I am away." Knowing her tender heart, he foresaw that soon it would be she who would be caring for poor Eleanor Mortimer.

But Isabel had grown impatient waiting for him and was in a tantrum as regal as her gown. "Why do I have to stay here with any of them? Am I not Queen?" she demanded. "Your first queen went everywhere with you!"

"Never campaigning," said Richard shortly.

"Madame de Courcy says you were wildly in love with her and slept with her every night. And that when she died you risked the plague to hold her in your arms. And that afterwards you burned down——"

"I will speak to Madame de Courcy."

Richard's eyes were cold as ice. Isabel had never known him to speak or look like that. And as he turned aside, experienced courtiers made way for him in apprehensive silence. They never heard what he said to that haughty, extravagant lady before he sent her packing. But hard-pressed for money as he was, he instructed Medford to settle all her bills, because she had been Robert de Vere's wife.

When he went to take his leave of Isabel he found her in floods of repentant tears. There was a different look about her and dark smudges beneath her candid eyes. It wasn't her fault that Roger had been killed, thought Richard with compunction, and that things looked very different for her, for him and for England. Roger's son was even younger than she, and there seemed scarcely time to wait for two children to grow up.

"I had no right to lose my temper just now, my poor sweet," he said, helping to dry her tears. "You must try to bear with me because I have so many worries."

"I am sorry, Richard. About adding to your worries, I mean," she told him, her voice still erupting with a stray sob or two. "But I love you with all of me, and you love me only as you love Mathe."

336

"You give me more than I deserve, and I am more grateful than you will ever know," he said. "But you must put all this ridiculous idea of rivalry out of your head. I allow *no* one—not even you, Isabel—to discuss *her*. But you are growing up and I owe you the truth." He set her before him and tried to make her understand. He was almost as white and shaken as she. "Nobody and nothing on earth can ever take the place of—my wife. But you are God's last solace to me, dear child, and I adore you. And some day soon, when I come back from Ireland, you shall come to London and really be my queen."

Her tear-stained face was transfigured. The streets of London were paved with gold for her as surely as Richard Whittington had told her they had been for him—years ago when he was a poor boy and not a rich Lord Mayor. "You promise, Richard?"

He kissed her gently on the forehead. "I promise."

She flung herself upon him. "Then come back soon, Richard! Come back soon!"

Richard had no idea when he would be back—or whether he would get back at all. Something completely outside his careful reckoning had happened when Roger had been killed.

When he went with his little queen to hear Mass he was conscious of the paradoxical selfless peace of a soldier going into battle whose fate is out of his own hands. Again that keen awareness of beauty invaded him. It uplifted him so that all cunning and bitterness seemed to fall away. It was difficult to believe that he was his uncle's murderer or—if he were—it seemed that God had in some miraculous way wiped out the guilt. He felt as if Anne and all those whom he had loved were very near him, and the veil dividing him from the company of Heaven no more impenetrable than the haze of incense rising before the altar. In this uplifted mood he waved the choristers to silence and chanted the beautiful words of the Collect as a solo. ". . . increase and multiply upon us Thy mercy . . . that we may so pass through things temporal, that we finally lose not the things eternal . . ." Priests and laymen listened spellbound. His true, sweet tenor was an inspired joy, and the memory of it lingered in the chapel of Windsor long after he was gone.

"Oh, Richard, I didn't know you could sing like that when you are really serious!" whispered Isabel, as they came down the aisle after the blessing.

"Didn't you?" he whispered back teasingly. "Then I must learn some wild Irish songs to frighten the life out of you with when I come home."

All the distinguished company streamed after them, and out in the sunshine their brightly caparisoned horses were waiting. At the west door pages served them with comfits and wine.

"What a funny meal!" laughed Isabel, trying to be gay as she was sure his first wife would have done.

"A sort of stirrup cup! Or is it a loving cup?" said Richard, dropping a sugared grape into her wine for luck.

He entrusted her solemnly to his uncle and made his formal farewell. "*Au revoir, ma petite reine*," he said, embracing her fondly so that many of the women wept. But as he went quickly to mount his horse, a warm, playful breeze caught at his cloak, the scent of lilac assailed his nostrils and the familiar reach sparkled enticingly in the sunshine. It seemed so senseless to be going to war. Half-way down the steps he stopped and turned, and saw the look on Isabel's face. She was scarcely twelve, and because of all the staring people she was trying so bravely not to cry.

He went back and lifted her in his arms, kissing her again and again. "Good-bye," he said, in plain homesick English, which was the only language to meet the elemental simplicity of his mood. "Good-bye, dear child, until we meet again."

CHAPTER XXXII

RICHARD landed at Waterford on the first day of June and waited almost a week for Aumerle and his detachment to arrive. Fuming, he marched his own men to Kilkenny, only to wait another fortnight before they caught up with him. Time, for Richard, was the prime factor of the enterprise; for though his face was set towards Dublin, half his preoccupation was with England. And all the while Aumerle grumbled about adverse winds and bad roads and lost equipment. How much of Aumerle's mishaps and excuses were due to inexperience and how many were deliberate, it was difficult to assess.

All through the wilds of Wicklow the English archers were harried by elusive hordes, who would swoop down suddenly from the hills to snipe, or lie in ambush behind boulders in some eerie glen. Their losses were heavy. Could they have stood on firm, familiar ground, the Irish—fine fighters as they were—wouldn't have stood a chance against their discipline and marksmanship. But Art McMurrough, who styled himself King of Leinster, was far too wily to come out into the open. Let the English pigs bog themselves again and again until their patience was exhausted, their fine clothes ruined and their baggage lost!

Richard wanted to meet him personally. He had done so before, and knew just how to appeal to the man's rough generosity and how to play on his childlike vanity. But, thanks to Aumerle, he had already been three weeks delayed. He was obliged to leave Gloucester's son to negotiate with Art and to press on to Dublin. But he gained little by entering the capital. Owing to McMurrough's guile and the young Earl's ineptitude, unconditional peace was all the Irish would discuss, offering no redress for the rising and the slaughter of their Lord

Lieutenant. In a fine fury Richard retraced his steps, searching fruitlessly for a chieftain with whom he could parley, and trying to bring the enemy to battle. Many of his best companies were cut off by bogs in the process, and in the end there seemed nothing for it but to get his depleted army back to Waterford.

And there, awaiting him, was the news he had feared from England.

" Henry has come from France;" wrote York, shakily.

" The Duke of Lancaster has landed at Ravenspur, in Yorkshire," reported the messenger, who had already been waiting some days.

" The only Duke of Lancaster I know is dead," snarled Richard ; and gave orders to his captains to have their ships ready to sail in two days.

But the grey sea looked high as the mountains. His fleet stood a good chance of being scattered. York's messenger had been weeks coming. Henry might be anywhere by now.

" Send Salisbury across first to rouse North Wales, while we wait for all the stragglers and then cross into South Wales," suggested Edward of Aumerle. " Then we can consolidate at Chester."

By this time Richard trusted Aumerle no farther than he could see him. But there was enough sense in the advice to draw backing from Salisbury, whose loyalty was above suspicion. Against his own better judgment Richard waited a week for the remainder of his morassed army, and let Salisbury embark. He had done a thing foolish enough to make the Black Prince turn beneath his burnished tomb at Canterbury. He had divided his army. ·

Aumerle had cozened him into making a false move at last. For two months Richard had been obliged to take his eyes off the game, and by the time he had brought the small remainder of his archers into Milford Haven the whole face of the checkerboard had been changed. His two knights, Bushey and Green, had been taken. Bolingbroke, by one of his brilliant flanking movements, was at Bristol. And the King in check indeed !

Rumour was rife even in the little South Wales seaport of Milford. And rumour had it that Salisbury's army had already been dispersed—some said by force, and some by treachery. Richard didn't believe it; but it was being so carefully fostered that even his own Cheshiremen began furtively tearing the white hart from their sleeves and letting each other over the town wall by night.

More reliable news had been gathered by the page left in charge of Mathe. It was Arundel's brother, recently promoted to the See of Canterbury, who had crossed the Channel the moment the King's back was turned and made it his business to tell Bolingbroke about the seizure of his father's estates. And the Archbishop had gone armed with a long list of signatures of important people who promised to support him if he came back and claimed what was his own. Northumberland and his son, Percy, had been among them. And Bolingbroke had needed no second bidding.

It had been easy for John of Gaunt's son, marching in a martyr's cause through Lancaster, to augment his little band of followers to the size of an army. But Thomas Arundel had been cleverer than that. Like his late brother, he was a master of propaganda. He had worked on the fears of a people ripe for panic. He announced that the King meant to impose unheard of taxes to pay for the Irish campaign, and that if they resisted he had arranged that his French father-in-law should send him aid. "I, your Archbishop, have just come back from France and it's the talk of Paris," he said. Even the Lord Mayor of London was willing to believe that Richard would take away the City's charters and privileges, as he had done once before. And as Bolingbroke marched westwards, so volunteers poured out to meet him, in such numbers that he couldn't feed them all.

Obviously it would be necessary to make a stand somewhere until such lying rumours could be disproved. But every plan or movement of Richard's seemed to reach Bolingbroke's ears, so that he was scarcely sorry when Aumerle openly deserted, taking a considerable part of their army with him. Richard sent a messenger to Salisbury altering their rendezvous from Chester to Conway, and set out immediately. In order to outwit the vigilance of enemy spies, he disguised himself as a travelling friar. Clothes, baggage and even his gold altar plate had to be abandoned. Only Mathe he hadn't the heart to leave, and a sort of rope sling was made for him between two horses.

It was almost impossible to keep an army together over the rough coastal tracks. Hungry, unwashed and weary, Richard and his little band of faithful followers pushed on. Carmarthen, Harlech, Carnarvon, Beaumaris. In each castle the Welsh were loyal enough, but they were pitifully poor. Owen Glendower, their national hero, was a king's man. But they had no rich banquets or state beds to offer. There were nights when Richard was thankful to throw himself down on straw like his groom, and sleep as soundly from sheer exhaustion.

But they reached Conway at last. Conway with her walled harbour. Conway with her beautiful white towers safely flanked by the sea.

Instead of bristling with activity, the great castle seemed half asleep. No one came out to meet them. Watchmen called down a careless challenge, mistaking their king for some medicant friar with a jaded, ragged band of pilgrims. Evidently his messenger had been murdered or waylaid. When Richard entered in under the hastily raised portcullis he noticed that the battlements were sparsely manned, and the stables in the outer bailey half empty. But Salisbury was there, a faithful if perplexed old friend. Watching him shuffle down the keep stairs, Richard realized that the best days of his soldiering were over, and a sharp reprimand died on his lips.

" What's wrong ? Where are all your men ? " he asked, as the old man went down on stiffened joints before him.

Salisbury pressed his lips to his master's hand, almost too agitated to speak. "I raised three thousand, but now——"
With one mailed hand he made the all too expressive gesture

of a man scattering seed to the wind. "We heard that Bolingbroke had dispersed your force in the south and that you—
were killed."

At that moment Richard wished he had been. Averting his
eyes from the earl's bared grey head, he looked hopelessly
around at the silent precincts of the castle. No boisterous
laughter from the guardhouse, no clatter of pans from the
kitchens. Only the monotonous scrape of shingle outside the
walls, and the sad shriek of curlews, grey against the wet
Welsh sky. What a welcome after six drizzling hours in the
saddle! "For God's sake, get us some food," he said.
"Mathe here is almost exhausted."

"Bolingbroke is at Chester!" said the Constable with bated
breath, as if such proximity were excuse enough for the paraly-
sis that had stricken his domain.

It was difficult not to smile at the circumvention of
Aumerle's proven treachery. But only the narrow county of
Flint lay between them now. It was sufficiently staggering.
Richard slid stiffly from his steaming horse and saw Edward
Dalyngrigge standing in the doorway of the keep.

Seldom had he been so glad or so surprised to see any man.
Weariness forgotten, he grasped the knight's massive hands
between his own. "My good Dalyngrigge, what brings you
here?"

"Before landing at Ravenspur, Bolingbroke and the Archbishop put ashore near Rye to rouse the men on the Arundel
estates," he explained. "And after that I made it my business
to watch their movements."

Richard could appreciate that Bolingbroke's movements
might be very much the business of any man who had been
concerned in the disappearance of Gloucester. "Well, what
have you gleaned?" he asked, as they mounted the steps
together.

"Nothing good, I fear," said Dalyngrigge. "The Duke of
York stood out as long as he could. But all England has risen
against you, sir. He had to give in."

Richard's thoughts went back to that last happy tournament with Anne, when prentices had thrown their caps in the air and young girls had strewn roses. "All England . . ." he repeated slowly.

"It's this grievance about the Lancastrian estates, sir. You know the Englishman's passion for fair play."

Only a man as hardy as Dalyngrigge would have dared to put it quite like that. Or was it that a hunted king counted for less?

"And the little Queen?" asked Richard, as soon as they had brought him water to wash with.

"She is still at Leeds, in Kent."

"Are they treating her kindly?"

"Even Bolingbroke would scarcely dare to do less, sir, seeing that she is the King of France's daughter."

Richard looked round at him, the towel still in his hands. "Meaning that it boots her nothing—being the King of England's wife?"

Dalyngrigge was no courtier, but what he lacked in tact he made up for in practical kindness. It was he who bullied the few flustered cooks into producing an edible meal, and he who served the King and saw that his followers and Mathe were properly attended to. After the lavishness of Bodiam, it irked him to see a castle so badly run.

But it was scarcely a cheerful meal. Men ate with their weapons beside them as if at any moment Bolingbroke might appear, and Salisbury kept bemoaning the capitulation of the Duke of York.

Richard turned to Dalyngrigge. "I take it that wasn't all you came these many miles to tell me about?"

"No," said Dalyngrigge.

While the others were still eating, the King led the way up onto the battlements and invited him to follow. The drizzle had ceased and a watery sun was gilding the sands left by an ebbing tide. It was chilly for August and Richard still wore his monkish habit, partly for warmth and partly because Standish and Tom were lovingly trying to cleanse and press his only remaining garments. He leaned his back against the machicolated wall, thrusting both hands through the heavy cord that girt his waist. " Well ? " he asked, bracing himself to hear the worst.

Dalyngrigge met his glance squarely. " They are drawing up an indictment to be presented to Parliament."

Richard's chin shot out. Shaven of his beard, he looked singularly like the arrogant young man who used to defy Gloucester and the Council. " There isn't any Parliament. And without me they can't call one."

Dalyngrigge shrugged the technicality aside. He knew more about ships than politics. " One of the accusations against you will be the murder of Gloucester," he said, as if the King hadn't spoken. " It is known that I was in Calais at the time and they would like to get me as a witness. I want you to know that I am prepared to swear on my mother's soul that he did not die by your orders."

" When you can slip safely away any dark night from Rye ? " Because he had met with so much defection, Richard's smile was almost tender. " What moves you to do this for me, Edward Dalyngrigge ? "

For the first time the forthright pirate showed embarrassment. He began to kick at a hardy leek that had somehow grown between the flagstones. " You let me have Lizbeth, and though her body has always been yours, you didn't betray my hospitality." He raised half-shamed eyes to the King's surprised ones. " Oh, I had her watched ! I know she's wanton. But all my life I've collected beautiful things—and I'm still hungry for her . . ."

Richard was too moved for words. He took a turn or two along the rampart. With his sandals and his tonsured, auburn head, he might have been a youngish monk pacing his cell. Presently he seated himself in a loophole of the battlements. " Tell me what really happened at Calais," he said.

"I swore to Mowbray that I wouldn't. He wanted your favour——"

"Mowbray's on a crusade. If I know anything about him, he'll fight in the forefront until he gets killed. It wasn't a light thing for him to be exiled from England." Richard was making conversation while the officer of the watch, going his rounds, saluted and passed by.

"What did Mowbray himself tell you, sir?" asked Dalyngrigge cautiously.

Richard watched the young Welshman turn an angle of the wall. "He told me—he had had him smothered."

"He lied," said Dalyngrigge. "He only meant to."

Richard leaned forward, his face tense. "You mean—Gloucester is still alive?"

"No. He died in his sleep."

A cloud seemed to roll from Richard's brain. He sprang up. It was too big a thing to believe. "And all these y-years——" he began incoherently. "Are you *certain*?"

Dalyngrigge came closer and began talking in rapid undertones. "Mowbray's men would have no hand in it. Mine, as you know, would skin their own fathers for a florin. That's why it had to be done sooner than he meant, before I weighed anchor."

Richard clutched at his arm, as if to shake the story out of him.

"I had promised nothing, as you know—except to take them across," went on Dalyngrigge, "but I'm human—and curious. I followed them up the stairs and stood just inside the room, behind Mowbray. There was a rush light burning beside the curtains of the great bed. As we opened the door it flickered in the draught, throwing light for a moment on the greyness of Gloucester's face."

Sun and wind and present danger were blotted out. Richard's eyes never left his face. "Go on!" he said. He was there—seeing it all happen—in Calais. . . .

"He lay on his back with his mouth open and I could have

346

sworn his eyes were open too, staring at us. Yet he made no sound, no movement of fear. I saw my men bend over and feel with clumsy fingers for the other pillow. Dan Burridge, the godless jailbird, stood stock still with it all ready in his hands. But suddenly he let it slide to the floor. ' He's already dead ! ' he cried, and crossed himself. Deschamps, his mate, let out a foul oath. ' What made you bring us here to smother a corpse ? ' he hissed at Mowbray."

" And then ? "

" And then I saw Mowbray bend over the bed with the rush-light and pass it across Gloucester's parted lips. And there was no draught this time. Not a flicker."

Richard leaned upon the wall, his face hidden in his hands. He might have been praying, or recovering from some shock which had shaken him to the core of his being. Dalyngrigge shifted his stance impatiently. This was no time for the King to be behaving as if he really were a monk—with all England rising and Bolingbroke only one narrow county away. But Richard wasn't even aware of his impatience. It wasn't Henry Bolingbroke before whom he had to justify himself, but God. So that he might go to Anne. And God had been extra-ordinarily good to him. He had been a murderer in intention, but not in fact. And for the venial intent, his confessor promised, there could be reparation. Gratitude filled his soul. " So bring us through things temporal that we lose not the things eternal . . ." His lips moved in self-dedication, remembering those uplifted moments at Windsor.

But was it God alone who had been good to him ?

He tried to compose himself. " What did they suppose—my uncle—died of ? " he asked, without turning.

" I don't know, sir. All I know is that he'd been terribly seasick, and that night we'd jellied lampreys for supper——"

" Tch ! My uncle's belly was as tough as leather ! " scoffed Richard. And then with seeming irrelevance, he put another question. " Do you know what happened to Mundina Danos ? "

"As far as I know, sir, she left the Citadelle the next day," said Dalyngrigge.

"After you had sailed?"

"Yes."

That seemed to tally with what Mowbray and Jacot had said. And from that point she had disappeared completely. Richard turned and faced Dalyngrigge. "Have you remembered yet where you picked up that little mother-of-pearl box you gave Lizbeth?" he asked abruptly.

Dalyngrigge's jaw dropped. He had supposed the unfortunate incident forgotten. "It was lying in that little closet behind the arras," he admitted.

"Was it empty?"

"Yes."

But Richard knew that it hadn't been—quite. That day at Coventry when he had helped himself to one of Lizbeth's comfits he had stirred them with his finger, seeking one to his taste—and noticed, subconsciously, a few grains of whitish powder in one corner. He remembered it perfectly.

"If you suspect foul play, it was by no order of yours," Dalyngrigge was saying. "Let them search for the real murderer."

But that was the one thing that Richard would never let them do. "Does it matter very much?" he asked wearily.

"Not matter?" expostulated Dalyngrigge.

Richard was quick to realize his own seeming ingratitude. He grasped the man's arms with a warm gesture. "My good friend, it matters everything—knowing myself innocent. You will never know what you have given me."

Dalyngrigge looked past him to the swaying masts in the harbour. "If you won't let me save you that way, at least let me take you back to Ireland—to Calais or Bordeaux," he urged.

But Richard only shook his head. Hitherto he had always saved himself by his own wits. And the idea of running away was repugnant to him. The drama was to be played out here.

The drama of his retribution. "There is so little now with which I can reward my friends," he said, glancing almost whimsically at the roughness of his habit. "The only way I can repay you is to order you back to Bodiam—and to Lizbeth. Until all this has blown over."

There was nothing for the bewildered knight to do but to withdraw.

Richard lifted his face to the limitless sea and sky. "I'm not a murderer! Dear God, I'm not a murderer!" he whispered over and over again, with the salt of tears on his face. He sank to his knees and knelt there for a long time, his tonsured head buried in his arms. Passing men-at-arms scarcely heeded him, supposing him to be some devout young monk at his prayers. Gulls circled and screamed above him. He heard neither Mathe barking down in the bailey nor the commotion of new arrivals.

"Oh, Mundy, Mundy, how could I have been so blind as not to guess?" he cried. "I, who considered myself sensitive and supposed that I had learned the whole gamut of love—while you, who once said you would give your body to be burned for me, took my guilt upon your own soul—here and hereafter —to make me fit to find my love again. . . ."

As he knelt there, apart from the world, it was as if Mundy's inestimable gift were drawing the evil out of him—soothing his bitterness and leaving him sane at heart—just as she herself used to do. He even managed to smile a little, wondering if she had left his box there purposely so that, whatever other people believed, he should know and understand. "Darling Mundy, you never did anything carelessly, did you?"

After a while he became aware of someone standing beside him. He got up slowly and stared at Salisbury as if he were some intruder from another sphere. Gradually the heavy present came back to him.

"Bolingbroke has sent Northumberland and that sanctimonious snake, Thomas Arundel," said Salisbury.

"I will come down," said Richard calmly. In spite of his sadness, a new serenity informed his mind. Even the colour of material things about him seemed to have changed from sombre purple to some ineffable clarity.

"So you take sides with my cousin of Derby," he said to the great Percy of Northumberland.

"There are ten thousand more besides me," replied Northumberland, with insolence.

"Then you have come to make terms?"

"Even if Bolingbroke had every man in England behind him he would scarcely be in a position to do that—whilst his eldest son is in your hands."

"True," agreed Richard, who had almost forgotten the lad's existence.

"In view of this the Duke has left his army in Chester and come with half a dozen followers to the castle of Flint—halfway between his army and yours," announced the Archbishop.

"The Duke?"

"The Duke of Lancaster."

"Ah, yes."

"'Give me back my son and my lands,' he says, 'and I will disband my men and renew my allegiance!'" quoted the Archbishop.

"It sounds so reasonable that I wonder he doesn't come and ask for them himself," remarked Richard. "If that is *really* all he wants——"

Northumberland laughed unpleasantly. "Conway is very strong and the sea lies at your gates. With the Duke and his son both in your hands——"

"Conway *is* strong, and the Welsh loyal," broke in Salisbury, his valiant old heart good for yet another losing fight. "We could hold out here, sir, until England has come to her senses."

But in this strange new clarity Richard could see things from the viewpoint of the man he had been when Anne was taken from him. He recalled Chaucer's warning words. It was not so much England that had lost her senses, as he. And with that excellent memory of his he remembered a bargain he had once made with Burley—and with himself. Before Radcot Bridge. " Let me fight just this once for the power that is my own, to rule as I will—and I swear on all I hold sacred that never again will I risk plunging England into civil war." Well, he had had his way. And those splendid eight years of his which had put England on her feet again. . . .

" How do I know that Bolingbroke has come to Flint in good faith with only half a dozen men ? " he asked, wondering why he must do all the trusting.

" We are prepared to swear it on the Host," offered Thomas Arundel.

Richard led them to the chapel and solemnly, in the sight of all men, they laid their hands upon the Lord and took their oath. After that, no man could doubt their integrity.

While they were served with food, Richard gladly exchanged his brown habit for the furbished up suit of green and gold and blue, and had Tom Holland put a gold circlet round his head to hide the tonsure. He would have liked to wear his ermine cloak, but it had been abandoned at Milford.

He left such soldiers as he had at Conway, and set out with only Northumberland, Arundel and his own personal followers. But half-way along the road, he was ambushed by Bolingbroke's men and led, a prisoner, into Flint castle.

It was checkmate this time. Henry came to meet him in the courtyard. Cold with fury, Richard noticed that he was even wearing the ermine cloak, which had presumably been looted by Aumerle. " I came prepared to give you back your father's lands," he said. " Was such treachery necessary—or becoming —in John of Gaunt's son ? "

Bolingbroke muttered something about sending an escort to protect him.

" About the same as you had at Radcot Bridge," reckoned Richard, glancing round at the closely ranged spears hemming him in. " Rather excessive, surely, to protect me from a few decent Welsh ploughmen and a flock or two of goats."

His cool voice had still the power to lash. In spite of sartorial disadvantages, there was no mistaking which man was king. And Bolingbroke was painfully aware of it.

"I want only what is my own," he reiterated. To brazen out his embarrassment he began snapping his fingers and making friendly overtures to an old hound ambling across the courtyard. The creature was so unkempt that he had no idea whom it belonged to.

But Mathe heard the snapping fingers and must have caught the familiar scent of the cloak. Many a time had he nuzzled and dozed comfortably against it. He padded towards the enticement, passing his master by, and rearing his lean body with an effort laid his two forepaws on Henry Bolingbroke's shoulder.

Henry saw the look on Richard's face. "I'm sorry. I didn't realize . . ." he muttered, pushing the bewildered hound aside.

Richard recovered himself almost immediately. He would have died sooner than let his enemies look upon the vulnerability of his real soul. All his life he had been like that. "Don't worry, cousin," he said lightly. "The dog is so blind I ought to have had a kindly arrow put through him long ago. But, as you see, he still likes to be in the fashion. And he is very wise."

"Wise?" Thomas Arundel had the effrontery to ask.

Richard looked through him as if he were not standing there. "He heard someone once say to me, 'Only a king is good enough for Mathe,'" he explained, looking straight into Bolingbroke's hard, predatory eyes.

CHAPTER XXXIII

THIRTY paces across from door to window, and thirty back again. Ten paces from door to empty hearth and then, if one took extra long steps, fifteen to the fat stone pillar in the middle of the room. After five months as a prisoner in Pontefract Castle Richard could gauge the distance with his eyes shut. He knew exactly where the iron brazier stood, and his narrow bed and the long refectory table where his meals were served.

Once more round the circular walls and back to the window again. Partly to keep warm and partly to keep fit. Foolish, perhaps, to mind so much about keeping fit when he was probably put away here to die. But for some reason which he himself scarcely apprehended, it mattered supremely. Instinctively, although he tried not to think about it, he was trying to fend off the foul fate of the second Edward. That horror with which his tender adolescence had deliberately been violated. It was because he had always been fastidious that he was trying to keep up his strength. " If they mean to kill me, at least let me go out with some sort of dignity," was his nightly prayer. And so far, although he had often eyed the cesspool beside the stables with apprehension and noticed a stairway leading down to some dark dungeon beneath his room, apparently nobody had suggested incarcerating him in either. All Bolingbroke's minions had done was to try to starve him, slowly.

Being no gross eater, he had reacted disappointingly to their endeavours. Never had he felt in more full possession of all his faculties. " And if I lose much more weight I shall be able to hide behind that pillar and hit Hodge over the head when he brings my miserable supper," he thought, limbering up his unused muscles.

But one couldn't go on exercising one's body without growing still more hungry. And it didn't take nearly as long to chalk up the dragging days and months on the wall as to live them. October, November, December of 1399. And then January and February of 1400. Nearly half a year in all. Well, at least he had lived into the new fifteenth century. And now it was St. Valentine's Day. How he used to ransack the goldsmiths' and jewellers' wares to send Anne a surprise gift on Valentine's day! Would that he could send her something to-day!

To one of Richard's temperament imprisonment was torture. And just as he was being starved of food, so here in the Round Tower he was being starved of beauty. At first Sir Thomas Swinford, the Constable, had let him use a room with a pleasant view in the Gascoigne tower and sit on a garden seat outside. Swinford had shown him what clemency he dared, remembering perhaps past kindnesses to his kinswoman, Katherine. Richard had been properly fed and warmed then. Thomas Holland had been with him, and humbler friends allowed to visit him. They used to come and tell him about Henry's grand coronation and find out for him what was happening to the little Queen.

And then John Holland, of all people, must needs rush back to England, to tempt fortune in his half-brother's cause. John Holland, who always brought trouble, running away when he was needed and striking violently when he should stay his hand. He had struck ill-advisedly again before the time was ripe. Before Parliament had had time enough to find out that one King costs as much as another, or the people to tire of Bolingbroke's heavy hand. Poor misguided Salisbury had joined him, leading a Richardian revolt to disaster. Stringent orders had come immediately from Westminster. And since then Richard had been in the Round Tower, completely cut off and helpless.

He minded even more for Isabel than for himself. Would Charles never heed his frantic messages and bestir himself on her behalf? For the hundredth time Richard reached up to test the iron bars of his window. But his captors were taking no chances; and outside he could see nothing but a square of snowbound sky and the top of a withered bay tree growing in the kitchen courtyard.

There was nothing to do but sink back upon the hard window seat and try to warm one's fingers over the brazier. And go over and over the brief, irrevocable events which had transformed a despotic King of England into a subject's helpless prisoner. The blasphemous treachery of the Archbishop, the veiled bullying of Bolingbroke. The excitement at Lichfield when he had very nearly escaped, letting himself down from a window to join loyal supporters who had repeatedly harassed Bolingbroke's hurrying army. After that Henry had taken away his horse and given him the meanest mounts he could find. Lest he try to escape a second time, he said. But Richard knew it for the vindictiveness of a man who feels inferior. Bolingbroke was seizing a chance to lessen his cousin's personal appeal to the people. A touch of buffoonery so soon strangles pity. And no one could out-king him entering into London on a winded, spavined nag. Richard, who had never in his life bestridden any horseflesh that wasn't blood stock, had tried to look unmindful of the insult and to ease the poor, chafed brute along as best he could. But even now he could not bear to recall the cruel ignominy of that journey.

He had been almost thankful when the Tower gates had closed behind him. At least they shut out ridicule, which was a new thing for him to bear—and the hardest of all for one as sensitive as he. But scarcely was he installed when a swarm of litigious Lancastrians had been sent to argue with him. They had argued endlessly and he had refused to answer, demanding only the right to meet Bolingbroke face to face. Bolingbroke had come at last, supported by Thomas Arundel and a very unwilling York. At sight of them, all Richard's Plantagenet rage had flared up. Scene followed scene. The kind of scene which left him devastated.

They accused him of murdering his uncle and unjustly impeaching Richard Arundel. Of violating his coronation oath by failing to maintain the laws and to do justice in mercy and truth. Of choosing unwise Councillors. Of failing to keep the peace within his own realm. And when they couldn't think of any more charges, they repeated the same ones over and over again in different words. When Richard heard them talking about mercy and peace, and remembered how often he had been contemptuously dubbed a peacemonger, he had laughed hysterically in their faces. But there was little he could do. They had appointed fresh ministers and sheriffs in his name, issued false writs and used his seal to summon an illegal Parliament packed with Lancastrian supporters. And finally they had brought him to Westminster Hall and read out their monstrous indictment and demanded his deposition. The lovely building he had perfected, and which he and Anne had hoped to use as the setting for so much happy pageantry, had become the scene of his final humiliation. Even if he ever got out of Pontefract alive, he felt that he would never again be able to re-enter that much loved place. Just to stand within the doors would be to relive that soul-crushing ordeal when he had been forced to forswear his holy anointing and give back his inherited crown. He had given it back to God. Not even that packed, hostile assembly had been able to make him say that he gave it to Henry. And now, lying awake on his prison bed through the interminable nights, he could still hear Henry's harsh voice urging some fantastic claim to the succession, and utterly ignoring the Mortimers. Pretending to the world that a perjured king had handed it to him like so much conscience money, of his own free will. " The most self-righteous usurper the world has ever seen ! " as the Frenchman Creton had reported to his own king in Paris.

Maybe it would have been manlier to have killed himself. The thought had often tormented Richard. But never again would he do anything which might separate him eternally from Anne.

The only thing he had brought himself to plead for had been that he might be allowed to see the little Queen. He scarcely knew how he could face her. But all that really mattered was that he could go and comfort her and try to bind up that broken, passionate young heart of hers. Making a show of magnanimity, Henry had promised that he might go to Leeds, in Kent, on his way north and bid her good-bye. But already ordinary citizens and yeomen were shocked by so ruthless a *coup d'état*, and the very reversion of their sympathies deprived him of a privilege accorded to any common criminal. Friendly demonstrations in so many towns and villages had frightened the officer in charge of him into disguising him in foresters' clothing and hurrying past Leeds castle, where feeling ran so dangerously high.

Richard got up and began to tramp the Round Tower room again. If only he could see Isabel and explain why he couldn't keep his promise about Windsor and why she must go back to France. That it wasn't because he didn't want her. . . .

The sound of Hodge's key turning in the lock cut short his reminiscences. The heavy oak door swung inwards. Any visitor was welcome, even if it were only the Constable. But today Thomas Swinford didn't even descend the three shallow steps into the room. "Your tailor has brought the suit he was making," he said, trying not to look at his prisoner's rather threadbare one. "He seems to think you must be cold." ·

"I am very cold," agreed Richard. "But won't you come in and talk a minute? I haven't the plague."

The Constable avoided the friendly overture with obvious embarrassment. "I don't think the King would mind his coming to try it on," he said in his vague way.

"The King?"

"King Henry."

"But, of course. How stupid of me!" apologized Richard. One must try to get used to it.

Swinford seemed only too glad to withdraw and make way for the visitor from the outside world. To him it was only a tailor come to try on a suit. To Richard it was someone from home. Someone who loved him and before whom he was a king again.

Jacot's face worked painfully. Clearly he was torn between joy at seeing his master and shock at finding him so shabby. Each tried to say the appropriate formal thing. Hodge was lounging in the open doorway, and presently a castle servant came in with a linen-covered basket, thumped it down on the table and departed. Jacot's fingers—usually so nimble— fumbled at the wrappings of his handiwork. " I shall have to take in all the seams," he said, tears gathering in his eyes as they noted the change in his master's figure since the cloth had been cut.

" Oh, come, Jacot ! You wouldn't have me bulge like my uncle of York, would you ? " rallied Richard. " My wife would have hated it, you know."

Jacot, already on his knees trying on the new hose, looked up in surprise. Never since the late Queen died had he heard the King speak of her so normally, or exhibit such sweet patience.

The dull February afternoon was closing in and the old familiar luxury of being fitted for new clothes made Richard forget for a moment his sorry status. " Get us a torch, Hodge," he ordered. There was still that quality in his voice which made people obey him. Hodge moved away and they could hear him on the outside staircase shouting to some underling.

" The little Queen ? " asked Richard, the moment his back was turned.

" Quite honourably treated," Jacot reassured him, in the same urgent undertone. " The Prince of Wales himself— begging your pardon, sir—young Harry Bolingbroke—rode out to pay his respects to her. And when her servants saw him coming she had the drawbridge raised."

Richard's face lit up with joyful affection. Even the new tunic he was putting his arms into was forgotten. But almost immediately a fresh thought tormented him. " You don't think Bolingbroke sent him purposely ? That he means to get a dispensation and try to keep her here for his son? To promote fresh haggles over France."

"It is in everybody's mouth——"

"But my messages to Charles of Valois? They were sent, Jacot?"

"Standish assures me so. But the French king is suffering from a bout of madness."

Then it was true, what Queen Isabella had hinted at St. Omer. But that the malady must afflict poor Charles at a time when his daughter so sorely needed protection!

"The next time young Bolingbroke went to Leeds he was clever enough to take your poor dog, who had been pining; and little Madame let them in. She kept the hound, but would have none of Harry!" chuckled the tailor. "And last week the new king found a sharp weapon in his bed. . . ."

Richard forgot that he was cold or hungry. Here was the sort of news that warmed a man through and through. "Who put it there, Jacot?"

"Some maidservant, probably. It is thought by Queen Isabel's orders." Jacot took immense pride in his royal countrywoman. But he began hastily taking in a seam as Hodge returned and stuck a lighted torch in the iron wall bracket.

"What sort of a weapon?" Richard asked cautiously.

Hodge was back at his leaning post, picking his teeth with a goose quill. In any case, it was improbable that he understood more than a word or two of French.

"A spiked mace. You know, sir. The kind of thing the Cœur de Lion used."

Richard stifled a delighted splutter of laughter and turned it into a cough. "Then I think it must have been—another lady," he said.

When Jacot suggested that he should stand by the raised window seat at the far end of the room for a final fitting, he went there in a kind of dream. It was as if all his friends were rallying round him again. "Oh, Lizbeth and Salisbury—and my sweet Isabel—that you should do these things for me!"

His heart sang. He smoothed the warm green velvet of tunic and matching houppelarde with appreciative hands. It was good to feel well dressed again, and Jacot had chosen his favourite shade and put his finest work into it. "It's really too fine to wear every day," he said. "I must keep the old checkered suit for when the weather gets warmer."

But the tailor was folding it purposefully into a parcel.

"Why?" whispered Richard, with a hand on his wrist and his eyes on the unpleasing silhouette of Hodge.

Jacot went down on his knees to search diligently for something he hadn't dropped. His back was towards the door, his lips mouthed the words towards Richard. "Because Thomas Holland is in Chester with three thousand men. He will put this on. Up and down the country, everybody has seen you in it. You and he have passed for each other before. As he marches southward people will think you have escaped, and more and more will flock after him. Already they are muttering against the usurper, and Northumberland swears he meant him only to get back his lands—not to lord it at Westminster."

Richard felt his heart racing: "It's a lean hope, Jacot," he whispered back, still watching Hodge.

"But still a hope, sir. Even Queen Isabel is planning to ride out and join them and has sewn all the white hart badges onto her people's liveries again."

Richard smiled tenderly. Fastening the purse she had made him onto his new belt, he remembered how laboriously she sewed. "Why should she and Tom take such a risk for me?" he sighed.

He would have liked to point out how hard it would be for her—seeing Tom coming, looking the spit of himself, and being just Tom. And Jacot would have liked to remind him of risks he—Richard Plantagenet—had often taken for his friends. But Hodge was beginning to shuffle impatiently and to rattle his bunch of keys.

Jacot rose to his feet. The King was standing in the window embrasure. The tonsured patch on his head and his small beard had almost grown again and, thanks to the new green velvet, he looked much as he used to look at Westminster or Sheen. Neither of them could think of any excuse to prolong the precious visit. "I almost forgot, I brought you a new purse, sir," said Jacot, noticing the shabby one.

But Richard only shook his head and smiled at him. "This one will last me," he said, stepping down from the window.

He shook his tailor by the hand. "Good-bye, and thank you—for everything," he said, and walked with him to the door. But as Hodge was fitting his key into the lock he spoke again as if inquiring casually after some mutual acquaintance. "I suppose you never really found out what happened to Mundina?"

Jacot started. "She—wouldn't want you to know," he muttered evasively.

Richard laid a hand on his shoulder. "Jacot, my friend," he urged, "it may be a very long time before I see you again."

Pausing in the open doorway, the tailor shifted his parcel more comfortably under his arm. "I only know that a tall, dark woman was suspected of alchemy and burned as a witch in Calais," he said.

Somehow Richard felt that he had always known it. Hadn't Mundy said that she would give her body to be burned for him? And was not the expiation enough? Might not a merciful God, who had accepted the sinner's spikenard, let her burn here, and not hereafter? "By the Governor's orders?" he asked, knowing already that Mowbray had double-crossed him twice.

The departing Jacot shrugged expressively, as only a Frenchman can. "At least he did nothing to prevent it. It was, perhaps—convenient——"

So banishment for life had not been too long. Not an hour too long.

When the door had clanged shut and Richard was alone again the silent room seemed full of these people who had loved him. He told over like the beads of a rosary all the things they had done for him, and all they were yet doing. Even if he were ill-beset, he had been rich in the gifts of love. Life was never as unfair as it seemed. He was no longer alone, caught like a rat in a trap—waiting to die, with his story only half told. He was in the middle of an adventure that spanned dissolution, and whatever happened—his story would go on and merge again with theirs. The hope of present rescue and freedom sustained him. A strange gaiety consumed him. Or was it, he wondered, just that he was growing a little light-headed with hunger ?

The smell of supper was unusually good. All the more so because Hodge appeared to have gone off duty. The round-faced country lad who brought it was at least clean. He set a great brass candlestick at one end of the long table and then brought a couple of dishes and a flagon of wine. " Quite a spread tonight, sir," he said, in his wide Yorkshire dialect.

Richard tried not to lift the covers too eagerly. Roast chicken and spiced venison. His nose had not deceived him. He hesitated, knife in hand. It might, of course, be poisoned. Gone were the days when a ceremonial taster stood behind his chair and kneeled for the first spoonful. But what risk was too high for the thrill of eating venison again ? He could have clumped the clumsy kitchen lad for dropping the sauceboat and wasting some of the precious contents among the straw.

He tried to restrain his exaggerated annoyance and eat with some semblance of good manners. " You look excited tonight, Perkin," he remarked good-naturedly, as the full plate of meat warmed him. " What is it—a wager or a wench ? "

Apparently it had nothing to do with Perkin's own crude life. " It's guests from London, supping in hall, sir. I got to hurry an' help clear. They said to be sure an' give you a good supper, sir. An' Sir Thomas, he sent the wine."

Richard looked up with arrested fork—an implement of table nicety he had brought from France. " You don't happen to know who the guests from London *are* ? Or anything of their business ? " he asked warily.

But as Perkin said—and as Richard was accustoming himself to feel—" Who'd be tellin' the likes o' I ? "

Moved by fellow feeling, Richard offered to wait on himself. And long after the lad had hurried away to the bustle and fun of the hall, he sat alone at his long table, leisurely finishing his meal. From time to time, before the door was closed, he had caught a snatch of song or drunken laughter from the guests. But he did not envy them. For the first time in weeks he was warmed and fed. He had even thrown his fine new houppe-larde over the back of his chair, leaving himself freer to deal with the dishes. It had been thoughtful of Sir Thomas to send the wine. In imagination, Richard Plantagenet was giving a feast for his own friends, talking to each one of them with wit and charm as he was wont to do. As time went on and the flagon emptied, he even began to sing to them—softly, in that caressing tenor of his. That French chanson that he hadn't sung for years :

> " *My candle burns at both its ends*
> *It gives a lovely light !*
> *But oh, my friends, and ah, my friends,*
> *It will not last the night !* "

He broke off abruptly on the last cadence, his glass still upheld against the candlelight that he might see the royal purple of the wine. He heard footsteps and voices. Heavy hurrying footsteps, climbing the stone stairs outside. The visitors from London, perhaps ? Their own party must have fallen flat and they had come to finish up at his. Let them come. He'd show 'em. What was it Anne had said ? " You and Robert could make a party out of a couple of candles and a bottle of Bordeaux, couldn't you ? " He rose to his feet hospitably, if a little unsteadily, waiting for the inevitable Hodge and the grinding of the lock.

But there was no Hodge. A gust of cold night air and the sight of four strangers sobered him instantly. But they weren't all strangers. The dark, beetle-browed man at the back was Sir Piers Exton, Henry Bolingbroke's squire. And each had a weapon in his hand.

So it had come at last. It was actually happening. Four men had come to murder him. He laughed shortly, remembering how he had made sure that Gloucester had a good supper at Bodiam before he died. As he set down his glass his fingers closed over a table knife. His eyes went light as steel. There was no need for words, and none were ever spoken. The intruders' intention was written on their faces. They huddled for a moment or two on the shallow steps, blinded a little by coming from the outside darkness ; and taken aback, perhaps, by the candlelit elegance of the man whom they had come to kill.

That moment's hesitation gave Richard the advantage. They had made no plans, expecting him to cower. Never had it occurred to them that their victim might take the initiative. He snuffed the candles with his palm and caught the first man under the chin before he had time to descend the bottom step. The knife drove straight into his throat as Walworth's had once driven into Wat Tyler's. The brutal lightning stroke had graven itself firmly in Richard's memory.

As the man pitched forward the others came at him like unleashed hounds. One of them stumbled over his dead comrade. They were armed only with clubs and axes. " Henry would rather produce my body whole," ran the thought in Richard's mind, as he backed behind the table.

Once his knife got Exton on the shoulder, but the man held back behind his hirelings as if reluctant to do the deed himself. And now they were coming round the table. The fat man on the floor had picked himself up. Richard dodged behind the central pillar. Round and round he dodged, missing their thwacks by a hairsbreadth so that they slashed sickeningly against the stone. It was like some macabre game, practised to perfection. Through the desperate exultation of the fight Richard remembered how he used to play it long ago. Four murderers and an archbishop. Usually Robert had been the murderers and he had been Becket. And sometimes—when he had been on top of his form—the Archbishop had escaped with his life.

But the real murderers were pressing him hard. If only Robert were here now! Doubling by the steps, Richard slipped on a stream of blood and a tall man with a face like a goat slashed at his left arm with an axe, severing a muscle. The pain was excruciating. But those interminable marches in Ireland and Wales must have toughened him. He reached up to the wall bracket and threw the torch to the stone floor, grinding it out with his heel.

With the room plunged in darkness, the advantage was his again. He could hear his assailants stumbling and cursing as he eluded them, moving catlike in his soft leather shoes. Six paces from pillar to chair, and he had picked up the trailing houppelarde. He let the fat man come within almost an inch of him, then threw it over his head and stabbed him.

It was then, leaning against the wall to get his breath, that he noticed the open door. So confident had they been that they had not thought to shut it, and even the meanest castle servant must have shrunk from the night's foul deed. From where Richard stood, it was only an arched oblong of faint light; but it was the way to freedom. If only he could reach it and turn their borrowed key on his assailants. Outside were the stars and the night air to cool his sweating body, and some wild chance of joining his friends.

He began to tiptoe cautiously along the wall. Only Exton and the goat-faced man were left. But their eyes were becoming accustomed to the gloom. The goat-faced man was after him, between him and the door. He was crouching to spring. Richard's right hand shot out into the darkness and toppled the heavy iron brazier against him. He went down clutching the table cloth. Wine, dishes and candlestick crashed over him. And, trying to free himself, he clutched at Richard's wrist. At his only usable wrist, so that he was powerless to shake him off. Richard set a foot upon his throat—pressing, pressing. . . . The goat-faced man's breath whistled in his windpipe, but still his frantic fingers were fast as a steel trap. Freedom was only a few yards in front, but Exton was somewhere in the darkness behind. Exton had heaved himself up onto the chair. Exton was swinging his cudgel upwards to strike. Richard struggled desperately to free himself. He dug his foot into the yielding flesh. God, would the man never die! Just as the clutching hand on his wrist slackened, Exton's cudgel came down on his head. Exton was a champion in the lists, and there was no need to strike twice.

Richard's whole world reeled. His knees sagged beneath him to the stone floor. A rush of blood beat at his eardrums. But out of the engulfing darkness he could still see the open door. And the light was growing brighter—an ineffable light, more splendid than the stars. It showed him the way to unimagined freedom. With an effort which was more of the spirit than of the body, he got to his feet and staggered a few steps towards it. He heard his own voice, glad and unafraid cry, "Anne! Anne! I'm coming. . . ."

BOOKSHELF SPECIAL!

ONLY 132½p (26s 6d) Plus 24p (4s 9d) postage and packing

This three-shelf bookshelf is specially designed to fit your paperbacks. There's room for up to 120 standard size paperbacks. Each shelf has its own adjustable bookend to hold the books snugly in place.

It's handsome! It's made of very strong, very lightweight metal. The shelves are beautifully finished in matt white, yellow and red; sides and bookends in gunmetal grey.

It fits anywhere! Height 21″, width 19″, depth 4½″ (approx). You can fix it at floor level or eye level, above a bunk or beside a divan. It's easy to assemble: full instructions are enclosed.

All Sphere Books are available at your bookshop or
newsagent, or can be ordered from the following address:

Sphere Books, Cash Sales Department,
P.O. Box 11, Falmouth, Cornwall.

Please send cheque or postal order (no currency), and allow
5p per book to cover the cost of postage and packing
in U.K., 7p per copy overseas.